PRAISE FOR

MY NEW AMERICAN LIFE

"Prose is dazzling in her sixteenth book of spiky fiction, a fast-flowing, bittersweet, brilliantly satirical immigrant story that subtly embodies the cultural complexity and political horrors of the Balkans and Bush-Cheney America."

—Donna Seaman, *Booklist* (starred review)

"Utterly charming. Savvy about the shady practices of both US immigration authorities and immigrants themselves, *My New American Life* is powered by a beguiling Albanian heroine and her hapless American employers. Entertaining, light yet not trivial, a joy to read."

—Lionel Shriver

"Prose succeeds by transforming anxiety into compassion—it's a little lever that gets tripped when we truly imagine what another person feels."

—*Los Angeles Times*

"Prose spins the many straws of American culture into a golden tale, shimmering with hilarious, if blistering, satire."

—Helen Simonson, *Washington Post*

"She's a perfect observer of American life in the opening decade of the twenty-first century. . . . Wry . . . witty . . . a book that brims with smart surprises."

—Ron Carlson, *New York Times Book Review*

"Fun and funny. . . . A satire of immigration and its discontents."

—*San Francisco Chronicle*

MY NEW
AMERICAN
LIFE

Francine Prose

MY NEW AMERICAN LIFE

HARPER PERENNIAL

NEW YORK • LONDON • TORONTO • SYDNEY • NEW DELHI • AUCKLAND

HARPER ● PERENNIAL

A hardcover edition of this book was published in 2011
by HarperCollins Publishers.

P.S.™ is a trademark of HarperCollins Publishers.

HarperCollins books may be purchased for educational, business, or sales
promotional use. For information please write: Special Markets Department,
HarperCollins Publishers, 10 East 53rd Street, New York, NY 10022.

FIRST HARPER PERENNIAL EDITION PUBLISHED 2012.

Designed by Fritz Metsch

Library of Congress Cataloging-in-Publication Data is available upon request.

ISBN 978-0-06-171379-8 (pbk.)

12 13 14 15 16   OV/RRD   10 9 8 7 6 5 4 3 2 1

To Howie

Chapter One

———— ◦◦◦◦ ————

THE DAY after Lula's lawyer called to tell her she was legal, three Albanian guys showed up in a brand-new black Lexus SUV. She had been staring out her window at the drizzly afternoon and thinking that the mulberry tree on Mister Stanley's front lawn had waited to drop its last few leaves until it knew she was watching. Obviously, this was paranoid and also egocentric, but in the journal that her immigration lawyer and her boss had suggested that she keep, she wrote: "October, 2005. Does a leaf fall in New Jersey if no one is there to see?"

Don Settebello and Mister Stanley would go nuts for a line like that. They were always telling Lula she should write a memoir about her old Albanian life and now her new one in the United States. Don even had a title, *My New American Life*. Lula had a better title, *Stranger in a Strange Land*, but she'd already seen it in the public library. Maybe she could still use it. Maybe no one would notice.

Raindrops beaded the SUV as it trawled past the house where Lula lived and worked, taking care of Mister Stanley's son Zeke, a high school senior who only needed minimal caretaking. In fact Zeke could do many things that Lula couldn't, such as drive a car. But since Mister Stanley believed that teenagers shouldn't be left on their own, and since he went off to Wall Street at dawn and didn't return until late, he had hired Lula to make sure that Zeke ate and slept and did his homework. Mister Stanley was very safety-conscious, which Lula found very admirable but also dangerously American. No Albanian father would do that to his son and risk turning him gay.

Lula's duties included making sure there was food in the house. Most afternoons, Zeke drove Lula to the supermarket in his vintage 1970 Oldsmobile. Considering how little they bought and how much of it was frozen, they could have shopped once a month, but they enjoyed the ritual. On the way, Zeke gave Lula driving tips: who went first at an intersection, how to speak the silent language that kept drivers from killing each other like they did constantly in Tirana. Zeke might have been explaining the principles of astrophysics, but Lula appreciated the gesture, just as Zeke liked feeling superior to Lula and better about having a nanny only nine years older than he was. The word *nanny* was never mentioned. Lula explained to Zeke that in her native country only party bigwigs were allowed to own the black deathmobiles that sped through Tirana in packs, and then the economy tanked and no one could afford a car, so now Albanians drove their hot or secondhand Mercedes like kids who'd had their licenses for about five minutes.

As had Zeke, who still wasn't legal to drive at night. But he'd grown up in a car culture, driving was his birthright. Every country had problems, but when Lula saw how Americans drove, how American *children* drove, she couldn't help feeling cheated for not having been born here. Her dad used to borrow her uncle's car, and then he sort of stole it and smuggled it over the border from Albania into Kosovo, where both her parents were killed in a car wreck. Lula had never mentioned this sad fact to Mister Stanley or Zeke. It would only have upset Mister Stanley and made Zeke suspect that his driving lessons might not be enough to put Lula on the road.

Mister Stanley said Zeke could have the gas-guzzling-pig Olds if he hardly ever drove it. If he had to drive at all, his dad preferred him in a tank. Zeke was so in love with the Olds that he kept it in the garage and rode the bus back and forth to school, and Mister Stanley parked his seven-year-old Acura minivan at the end of the driveway. Officially, Zeke was only allowed to drive to The Good Earth Market, which his father liked, because it was close and had organic choices, and which Zeke also liked (it was practically the only thing he and his father agreed on) because he believed in staying small and locally owned and off the corporate grid, though his actual food tastes ran to mesquite-flavored corn chips and microwavable ramen. Zeke didn't notice the other shoppers looking down their rich straight suburban noses at what he and Lula bought. Probably theirs was the only household in which the Albanian girl let the American teen decide. Lula had cooked vegetables, many times, but Zeke refused to eat them. Let his wife worry some day.

After she and Zeke got back from the market, Lula mixed them each a mojito, a splash of alcohol in Zeke's, a healthy splash in her own, heavy on the sugar and mint. Zeke sat on a kitchen stool and watched Lula make dinner. Most nights they ate pizza with frozen crust, tomato sauce from a jar, and moz-zarella that, refrigerated, would outlive them both. Sometimes Lula unpeeled tiny ice-dusted hamburgers, which, steamed in the microwave, were surprisingly delicious, surprisingly like a street snack you could buy in Tirana. Bad food made Zeke feel rebellious, which every teenager needed. The better Zeke felt about himself, the more secure Lula's job was, and the likelier her chances of staying in this country, though Mister Stanley and Don Settebello had made it clear that their helping Lula was not about her working for Mister Stanley and being good for Zeke.

And now, hooray, she was legal! Lula inhaled and shuddered, half at the shiny black Lexus still patrolling the block, the other half at her daily life. The life of an elderly person!

Last night, like every weeknight, Lula and Zeke had eaten dinner in front of the TV. Lula made them watch the evening news, educational for them both. The president had come on the air to warn the American people about the threat of bird flu. The word *avian* was hard for him. His forehead stitched each time he said it, and his eyelids fluttered, as if he'd been instructed to think of birds as a memory prompt.

"At home," Lula marveled, "that man is a god."

"You say that every night," Zeke said.

"I'm reminding myself," she'd said. Her country's love affair with America had begun with Woodrow Wilson, and Clinton and Bush had sealed the deal by bombing the Serbs and rescuing the Kosovar Albanians from Milosevic's death squads. Even at home she'd had her doubts about the streets paved with gold, but when she finally got to New York and started working at La Changita, the waitstaff had quickly straightened her out about the so-called land of opportunity. And yet for all the mixed feelings shared by waiters and busboys alike, the strongest emotion everyone felt was the desire to stay here. Well, fine. In Lula's opinion, ambivalence was a sign of maturity.

Yesterday night, as always, she'd felt sorry for the president, so like a dim little boy who'd told a lie that had set off a war, and then he'd let all those innocent people die in New Orleans, and now he was anxiously waiting to see what worse trouble he was about to get into. He seemed especially scared of the vice president, who scared Lula, too, with his cold little eyes not blinking when he lied, like an Eastern Bloc dictator minus the poufy hair.

"There is no bird flu," Lula had told Zeke. "A war in Iraq, Hurricane Katrina, sure. Maybe one chicken in China with a sore throat and a fever."

But by then the city police chief had appeared on the screen to announce that the alert level had been raised to code orange because of a credible terrorist threat against the New York subway system.

Lula said, "There is no threat."

"How do you know everything?" Zeke asked. "Not that I don't agree it's all bullshit."

She'd been about to tell Zeke—again!—about having grown up in the most extreme and crazy Communist society in Europe, ruled for decades by the psycho dictator Enver Hoxha, who died when Lula was a child, but not without leaving his mark. The nation was a monument to him, as were the seventy thousand mushroomlike concrete bunkers he'd had built in a country smaller than New Jersey. But before she even had a chance to repeat herself, she'd been distracted by an advertisement for the new season of *ER*.

"Look, Zeke," she'd said, "see that gurney rushing in and doors flying open and all the nurses throwing themselves on the patient? Other countries, no one rushes. No one even looks at you till you figure out who to pay off."

As a reward for sitting through the news, Zeke got to watch his favorite channel, which showed grainy reruns of a cheap black-and-white 1970s series about a small-town mom and daughter both in love with the same cop who grew fangs and bit girls' necks. Zeke was obsessed with vampires and with the 1970s. He predicted that vampires were going to be huge.

"One problem with vampires," Lula told Zeke, "in my part of the world, harmless people are always being burned at the stake because their neighbors think they are blood-sucking bats." She hated lying to Zeke. But vampire lynchings had happened. She'd just changed one little phrase, *always* instead of *used to*, and put it in the present tense. She never, or hardly ever, used to lie at home, where for decades mass lying had been a way of life, where you agreed that day was night if you thought it might help keep your children safe. She'd almost never lied at all until she'd applied for her U.S. tourist visa. But ever since she got here, she couldn't seem to stop.

Zeke said, "Why would people do evil shit like that?"

"Because they wanted their neighbor's house or husband or wife?"

Zeke said, "That doesn't happen here. Vampires are a metaphor."

"A metaphor for what?" Lula asked.

"For everything," Zeke replied.

After dinner, Lula plastic-wrapped the leftover pizza in case Mister Stanley came home hungry, which he never did. She'd worked for Mister Stanley for almost a year and still had no idea what he did for food and sex. Maybe he was a vampire. Mister Stanley's milky skin was so translucent that, until she tired of it,

Lula liked standing where she could see him backlit so that his bat ears glowed like a pair of night lamps.

NOW AS SHE watched the brand-new SUV prowl the suburban street, she was sure, or almost sure, it had nothing to do with her. For one thing, she didn't know anyone in this snooty town, and no one knew her. Mama dead, Papa dead, may their souls rest in peace, not that she believed in the soul. She hoped they were in a heaven (which she also didn't believe in) that was as little as possible like Albania. But would they have wanted that? When her dad drank, which was constantly, he said he would die for his homeland, and in his own way, he had.

Lula still had a few aunts, uncles, and cousins sprinkled around Albania and Kosovo, but they'd lost touch. An Albanian without a family was a walking contradiction. Of course she hadn't said this to the embassy officer in Tirana who'd approved her tourist visa. She'd brought in pictures of neighbor kids, whom she'd claimed were nephews and nieces she could hardly bear to leave for that last-fling vacation before she came home and married her childhood sweetheart. She said "Christmas wedding" a dozen times so the guy wouldn't suspect she was half Muslim. Dad's mom, her granny, was Christian. Wasn't that enough? Anyway, Muslim meant nothing in Communist post-Communist Albania. An American wouldn't know that. Muslim meant Muslim to him.

She'd said, "I want to see the world, starting with Detroit, where my aunt lives." The officer smiled. How cute! His heart flopped for the Albanian girl so innocent she thought Detroit was the world. One look at Detroit, she'd jump on the first plane home and shrivel into a raisin before she was thirty-five. Lula crossed and uncrossed her legs. On the visa officer's wall was a poster of the Statue of Liberty. Give me your tired, your poor, your huddled masses. Lula had to convince him that she wasn't planning to stay. Everyone lied to the embassy. It didn't count as a lie. Since 9/11 they made you lie, but that hadn't stopped one Albanian girl or boy from wanting to come to New York.

The Lexus turned and passed the house.

Mister Stanley had given Lula a cell phone that he liked her to keep charged, though she never called anyone, and no one had called her, not since her best friend Dunia had left the country and gone home. Mister Stanley had programmed in their home phone number, Mister Stanley's cell and work phones, Zeke's cell phone, and Don Settebello's office. She was the only person on earth with five numbers on her phone!

She was like the girl in the fairy tale. The princess in the tower. One of the made-up "traditional" folk stories she'd written for Mister Stanley and Don Settebello was about a beautiful maiden imprisoned in a castle. A prince sees her at the window, falls in love, and, unable to reach her, transplants a strong, quick-growing vine from his native region. The good news is, he climbs the vine and rescues her; the bad news is that the vine grows and grows and wipes out the local farmers, their punishment for locking up the princess in the first place. Don especially liked that one, which, he said, proved that indigenous folk cultures foresaw the threat of species importation and genetic engineering.

Next fall, Zeke would leave for college, and Lula would have to figure out the next phase of her new American life.

That is, if things went according to plan, though Lula couldn't have said what the plan was, or who'd designed it. She'd saved fifteen hundred dollars, which was reassuring, though hardly the astronomical sum she might have thought before she saw the drink tabs at La Changita. She kept the money in cash in the secret compartment of the old-fashioned desk in her room, the so-called guest room, though Zeke said they'd never had guests. Next September was the cutoff date, her target day for leaving. By then she would have spent almost two years at Mister Stanley's, a fact she tried not to dwell on. She was too young to have her life fall away in chunks like the glaciers crumbling nightly on the Nature Channel.

Deep autumn had already come on when she'd answered Mister Stanley's ad on Craigslist. Dunia was still in the country, their tourist visas were expiring, they were waitressing illegally at La Changita, near Tompkins Square. All evening, Lula and Dunia drank what the loud, young, undertipping Wall Streeters left in the sweating pitchers painted with happy monkeys. After the owners, Rat Face and Goggles, went home, Luis the cook fed the waitstaff his special *ropa vieja*, and everyone got drunk and bet on who'd get deported first.

They knew it wasn't funny. The day after Eduardo the busboy didn't show up for his shift, his wife came into the restaurant, crying. Eduardo had gone to settle a parking ticket, and now he was somewhere (his wife hoped) between New York and Guerrero. Tears bubbled through the curtain of her little son's lashes. Bleeding heart Lula and Dunia had to talk each other out of adopting Eduardo's family and bringing them home to share the tiny Ludlow Street walk-up that wasn't even theirs.

By that point Lula's visa problem was keeping her up at night. She told herself not to worry, the government had plenty of people to deport before they got around to her. Busboys like Eduardo, Arab engineering students, hordes of cabdrivers and cleaners. On the other hand, who would a bored horny INS dude rather have in detention: Eduardo, some Yemeni geezer in a skullcap, or two twenty-six-year-old Albanian girls with shiny hair and good tits?

Lula and Dunia had shared a one-bedroom on the Lower East Side with a Ukrainian girl, an unemployed dental assistant who was never home, and a beanpole from Belarus who wanted to be a runway model and gave them a break on the rent if they pretended not to hear her puking in the bathroom. Lula said they had to do something about their immigration status, but Dunia said if they did nothing, something good would happen. Dunia's mother was a Christian Scientist, a rarity in Albania, and sometimes Lula heard the mother's soft prayerful voice under the daughter's raucous smoker's croak. Lula believed in watching out, in contingency plans, common sense. Dunia had often told Lula that she should try being a half-full-glass person instead of half-empty-glass person. In Lula's opinion, she and Dunia traded off, half-emptiness and half-fullness, but you couldn't argue with Dunia, so she'd let it go.

When Lula showed Dunia Mister Stanley's Craigslist ad, "Divorced man looking for companion for teenage son, Baywater, New Jersey, ten miles from downtown Manhattan," Dunia said ten miles if you swam. Dunia also said that a Slovakian girl she knew answered an ad like that, and it was an escort service. Genius Dunia was back in Tirana now. Or so Lula hoped. Not long after Lula moved to New Jersey, Dunia phoned, yelling above the La Changita racket, babbling in Albanian (which they'd mostly stopped speaking by then) that two men in black suits had come looking for her at the restaurant, and she was going home before they deported her. Since then, Lula's e-mails had bounced back, and no one answered when she called Dunia's mom in Berat. She'd looked on Facebook and MySpace, but Dunia wasn't there. She tried not to think about the things that could have happened to her friend. What if the men in black suits were worse than INS agents? Lula didn't know how to look for Dunia, short of going back to Albania and hiring a detective.

Lula and Mister Stanley had arranged to meet for the first time in the Financial district, for coffee. Even in the Starbucks gloom it was clear that Mister Stanley wasn't looking for a girlfriend or even occasional sex but, like his listing said, for a responsible person to watch his kid. From a distance, Lula had tagged him as a depressed mid-level accountant, but up close he turned out to be a depressed something higher up, which meant he could pay Lula very well for doing almost nothing. At the interview, Mister Stanley explained that his wife had left—abandoned—him and Zeke and traveled to the Norwegian fjords because she wanted to start over, somewhere clean and white.

"Ginger," he said. "My wife." His voice had the pinched, slightly nasal timbre of a chronic sinus sufferer.

"That's a scream," Lula had said. It was funny, a woman named Ginger, like being named Salt, and funny that a woman would want something whiter than Mister Stanley.

Then Mister Stanley had told her that just before Ginger left, she'd developed—she'd *begun* to develop—some serious mental-health issues. He'd tilted his head toward Lula to see if she knew what he meant, if what he was saying translated into whatever Lula spoke. Lula knew, and she didn't know. She'd found his unspoken doubts about her comprehension, like so many things in this country, at once thoughtful and insulting. An illness, Mister Stanley had said, for which no one had managed to find an effective medication, or even a diagnosis.

Christmas Eve, said Mister Stanley, would be a year since his wife's departure. They'd managed, him and Zeke. But he worried about his son, alone for so many hours. Then he'd asked what Lula *was*. Meaning, from what country. He said he wouldn't have thought Albanian. He seemed to find it amusing.

Lula said, "I grew up in Albania. But my parents were visiting my dad's cousin in Kosovo, and they got stuck there when the war broke out and the Serbs came and tried to murder everyone. They couldn't get home to Tirana. They were killed in the NATO bombing." The smile dribbled off Mister Stanley's face. It was the perfect moment to mention that her visa was running out. Mister Stanley said he had a childhood friend, Don Settebello, a famous immigration lawyer. There'd been a profile of him in the *New York Times*. Don was a miracle worker.

A few days after the interview, Mister Stanley drove Lula out to meet Zeke and see his brick battleship of a house with wavy leaded-glass windows and a curved porch bulging from one side, like a goiter. A gnarled tree in the front yard had purpled the sidewalk with berries. She hadn't thought there were houses like that so near the city, nor fat crows that sat in the mulberry tree and warned her not to take the job.

"Mind your own business," she told the crows.

"Excuse me?" said Mister Stanley.

"Albanian superstition," a lying voice explained through Lula's mouth.

Zeke's hair was as black as the crows, but duller, and a thick octagonal silver bolt emptied a space in one earlobe. Zeke's excessive smile was a mocking imitation of someone forced to communicate pleasure or harmlessness or just simple politeness. Zeke shook her hand, his long body slumped in an S curve, checking her out even as he acted too annoyed to see her. Veto power was all he had. It was easier if he liked her. And Lula was hardly the wicked-witch prison guard he'd imagined his father hiring.

Mister Stanley had left the two of them in the living room.

"What do you do now?" Zeke said.

"I'm a waitress. In the Mojito District. So is Zeke your real name?"

"Why do you ask?" Sunk in the couch across the room, Zeke peered at her from beneath his inky slick of hair.

"Because it sounds like someone frightened. *Zeek ʒeek ʒeek.* Or like a little bird."

"It's my name. How did you learn English?"

"In school. In Albania."

"You speak perfect English. You sound like a British person."

"Thank you. Our teacher was British. Plus I took private tutoring from an Australian." No need to tell this innocent kid she'd paid for those lessons with blow jobs. "The next generation younger than me, they all learned English from Sponge-Bob SquarePants."

"SpongeBob is gay," said Zeke.

Lula said, "So what?"

"Ezekiel," said Zeke. "Like in the Bible."

Lula said, "I never read the Bible. I grew up atheist. Half Muslim, half Christian." Normally, she never mentioned the Muslim part, so already she must have felt that Zeke could be trusted not to think she was plotting to wage jihad on McDonald's.

Zeke said, "There's an Iranian kid in my class. He kept getting his ass kicked in public school, so they put him in my school where everybody's super tolerant. His dad's a famous eye surgeon. They live in a mega-mansion."

"Albania is the most tolerant society in the world," said Lula.

"Good for it," said Zeke. He turned on the TV, and together they watched a hard-looking Spanish girl make out with male and female contestants, deciding which she liked better. Lula sensed she was being tested, not on her response to the show, but on her response to Zeke watching the show. What was her reaction? Boredom passed the test.

Zeke heard his father in the hall and switched off the TV. "What restaurant did you say you worked at?" "La Changita," Lula said. "The little monkey."

Zeke asked if she could make mojitos.

She'd said, "We'd need fresh mint."

Mister Stanley appeared in the doorway. "I see we've found plenty to talk about."

Mister Stanley often said "we" or "one" when he meant "you" or "I." Sometimes Zeke imitated him, but only under his breath, so his father could pretend not to hear Zeke say, "One would one might one should," in Mister Stanley's voice. At first Lula wondered if this usage was correct, if there was something wrong with *her* English. None of the younger Wall Street guys talked like that. The mystery of Mister Stanley's career was solved when Zeke explained that his father used to be a professor of economics until he let himself get recruited by a bank, which he seriously regretted, even though he made lots more money than he had as a teacher.

Maybe nobody else applied for Lula's job. Maybe no one wanted to live with the sad-sack father and son. Maybe Mister Stanley thought Lula was a war refugee, which strictly speaking was true, and that he was doing a good deed, which strictly speaking was true. Lula wouldn't have hired herself to take care of a kid. She would have asked more questions, though Mister Stanley asked quite a few. It was unlike him not to require notarized letters of reference. But she had turned out to be good with Zeke, so maybe Mister Stanley had sensed some maternal feeling burbling up inside her, or the decency that Lula prided herself on maintaining despite her many character flaws and the world's efforts to harden her heart.

Lula was twenty-six. Old, she thought on dark days. Only twenty-six, on bright ones. She had time, but she had more time if she stayed in this country. She wanted to learn that American trick, staying young till forty. Some American girls even got better looking. Not like Eastern Europeans, who started off ahead but fell off a cliff and scrambled back up a grandma. Maybe the pressure to marry aged them before their time. But there was no pressure on Lula. If her ancestors wanted grandchildren, they were keeping quiet about it.

To make everything official, Mister Stanley had taken her into his so-called library, the dank, mildew-smelling, manly lair where he hardly ever went except to pay bills. The shelves were empty but for a few rows of dusty books that Mister Stanley must have used in his university courses. He said, " 'Come into my parlor,' said the spider to the fly. I suppose we should talk about terms."

Over Mister Stanley's desk was a framed antique print of an exploding volcano. Lula had watched its sparks fly as Mister Stanley spelled out the rules. Be there when Zeke got home from school. No drinking or smoking in the house. No driving in bad weather. In fact no driving anywhere except to The Good Earth. Make Zeke eat an occasional vegetable. No overnight guests, except relatives, with Mister Stanley's approval. Always lock up when she left. Mister Stanley used to subscribe to a burglar alarm service, but he'd had it discontinued when it turned out that the service was robbing houses.

When she'd asked Mister Stanley to pay her in cash, he assured her banks were safe. She'd said she was sorry, but Albanians had such bad history with banks . . . her voice trailed off into the economic catastrophe and massive social unrest that came after Communism, like those last scenes in the horror films when the maniac pops from the grave. "You've heard about our pyramid scheme? Offering investors fifty percent. What was anyone thinking? The government was in on it, too, everybody got wiped out."

Mister Stanley had nodded tiredly. He said, "Of course I remember. Scary stuff. It could happen anywhere. Sure, we can do this in cash." Probably it was wiser, seeing as how Lula didn't yet have a work visa, though Don Settebello would fix that. Mister Stanley said, "If I ever get tapped for a government job, you'll have to deny you know me."

"Sure," said Lula. "We never met."

"Joke," said Mister Stanley.

Lula knew that some Americans cheered every time INS agents raided factories and shoved dark little chicken-packagers into the backs of trucks. She'd seen the guys on Fox News calling for every immigrant except German supermodels and Japanese baseball players to be deported, no questions asked. But others, like Mister Stanley and Don Settebello, acted as if coming from somewhere else was like having a handicap or surviving cancer. It meant you were brave and resilient. And being able to help you made them feel better about themselves and their melting-pot country. Their motives were pure, or mostly pure. They liked power and being connected, they liked knowing which strings to pull.

Now Lula would be able to stay. Everyone would be happy. The Balkans had no expression for "win-win situation." In the Balkans they said, No problem, and the translation was, You're fucked.

WATCHING THE BLACK Lexus SUV turn and crawl down the block, Lula wondered if Zeke was in trouble. In her opinion, he was just a semi-depressed American teen, but American TV survived on the blood spilled by semi-depressed teens. As the shooters' neighbors always said, Zeke was a good boy. Quiet. But that unlikely piece of bad news would arrive in a police car.

Her next thought was immigration. Then she thought, with joy and relief, Since yesterday I'm legal! Then she remembered, Big deal. This was Dick Cheney America. Native-born citizens worried. It was just a matter of time before someone on Fox News got the bright idea of sending back the Pilgrims who'd landed on Plymouth Rock.

Lula's lawyer, Don Settebello, had grown up in the same apartment building as Mister Stanley. The first time Lula went to Don's office, she gave a long impassioned speech, all true, about how she loved this country and how badly she wanted to stay here. Don held up his hand. Time was not money but something more precious than money. Time was time. All his clients told him how much they loved it here. He could make it happen. And he had. He'd called in favors, done the impossible. Lula had a visa. Heroes could do that, said Mister Stanley, who several times said he worried that Don would push too hard and ruin his career, or worse.

Probably everywhere was the same. You paid and paid, and when you stopped paying, the favors stopped. Also this was New Jersey, the Mafia's home state. Lula watched *The Sopranos* with Zeke and Mister Stanley. Maybe the black SUV had come because Mister Stanley or Don quit paying a few months early.

The SUV reached the end of the block and pulled into a driveway. Lula watched it turn again and head back down the street. She wished she weren't alone in the house. Why was she so edgy? Could it be the residue of her Communist early childhood? Blame her delicate nervous system on growing up under a system that thought the Soviet Union was too liberal and was best friends with China until the dictator decided that China was too liberal, and China cut them loose. Blame it on the neighbor woman in Tirana who got sent away because her son rotated the roof antenna so he could hear a chesty Italian girl sing his favorite song. The reception was too fuzzy to see, but the audio was enough to get his mom dragged off in broad daylight. It was one of Lula's first memories. Everyone was afraid. Her dad was taken away for one night. But the next day, he came home.

Even though Lula's immigration status was secure for now, she felt her future depended on the web of lies she had started spinning the first time she'd met Mister Stanley. It was Mister Stanley's fault for asking her a question he could have answered, though she knew it was something any prospective employer might wonder.

"Why did you leave Albania?"

She'd gazed into her Frappuccino. "Listen. Mister Stanley, you have to understand."

"Call me Stanley."

Of course. Stanley. Mister Stanley had to understand that in the part of Albania where Lula grew up, blood feuds still raged for generations. Revenges. Bride kidnappings. Their idea of courtship was still the fireman-carry and rape. Her Cousin George was involved in one such case. The couple holed up in a cave and the girl's relatives blocked the mouth of the cave with stones, and the lovers suffocated. Lula thought it was smart to emigrate while she was several rungs down the hit list.

"Dear God," said Mister Stanley.

So it really was his fault, falling for such a story. Hadn't he been a professor? Shouldn't he have known better? She did have a Cousin George. But the story happened in the time of her great-great-grandfather, when the family slept in the same room with their donkey on a mountaintop in Shkodër. Her actual Cousin George had one of the bigger Mercedes dealerships in Tirana, and when she imagined him holed up in a cave, she saw him yelling about bad cell phone reception and blaming his wife, who looked like a fatter, older Donatella Versace. Besides, no one considered a woman or child worth the bullets and ill will. A woman's blood was worth less than a man's. Now the blood feuds were all about real estate. Very unromantic.

Mister Stanley should go to Albania if he wondered why she'd left. Who would choose Tirana over a city where half-naked fashion models and their stockbroker boyfriends drank mojitos from pitchers decorated with dancing monkeys? The land of opportunity. Hadn't Mister Stanley heard? But America was like Communism and post-Communism combined. You weren't supposed to be materialistic until you got successful, after which it was practically your duty to flaunt it in everyone's face.

The lie about the blood feud had been a mistake. Mister Stanley asked if those vendettas ever carried over here. Lula said her clan was superstitious about crossing water. Anyway, her family hadn't lived in that part of Albania for generations. Her great-grandparents, rest in peace, had left the north for the capital, where she'd studied English at the university. When her parents got caught in Kosovo, she'd stayed behind at school in Tirana. After they died in the war, she'd graduated from university and lived with her aunt and uncle and taken more English lessons until she'd figured out what to do next.

Mister Stanley complimented her English. He'd said, "That story about the cave . . . you should write it down."

Lula said, "That's what I should do when your son is at school."

Maybe that was part of the reason she was hired. Mister Stanley got a babysitter and his own private art colony for the same low price. The Lorenzo de Medici of Baywater, New Jersey.

Mister Stanley was all business, working and doing his job. He slept through most of Saturdays, which Zeke spent with his friends, girls and boys, all with dyed black hair and facial hardware. Neither Mister Stanley nor Zeke was big on family life, but Lula felt it was only friendly to offer to cook them Sunday breakfast. Mister Stanley said, Thank you, that would be nice, but no bacon, egg whites only. Cheerios or oatmeal. His bad cholesterol numbers were high.

No one talked at these Sunday meals. Zeke's chair was not even a dining room chair but an armchair pushed to the table, so Zeke could nod off, or pretend to. It was awkward, eating egg-white omelets with silent Mister Stanley and his snoozing son. It was as if there were two Zekes: the agreeable boy he was with Lula, and the furious troll he became around his father. Lula told Zeke he should be nicer to his dad, and Zeke agreed, but he couldn't. It would have meant going against his culture.

Sometimes Mister Stanley got annoyed at his son. But his impatience or disappointment or hurt (it was hard to tell) expressed itself as sadness rather than anger. By Albanian standards and even, Lula suspected, by American ones, Mister Stanley had a narrow emotional range. Nothing in Lula's past had prepared her for his baby-bottle lukewarmness. Especially when they'd been drinking, her father and her uncle believed that pointless yelling was not just the prerogative but the proof of maleness. Because they did so much shouting, no one paid attention, so the end result wasn't so different from the end result of Mister Stanley's composure.

At home, family parties always ended in fights, but never once was there anything like a family gathering at Mister Stanley's. Wasn't there an Albanian-style widowed aunt or grandma who could have moved in with the dad and son and kept house? Mister Stanley had neither parents nor siblings, and on those rare occasions when Ginger's parents phoned from Indiana to speak to their grandson, Zeke instructed Lula to tell them he was out.

On Sunday afternoons, father and son did father-son things—baseball, tennis, the park—inspired, Lula sensed, by their need to prove something to the disappeared mom: how well they were doing without her. Mister Stanley had a boyish love for buying sports equipment, and he was at his most cheerful (not very) when he and Zeke left to try out a new racket or catcher's mitt. Each time they returned, Zeke had sustained some minor injury that required a bandage or ice pack, which his father seemed to enjoy providing. The happiest moment of the week arrived on Sunday nights when Lula and Zeke and Mister Stanley watched Tony Soprano and his even more messed-up family drive their gigantic vehicles through neighborhoods flatteringly near Baywater.

Mister Stanley had mentioned his Sunday outings with Zeke at Lula's job interview. Meaning he wasn't adopting Lula, she shouldn't expect to be invited. That was fine, Lula said. That was when she mentioned that she didn't drive. Mister Stanley had said *that* was fine, but she might feel trapped in the suburbs, and she'd said, No, that was fine, she was a big reader, it was how she'd learned English, and Mister Stanley said that was excellent. Zeke wasn't much of a reader, maybe it would rub off. The sweet little public library was within walking distance.

Lula worried she would be expected to have books around the house. She was reassured when Mister Stanley didn't ask what she liked to read.

Lula had told Mister Stanley she wanted structure. Well, structure was what she'd got. Walls, a roof. A front yard. Be careful what you ask for.

Sometimes on weekends Lula went into the city. The happy shopping couples, the giggly groups of girlfriends, could see how lonely she was. Sometimes she thought they were laughing at her. Stranger in a strange land. She was always happy to get back to New Jersey.

Another problem with lying was how often lies came true. Now, for example, since the public library was one of the few places she could walk to, she had become a reader. She'd looked up Albania and spent hours reading the novels of Ismail Kadare, her country's greatest novelist, who until now she'd only pretended to have read. Trying to imagine the words back into Albanian was good for her English. Not having gotten one piece of mail—let alone a utility bill—at Mister Stanley's, she couldn't apply for a library card. But now that she had her work visa, maybe she'd try again.

She had also started writing, another lie come true. Zeke let her borrow his laptop when he was at school. He made her promise not to look at his files. Touched by his trust, Lula never mentioned the beautiful girls who kept popping up, asking Zeke to get back in touch. Who knew if they even looked like that, or how old they thought Zeke was? Lula e-shopped for luxury items—garden furniture, scented candles, motorboats—she would never buy, priced itineraries to places she would never travel.

Eventually, Lula buckled down and wrote a story in English, with the help of a dictionary and a thesaurus she found in Zeke's room. In the flyleaf was an inscription. "To Zeke, Happy Birthday from Mom, may words give you wings!" What heartless witch gives a teenage boy a thesaurus for his birthday?

Trying not to think too hard, Lula wrote a story about the blood feud in her great-great-grandfather's time. She pretended that her Cousin George was the bridegroom's brother and added a long poetic passage about the bride walled in, stone by stone. There was also a lot about muskets, information that came easily, her dad having been a gun nut, and finally lots of folkloric stuff, curses and proverbs she found on Albanian online forums. She put in everything but the sound track of Albanian folk songs.

Mister Stanley liked her story so much that it became part of the package they gave Don Settebello, who now listed writer among her skills, along with translation and childhood education. Independently, or maybe not so independently, Mister Stanley and Don suggested she write a book. Lula couldn't imagine why a country would want a citizen from a long line of blood feuders. So to tip the scales in her favor, she wrote a sad story about the day she heard that her parents had been killed in the NATO bombing.

"I'm so sorry," Mister Stanley said.

"I'm okay," Lula assured him.

It was true, they'd died in the war. So what if they hadn't really got stuck in Kosovo when the war broke out, but had sneaked across the border when it was almost over? Thousands of refugees had been fleeing from Kosovo into Albania, from the Serbs and from NATO. Only her crazy father had stolen his brother's car and, fueled by drink and misguided patriotism, driven himself and her mother in the wrong direction. His Kosovar brothers needed him! Her dad had gotten it into his head that the Kosovo Liberation Army could use his collection of tribal muskets. So what if it wasn't the NATO bombing that got them, but an auto crash, and her dad was driving drunk? They'd hit a NATO tank. Lula's private opinion was that he'd been on a suicide mission. The six years since her parents died sometimes seemed like an eye-blink and sometimes like forever. Some days Lula could hardly remember them, some days she couldn't stop seeing their faces. She still cried whenever she thought about her dad's funny porkpie hat, a style increasingly popular with hipster boys in Brooklyn.

"You should write a memoir," Mister Stanley had said, that first conversation.

"Maybe short stories," said Lula.

"I don't know," said Mister Stanley. "Don says nonfiction sells better. A memoir of immigrant life. Coming from the most backward Communist country and moving here—"

"Not the most backward," said Lula. "You're forgetting the stans. Turkmenistan. Uzbekistan."

"Sorry," said Mister Stanley. "That was thoughtless."

"Don't mention it," said Lula.

BY THE TIME the Lexus had passed the house four times, Lula had progressed from being sure it had nothing to do with her to thinking it was no wonder that the car had come to punish her for lying.

The Lexus stopped. Three guys got out and ambled toward

Mister Stanley's. No double-checking the address. They acted like they lived here. All three wore black jeans streaked with white dust. Maybe they were in construction. Had Mister Stanley hired someone to fix the house and not told her?

One of the men wore a red hoodie appliquéd with the black double-headed Albanian eagle. Not exactly regulation INS business wear. So it made sense, of a kind. How many Albanians were there in the metropolitan area? The odds were against this being a random home invasion. Which wasn't to say that her fellow countrymen wouldn't rape and kill her for fun. But the odds were also against their doing that to an Albanian girl they didn't personally know.

Had Mister Stanley called Albanians to work on his house? Surely he would have said. Lula sometimes watched a TV show that warned you about the latest dangers—phone scams, dust mites, black mold, carjackings. But the series was in rerun, so you couldn't tell if the threat was current. Not long ago she'd seen a segment about a gang that went door-to-door and offered to fix your roof, and if you refused your house burned down.

The three guys were like a comedy act. Two of them looked like twins. Same body type, black cop shades, overly gelled spiked hair. Stocky, big hips, fat asses. She'd gone to high school with guys like that. Maybe she even knew them. The one without the hoodie wore a long black leather coat.

The third was taller, red-haired, and fell in behind the other two. Cool, both hands in his pockets. Cute. He glanced up at the window and saw her. He had a mustache and longish hair. He reminded her of a boyfriend with whom she'd sniffed glue when she was young and crazy and going to raves in the bunker fields. Now that the Cute One had seen her, pride wouldn't let her lock herself in the bathroom and pretend not to hear the doorbell.

The third time they rang, she opened the door but kept the chain on. She looked at them hard, each in turn. Strangers. She would have remembered.

"*Miremengyes*," they said. Good morning.

"*Miremengyes*," said Lula.

"Lula," the Cute One said. "Little Sister."

How had these guys found her? How did they know her name? Maybe they knew Dunia. Had she sent Dunia her new address? Oh, Dunia, Dunia, where was she? Best not to think of that now.

"Whassup?" said Leather Jacket. On the street they might speak Albanian, their secret code, but on this American doorstep, they showed off for each other in the street slang of their new country.

"Remind me how we're related," Lula said.

"All Albanians are related," said Hoodie. "Brothers and sisters." His eagle sweatshirt was half unzipped. Around his neck, on a silver chain, hung a double-headed silver eagle.

The Cute One gestured at the SUV. "We're good friends and customers of your Cousin George." Then he curled his lips in a way that transformed his pretty mouth into Cousin George's fat liver lips. Lula laughed, partly because it was funny and partly because it was nice to meet someone who could imitate her cousin.

"Brothers and sisters," said Hoodie.

"Okay," said Lula. "Got it."

Leather Jacket said, "Congratulations. Congratulations on your work visa."

"How do you know about that? My cousin doesn't know yet."

The Cute One's smile uncovered a gold tooth. "Don't worry how we know. My girlfriend works in immigration."

Lula said, "I have a great lawyer. My boss——" The quick sharp looks the men exchanged made Lula sorry she'd boasted. Her Balkan survival instinct had been blunted by the spongy atmosphere at good-guy Mister Stanley's.

Lula undid the door chain. Please don't let them steal Mister Stanley's television and Zeke's computer. But who would want Mister Stanley's ancient Motorola, or Zeke's student laptop? Maybe that would make Mister Stanley finally buy a flat screen, which would make Zeke happier than the therapist he'd seen weekly when she'd first got here and then decided to stop seeing, a change that inspired Mister Stanley to give Lula a little raise. There would be no more little raises if Mister Stanley found she'd invited these guys into his house. And maybe no green card, no citizenship. Disaster. On the other hand, they were Albanian. They called her "Little Sister" and knew her Cousin George. The Cute One was cute. And nothing else remotely this interesting was going to happen today.

The men brushed past her, then turned and, one by one, shook her hand. Two of the handshakes were ceremonial. The Cute One's was a caress. How long had it been since anyone touched her, not counting the restaurant customers grabbing her ass? She could always tell which guy it would be, and after how many mojitos. The last time she'd had sex was with a waiter, Franco, who took her to his loft in Long Island City, which he shared with three roommates. He'd showed her the sculptures he made from mattress springs he'd found on the street. She'd said they looked like space aliens, apparently the right answer, and then he told her he called it his Bedbug Launching Pad series, very nice considering that they were about to get in his bed. Mostly she remembered her surprise that a guy that drunk could get it up at all. She'd drunk quite a bit herself, or she wouldn't have been there.

"I thought you guys were brothers," said Lula. "Up close not so much." The same way of muscling into space was the main resemblance.

"You think I look like this guy?" said Hoodie. "Are you kidding me, or what?"

"Brothers with different mothers and fathers. Blood brothers." Leather Jacket slashed a finger across his upturned palm. "No joke."

Hoodie said, "Every Albanian is related by DNA."

"So we're family," Lula said flatly. Then she waited to find out what her three long-lost brothers wanted.

The Cute One hung back, scanning the living room as if searching for a place to hide something or a place where something was hidden. Only when Lula looked through his eyes did she see what a dump it was. Heaven, compared to Albania. All the creature comforts. Still, it was sad to have come this far and to have wound up here.

She could have made the house more pleasant, or at least less musty and smelly, but Lula wasn't the type to redecorate someone else's space. Everything from Ginger Time remained as Ginger left it—the puffy grandmother furniture, the piano no one played. Lula had developed a wary and disapproving relationship with Ginger, based on her examination and appraisal (negative) of Ginger's stuff, and on what little she'd heard (more negative) from Mister Stanley and Zeke. One bleak morning, Lula had gone through Ginger's dresser, holding the baggy cargo pants and roomy dashikis up against her body. The stretched-out granny underwear explained a lot, though not the question of why Ginger had been the one to leave. How could a woman—a mother—walk out on two helpless babies like Zeke and Mister Stanley? Mental health issues. What did that mean? Mister Stanley hadn't said.

The Cute One looked around and sniffed. What was he comparing it to, his sumptuous walk-up in downtown Bayonne? Or maybe some shack in Durrës? Why should Lula feel protective of Mister Stanley's home?

"What's that smell?" said Leather Jacket.

"The grave, I think," Hoodie said.

"It's my boss's house," said Lula. "My job is watching his kid."

"We know that," said the Cute One.

Lula hoped he wouldn't go over to the fireplace. She hoped he wouldn't look at the family photos. If she couldn't change the lamps or move the end tables, what were the chances of her saying, Mister Stanley, Zeke, are you sure you want to keep a mantelpiece full of mementos of your life with a lunatic who left you for a glacier?

The family had traveled a lot. Many of the snapshots were posed against natural wonders, mountain peaks and canyons. Their smiles were frozen, and they always looked cold, even in the desert. Apparently, they weren't the type to ask strangers to snap their photos, which showed Mister Stanley and Ginger,

Zeke and Ginger, but never Zeke and Mister Stanley. Ginger seemed not to take pictures, but the travel was her idea. Lula couldn't imagine Mister Stanley and Zeke going anywhere on their own.

The Cute One held a picture toward her. From across the room, Lula saw Ginger and Mister Stanley posed against rocks at a beach. For the first time she noticed that their arms were around each other's shoulders.

"My boss, Mister Stanley," Lula said.

"Tarzan!" The Cute One curled his lip.

"And her?" the Cute One asked.

"Ginger. His wife. His former wife."

"Ginger the person? Ginger the cookie!"

He handed the picture to Leather Jacket, who said, "Ginger the Spice Girl. Hah!"

In a soft voice, Hoodie started chanting Albanian names and their English translations. "Bora snow, Era wind, Fatmir lucky. Beautiful Albanian names, ugly words in English." He took a deep breath and resumed, rapping himself into a trance. "Jehona echo, Lula flower—"

"Shut the fuck up, you fucking idiot," said Leather Jacket.

"Guys," the Cute One said warningly.

Hoodie emerged from his name-trance like a child waking up cranky. He said, "So you and the boss . . . ?" He joined his left thumb and forefinger and poked his right index finger through. The Cute One shot him a look.

Leather Jacket said, "Sister, disregard this ignorant donkey bent over one too many times for the Greeks."

The Cute One said, "Okay, guys. Cut it out. I'm Alvo."

"Pleased to meet you, Alvo," said Lula.

"This is Guri," said Alvo, pointing at Hoodie. "And Genti." He indicated Leather Jacket. "Better known as the G-Men."

Lula said, "So . . . what do you guys do?"

"Listen to her," said Hoodie. "Already asking her brothers the rude American question."

"Contracting," Alvo said.

"And you're here because . . . ?"

Their expressions were like conversations reaching back to her childhood. She said, "Would you like some coffee?" If there was ever a moment to be Albanian, this was it. A shift in the pitch of their shoulders told her she'd done the right thing.

Hoodie—that is, Guri—and Leather Jacket Genti rearranged the furniture so the comfortable chair, Zeke's chair, was at the head of the table. Alvo sat in the soft chair, the others on either side. They reached into their pockets and pulled out cigarettes.

She said, "Please don't smoke. My boss—" Zeke wasn't supposed to smoke or drink. Tobacco was disgusting. Lula's father's machine-gun cough still interrupted her dreams, less so after her hair stopped smelling of smoke, as it had when she'd worked at La Changita. She didn't think Zeke's super-weak mojitos counted as drinking. Lula bought the rum with her salary, not with the food allowance Mister Stanley gave her.

"Please," she repeated. "If I get fired . . . what then?"

Hoodie said, "One cigarette each. Trust me. No one will know."

Lula plunked down a soup bowl for them to use as an ashtray and stomped off to the kitchen. She ground a lot of coffee. Mister Stanley wasn't picky about much, but he did like his whole Starbucks beans. This was not a job for the timid electric coffeepot. She boiled the coffee in a pan. She had to wash off a coating of grime, but Ginger's Zen tea set would do nicely. Lula decanted the tarry sludge into delicate Japanese cups.

She brought four cups on a tray. The men thanked her. She sat in her Sunday breakfast seat, next to Leather Jacket and across from Hoodie. Leather Jacket took a bottle of clear liquor from his pocket and splashed some into the men's cups. When he looked at Lula, she nodded. The alcohol burned deliciously. Spiked coffee at ten in the morning!

"Delicious," Lula said.

"Raki," said Leather Jacket. "From my grandfather's mulberry trees in Gjirokastra."

"*G'zoor,*" they said. Enjoy. Good health. Long life. They drained their cups.

If Lula had hoped for a rush, she was unpleasantly surprised when the caffeine and alcohol melted her into a puddle of self-pity. How pathetic her life must be if she was ecstatic because three Albanians had home-invaded Mister Stanley's and dosed her coffee with lighter fluid.

"Thank you," Alvo repeated. "Little Sister, the reason we're here is we need to ask you a teensy favor."

Lula braced herself. *Teensy favor* could mean fly to Dubai and back, coach both ways, with a dozen condoms full of heroin up her ass.

"We need you to hold on to something for us. It's nothing." As Alvo leaned toward her, his handsome smile emphasized that it was nothing.

Lula pictured columns of shrink-wrapped white bricks

stacked in Mister Stanley's garage. Good-bye sweet library walks, good-bye innocent cocktail hours with Zeke. From now on, she would constantly be looking out the window.

Lula said, "You don't even know me—"

"My point exactly," said Alvo. "There is no Reese's Pieces trail for ET to follow from us to you. Except for your Cousin George and my aunt in the immigration office."

His aunt? Five minutes ago it was his girlfriend. But who was Lula to judge someone for not keeping his story straight? Better an aunt than a girlfriend. She was pleased to hear it.

"Hold on to what?" she said.

"A gun," said Alvo. "A little gun."

Lula sighed. She should have known. Maybe the white dust on their jeans was an illegal substance. Who drove SUVs like that except coke dealers and pimps? Contractors so rich and successful they had to go around armed?

Lula said, "What kind of little gun? I know about little guns. Also bigger guns."

"Seriously?" said Guri. "No insult, you're a girl."

"Seriously." Lula ignored the girl remark. At twenty-six, she liked it.

"My dad was a gun nut," she said, then decided to leave it at that. For weeks they lived on polenta, but Papa got his semi-automatic. She knew each gun's uses. Assassin guns, hunting guns, snake guns. Her father was a pussycat, but he could get reckless when he drank. Then her mother would lock up his guns, and they would yell about that. They'd wrestle over the car keys, and sometimes—this had turned out to be the fatal part—sometimes her father won.

He used to borrow her uncle's car and, not having a son,

take Lula for target practice in a garbage dump or picnic spot, depending how hard you looked. This was after Communism, when you could get Italian movie magazines, from which he'd tear photos of Madonna and nail them onto a plank and teach Lula to aim for the heart. He had nothing against Madonna, he just had a strange sense of humor. He'd probably thought it was funny to aim his car at the NATO tank and stomp on the gas. He'd lost all their money and their house in the pyramid scheme and sneaked over the border to sell guns, as if all the Kosovo Liberation Army needed was a middle-aged guy hawking tribal muskets and broken Nazi pistols. Lula had grown close to her Aunt Mirela, with whom her family lived before, and with whom she moved in again after university. When Aunt Mirela died of a kidney ailment that could have been cured somewhere else, Lula spent her tiny inheritance on a ticket to New York.

Alvo said, "Small enough for a shoe box. Easy."

"Easy," Lula said. "Famous last words."

Leather Jacket said, "Easy is one word."

"Shut up, asshole," said Hoodie.

"Easy," Alvo repeated.

She wished she knew what the gun had done and why they needed to hide it. Why couldn't they just throw it down a storm drain? But why waste a good gun when they could find an Albanian girl to sit on it like a hen until it hatched baby guns? The Americans had laws for everything having to do with guns. Her father would hate it here. He would have been one of those who said all the wrong people had guns. If someone found the gun, Lula could get deported, visa or no visa.

She said, "I'm hiding your gun because——?"

Alvo rose out of his chair.

"What good would it do for you to know? Would it be better for you? Or me? The less you know about us, the better."

"Suppose I need to get in touch with you?"

"You won't," said Leather Jacket. "We'll be in touch."

"Okay," Lula said. "I'll keep it. But I don't know how long I'll be living in this house."

"No offense," said Alvo. "But I don't get the feeling you're going anywhere soon." He twitched one shoulder at Leather Jacket, who produced a brown paper lunch bag and set it on the table. They all stared at the bag. Alvo nodded, and Hoodie took out an evil-looking snub-nosed revolver. Then they all stared at the gun. For Lula, it was as if her father's spirit had entered the room and given his ghostly approval to her new American life.

"When will you come get it?" Lula said and promptly burst into tears.

The men couldn't have looked more shocked if she'd picked up the gun and shot herself. Lula hadn't planned on crying, no more than she'd planned on not being able to stop. Maybe it was the eagle on Hoodie's shirt, or the taste of raki, or some magnetic force that dragged her back to her granny's house, when Granny was alive, telling that story about the woman who went around collecting women's tears and selling them in vials, the ultimate high-end cosmetics, until a neighbor denounced her and she was about to be sent away, but a party official's wife asked for a sample, and the dealer in tears was pardoned in return for a steady supply. Most likely the gun made her cry.

All this time Lula was sobbing. How she missed her mother and father, and especially her grandmother! She would never

see her again. There was no one here who knew these stories, who knew Lula or her granny. Lula cried for her granny
and her parents and her childhood, for her home, all lost, for
Communism, good riddance, for the lawlessness, the riots, the
violence, the problems grinding on. For her once-beautiful
homeland now in the hands of toxic dumpers and sex traffick-
ers and money launderers. She cried for missing her country,
for not missing it, for having nothing to miss. She cried for the
loneliness and uncertainty of her life among strangers who
could still change their minds and make her go home.

She blinked. The three guys were staring at her, as if through
a rainy windshield.

"Get over it!" Guri yelled. Lula stopped crying, instantly
cured, as if from a case of the hiccups.

"We'll come check on you," Alvo said.

Squeegeeing her tears with her hand, Lula couldn't help asking, "When?"

"Don't worry," said Leather Jacket. "You'll see us when you
see us."

Chapter Two

———— ◦◦◦ ————

Lula watched her three new brothers ease themselves, like fragile cargo, into the SUV. Leather Jacket in the driver's seat, Hoodie beside him. Alvo in back.

"See you soon," she bleated.

The house swam into focus. In two hours Zeke would be home, and the site of a tough-guy sit-down would have to be restored to the suburban haven where a responsible dad was raising his son in the wreckage of his marriage.

Lula took the gun upstairs. She paused in her bathroom doorway. One advantage of living here was having her own bathroom. How quickly she'd switched from making do with a filthy communal apartment-block latrine to needing her middle-class personal space. She was glad not to have to use the same toilet as Mister Stanley, nor to have to wait while Zeke did whatever he did, locked in for an hour every morning. Lula liked being able to keep her bathroom clean and modestly stocked with the beauty products she'd bought in the East Village with Dunia, and which she grudgingly replenished after hoarding every precious squirt of shampoo.

She thought of that scene in *The Godfather*: the gun taped inside the toilet tank. No need for such contortions to hide something at

Mister Stanley's. Her impulse was to put it in the same drawer with her money. But not even sensible Lula was that unsuperstitious. "Don't keep your gun with your money" was probably, or should be, an Albanian saying.

Finally she slipped the gun in her underwear drawer. In a normal house with normal men, that would have been the last place. But neither Mister Stanley nor Zeke would look there. It was very American, following the rules of privacy and respect designed to help men and women have happy, healthy relationships. At home, there were different rules: You pretended to be fascinated by everything your boyfriend said until you got the ring, and he pretended to listen to you until you agreed to have sex. After marriage, you could go back to ignoring or putting up with each other and leading separate lives. For now, it was exciting to keep Alvo's gun in her underwear drawer. Almost as if it were Alvo.

Given the state of her underwear, she was glad the gun *wasn't* Alvo. Mostly she wore cheap synthetics from outdoor bins on Fourteenth Street, except for one fancy bra and silk panties, lavender laced with dark pink ribbon. The bra alone had cost her a week of tips at La Changita. She'd read in a magazine that one of the top ten secrets of successful women was wearing expensive underwear under their business suits. I wear it for myself, explained one female CEO. It's my secret message from myself to myself. Lula bought the costly underwear, but had never worn it or gotten the secret message, which might have been: Who do you think you're kidding? She hadn't bought the underwear for corporate success, but for the future boyfriend. Buy it, and the boyfriend will appear. But the boyfriend had never appeared. Maybe it would work magic if she wrapped the Cute One's gun in her good lingerie. It was nice to have a reason to wish she believed in magic.

Downstairs, Lula dragged the dining room chairs back to their usual places. But furniture wasn't the problem. How could three little cigarettes have left so much of themselves behind? Hoodie and Leather Jacket smoked black cigarettes that reminded her of her grandpa, who'd grown his own tobacco. Alvo smoked Camels. The basement furnace wheezed and complained as Lula pumped the front door until the chilly house smelled like the Tirana train station in the dead of winter.

At four, when Zeke got home from school, Lula was in the kitchen.

"You're cooking?" he said. "What's with that?"

Lula watched the bubbles of steam leave ragged craters in the thick red paste. Every fall, her granny used to simmer bushels of red peppers down to a sort of ketchup from which she made delicious sandwiches with cream cheese. It was destiny that, on Lula's walk home from the library yesterday, she'd spotted a box of red peppers outside the corner grocery that ordinarily never sold anything fresh, except a few shriveled lemons and cucumbers halfway to being pickles. Maybe Granny, wherever she was, had sent Lula the peppers with their witchy power to trump tobacco.

Zeke said, "How come it smells like cigarettes in here?"

Lula said, "Gas, not smoke. Matches. I had to light the burners. The pilot light went out."

"Did you start smoking? I wouldn't blame you for needing something to cut the boredom."

The boredom? If Zeke only knew! She'd spent her day with guys whom Zeke would pay money to meet. She said, "You think I'm crazy enough to start smoking when cigarettes are fifteen dollars a pack?"

"Seven dollars. Oops. Was that a trick question?"

"Please don't smoke," said Lula.

"I don't," Zeke said. "One cigarette a week."

"That's too much."

"Okay. One cigarette a month." Zeke picked up the newspaper. "Awesome old lady."

This morning, Lula had walked into the kitchen to find the newspaper left open to a feature story about Albanian sworn virgins dressing and living like men to support their widowed mothers. The pretext for the article was that the custom was dying out, but really it was an excuse to run a photo of a butch Albanian lady in cowboy drag, her knees apart and a rifle slung across her lap.

Lula said. "Every time the paper has something on Albania, your dad leaves it out for me to read."

"Do you think my dad has a crush on you?"

"No," Lula said. "I think he misses your mom."

Zeke said, "I don't know. Mom calls every so often and asks for money, and he sends a fat check wherever she is. So he must still care or feel guilty. Or something. Did you know any old ladies who dressed up like that?"

"No," said Lula. "But I had this great-aunt . . . once someone stole some of our firewood, and she shot the guy."

"Did she kill him?"

"No. But she popped the guy in his kneecap from ten meters away." The firewood had been a good touch. So had the shattered kneecap. If Zeke asked if her story was true, she'd confess she made it up.

Zeke said, "How long is a meter?"

"Look it up. You're a senior. Don't you study math?"

Zeke said, "Do you think you got her DNA?"

"She never married. Nobody got her DNA."

"Don't you know anything about DNA? You could both have Genghis Khan's DNA. Didn't you study science?"

Was it Hoodie or Leather Jacket who'd said all Albanians had the same DNA? Would sex with Alvo be incest?

"What's the matter?" Zeke said.

"Why?" Lula said.

"You looked weird for a minute."

Lula said, "It's hostile to tell people they look weird. Or tired. This waitress at La Changita was always telling people they looked tired and ruining their whole evening. Every time she said it, they had to run look in the mirror."

"Does weird always have to mean bad? Couldn't someone look weird good?"

Lula said, "Do you want a sandwich? Red pepper paste and cream cheese."

"No thanks," said Zeke. "I don't eat anything the color of blood."

"Pizza is the color of blood. Ketchup is the color of blood."

"They're the color of tomatoes."

"What kind of vampire are you?" Lula said. "Okay, I'm making pizza."

Stewed peppers and microwaved tomato sauce canceled out three cigarettes. All the same, Lula kept sniffing the air. When Mister Stanley got home, his nostrils didn't so much as flutter. Lula leaned against the counter while Mister Stanley sipped a glass of cold water into which he had squeezed the juice of a lemon he cut into wedges and kept, plastic-wrapped, in the fridge. Lula liked Mister Stanley, who was kindhearted and decent, who only wanted the best for his son, and who always treated Lula with perfect consideration. So the fact that she was sometimes revolted by the sight of him drinking his nightly glass of water filled her with guilt, and also with anger at herself that spilled over onto Mister Stanley, like the droplets that sometimes dripped down his chin.

"How was work?" asked Lula.

"Uneventful," said Mister Stanley. "Another day of wishing I'd never quit teaching."

"You could go back," said Lula.

Mister Stanley said. "My life is very expensive, as my wife was quick to point out before she made it more expensive. One only hopes she's getting the help she needs, though she never seems to stay in one place long enough to . . . Well, on a brighter note, how's Zeke?"

"Fine."

"Homework?"

"Done."

"Did you read that article?" Mister Stanley said. "About those Albanian women dressing like men? Imagine wanting to—or being forced to—live like that."

"People do what they have to." It was the kind of gloomy statement Lula counted on to silence Mister Stanley when she was tired of talking. But why was she feeling sullen? She'd had an interesting day! She briefly considered mentioning the sworn virgin in Shkodër who was a Party official responsible for the deaths of many innocent people. But it was a long ugly story she didn't feel like telling. She said, "My granny was a ball buster. Except that she got married and had kids and wore a dress."

A smile wobbled on Mister Stanley's face. "Where did you learn an expression like . . . *ball buster?*"

Lula knew some English expressions that Mister Stanley probably didn't. It was touching that he'd found it hard to say. But how could he work on Wall Street and be so clean? She'd learned the phrase at La Changita, from young guys who were probably angling for Mister Stanley's job. You learn a word the first time you're told not to *be* that word, implying you already are.

"I don't remember," said Lula.

Mister Stanley said, "You were saying about your grand-mother?"

"She loved pro wrestling. She made my grandpa get an illegal TV antenna so she could watch the matches from Bavaria. He could have gotten sent away for that." That part at least was true.

"Write it down," said Mister Stanley. "Another terrific story. I'll pass it along to Don. Speaking of which, I almost forgot the most important thing. You and I and Zeke are having dinner with Don on Saturday night to celebrate your work visa coming through."

Lula said, "Don't you think that's bad luck? Can I get you a snack? I made this delicious red pepper paste my granny used to cook."

"No thanks," said Mister Stanley. "I'd love to, but red peppers give me heartburn. What's bad luck?"

"Celebrating," said Lula. "Celebrating anything."

Mister Stanley said, "Lula, when you apply for citizenship

and you go for your interview, do me a favor. Don't say you think it's bad luck to go out to a pricey restaurant in Manhattan and raise a glass to a positive change in your immigration status. And have someone else pick up the tab. It's deeply un-American."

Lula said, "Sorry. I know. I'm grateful. I can't believe that you and Mr. Settebello would do this. I mean, in addition to—"

"Please," said Mister Stanley. "We're happy for you. In fact, what about a little bonus in case you want to buy something to wear to the dinner? Only if you want to . . . only if . . . I wouldn't—"

"Thank you," Lula said. "That's so nice of you. I'll go into the city this week."

"Be careful," said Mister Stanley. "Watch out."

Had Mister Stanley gotten a secret tip from Don? Was there some kind of crime wave? Had the code level been kicked up to red in honor of Halloween? Lula and Zeke had watched the terror threat level rise before each holiday, as if suicide bombers thought that blowing themselves up on Presidents Day would put them on the fast track to the Garden of the Martyrs. Lula often told Zeke how governments loved keeping people scared, how Enver Hoxha had built all those bunkers for people to defend themselves against an attack by . . . whom, exactly? The Greeks? The Serbs? The United States? No one ever said. It didn't matter. All that mattered was fear. The bunkers had turned out to be indestructible, just as the dictator promised, which meant that seventy thousand cement cow pies remained, plopped along the roadsides and on people's lawns.

Lula had been in Tirana on 9/11, which she'd watched on blurry TV with tears streaming down her face. She and Dunia had wept again as they stood on the platform above Ground Zero. Dunia said that at home the hole in the city floor would already have become a picnic site. Picnic site, toxic dump site. Shit happens, Dunia said. Lula and Dunia used to compete in acquiring American slang.

At the site Dunia had tried to pick up a good-looking cop, but it stopped being fun when he told them that leaving his shift early would dishonor the memory of the dead. When Lula asked Mister Stanley where he was on 9/11, he'd said, "Well, as you know, I work downtown. At first one talked about it a lot, but then I stopped, and I find I no longer want to."

"Be careful of what?" Lula asked now.

"I don't know," said Mister Stanley. "Just be careful is all."

EVEN THOUGH NEITHER Mister Stanley nor Zeke suspected that the three Albanians had paid Lula a visit, she was glad when, the next morning, Estrelia came to clean.

Lula had been relieved at the beginning when Mister Stanley said cleaning wasn't part of her job. Estrelia had been with them forever; she came every Tuesday. Don Settebello had been very helpful to Estrelia and her husband and son.

Butterball Estrelia radiated sweetness but hadn't learned much English, probably because she spent her days in empty houses. Had she talked to Ginger? Lula had no language in which to ask. She liked Estrelia but preferred to be out of the house while she worked. It was awkward, standing around, watching Estrelia shake her head at the stacks of newspapers and magazines Mister Stanley didn't have time to read, the papers and books Zeke lost track of, the wadded up T-shirts and single sneakers kicked into corners. Estrelia neatened the stacks and herded the shirts and shoes, glancing guiltily at Lula, whose shrug meant, I don't blame you.

Estrelia's vacuum purred, and Estrelia purred along with it. Let the crime scene detectives come now! Any skin flaked off Hoodie's ankle was just more dust to Estrelia.

After a brief conversation about Estrelia's son Sebastian (fine) and her husband (also fine, *gracias*), Lula and Estrelia played a translation game, exchanging basic vocabulary in English, Spanish, and Albanian. Estrelia knew all the furniture words, and they had moved on to colors. Estrelia picked up a cushion and pantomimed what green it was—trees no, birds no, river yes, dive in the river. Lula said Nile green, then in Albanian, river green, and Estrelia said something *verde*. Then on to the crocheted blanket, but there were no words in any language for the shades of acrylic in this item of hand-made Ginger decor.

Estrelia was finishing up in the dining area, and Lula was about to go to her room, because it was even more awkward loitering outside the bathroom and comparing the Spanish, Albanian, and English words for toilet brush. But just then, Estrelia poked the vacuum hose into the chair in which Alvo had sat yesterday. The vacuum coughed, and Estrelia extracted a scrap of paper she handed to Lula.

Lula smoothed it out on the table. In faint purple type was the address of a supermarket in Manhattan. One quart orange juice, 2.59. Cigarettes, 7.95. Unless Mister Stanley had started smoking (impossible) or Zeke had gone into Manhattan to buy cigarettes (unlikely) or the receipt had been here since Ginger Time (Estrelia was way more thorough than that), the only logical conclusion was that it had fallen from Alvo's pocket.

"Oh, thanks, it's mine," Lula said. What would she do with a sales receipt? Treasure it as a memento? Use it to stalk Alvo to his neighborhood market? "Thank you. I lost this. I need it. Taxes." Taxes? She put the receipt in her pocket, and motioned for Estrelia to follow her into the kitchen.

Estrelia froze. Did she think some subtle status shift had raised Lula from coworker to boss, no longer a friendly young person but a harsh taskmaster about to point out some neglected duty? Lula cradled Estrelia's elbow with a pressure meant to seem affectionate but which probably felt like the grip of a cop collaring a suspect.

Estrelia sat at the kitchen table while Lula made her a sandwich of red pepper paste and cream cheese on a sesame roll.

She said, "Zeke and Mister Stanley won't taste it. There's only so much I can eat." Estrelia nibbled at the bread and, nodding vigorously, smiled. Then she furrowed her penciled-on brows in a friendly question directed at the sandwich.

Lula would have liked to tell Estrelia about her granny. She would have liked to ask if Estrelia had a granny, if she was alive or dead. Lula didn't even know the Spanish word for granny. She pointed at the sandwich, then hunched over, pretended to walk with a cane, and rocked an invisible baby.

Estrelia got it, or got something.

"*Sabroso*," Estrelia said.

EVERY TIME LULA went into Manhattan, she could hear Dunia saying, "Ten miles if you swam." On dry land, you had to take the George Washington Bridge, the tunnel, or the train. The least miserable route involved two small buses and then a big bus that took you to midtown, from where you could take the subway to anywhere you might actually want to go. Lula would be lucky if she could find something pretty to wear and get back in time for Zeke's return from school. Zeke could take care of himself and would never tell his father if she wasn't there when he arrived. In fact he'd probably like a break from Albanian watchdog Lula. But being present so that Zeke wouldn't walk into an empty house had been one of the few promises that Mister Stanley had extracted from her, and Lula was determined to keep it.

New York had been fun with Dunia, shopping for items they couldn't afford, egging each other on to ask the price of luxury items they wanted and were scared to touch. Of course they'd gone shopping in Tirana, at street markets when they were teenagers and then at the boutiques that had started springing up in Blloku, the understocked, overpriced shops, still smelling of fresh paint, that Mafia guys were opening so their bored childless mistresses could buy stolen designer shoes from each other. New York had confirmed what Lula and Dunia had long suspected, that the nicest store in Tirana was a sandbox in the nursery school of real-world consumer culture. At first Lula had felt almost angry at the gorgeous variety and obscene profusion of stuff for sale. But being with Dunia had alchemized her anger into humor. Together, they were twice as strong and could pretend to be superior to all that unattainable splendor. They'd been each other's armor, protective gear against the serenity of the American girls letting strangers paint their faces, against the trancelike calm of the women pawing through swaying garments.

Oh, Dunia, Dunia, where was she? Every week the TV ran a

story about sex-trafficked girls, and though Lula was certain, or pretty certain, that Dunia was too smart to let herself get caught up in anything like that, Albania was Albania. Anything could happen. People fell down potholes in the sidewalk and were never heard from again.

Today, Lula missed Dunia with a particular pang as she performed the humbling yoga of trying on a sweater and skirt in the communal dressing room of the store whose designer bargains were legend even in Tirana. Like the women around her, Lula faked indifference to the range of female bodies in the mirrors. At home no one thought about weight so much. Poverty and fear kept you thin, though strangely, in this country, they had the opposite effect.

But no matter how hard Lula tried not to notice, she couldn't help surreptitiously watching the girl beside her stuff a blouse into her backpack while, as a distraction, her friend argued with the woman guarding the dressing-room door. Would the clerk get fired when someone found out the blouse was stolen? Probably not. She shrugged when another customer gave her a handful of antitheft devices she'd found in a jacket pocket. Lula could probably steal the sweater and skirt and keep Mister Stanley's money. But she'd just gotten her visa. How embarrassing to get deported for shoplifting an outfit to wear to a party to celebrate being legal.

Lula studied her reflection. She still looked okay in the street-bin underwear, a miracle considering her sedentary life, the nightly mojitos, the frozen burgers and prepackaged pizza. Granny would die all over again if she knew how Lula ate. She shifted from hip to hip, appraising the short black pleated skirt, the white V-necked sweater, schoolgirlish, cheerleaderish, just sexy enough to turn heads without going all-the-way slutty. Lula also decided on a deep Goth-purple sweater. Maybe Zeke would imagine she'd dressed in funeral colors for him, while Don and Mister Stanley would think her look was exotic Albanian.

The skirt and sweaters came to a hundred and thirty dollars, which left her with change and a pleasant feeling of sensibly saving for the future, plumping up the safety cushion in the secret compartment of the desk that, Zeke said, had belonged to Ginger's mother. The swing of the shopping bag on her arm filled her with optimism. Not only did she have new clothes, she had a future in which to wear them.

She knew how to live in New York, how to take the subway to the first of the buses that would take her home to New Jersey. One Sunday morning, she and Dunia had drunk a bottle of wine and memorized the subway map. The web of colored lines materialized before her eyes, like the chart of the veins and arteries on the poster of the skinless body that Zeke had tacked to his bedroom wall.

Every seat on the train was taken. Lula's heart ached for the souls damned to ride both ways, mashed together in rush hour. At least she had been spared that. Thank you, Mister Stanley.

Finally someone got up from one of the two-seaters at the end of the car. A little kid made a run for it, but Lula stopped him with a look. A woman whose skin seemed to have been baked from some rich flaky pastry shut her book, sighed theatrically, and slid over to make room for Lula, then sighed again and went back to reading *Daily Affirmations for Women Who Do Too Much*.

Across the aisle was a young Hispanic couple, a skinny

hypervigilant guy in jeans and a light sweater pushed up to reveal a muscular arm bulging with Maori tattoos. His heavily made-up transvestite girlfriend had nodded off on his shoulder, so the ends of her long glossy curls swung against his chest. You only had to look at them to know they were in love. It wasn't what they planned or wanted, but love was love, what could they do? Lula knew she shouldn't stare, but she couldn't help it. No one could, including the woman beside Lula, who glanced up from her book and shifted in her seat, sighing her critique of the sinner perverts doomed to burn forever in hell. Lula stared at her neighbor until the woman had to look back. Her eyelashes curled like a moth's antennae. What did she see in Lula's face that made her own face clench so tight?

Lula said, "We're all God's children, don't you think?"

Why had she said that? She didn't believe in God or Jesus or Allah or Buddha. Some new American language was erupting through her, the same language that had her cradling and rocking her arms as she tried to tell Estrelia about Granny's red pepper paste.

The woman regarded Lula coolly, then almost smiled, then decided not to. She said, "Maybe you're right. Jesus wouldn't have made them unless He had His reasons." With which she returned to her book.

The boyfriend gazed at Lula over the head of his sleeping beloved, and a flicker passed between them, almost as if he'd heard her above the roaring train. Maybe this was Lula's new role in her new American life, opening blocked channels of communication, bringing these strangers a gift from a country where tolerance was the best result of everyone forced to be the same.

Who cared if the three Albanian guys never showed up again? Here she was, in New York! How much friendlier the city looked when she had money and a mission. What she'd just witnessed would never happen at home. For one thing, there were no subways. For another, no Puerto Ricans. Or cross-dressers, for that matter, except for one club in Tirana where they still changed in the back room. No doubt about it, there was more freedom here. You just had to watch your back and not shoot off your mouth or do anything stupid that would get you locked up or kicked out.

How appealing her fellow passengers looked in those ingenious vessels—their bodies!—so brilliantly designed to contain all their hopes and fears, their dreams and experiences, bodies designed to change as their souls were changed by every minute on earth. She wanted to stay in this city with them, she wanted to have what they had. She wanted it all, the green card, the citizenship, the vote. The income taxes! The Constitutional rights. The two cars in the garage. The garage. The driver's license. The good sense to appreciate what Don and Mister Stanley were doing to help Lula belong to this crowded, overwhelmed, endlessly welcoming city, where sooner or later, like on the subway, someone would scoot over and make room.

Chapter Three

⟨⟨⟨—

AT THE very last minute, dressing for Don Settebello's dinner, Lula vetoed the knee socks that would have nudged her outfit over the line from college girl to role-playing escort-service college girl. She took the filmy black scarf she'd gotten last Christmas from Zeke, draped it around her neck, and tied it in a sort of noose, accentuating her pallor and giving her look a subtle vampire edge that Mister Stanley and Don might appreciate, if only on a subliminal level. Zeke would like it a lot.

Lula dreaded coming downstairs and finding Mister Stanley and Zeke waiting for her and feeling obliged to say how nice she looked. So she was preemptively ready, on the couch with her coat on, when Mister Stanley appeared in a suit and, twenty agonizing minutes later, Zeke clomped downstairs in a black shirt, black jeans, and a black bomber jacket.

Lula said, "You look good, Zeke."

"Doesn't he?" Mister Stanley said wistfully.

Zeke held his phony smile for so long that no one could mistake it for the real thing. Then he said, "Awesome! Lula's finally wearing the scarf!"

"Your Christmas present from Zeke," said Mister Stanley. "I remember! How sweet!"

The dead tree Mister Stanley lugged home last Christmas Eve bumped across Lula's visual field. By Christmas morning it had dropped its needles on the scarf, an envelope containing a hundred-dollar bill from Mister Stanley to Lula, an iPhone for Zeke, and two Banana Republic shirts Zeke would never wear. Lula had given Zeke the *Coumadin Rat Bleed-Out Live* CD he wanted, and for Mister Stanley, she wrapped up the stubby ceramic pitcher she'd tossed into her suitcase in Tirana. When she left, she would ask for it back. Zeke gave his father a card promising to be nicer in the coming year, a promise he broke (silently, for Lula's benefit) even as Mister Stanley read the card aloud to Lula.

All Christmas Day, Mister Stanley kept saying how nontraditional it was to have holiday dinner at Applebee's and catch a movie at the mall. They'd watched gladiator blood spurt across a giant screen and waited for the day to end. No one mentioned that it was the anniversary of Ginger's departure. When they got home the answering machine was blinking. "Merry Christmas, honey, it's Mom. Love from Ubud. Bali. I think. I meant to send you a present, but the post office was so . . . and these—" The machine buzzed, and Ginger's voice sank beneath the ocean between them. Mister Stanley had said, "Mom sounds better, don't you think?" and Zeke ran up to his room.

Now Zeke said, "I knew that scarf would look awesome. Let's go. We're late. Don will be waiting."

"That's my line," said Mister Stanley. But Zeke was already out the door.

In the months that Lula had lived here, the three of them had been in the car together so rarely that their seating arrangement hadn't been worked out.

Zeke said, "It's your party, Lula," and dove into the back seat.

Mister Stanley pulled onto the street, headed toward the highway, and merged into the onrushing traffic. How unlikely, that every driver should choose to observe the rules of the road over suicide and murder. Lights parted to let them through. Why should driving seem harder than escaping from a coffin underwater? Everybody drove. Everybody was born and ate and slept and had sex and died. And drove. It wasn't Lula's fault that she couldn't. Where she came from, driving was more of an extreme sport than an everyday method of transportation.

Eventually her father had aimed his brother's ancient Zastava at the armored personnel carrier, and that was the end of that. A cousin of a cousin had arranged to have her parents' bodies shipped back to Tirana along with the corpses of Albanian boys who'd gone to fight with the KLA. Lula and her uncle and aunt waited at the airport, together with the families of the dead freedom fighters. Lula knew better than to ask to see what remained of her parents. The image she wanted to remember was her father's stubborn potato face when Aunt Mirela yelled at him for heading into a war zone for no good reason. A very good reason, her father had said. I'm helping where help is needed. It was lucky that Aunt Mirela and Uncle Adnan didn't blame Lula when her father stole their car for her parents' final trip across the border to Kosovo.

The lunar glare of security lights in an office park strobed past, shocking Lula out of her melancholy reverie just in time to note the tipsy invitation of a tilting neon martini. Twice, they passed a black Lexus, and Lula turned around so sharply that Mister Stanley asked what was wrong.

"Lexuses are cool," said Zeke. "The company should make hearses."

If Lula had been alone with Zeke, she would have told him to knock on wood and shut up about hearses.

Mister Stanley said, "Zeke, these wet dead leaves are almost as bad as black ice. Not almost. As bad. Be careful."

Zeke made a snoring sound.

Mister Stanley said, "Your mom called. She telephoned me at work."

The fake snoring stopped.

This was when Mister Stanley informed Zeke that his mother had called? On the way to Lula's party? But really, it made sense. He didn't want to be alone with his son, or even looking at him, when he told him.

"So . . . what did she say?"

"She said she's doing better. She sounded less upset, or anyway, less angry."

Zeke said, "What's *she* got to be angry about?"

"I wish I knew, son," said Mister Stanley.

After a silence, Zeke asked, "Where is she?"

"Sedona, Arizona."

"What's there?"

"Red rocks. Indian spirits."

Zeke said, "Mom's kind of town."

"She said she wants to see you. She wants you to come visit." Mister Stanley tried and failed to keep the worry and begging out of his voice.

"That's not going to happen," Zeke said.

"Right on," said Mister Stanley. "I like your thinking on this. So okay, let's forget it, for now. This is Lula's night. Poor Ginger! I wish there were some way we could help. But she doesn't want our help."

"Let's have fun!" said Lula weakly.

"Definitely," said Mister Stanley.

The fleet of hired cars double-parked in front of the restaurant promised that the wine would be good. The wine and the steak. There were places like this in Tirana, where Party bigwigs went and later gangsters. Guns in every armpit. A guy in a tuxedo and a black bow tie sprinted toward the car. Mister Stanley shrank back, and the parking valet had to pry the keys loose from his fist.

"Dad," said Zeke. "Take it easy, okay? Valet parking is awesome."

Inside, a group of beauties flitted like moths around the glowing lectern that held the reservation book, a shimmering tableau shattered by the arrival of Mister Stanley's party. One girl split off from the rest to guide them toward Don Settebello, who had risen from a banquette and was waving as if to beloved passengers sailing into port.

Crossing the restaurant, Lula turned a few heads and was glad, for Don and Mister Stanley's sake. They deserved to have dinner with someone who made other men momentarily forget what they were saying.

Don gathered Mister Stanley and Zeke in one exuberant hug. In his office, Don greeted Lula with a formal handshake, but tonight he stood on his toes to kiss her cheek. This was a celebration! Don's round bald head and belly reminded Lula of a bowling pin for giants. Don had many qualities—intelligence, kindness, generosity, power—that women found attractive. Lula wished she were one of those women, instead of the kind who was drawn to the sort of guy who asked you to keep a gun for him and didn't let you ask why.

Peering around Don, Lula saw a child's head on a platter. Don's daughter had rested her head on her plate to express how depleted she was by the boredom of watching her stupid father welcome his stupid friends.

"Hi, Abigail," said Zeke.

Abigail thrust out her tiny pink tongue and licked the empty plate.

"Abigail!" said Don Settebello. "Be polite, please!"

"Nice to see you," Abigail droned.

Don and Mister Stanley dropped back as Lula and Zeke approached the table. Lula heard her lawyer tell her boss, "Betsy must think I'm stupid enough to believe that people get last-minute opera tickets on Saturday night. She loves to wait until it's too late to get a babysitter so I can't go out and commit all the chauvinist-pig misdemeanors she thinks I've been waiting to do all week. Heinous macho crimes against the female gender, which I obviously can't perpetrate if I have Abigail with me."

"At least Betsy calls you," said Mister Stanley. "Unlike Ginger." Hadn't he just said in the car that Ginger had phoned? Lula sensed competition over whose estranged wife was more exasperating. Mister Stanley admired Don, but they'd grown up like brothers, and there was an edge of brotherly rivalry, an odd note that crept into Mister Stanley's voice when he worried out loud about Don pushing his luck in choosing to fight Washington with every case he took on. It wasn't clear, exactly, what he feared might happen to Don, though several times he'd mentioned how shocking it was to think that his friend might be made to suffer for having a conscience and speaking out.

"How shall we arrange ourselves?" Don asked. Abigail wasn't budging from the center of the banquette. Zeke slid in beside her, Don sat on her other side, Mister Stanley beside him. Lula was exiled to the end, celebrating her party from the far edge of the children's section. Even though they liked Lula, the men would rather talk to each other.

"Of course you win," Don told Mister Stanley. "Ginger has always taken the cake." Lula couldn't ask what Don meant by "the cake" with Zeke and Abigail listening.

Lula had promised herself not to drink much, no matter how good the wine was. The watery mojitos had probably lowered her tolerance to the point at which she might say something that made no sense, or more sense than she wanted. But the seating arrangement was making her ill-tempered and reckless. Put her at the children's table, and she'd be the baddest child. When the waiter appeared with the wine, Lula beamed up at him and mimed upending the bottle into her glass. Unamused, he filled it to the precise level he'd learned in red-wine training. La Changita had a rum sommelier, a conga player whose English was so bad he could fake knowing one rum from another.

"To Lula and her new American life!" said Don, and all except Abigail raised their glasses.

"To peace in our time," said Mister Stanley.

"Amen!" said Don. "To bringing the troops home from Iraq!"

"That's not going to happen," said Lula.

"To our little Albanian pessimist," said Mister Stanley.

"Realist," muttered Zeke.

"*G'zoor*," said Lula.

"*G'zoor*," said Mister Stanley and Don.

"To whatever," toasted Zeke. He was bringing his water glass to his lips when Lula grabbed his arm.

"It's bad luck to toast with water!"

"What am I supposed to do now?" asked Zeke, horrified by the attention.

Lula pinked Zeke's water with a few drops of wine, ignoring Mister Stanley's dirty look. Two drops. Why couldn't he be charmed, as always, by her quaint Old World customs, instead of worried that he was paying her to turn his son into an alcoholic? Then Mister Stanley remembered—European!—and relaxed back in his seat.

"I already took a sip of water," said Zeke. "Does that count?" Zeke stared into his water glass as if he was watching bad luck rise from it like a genie.

"One sip doesn't count," said Lula, wishing it were true.

Lula's first mouthful of wine tasted like drinking velvet or pipe smoke or liquefied brocade. A cascade of flavors brightened the future enough that, if she didn't feel happy yet, she could imagine feeling happy before the night was over. To speed along the process, she drained her glass and signaled the waiter to refill it. Only a few times in her life had she drunk wine this good, always when a table at La Changita ordered from the top of the list and then got so blasted they left half the bottle, which Lula hid so that she and Dunia and Luis and Franco could finish the two-hundred-dollar Amarone.

"Jesus," said Don Settebello. "Speaking of bad luck. One of my clients, Salvadoran guy, he's just got his green card, the guy was a journalist back home and now he's got a job with CNN, he's on his way to sign his contract, crossing Broadway and Fifty-first, a taxi jumps the curb, the driver's first day on the job, the fucking stupid moron—excuse me, kids—runs over my client's foot."

"Nightmare!" said Mister Stanley. "That's why defensive driving is so critical, Zeke. The streets are swarming with nut jobs."

"Wait. It gets worse," said Don. "The guy's foot is smashed, they operate on him for hours, chewing-gum and duct-tape everything together, good as new, or practically. They're writing him a scrip for physical therapy when somebody notices he has no health insurance, and they deport him because no facility will take him."

"Deport him deport him?" said Mister Stanley.

"From the country," said Don.

"Can they do that?" asked Lula.

Don shrugged. "My dear, we all know goddamn well they can do anything they goddamn want."

"So where is he now?" asked Mister Stanley.

"Juarez, for all I know. They dump the poor bastards over the border. All my e-mails keep bouncing back, which is never a good sign."

Lula felt as if her wine had been replaced with some icy acidic punch. Instantly sober, she said, "I have this friend—"

"Health insurance," said Mister Stanley. "Who would bother working otherwise?"

"You would, Stan," Don said. "And you know why? Because you're the only guy in America still waiting for Wall Street to keep its promise. How long has it been now?"

"Twelve years," Mister Stanley said glumly.

"How time flies!" said Don. "Bill Clinton's first year in office, Good Guy Stan lets himself be lured down from his ivory tower by these headhunters—don't you love that expression?—who claim they're about to start a new program, a socially conscious Grameen-bank kind of thing, small loans to small businesses. Help the little guy. Good deeds and good money. Who could resist? Except that the good deeds part never happened, as I remember warning you. Remember what I said? I said, Lie down with the big dogs and you get up with the big fleas—in a corner office! So now you get to foreclose on the same little guys you thought you were going to help, and even now, even now some part of you still believes that things will turn around and you'll get to do some—"

"Badgering the witness!" Mister Stanley said.

"Lula," said Don. "Did Stan ever tell you that the young guys in his office call him the Professor? Did he ever tell you how when we were kids back in Rockaway, the neighborhood bully offered Stan ten bucks, a fortune back then, to steal a beer from the corner store? Stan did it, not so much for the money itself, which trust me his family needed, but because he believed the kid would pay him. Even then Mr. Big Heart thought that people did what they promised. So of course he got caught and his poor dad had to go in and apologize and pay off the owner not to call the cops and—"

"Dad, you stole a beer?" said Zeke. "That is totally cool."

"I was eight," Mister Stanley said. "Half your age. A child. I didn't know any better. Tell Lula what *you* did, Don."

"I tracked down the little bastard bully and beat the crap out of him. From there it was a hop skip and jump to the DA's office, until I got fed up with persecuting the poor and deporting the innocent. My point is, it's never too late to come over, or back, to the side of the angels."

"You would too, Don," said Mister Stanley, his pale cheeks pinking with every gulp of wine.

"Would what?" said Don.

"Keep working if it weren't for health insurance. Because you can actually do some good. You're helping people. Like Lula."

"*G'zoor* to that," Lula said. She toasted the air and drained her glass. It was semi-interesting, what Don had said about Mister Stanley, but her attention had been hijacked by Don's client with the broken foot. She hated stories about how if you'd only stopped to pick up that piece of trash or ordered that second cup of coffee, if your Metrocard hadn't failed to swipe, your whole life would have been different. She also hated stories about people being deported and stories about car wrecks. Lula would ask them about Dunia. They would know what to do.

"On second thought," said Mister Stanley. "I'm not so sure I would keep working without the coverage. Every day I ask myself why I get up in the dark before dawn and drive through the filthy smelly tunnel—for what? To transfer money from one pocket to another? Other people's pockets. And it's all going into the same pocket. Okay, the same five hundred pockets. What if I quit tomorrow? Whose life would it change but mine? Not the guys we turn down for loans, not the families—"

"Hear, hear," said Don Settebello. "My old friend Stanley discovers the pimply fat face of capitalism."

"The main thing that will change if you quit," said Zeke, "is that you won't be able to pay for my college."

"That won't change," said Mister Stanley. Then he put his head in his hands.

Don signaled the waiter for another bottle.

Lula said, "Something like that happened when I worked at the restaurant. There was this busboy, Eduardo . . . and I have this friend, Dunia."

The waiter loomed over Don's shoulder. "Ready to order, sir?"

"If we had menus," Don said.

The waiter stomped off and returned with a stack of leather-bound tomes. None of the entrees were under forty-five dollars. A hamburger was thirty, but Lula would feel embarrassed ordering a burger here. A plate of home fries—fifteen bucks! Lula knew that the waitstaff had nothing to do with the pricing. Even so, she felt as if they were conspiring to relieve Don of the maximum amount of his hard-earned cash. How odd to find herself on the customers' side of one of those undeclared wars that sometimes broke out between customers and waiters.

Mister Stanley said, "I'll have the rib eye."

"Me too," said Zeke.

"Make that three," said Lula.

"The porterhouse," Don said. "And I want to hear mine moo."

A wail went up from Abigail. "What about me? Isn't anyone taking *my* order? Am I not here?"

"What would you like, honey?" Don said. "Order anything you like."

"You know I'm a vegetarian. Dad, why did we even come here?"

"We have a very fresh swordfish tonight," the waiter said.

"Is swordfish a vegetable?" Abigail demanded. "Dad, is swordfish a vegetable? Does it have a face or a central nervous system? Because I'd really like to know if it has a face or a central nervous system."

Lula glanced at Zeke, who seemed delighted by Abigail's courage. Lula sent him a telepathic message. Don't be fooled. You can count on a vegetarian to eat little boys like you for breakfast.

"I'll have the creamed spinach," Abigail said.

"That's all?" Don gave Mister Stanley a searching look, asking for a ruling on whether Abigail was just messing with his head or if she'd developed a full-blown eating disorder. Mister Stanley shrugged. What did he know about girls?

"Appetizers?" said the waiter. "Sides?"

Defeated by his daughter, Don surrendered to the waiter. He said, "We're in your hands." Lula wanted to cry out, No!

"We'll bring some appetizers and sides," said the waiter, ignoring Lula's furious stare. *Ka-ching*, she thought. *Ka-ching*.

Don said, "What's up with that bottle we ordered? Sooner rather than later."

Mister Stanley put his hand over his glass. "I'm fine. I have to drive the family back to New Jersey."

The family? Lula was family? Sweet dear Mister Stanley!

"What about you, Lula?" said Don. "I'm not drinking alone, am I?"

Lula raised one eyebrow and nodded. Deal me in.

Don's smile conveyed a loopy familiarity, as if he and Lula had agreed to embark on some joint project. In Lula's experience, the end of that particular project—drinking—was usually sex, but she couldn't tell if that was what was on Don's mind. She'd known it was on Franco's mind, that night when, after La Changita closed, he stood behind her chair and pressed his groin into her back. What a gentleman! How did guys like Don Settebello signal erotic interest? Probably just like other guys, but Lula wasn't sure. Besides which, he was her lawyer. If they had sex, a principled fellow like Don would feel he had to recuse himself from her green card application, which would make having sex with Don a lose-lose situation. Unwelcome thoughts of Alvo crowded into her mind. Or maybe not so unwelcome. Lula picked up her glass and resumed her progress along the road to tipsy well-being.

A convoy of waiters closed in on them, thumping down shrimp cocktails, wooden boards draped with pâté and cured meats, cheeses, pickles, platters of tomatoes ripened in costly winter sunlight, every red slice bundled beneath its own snowy blanket of mozzarella. The plates would not stop coming. There was twice as much as they could eat. Half would go back to the kitchen. The waiters would eat well tonight. As they should, thought Lula.

She helped herself to a shrimp, amazingly firm and fresh and sweet, considering the season. Nauseating, nonetheless. Lula picked up her wine glass and put it down without drinking, glad now that she was sitting so far from Mister Stanley and Don.

Zeke and Abigail stared ahead as if they were at the movies. It was easy to get Abigail's attention, but hard to know what to do with it. Her laundry-bleach blue eyes scared Lula into asking, "How do you like school?"

"My school sucks shit," said Abigail. "My dad pays thirty grand a year so I can call my teachers by their first names."

"Every school sucks," said Lula.

Abigail was having none of it. "You want to know how bad mine sucks? Have you ever read *Macbeth*?"

"I read *Macbeth*," said Zeke.

Abigail said, "We had to memorize a section of the play and recite it in front of the class, and I did the witches' speech—"

"Obviously," said Zeke.

"Right? Except that my teacher said I was taking the easy way, because it rhymed, but she'd pass me because I said it with energy and passion. Energy and passion. How gross is that?"

"Extremely gross," agreed Zeke.

"Scum-sucking bitch." Abigail screwed up her face and croaked, "Double double toil and trouble."

Had Don and Mister Stanley heard that? It was not Lula's place to tell her lawyer that his precious little daughter cursed like a Hungarian.

Zeke couldn't stop looking at Abigail. Lula's plate, on which there was one lone shrimp tail, vanished before she had tasted the cheeses and pâtés. Annoyance turned to outrage and then, shockingly, to bereavement. She had missed the cold cuts at her own celebration. Platters of home fries and bowls of creamed spinach signaled the imminent arrival of the meat. It seemed like a mockery to set a bowl of creamed spinach down before Abigail, a separate portion identical to all the other bowls of creamed spinach she could have had, for free. But not for free, not free at all. This was costing Don a fortune.

Deliciousness steamed off Lula's steak, aswim in its pool of blood. Not having fun wouldn't save Don money or bring the cow back to life. It wasn't her fault if Eduardo the busboy and Don's client had been deported. Or if Dunia had disappeared. Lula too could disappear. Enjoy yourself while you can.

The conversation stopped as everyone chewed. Abigail masticated dainty bites of spinach with theatrical distaste. After a while Don Settebello asked everybody how their steak was, and everybody said good. Great.

Don said, "How's the writing going, Lula?"

"Great," said Lula. The same word she'd used for her steak. The last thing she'd written was, "Does a leaf fall in New Jersey if no one is there to see?" The day the Albanian guys showed up. She hadn't written one sentence since. She hated lying to her journal. It was the one place in her life reserved for unadulterated truth. But if she wrote the truth, she would have to mention how much time she'd wasted lately thinking about Alvo. If she couldn't write about that, best not to write at all. It would spare her the dilemma of how much to say or not, how much to admit to herself about being the kind of person who would hide a stranger's gun in her trusting boss's house.

She said, "I'm writing a short story now. It's about this government bureau that analyzes people's dreams, and everyone has to report their dreams, and they're on the lookout for any dreams that might indicate that someone is plotting against the state." Lula held her breath. Neither Don nor Mister Stanley showed any sign of recognizing the plot of a novel by Ismail Kadare.

"How does it end?" asked Mister Stanley.

Don said, "What are you thinking, Stan? Never ask a writer a question like that."

"I don't know yet," Lula said.

"See?" said Don Settebello. "I hate to imagine what would happen if that story got out. Can you picture FBI agents shaking down therapists?"

"Hell, yeah," said Zeke. "That shrink Dad sent me to would bend over for anybody with a badge."

Don said, "I never trusted those prying bastards, all that money changing hands, a whole economy based on helping the comfy middle class deal with their comfy middle-class problems."

"Not always so comfy," said Mister Stanley. "Ginger's doctor seemed like he was doing her a lot of good until she decided he wasn't."

Don said, "After the divorce, when I had that little fling with a younger, not *that* much younger woman, Betsy said it would impact Abigail. But I don't think it has. Do you? Anyway, that's all I need, some nervous-nelly doctor blabbing my secrets to some FBI goons who could then spread the lie that the country's ballsiest immigration lawyer is in treatment for pedophilia. It's sort of like what Lula said. I mean, the plot of her story. I bet Dick Cheney insists on personally vetting the videotapes of sessions with hot young starlets in therapy for sex addiction."

"Poor Lula," said Mister Stanley. "We shouldn't joke like this around her until she's got her green card."

"Who's joking?" said Don.

Mister Stanley said, "Let's leave her with a few illusions about the country where she's trying to stay."

"*If* I get my green card," Lula couldn't help saying.

"You will," Don said. "Trust me. Meanwhile you can think anything you want. But just to be on the safe side, you should probably watch your mouth. Do I sound paranoid? I *am* paranoid. We'd be insane if we weren't. By the way, how *is* Ginger? Excuse the mental leap."

"Better, I think," said Mister Stanley. "She called from Arizona. Only once did she allude to hearing holy messages from the red rocks in some canyon."

Lula and Zeke exchanged quick looks. Mister Stanley hadn't mentioned that part in the car.

After a silence, Mister Stanley said, "It must be tough for Lula. She sees what's happening to this country. But she comes from a culture where America is God."

In one corner of Mister Stanley's garage, two John Kerry/ John Edwards placards leaned against the wall, and several times Mister Stanley told Lula that he'd donated serious money to get Bush out of office. Lula was impressed by his freedom to say this. She was impressed by the freedom of the American press to tell the world that their vice president accidentally shot his friend in the face. At home, it wouldn't have been accidental. And he would have succeeded. Still, you had to watch out and not criticize, same as anywhere else. You could never predict when Americans, even Mister Stanley and Don, would get all defensive and huffy.

"It's hard for everyone to see what's going on here," said Don.

Lula said, "Everywhere it's common sense to keep your mouth shut. Growing up under Communism wasn't such a picnic."

"Amen," said Mister Stanley.

Don said, "I promise you, Lula, this is a free . . . My God, I almost said free country. Knowing what I know." Staring into his wine glass, Don said, "The thing that kills me is . . . the beauty of the U.S. Constitution. I love that fucking document, it still makes me cry, the sheer goodness and purity of the Founding Fathers' hopes and dreams, their ideas about what humans deserve and how they should be treated. The way these guys in Washington are trashing it . . . Christ, I've got to quit drinking. Every night's the same. The fourth glass of wine, I'm crying about the Bill of Rights and ruining everyone's fun—"

Abigail said, "Oh? Were we having fun? I must have missed the fun part, Dad."

Lula said, "Mister Stanley's house is a wonderful place to write."

Don said, "It's adorable, Stan, the way Lula calls you Mister Stanley. Like some servant girl from the nineteenth century."

Mister Stanley shook his head. "I've begged her to call me Stan."

Lula shrugged. She didn't know what to call Don Settebello, so she didn't call him anything.

They went back to tearing at their steaks. Abigail ate one last dab of spinach and pushed her bowl away so hard it spun. The others watched till it stopped.

Don said, "It's a miracle when the system functions. More often it's like with my Salvadoran client—all your ducks are lined up, actually your clay pigeons, one of them gets shot down, and it's back to square one, the poor guy is sent back to wherever. If he's lucky. And then you have a case where it works, and a person with Lula's brains and heart and talent gets to live here."

Mister Stanley said, "Here's to Lula. And Don."

"And Stan." Don's swallow of wine lasted so long that even Zeke and Abigail watched his Adam's apple bob up and down.

Lula said, "Thank you. I'm happy and grateful to be here."

"We want you here," said Don Settebello. "Fresh young blood. You're what keeps our country young."

Zeke stage-whispered to Abigail, "Fresh blood? That's so vampiristic."

Abigail said, "Are you actually listening to Dad?"

"Shut up, young lady," Don told her. "Okay, here we go." Don clinked his spoon on his glass, and half the restaurant turned. Don waited till the eavesdroppers went back to their meals.

"Dear friends, I've got an announcement. This is a celebration for me, too. Just because my life isn't already busy and difficult and frustrating and overextended enough, I've decided to take on a new project. I'll be doing some Guantánamo work, going down there and trying to get those guys to trust me. Do whatever I can. Not that I have high hopes, or any hopes at all, but I can't just sit back and watch. Plus to be honest with you I was flattered. They've got the top guys on this. The sharpest habeas corpus guys, the heavy-duty death penalty guys, famous law professors from Germany and France. And who am I among these superstars? Don from immigration—"

"You're hardly Don from immigration," Mister Stanley said. "Not for ten, fifteen years now. You have a very public career. You're a hero."

"Stan," said Don. "Are you listening? Did you hear one word I said?"

"I'm still processing," Mister Stanley said. "Guantánamo. Jesus Christ, Stan. I don't know what to say. I mean . . . how did all this happen?"

"Actually, I was recruited. This old friend of mine from law school—"

"Amazing." Mister Stanley didn't want to think about Don having other old friends besides him.

Abigail said, "Don't do it, Dad. Don't go. We all know you can't keep your big mouth shut. They'll probably keep you there. They'll lock you up in one of those orange suits and say you're Osama bin Laden."

"Darling!" said Don. "It makes me so happy that you not only know where *there* is, you know what goes on there. Stan, Zeke, Lula, do you realize that this . . . child understands more than most adults. It makes me want to keep doing it, to preserve the beautiful country in which my daughter is growing up."

Abigail said, "Think about *me* for five minutes."

"And what's more," said Don, "she seems genuinely concerned about my welfare."

"God," said Abigail. "Do you think I'm stupid? If you get sent to jail, it goes on my permanent record. Fat chance of my getting into boarding school and getting away from Mom once they find out my dad is a terrorist."

"Let's raise a glass to Don," said Mister Stanley. Everyone's glass was empty. Mister Stanley waved over the waiter, who was so perturbed to be getting instructions from him instead of Alpha Don that he filled Mister Stanley's glass to the top. Mister Stanley spilled a few drops. Lula watched red flowers bloom on the white cloth as Mister Stanley said, "We're grateful to you, Don. As your friends, as Americans, as citizens of the world!"

Lula lifted her glass to Don Settebello, then to Mister Stanley, then Zeke. Abigail wouldn't look at her.

"Cheers," said Lula. "*G'zoor.*"

NOW THAT LULA's big night was over, Zeke grabbed the passenger seat, and Lula climbed in back. A few blocks from the restaurant, Mister Stanley ran over a curb on which, miraculously, no one was waiting to cross. Furious honking pursued them, but Mister Stanley didn't notice. Zeke turned around to Lula and pantomimed pouring something down his mouth. Wasn't he worried that his father would see? It worried Lula that his father didn't see.

"You want me to drive?" asked Zeke.

Mister Stanley said, "Are you kidding, Junior? Your learner's permit specifies no night driving."

"What learner's permit? I've got a license," said Zeke.

"No night driving," said his father. Lula was reassured that Mister Stanley was sober enough to remember. If only she could drive! But that was the red wine talking. Even if she had a license, she'd drunk twice as much as Mister Stanley and was probably half his weight. Drunk or sober, her father was always a terrible driver. He'd learned too late to have the reflexes. His whole generation had. And soon it would be too late for her as well. Lula fastened her seat belt and braced herself as they sped toward the tunnel.

"Dad, that's a red light!" Zeke cried.

Mister Stanley slammed on his brakes and fell silent until they'd passed the Newark exit, when he said, "Do you think Don could be developing a tiny bit of a drinking problem? Poor Don. Who could blame him for tying one on, with that daughter? All that great work he's doing, and that girl treats him like . . . Jesus, I hope we don't get stopped. I should have stuck to club soda. Let this be a lesson to you, Zeke."

Zeke said, "What lesson would that be?"

"I don't know," said Mister Stanley. "Maybe about the downside of living in the moment."

Again Zeke wheeled around in his seat. "Did you hear that?"

he asked Lula. "Dad thinks his problem is too much living in the moment."

"Fasten your seat belt," said Mister Stanley. "Or I'm pulling over."

Zeke said, "This kid in my school wound up in the ICU because someone told him if you eat mothballs you can pass the Breathalyzer test."

"That's a myth," said Mister Stanley. "Deadly deadly deadly."

"Concentrate, Dad," said Zeke.

Lula shut her eyes and thought of everything she'd ever done wrong, sins against her parents, boyfriends, girls whose boyfriends she'd slept with, every lie she'd ever told Mister Stanley, Don, and Zeke. She decided to count her sins, starting from the first, but she kept losing track and having to go back to the neighbor boy whose hand she purposely stepped on and broke his pinkie and almost got her whole family sent away because the kid's dad was secret police. Then Lula gave up counting and apologized for each one. Sorry, Granny, for not returning the change when you sent me to buy butter. Sorry, Papa, for telling Mama we used Madonna for target practice. Underneath were the real sins. The time she chose to play with her friends and refused to visit her dying grandpa. The secret gladness she'd felt when her parents left for Kosovo, and then after graduation when there was so much more room for her in Aunt Mirela's apartment. But why was she even thinking this way, when there were monsters at home who'd sent innocents to their deaths during Communism and never apologized, never felt guilty? What about the Dictator? Had he woken in the middle of the night, worried he'd hurt someone's feelings?

Against all odds, Mister Stanley seemed to be parking in front of the house.

"Thank you, Mister Stanley," she said. "Thank you, Zeke."

"Why are you thanking *me*?" said Zeke.

"Because we're alive," said Lula. "Safe."

"No one's safe," said Zeke. "Full moon."

LULA HAD TO grab the banister on her way upstairs. Maybe that was why the wine cost so much, for waiting politely until you got home to slam you against the wall. Lula sat on the edge of her bed. Beyond her tented fingers, the revolving room picked up speed. A bath would feel nice, a cold bath, shocking the dizziness out of her, boiling off the alcohol just to keep warm. Hand over hand, she made her way to the bathroom and sat on the toilet lid.

Something was wrong. Out of place. The shower curtain was drawn. Lula never took showers. Could Estrelia have left it that way? Lula had taken several baths since Estrelia cleaned. Why would Zeke or Mister Stanley rearrange her shower curtain? Was that a shadow moving behind it?

Lula pulled back the curtain. She must have closed it and forgotten. She was turning the knob that stoppered the tub when she noticed that her soap was not in its dish. Now that was strange. Lula was obsessive about her soap, hand-milled in France by monks consecrated to silent prayer and shampoo. The soap lay beached against the drain, in a milky puddle. A sudden rush of nausea felt like a new kind of thirst that could only be slaked by immersing her body in water. But how could she bathe in a tub in which a stranger might have been? *Might have?* The tiles were wet.

And what was this? A curly red hair inscribed in the gooey lavender skin of the soap. Oh, hideous. Disgusting! Lula grabbed a swatch of toilet paper, and, averting her eyes, swabbed the soap with the paper, which she flushed down the toilet. Pretend it was one of the Lower East Side water bugs, puny wimps compared to the roaches that used to chase her around Aunt Mirela's apartment.

She would have been more frightened if she hadn't been drunk. Alcohol was so skillful at widening the distance between the self that knew what was happening and the self that felt compelled to do something about it. This was not her imagination. Something had to be done. Lula flung open the closet doors, then crouched and looked under the bed. What about Zeke and Mister Stanley? What if the red-headed serial killer had showered as ritual preparation for stabbing them in their beds? It would be her fault. Those guys with the gun, who were they? She had no idea. But she'd let them into the house.

She stepped into the silent hall. Propping herself against the wall, she listened and heard nothing but the distant buzz of Mister Stanley snoring.

A sense of peace overcame her, a feather quilt of fatalism. Let what happens happen. Most likely, it would be nothing. She was tired. She needed her rest. Things would sort themselves out. If she was murdered in the night, it would mean she'd made a mistake. Just before she fell asleep, she had a disturbing dream in which she saw Don Settebello, blindfolded and in shackles, his head gleaming behind the window of a plane painted camouflage green and black, bouncing over the ocean.

Chapter Four

———∞———

THE BURNING coin of pressure glowing between Lula's brows made it hard to remember why she was supposed to feel grateful to be waking up at all. Maybe because she hadn't been bludgeoned in her sleep by the killer who'd left his hairy signature scrawled across her soap. That is, she hadn't been murdered *yet*. It was only 4:00 a.m.

In the darkness, Lula ran her hands along her arms and legs. Unhurt, but for the hangover. Maybe the so-called intruder was a wine-fueled hallucination, a byproduct of rich beef protein and the frightening drive home. But she could picture the red hair, the winking copper wire. Someone's hair was that red.

Alvo's. It was Alvo's.

The possibility that Alvo had sneaked in and showered in her tub seemed marginally likelier than a quick cleanup by some random psycho. So it wasn't so scary. But troubling, she had to admit. And weirdly, sort of hot. It was foolish and stupid to have feelings for your stalker. As Lula got older, she seemed to be growing less mature about boys. At university in Tirana, her sensible younger self ended a brief romance with a guy just because she didn't like something she saw in his eyes during sex. Later Dunia's cousin went out with him, and he held a rotisserie skewer to her throat in bed.

Unless Alvo's late-night visit had nothing to do with her . . . Lula switched on the night lamp and vaulted across the room.

"Thank you," she whispered. Thank you? The gun was still in her underwear drawer. Then she remembered her money, and a fresh surge of adrenaline propelled her to the desk where—thank you again!—the envelope of cash was where she'd left it. She was deranged to think first about the gun and only then about her money.

They needed to put new locks on the doors. If something happened to Mister Stanley or Zeke, Lula would never forgive herself. In the morning she would have to figure out what to say. Mister Stanley, I made some new friends. I was so happy to meet Albanians, and one of them was cute, so I agreed to keep their gun. And now there's this little detail, they're breaking into the house when we're out. Showering in my bathroom. Bye-bye job, good-bye green card, farewell new American life.

She rolled onto her side and crossed her arms over her chest like a mummy. Both arms were numb when she awoke again at seven-thirty.

In the morning light, her imported soap was dry and smooth, her shower curtain open. Maybe she had dreamed it. No need to alarm Mister Stanley, especially if the hair belonged to Alvo, which it probably did. It was definitely his hair color. Maybe stalking was a courtship thing for him, a New World improvement on the old-school bride kidnap. She wondered if she could ever ask Alvo about it some day, or even make a joke. If she ever saw him again, unless she caught him creeping around.

It was Sunday, her day to cook breakfast for Zeke and Mister Stanley. She stripped off her slept-in party clothes, scrubbed the bathtub, rinsed it, and filled it again. She slid beneath the water to her chin and let the hot steamy bubbles melt away the soreness. By the time she got out, it was like any other Sunday. Sunday with a headache.

Lula threw on her jeans and a sweatshirt, then hurried downstairs, where she found Mister Stanley, drinking coffee at the dining room table, his back bowed over the Sunday paper. Lula made a quick tour, checking for shattered windows, busted doors, anything to track the route that Alvo, or someone, had taken. But there was only the usual mess, the usual sad Mister Stanley. How glad she was to see him. Mister Stanley wasn't hurt or even, it seemed, aware that anything unusual had occurred.

Maybe she could turn this into one of those cultural comparisons that Mister Stanley and Don so enjoyed. In her country, under Communism, if someone broke into your place and didn't take anything, it meant you were in trouble. Whereas after Communism, no one would bother breaking in unless they were planning to take something. Under Communism, there had been nothing to take. Every night, she and Zeke watched a news story about the White House insisting there should be more spying on private citizens. People acted shocked, as they should be, even if it was naive. In Europe, people admitted that the desire to spy on your neighbor was basic human nature. . . . They could discuss this in the abstract, but it wouldn't be long before Mister Stanley realized that Lula meant something specific.

Mister Stanley said, "I'm sorry, Lula. I overindulged last night."

"Sorry for what?" said Lula. "Nothing bad happened."

"The drive home couldn't have been fun," he said. "I shuffer . . . Shuffer? I shudder to think what could have happened. I will never do that again, I promise, never—"

Why was he looking to Lula, of all people, to absolve him? Because she was the only one here. She wanted to give him a consoling pat on the shoulder, but she never touched Mister Stanley, and she didn't want to start now, both of them weakened in body and spirit, both perhaps seeking relief from the damage that alcohol had inflicted on their bodies. Mister Stanley wasn't the type of guy to hit on the nanny, but every guy was a hangover away from being that type of guy. Even a friendly shoulder squeeze was a door best left unopened. Meanwhile, a surge of fondness almost persuaded Lula to tell him about her shower, the soap, her suspicions. It would be a relief to share her worries with him. And wasn't it her duty, as his employee? The impulse hovered in the air, spinning like a smoke ring. Lula told herself: No one's in danger. Relax and see what happens.

"We survived," she said. "No one got hurt. The car didn't even get scratched."

"I'll never do it again," Mister Stanley said.

Maybe she had imagined the incident with the soap. Her father used to say, My daughter Lula has some imagination. He'd made it sound like a genial way of calling her a liar. Imagination was part of what had gotten her this far. It was a tool in the arsenal that armed you for survival.

"Did you see this?" Mister Stanley slid the paper across the table. Another munitions dump had blown up near Durrës.

"Great," Lula said. "My country is practicing for the future nuclear reactor."

Mister Stanley said, "You know what it was? A factory full of little kids some gangsters paid to disassemble Kalashnikovs and stockpile explosives."

Lula said, "I told you things are bad there. You think it's all sworn virgins and blood feuds and paranoid dead dictators?" In case everything fell apart and she was deported for the crimes of her Albanian brothers, she wanted Mister Stanley to know what she would be going back to.

Mister Stanley glanced up. His face reminded her of how Estrelia had looked when Lula marched her into the kitchen to taste Granny's pepper paste. Lula said, "Everywhere seems romantic until you actually—"

Mister Stanley said, "One was never under the impression that Europe's most repressive dictatorship was romantic."

"It was the hangover talking," said Lula. "Sorry."

Mister Stanley's expression was uncharacteristically chilly and removed, as if he was looking at her and seeing someone else. Maybe Ginger.

He said, "You women always come at things from a crazy angle."

You women? This conversation had to stop before their hangovers exchanged one more word. Lula was heading into the kitchen when Mister Stanley said, "Anyhow, it was fun last night. Don's quite a guy. A hero."

"A hero," Lula agreed. "I wouldn't have the courage to do what he does."

Mister Stanley said, "I don't know. People do what they have to."

Where had Lula heard that before? She'd said it to Mister Stanley. A ribbon of pain cinched Lula's temples. She went into the kitchen and started separating eggs. The third yolk slipped into the bowl with the whites, and loudly, in Albanian, she cursed the eggs for fucking their mother.

Through the door she heard Mister Stanley say, "Good morning. Finally, Zeke!"

How could Mister Stanley and Zeke sit at the table without even making small talk? Maybe Ginger had been the talker. At La Changita, Lula had often seen mothers and girlfriends propping up the conversation, while the husbands and sons sulked or drank. It was easier in Albania, men and women divided, no one expecting the other sex to say anything much worth hearing. Lula brought in a bowl of Cheerios and an egg-white omelet for Mister Stanley, plates of scrambled eggs and toast for herself and Zeke.

Mister Stanley chewed his cereal. *Crunch crunch* pause *crunch crunch* pause. He said, "I want my low cholesterol back. I want to be young again."

Zeke said, "Dad, don't be depressing." The eggs were runny and undersalted, but Zeke seemed to enjoy them. Lula made a resolution to cook more. Kids appreciated it when adults made the effort.

Mister Stanley said, "Did you hear what Don's doing, Zeke?"

Zeke said, "I used to think Abigail's school was cooler than mine, but now it sounds like it sucks."

Mister Stanley said, "Don pays a fortune in tuition. Here's a guy who does nothing but good, who has nothing but decency in his heart, and that daughter of his, poor guy—"

"Abigail's awesome," Zeke said.

"What year is she in?" Lula asked.

"She's a senior, like me."

Lula said, "I thought she was twelve."

"Food issues." Mister Stanley contemplated his remaining Cheerios and wedge of egg-white omelet. "Tragic. Speaking of being a senior, Zeke, I got a call from a Mrs. Sullivan, the college counselor at your school."

Zeke said, "Do we have to do this now? I'm actually enjoying my breakfast. You want me to wind up like Abigail? I could quit eating too."

Mister Stanley said, "Not only have you not been to see Mrs. Sullivan, Zeke, but she thinks you haven't applied to one college, nor have you handed in the list of colleges you plan to apply to."

"I forgot," said Zeke.

"No one forgets something like that," said Mister Stanley.

"Okay, I was busy. Like you, Dad. And Mom wasn't here to help."

"You must be thinking of Old Mom. By the time New Mom left, she couldn't have helped anyone much, including herself." Normally Mister Stanley went overboard not to criticize Ginger. His tone made Lula suspect they might be headed for a dark place disguised as Zeke's college plans.

"I could have helped," said Lula. The idea that Zeke might not go away to school filled her with claustrophobic panic. No one was holding her prisoner here. She didn't have a contract. She could leave whenever she wanted, even if Zeke never left. Don Settebello and Mister Stanley had promised to help her become a citizen whether she worked here or not.

Zeke said, "No insult, Lula, but it's not like you know anything about the American college application process. You said Albanian girls got into the popular majors by blowing the professors."

When had Lula said *that*? Probably during an evening of mojitos, junk food, TV, and Lula speaking too freely. It was fun, trying to shock Zeke. Fun, but not very smart.

"You *said* that? You told *Zeke* that?" asked Mister Stanley.

"I don't think so," said Lula. "We had exams, like here."

"You did," said Zeke. "You told me that."

"You must have misunderstood," said Lula.

"These eggs are awesome," Zeke said.

"Have some more," said Lula.

"Watch the eggs, Zeke," said Mister Stanley. "You'll probably inherit my cholesterol numbers. It's never too early to develop healthy nutritional habits."

"That's what I mean," said Zeke. "This is exactly how Abigail got that way."

Mister Stanley said, "Mrs. Sullivan suggested we use the Veteran's Day weekend to visit a few New England colleges. She wrote down the names and Web sites. We're already late with this—"

"No freaking way," said Zeke.

"Lula could come with us," said Mister Stanley.

"I'd love to!" Lula said. A road trip was a road trip. America awaited her out there. She'd never been farther than New Jersey. She'd never even been to Detroit, where she'd told the visa officer she was going.

Mister Stanley said, "Come on, Zeke. We used to travel all the time."

"All right, fine," Zeke said. "Maybe we'll have a car wreck, and I can miss the rest of school."

"Knock on wood!" cried Lula.

"I thought Albanians weren't superstitious," said Zeke. "That's what you're always saying, but then you knock on wood."

"Be careful what you wish for," his father said. "Even Protestants believe that."

MONDAY WAS COLD but sunny, and Lula decided to take a walk. After a full weekend of Zeke and Mister Stanley, it would be pleasant to sit and read in the cozy library with the steam pipes clanking. And she didn't want to stay home. She knew the feeling would pass, especially if nothing else happened, but for now the idea of a stranger using her shower had spoiled her pleasure in being alone at Mister Stanley's. Most likely it was a one-time event.

Yet if the intruder was Alvo, maybe he would return. What if he came back today, and she missed him again? She weighed the odds, and chose to bet on the chance that Alvo might reappear. If the psycho stranger showed up, she would have calculated wrong.

Lula spent the day alternately looking out the window and trying not to look out the window. No one drove by, no one walked past but the mailman. The most exciting event was the *plop-crunch* of letters sliding through the slot.

How much mail Mister Stanley got, and how much went into the shredder! The three envelopes that arrived today—two invitations to upgrade credit cards and a charity solicitation—seemed destined for the same fate, but another item whispered to her as it skimmed across the floor. On the thick, hand-tinted, old-fashioned postcard two sepia rock formations rose like craggy penises. The caption said, "Red Rocks National Monument. The Scout and the Indian Maiden."

The postcard was addressed to Mr. Ezekiel Larch. Lula knew she should leave it for Zeke. But postcards weren't like letters or e-mail. Postcards dared you not to read them.

Written in brown fountain-pen ink and chicken-scratch handwriting, it said: "My dearest darling Zeke, I hear you're almost headed for college. There are some Great places out here where the air is clean and the magic isn't sick and filthy and Polluted. Or anyway, not Yet. Come here for school? College? Kindergarten? Seems like Yesterday. Keep in touch. Love, Mom."

There was no return address, the smudged postmark was illegible, and the capitalization was quirky, to put it mildly.

Lula put the card on the counter where Zeke couldn't miss it, then returned upstairs to resume her vigil, watching and not watching for the black SUV until she heard Zeke's footsteps.

By the time Lula got downstairs, Zeke was reading the postcard. She shouldn't have left it out. She should have put it somewhere he would find it after he'd fortified himself with juice and a snack.

Zeke said, "College between two penis rocks? I'd rather stay home. Forever."

"I don't think that's an option," said Lula. "Staying home forever."

Zeke said, "Dad would like that."

"Untrue," said Lula, reflexively, though maybe Zeke was right. Albanian eagle parents pushed their offspring out of the nest as soon as they could fly, but maybe that was just to make sure they flew back after their divorces. Lula had no nest to return to. Problems or no problems, Zeke was a lucky baby bird.

Lula said, "Are you looking forward to the college trip with your dad?"

Zeke said, "You're joking. Dad and I saw this *Sopranos* episode before you got here. Mom hated me and Dad watching it, but it was almost the only thing Dad insisted on. Tony killed this guy while Meadow was at an interview on her college tour. Something like that would be cool."

Lula said, "Something like that would not be cool. Come on. You get time off from school. I get out of the house. We both get a change of scenery. It's a win-win situation."

Zeke said, "You've never traveled with my dad." Staring into the refrigerator, he asked, "Do you want to hear about the worst summer of my life?" Lula's dad used to talk like that, addressing himself to the icebox. So did Mister Stanley. It was strange how men preferred deep conversation with a kitchen appliance.

Zeke said, "This was after eighth grade. We took a family cross-country road trip. From New York to Chicago Mom and Dad fought about the air conditioner. Dad said it couldn't be fixed, and Mom said that was Dad in a nutshell: Nothing could be fixed. Dad wouldn't let Mom drive, he did the crawly speed limit. We were in Nebraska for like twenty years. We only stopped to sleep or eat or piss until we got to the West, and then we'd stop at every national park, and I'd get out and kick some pebbles, and my mom would cluck her tongue and say weird spiritual shit about nature, and Dad would give me a lecture full of fascinating facts he'd learned in college geology, and Mom would look like she wanted to kill him. Then I took pictures of Dad and Mom against the natural wonders, and my dad took pictures of Mom and me. Then we'd get back in the car and drive fifteen hours to the next national park."

"That was your worst summer ever?" Lula said. "Everywhere in the world kids are being kidnapped and drafted as child soldiers. Or blown up in munitions plants. I'll bet when Don Settebello starts going down to Guantánamo, he meets kids—prisoners!—not much older than you."

Zeke said, "Don should stay home and take care of Abigail. Are you trying to guilt me or what?"

Lula said, "Okay. Sorry for the lecture. So is that why your mom left? Boredom?"

In all of Lula's time here, she had never asked Zeke directly about his mother's departure, and he'd never volunteered. It wasn't that she didn't care or wasn't curious, but she was afraid that Zeke would hate her if he told her. Men were like that, even young ones. Her first boyfriend in Tirana told her his uncle used to sneak into his bed and fondle him, and the next night he broke up with her. Another guy to whom she'd practically been engaged told her he'd stolen from the church when he was an altar boy, and then he left her too.

"I *wish*," said Zeke. "To say you're bored in this house is like saying the sun rises in the east. It *is* the east, right?"

Lula remembered a grade-school play about valiant Chinese people all working together to feed their population. She'd played the wife of a rice farmer, and in the end they all sang a Chinese song, translated into Albanian, about the sunrise.

"I was joking," Zeke said. "About the sun. My mom went

kind of nuts. One day, I was riding the school bus home, I saw her standing on the corner. From her expression I thought she'd come to tell me Dad was dead. She said she needed to ask me something private. She said, 'Zeke, pretend I'm a stranger, and you're walking home, and you see me. What do I look like?' "

"What did she look like?" said Lula.

"Like a bag lady," Zeke said. "But I couldn't say that."

"Good boy," said Lula. "Smart boy."

Zeke said, "Hey, are you wearing makeup?"

"Not really," said Lula. "Go on."

"After that she turned into a clean freak. She burned through two washing machines in a year. They were still under warranty, they just gave us new ones. I had to hide my T-shirts. She shrunk them into doll clothes. She started making Estrelia wear fluffy slippers when she cleaned the house."

"Poor Estrelia," said Lula.

"Poor me," said Zeke. "Poor Dad."

"Poor everybody," said Lula. No wonder Mister Stanley had hired her. They were lucky to get someone sane.

"Dirt and filth and pollution were all my mom ever talked about. Her face would get twisted up—" Zeke attempted to demonstrate. He got as far as clenching his teeth and narrowing his eyes until a shudder shook his features back into slacker default mode.

"She wouldn't like Albania," Lula said, just to say something. "For them a garbage dump is a clear mountain stream or the side of a country road."

"Not here," said Zeke. "Here you have to be a corporation to get away with that. Anyway, my mom stopped leaving the house except to go to this support group in the Lutheran church basement. Tree-hugging twelve-step crap. That's when she started talking about working her way back to cleanness."

"Didn't your dad make her see a doctor?"

"He did. She hated the guy. He put her on meds she refused to take. Finally one evening Mom sent us to the store for dish-washing detergent and laundry soap, and when we got back she was gone. I'm pretty sure she knew The Good Earth would be closed on Christmas Eve. We had to drive to the Shop-well, which was closed too, by the way. It gave her more time to escape. She took her passport and a big suitcase. Maybe she was nuts, but she was sane enough to write herself a huge check from my parents' joint account. Christmas Eve, did I say that?"

"You did," Lula said. "How do you know about the check?"

"I heard Dad telling Don," said Zeke. "Christmas Eve. Really nice. I wanted to call the cops, but Dad said give it a week. He said that's what the police would say. Sure enough, a week later, we got that postcard of glaciers in Norway."

Lula asked, "Do you miss her?"

"I think I miss a feeling from before she got sick. Dad says she has an illness."

"Sounds like one," Lula said. She tried to recall the message on the card Zeke was holding. Pollution had been capitalized, she was fairly certain. "Do you think she's happier now than before she left? Or less angry, like your dad says?"

"I think she's pretty cracked."

"Cracks get mended," said Lula.

"Some do, some don't," Zeke said.

"Now you sound like me," Lula said.

That night, when Mister Stanley asked how Zeke was, Lula told him he'd gotten a postcard from his mother.

"What did it say?"

"It said maybe Zeke would go to college out West, where she is."

"That's not going to happen," said Mister Stanley.

"That's what Zeke said," said Lula.

"Good." Without turning to face Lula, Mister Stanley glided from the refrigerator to the window and stared into the darkness.

After a while he said, "You know, there are some pictures one really wishes did not exist in one's head. The problem is, they crowd out all the other pictures, the good pictures, the memories from when one was young and happy. Or anyway, from when one was young. So one must have been happy. Do you know that Ginger taught second grade and, though I begged her not to, she quit to take care of Zeke? Do you know that Ginger used to be a beautiful, caring person?"

Lula shook her head. She didn't ask what Mister Stanley's mental pictures were, the good ones or the bad. She thought of Zeke's lip quivering when he'd tried to look like his mother, and of him saying he missed a feeling from before his mother got sick.

She said, "Young doesn't always mean happy."

Mister Stanley said, "One forgets sometimes. Thank you. Good night, Lula."

THE NEXT MORNING, the black Lexus pulled up to the curb. Partly from nervousness and partly from superstition, Lula ran through a series of disappointing scenarios, beginning with it being some *other* Lexus—unlikely!—and progressing through the scene in which Alvo waited in the car while Hoodie and Leather Jacket, Guri and Genti, came in and retrieved the gun.

Alvo and the G-Men ambled up the path. Lula straightened her sweater and skirt. She'd been putting on makeup since the first time they came. She ran downstairs, then waited to open the door until they rang three times. Hoodie and Leather Jacket shook her hand. Alvo gave her a brotherly kiss on both cheeks. He smelled like smoke and beach sand.

She said, "Can I get you guys coffee?"

The other two watched Alvo nod.

"Please," she said. "No smoking this time."

"We just smoked in the car," said Hoodie.

Lula took her time in the kitchen brewing the muddy coffee. They thanked her, then Leather Jacket said, "No one here smokes? No one in this house eats or sleeps or breathes or fucks? Or farts?"

Lula said, "They eat and sleep and breathe. No, wait. I don't know if the boss eats."

"What's their problem?" asked Hoodie.

"Shell-shocked. Before she left, the mom tried to poison them." Why had Lula said that? Because the true story of their loneliness, of Ginger's housewifely discontent shading into a mentally ill obsession with dirt, made the Larches seem even sadder and more pitiful than they were.

"No shit? What with?" asked Leather Jacket.

"Dishwashing liquid," Lula improvised.

"Stomach ache," Hoodie said. "Not fatal."

Alvo regarded his cup. "Maybe we should feed the coffee to the dog first."

"There is no dog," said Lula.

"Is the dog dead too?" said Alvo.

"I don't think there was a dog," said Lula.

"We know there's no dog," said Alvo. Had he factored that information in when he'd sneaked into the house? Or was he simply remarking that he'd noticed there was no dog?

Lula said, "You guys want your gun back?"

Alvo said, "Little Sister, we are not here about the gun. The truth is, we worry that you don't get out of the house enough."

Did she look pale? Tired? Sick? She needed to check herself out in the mirror.

Alvo said, "Because we are family, practically cousins of your Cousin George, we've come to take you for a ride, so you can breathe the fresh air."

Lula loved how he talked.

Hoodie said, "The fresh New Jersey air. You're a comedian, boss."

Lula said, "Is this the part where I wake up tomorrow morning in some sheik's harem in Dubai?" How could she joke about such things with Dunia out there, lost?

Ha ha, the three men laughed. Then Alvo asked Lula, "Is something wrong?"

Lula said, "I have this friend—"

"Those sheiks want twelve-year-old virgins," said Hoodie. "Little Sister is overqualified."

"Thanks a lot," said Lula.

"Shut up, shithead," Alvo said. "Come on, Lula. We've got errands. Business. Come for the ride."

What girl wasn't a sucker for male business errands? Not the former little girl whose papa had taken her into the homes of tribal warlords up north from whom he'd bought vintage muskets. Not the former teenager whose boyfriend had brought her to pick up an ounce of dirt weed he cut with wild parsley to resell at the bunker-field raves. It was pleasant to tag along, hardly noticed but there, subtly raising the temperature with your female physical presence.

She said, "I need to be back before Zeke gets home."

Hoodie looked exasperated. "You think we have all day for joyrides?"

They had places to go, people to see. Important things to do besides chauffeuring some loser Albanian nanny around northern New Jersey. But if they weren't kidnapping her, then what? That Alvo might want to spend time with her was too much to hope for.

"Let me get my coat," she said.

"Don't leave any notes," said Hoodie. "And we'll need to take your SIM card."

Lula knew he was kidding. Still, closing the door to her room, she had the sickening feeling she would never see it again. When you prepare for a journey, her granny used to say, prepare for death. What gloomy people she came from! No wonder her glass was half empty. But what if Zeke and Mister Stanley came home to find her gone? They would think it was their special curse. Or just something women did. Maybe Lula too had vanished in search of greater whiteness. In this case, the white sands of the emirates.

Hoodie paced as she took the coffee cups into the kitchen and washed them. Another mistake. In hiding the traces of her secret life, she had destroyed precious DNA evidence that might help the authorities find her. Get a grip, Lula told herself. Three friends of her Cousin George's were taking her out in a Lexus.

Leather Jacket and Hoodie lunged for the doorknob, but Alvo said, "After you." There was a pile-up, almost a scuffle, as the two guys stepped back and let Lula, then Alvo, through.

"Albanian cavemen," muttered Alvo. As Lula scrabbled in her purse, searching for her keys, Hoodie patrolled the front walk until Alvo said, "Cut that shit out," and Hoodie waited under the mulberry tree, where Leather Jacket joined him.

Alvo said, "Neanderthals. They still think women should follow five paces behind. Like my granny, rest in peace. Fifty years of eating my grandpa's dust."

"My granny too," said Lula. "My keys are in here somewhere." Did Alvo wonder why she was bothering to lock the door when guys like him could stroll in and shower whenever they wanted?

"Our friend Spiro," said Alvo, "he finds this high-powered Albanian girl, Columbia B-School graduate, no one believes such a smart girl would marry Spiro. But women are desperate, I guess. They get engaged, fly up to meet his family in Toronto, and he asks her if she could walk into the house behind him. Just this once. So this girl gets behind Spiro and takes off her nine-hundred-dollar Manolo Blahniks and smashes the high heel into his skull so hard he bled like a goat."

"I guess that ended the engagement," Lula said.

"They're married! They hold hands now. They both work on Wall Street. The modern Albanian couple. My granny should have done that. She didn't have the right shoes."

"I got the keys!" sang out Lula. Alvo was careful to walk beside her and not hurry ahead, a positive sign of reconstructed Balkan male behavior. That Lula should even register—and appreciate—this was depressing. But comforting, in a way. She liked being with someone who knew what it was like to watch your genius granny tag after your birdbrain grandpa. It was so hard to live among strangers with whom you shared no history, no knowledge of a way of life that went back and back.

Halfway to the car, Alvo put out his arm. "Let them get in first."

"In case the car blows up?"

Alvo's smile was all tolerance at her failure to appreciate his gesture of macho courtesy, making sure the vehicle was warmed up for the lady. Beneath the grin was a question. Why was Lula so jumpy? Lula's smile said, No reason. Really, no reason at all!

Alvo opened the door for her, and Lula slipped inside. On the dashboard was a TV screen, and as Leather Jacket left the curb, a blinking violet cursor imitated everything they did. Albanian hip-hop boomed out of the speakers.

"What group is that?" asked Lula.

"Keep It Bloody," said Hoodie. "You know them?"

"Sort of," Lula said. Regardless of the language, it was always the same guys yelling about how tough they were. The difference was the bitches whose asses these guys were going to kick were Serbs.

"Sort of?" said Hoodie. "Either you know them or you don't."

"Let it go, dumbass," said Alvo.

Lula said, "A bunch of guys driving a Lexus with black windows, and you play this music, this loud? How often do you get pulled over?"

Alvo said, "Good question. I like how this girl thinks."

Leather Jacket said, "Never. New Jersey's finest know better than to fuck with us." He took the prettiest streets, past mansions with white pillars and brick facades veined with dead ivy. They floated so high above the road they could have been in a balloon. Lula touched a button, and her window slid down to admit a gust of chill air, perfumed with leaf mold.

Leather Jacket pulled into a strip mall and parked in front of a supermarket with hand-lettered signs in the window.

"Need anything?" said Alvo.

"No, thank you," Lula said.

"Want to come in?" Alvo asked.

As Lula and Alvo crossed the parking lot, she felt buoyed by an updraft of something like exultation. Everything seemed natural, effortless, as if she and Alvo were a couple, young, in love, enjoying their courtship freedom before they had the two kids and bought the brownstone in Brooklyn. Where had *this* fantasy come from?

The few elderly shoppers stared at Lula and Alvo as if they were celebrities they couldn't quite place. The dying fluorescent light and sour-milk smell were happy reminders of Tirana. Alvo paced the aisles, checking out the cans and packages but also the walls and the ceiling. He said, "We are in construction. I mentioned that, right? I notice construction details."

"What kind of construction?" said Lula.

"Commercial only," said Alvo. "Residential is asking for headaches. First the client wants wallpaper, then she wants it ripped out. Businesses, they know what they want. Aisles, cash registers, shelves. Especially cash registers."

Alvo seemed to know what he was talking about, and the sound of the words—commercial construction—was honest, industrious, solid. And the gun? This was New Jersey. You'd be crazy to be in the building trades and not carry a weapon.

Alvo picked up a quart of orange juice and a carton of Camels. So that *was* his sales receipt Estrelia found in the cushions. Lula had saved it in her desk. Alvo's shoulder brushed against hers as they—ladies first—left the market.

But as they approached the SUV, Lula felt the temperature between them drop. She said something lame—testing, testing—about the weather, but Alvo didn't answer. This time he opened the door on his side and let her open hers. This time Hoodie took the wheel with Leather Jacket beside him. Alvo frowned into space. Lula had no idea what had gone wrong, or how she could fix it.

Hoodie's aggressive driving style matched the new mood inside the Lexus. The cursor on the GPS danced across the screen, and its female voice cried plaintively, "Reconfiguring, reconfiguring."

After a while, Alvo said, "My friend Spiro, the one with the stiletto heel in his head? That's why you don't want an Albanian boyfriend, Little Sister."

Little Sister. Alvo's fraternal romantic advice made her heart hurt. But why had she even thought that Alvo wanted to be her boyfriend? Maybe Lula was losing her charms. Welcome to twenty-six.

Lula said, "I dated this Argentinean guy, Franco, he was ten times crazier and more jealous than the worst Albanian shithead."

Alvo said, "What did he do, this Franco? For a living."

"An artist," Lula said.

Alvo glared at her. "Let me get this straight. You fucked an Argentinean?"

"No," lied Lula. "I said dated." First he'd told her not to go out with Albanian guys, and now he seemed ready to honor-kill her for dating an Argentinean.

"Glad to hear it. Dated." Alvo nodded at the front seat. "My gorilla pals here get very upset when they see Albanian girls going outside the community."

Lula said, "Good luck telling an Albanian girl what to do."

"Funny," said Alvo, mirthlessly. "Here we are. Home sweet home." How had Hoodie managed to find all new streets and arrive at her house without her realizing they were close? The SUV jerked to a stop. No one spoke. No one mentioned seeing Lula again, and the Lexus roared away before she'd unlocked Mister Stanley's front door.

Chapter Five

Days passed, then more days, with no sign of Alvo. What did Lula have to look forward to? The college trip with Zeke and his dad? Zeke's departure for school promised deliverance, of a sort. But Mister Stanley would find a reason to keep Lula around. He would pay to have another human watch him sip his water. How would Lula break away? Home comfort was seductive.

Oddly, the gun reassured her. But was that really so odd? Lots of people felt that way. For example, her father. Lula told herself that the three guys would return, if only to pick up the pistol. Handguns were costly, hard to obtain. Meanwhile her challenge was to keep busy and stave off worry about her future.

One morning, frustration drove Lula to travel into the city and check out the supermarket from which Alvo's receipt had come. Useless, as she'd known it would be. What did she think would happen? That destiny would deliver them both there at the same moment? What a coincidence, our meeting here like this! So now it was her turn to be the stalker in this romance.

Parked outside the supermarket was a construction van. From the door she could see that repair work was being done. She peeked through a gap in the plastic curtain. The workers were Chinese. Maybe her friends were in charge. She knew that a lot of

Albanian guys ran construction crews. She'd met some of them in a bar on Second Avenue on the night Albania competed in the World Cup.

She walked down the supermarket aisles, pretending to look at food, until she saw a checker watching her in the security mirror. She bought the costliest peanut butter, hand-shelled on a farm in Georgia, along with a jar of organic strawberry jam from Vermont.

She was taking off her coat when Zeke walked in the door.

"What's this?" Pointing accusingly at the peanut butter and jelly, he seemed upset that Lula had gone grocery shopping without him.

"I went into the city," Lula said.

"You went into the city to get peanut butter and jelly?"

"I got it especially for you. I read about this brand in the paper. Try it. Trust me, okay?"

Zeke said, "Did you get crackers?"

"Use a spoon," Lula said.

THE WEATHER TURNED even more dismal, and after a week of gloom, Lula powered up Zeke's computer and closed out a cascade of girls in bikinis wanting to chat. She imagined her own cascade, snapshots of lost keepsakes and loved ones gone forever. Back home in '97, when the economy tanked, everything went missing: doorknobs, letterboxes, public toilets, storm drains. Thieves would come in the night and steal the swings from the children's playground, the drinking fountains from the park. But who would want to read about that? Who would care about the neighbor who almost got lynched for stealing paper from the communal toilet?

The true stories of her childhood were tales of grubby misery without the kick of romance, just suffering and more suffering, betrayal and petty greed. It was nicer to mine the mythical past. Wasn't that the Albanian way? Five minutes into a conversation, Albanians were telling you how they'd descended from the ancient Greeks. The Illyrians. Those folktales had come from somewhere. Hoodie said they were all related. Every Albanian fairy tale was someone's great-granny's life story. Little Sister, they'd called her. For all Lula knew, it was true.

She could write the most famous legends and pretend they were family stories. For example, the tale of the heartless girl everyone called Earthly Beauty, who put her prince through hell before he could make her his wife. Lula wrote, "My grandfather's half brother fell in love with a woman known as the Earthly Beauty. She charged him money for peeks at her—a finger, a hand, an arm. He paid for every inch of flesh he saw, he spent his dead papa's fortune. And every inch, every beautiful inch, made him want her more."

Don and Mister Stanley were so good to her. It was sinful that fooling them should be easy and even entertaining.

Oops. Now came a part about the boy finding a hat that made him invisible. Lula would have to leave that out if she wanted her story to have any credibility whatsoever. The same thing went for the bottle from which genies appeared and threatened Earthly Beauty on our hero's behalf, genies whose power she turned against him by making them work for her. Lula imagined Earthly Beauty looking like Angelina Jolie. She turned the genies into thugs whom Earthly Beauty seduced, but ended the scene just short of her having gang-bang sex.

But still the tale had one final twist. The hero finds some enchanted grapes, red and green. The red grapes make horns grown on Earthly Beauty's face. The green grapes make the horns drop off. Magic cosmetic surgery. So the red grapes let the prince wreck his beloved's looks, and the green grapes turn her back into Earthly Beauty. After which she's so grateful she marries him, even though he was the one who destroyed her face in the first place. But then he fixed it. And he loves her.

She wrote, *My grandfather's half brother found some grapes.* No wonder there was such bitterness between Albanian men and women. This was their version of Cinderella. What do you do if the girl doesn't like you? Throw acid in her face, then pay for the plastic surgeon. If you believed the story, Earthly Beauty deserved it, stealing the guy's money for a glimpse of her hand. But that was how women were! That was why you took your girlfriend out for an expensive dinner and then refused to pay for your wife's dentist and let all her teeth fall out. If you still had any money left, you divorced her and found a younger wife who still had her own molars.

Lula deleted the last line. Then she typed it again. "My grandfather's half brother found some grapes."

She saved the file under "Earthly Beauty" and shut down Zeke's computer. She put on three sweaters and a coat and grabbed an umbrella and headed out the door.

The library was deserted except for nice Mrs. Beller, who had introduced herself early on and who always seemed personally disappointed that Lula could never provide the documentation required for a borrower's card. Were Mrs. Beller's tremors worse today, or was some bad news on her computer making her shake her head? She didn't acknowledge Lula. Had Lula offended her somehow? Could the librarian have unearthed some awful secret about her?

Lula went to the magazine rack and was soon engrossed in an article about a Texas dynasty literally and figuratively screwing each other for generations, when they weren't crashing cars into trees or jumping off the roof. The story cheered Lula. It sounded like a family you might hear about at home, though the money would have been different, as would the trees and cars and roofs. An hour passed, then another. Without the quiet welcome of this undemanding place, she might have fled Mister Stanley's long ago. Which might have been a good thing. Who knew where she would be now, how much better off, or worse?

Eventually, she made herself stand up and put on her coat. She was relieved when Mrs. Beller said, "See you soon, dear. Stay dry."

On the way home, Lula passed a drenched terrier guarding its owner's front porch. Ugly Dog to Earthly Beauty. What if the magic fruit didn't make you grow horns but created some more believable, less disfiguring problem? A bad mood. Bipolar depression. The magic green-grape cure could be some ancient folk pharmacology that would thrill Don and Mister Stanley.

Back in the house, Lula tossed her wet clothes into the laundry room and went up to her desk, where, she was surprised to see, she'd left Zeke's laptop on. She was always careful to shut it down, especially when it was raining. Many friends at home had had their hard drives fried by lightning.

Obviously, she was losing her mind. She'd left the Earthly

Beauty file open. The cursor blinked at the end of the text. Lula read through the final section.

My grandfather's half brother brought Earthly Butey the pretty red grapes, but they were poison. She fell ill and almost died while he searched the world for help. Finally he found an old heeler in the mountains who said, feed her green grapes. That wouldn't have been the guy's instinct, the red grapes had done enough bad. But he did what the heeler said, and Earthly Butey got better and fell in love with him and they married and had fifteen children and lived happily ever after, and she never complained when the guy had young girlfriends well into old age.

Lula hadn't written this. She knew how to spell *beauty* and *healer*. Her story wasn't about poisoning a girl and then curing her and she's yours. Fifteen children? The wife who doesn't mind the old guy having young girlfriends? What sicko male pig wrote that? A male pig who couldn't spell.

Or maybe someone was trying to make her think she'd lost her mind. She and Dunia had watched an old black-and-white movie on the Belarusian model's TV about an evil husband convincing his wife she'd gone mad so he could put her in an asylum and steal all her money. But Lula was sane enough to know that someone had sat here and read what she wrote and finished her story for her.

This was creepy in the extreme! Had Lula come home sooner, her chair might have been warm from her self-appointed ghost-writer's ass. Frantically, she searched the house for signs of alien presence. Nothing had been disturbed. She should run back to the library and throw herself on Mrs. Beller's mercy. But what would happen when Zeke came home to find the intruder still here? Lula should dial 911 and tell the police that someone had broken into the house to write fiction on her computer. She'd like to hear how that went. Anyway, no self-respecting Albanian called the cops for any reason, good or bad.

Lula checked the house again. She even went down to the basement, which scared her in the best of times. Really, it was fortunate she didn't believe in ghosts. When Franco, the waiter-sculptor, took her to his loft, he'd told her a story about angels finishing an artist's work while he was away. Franco must have believed that spirits worked on his crappy sculptures, assembling the rusty bedsprings into outer space creatures while he was off serving red beans and rice. It was one of those things guys said when they wanted you to get you in bed. Could Franco have tracked her down and done this? Franco was grateful that she'd never once mentioned their one-time-only drunken night of awkward sex.

Unless Lula had written some notes to herself and forgot, notes so rough she never bothered correcting the misspellings? She would have remembered. She had to be logical, look at the facts, be her own detective.

It had to be an Albanian person who knew about Earthly Beauty. It was Alvo. It had to be.

Maybe Alvo's ending wasn't so bad after all. Readers might prefer the randy Albanian codger with the fifteen kids and the harem. And what became of the Earthly Beauty? Whiskers, sagging breasts. Most people would think she got what she deserved for making her boyfriend suffer.

Lula corrected the spelling and grammar and printed out

the story, and that night asked Mister Stanley if he would mind looking at something she'd written. From across the kitchen, she watched him read. As he turned the last page, he said, "This is excellent. Can we share this with Don?"

"Naturally," Lula said.

THE NEXT WEEK, Don Settebello called and asked Lula if they could have lunch tomorrow. Just the two of them. During her work-visa application process, Don had several times taken her out for a burger to keep her informed about her case. All very proper and professional, the kindly hip avuncular lawyer reassuring the client in whom, he said several times, he saw his daughter, grown up. Surely he didn't mean Abigail, who had better start eating right now if she planned to turn into Lula. She'd assumed that Don meant his feelings for her were the purely paternal good wishes that a powerful older man feels for a bright, deserving young woman.

Don said, "Let's go to Mezza Luna. At the moment it's very hot, but I'm sure I can get in. The line cooks are all my clients. I need to ask you a little question. Maybe two little questions."

Lula couldn't say no, though it made her uneasy to recall that subliminal sexual thrum she'd picked up from Don at the steak restaurant. Dear God, don't let him hit on her and make life complicated. She had to admit it was flattering that an important guy like Don would knowingly violate the ethics of his profession for a shot at Lula, who lately had not exactly enjoyed an excess of male sexual attention.

"Two little questions?" repeated Lula. She hadn't meant

to sound provocative. Could one be: Will you blow me? Don would never say that.

Lula dressed up in her new clothes, this time without Zeke's scarf, and took the three buses that, against all odds, got her to the restaurant on time. Don rose to kiss her cheek. On the table were a glass and a half-empty bottle of red wine. Half full, Lula reminded herself.

"Something to drink?" asked the waiter.

Lula pointed at Don's bottle, and the magician-waiter produced a glass from thin air.

"Brilliant choice," Don said.

Don asked after Stan and Zeke. Fine, they were fine, everybody was fine. When Lula asked Don how his cases were going, he stared into his wine and was silent for so long she wondered if he'd heard her. He said, "I went to Guantánamo."

Lula said, "What happened?"

"It took me two days before they'd let me talk to anyone, and then another two days before anyone would talk to me. And then . . . the stories they told me, it was worse than you can imagine." Don closed his eyes for a few moments, leaving Lula free to look him in the face and see more anger and torment than she wanted to see in her lawyer's face, or in anyone's, for that matter. "You know what they call torture? Enhanced interrogation techniques. You know what they call a beating? Non-injurious personal contact. A suicide attempt? Manipulative self-injurious behavior. If I told you what I heard there, they'd have to kill us both. I could lose my security clearance, and my poor client would be fucked. Except he's already fucked. I'm not going to tell you his name, he's a Harvard-trained Afghan cardiologist, he went home to start a clinic, and some piece-of-shit neighbor got two grand for turning him in as a Taliban leader. The neighbor probably wasn't even a shithead, just some desperate slob who needed the money. Meanwhile my guy gets three years of torture. No sleep. No food. Constant loud noise. Made to eat his own shit. Shackled and hung from the ceiling. Razor cuts on his penis."

Lula put her hands over her ears and lip-read Don saying, "Fucked."

"It's great you're doing something," she said. "Or even *trying* to do something."

"Who knows what I'm accomplishing," said Don. "Making myself feel better. But what will they let me actually *do?*"

Why were Don and Mister Stanley always asking Lula questions that had no answers? She said, "During our dictatorship these things also happened—"

"Meaning what exactly?" said Don

"Meaning these things happen," said Lula. She hoped the food here was good. "Human nature, maybe . . ."

Don said, "I don't know what else to do. Once you know, once you've seen . . . So I take my life in my hands from the minute I get on that ridiculous toy plane with rust holes in the fuselage and nowhere even to piss. At least I give these guys some courage, some heart. Let the so-called Justice Department know that someone is paying attention. Then I come back and eat this fancy food and drink this fabulous wine, and maybe the guy gets tortured worse because I tried to help him."

"That's what happens," said Lula. "Like I said, human nature."

Don said, "You've got to stop saying that. I never said shit like that when I was your age. I was Mr. Idealism. I was the guy who was going to save all the little guys from the big bad bullies."

Lula shrugged, very Balkan. "You should have grown up where I did. We knew the truth from birth."

"And what truth would that be?"

"Put the little guys in power, and overnight they turn into the big bad bullies."

Lula stopped. Were they arguing? She didn't want Don to think she was calling him naive. But it never hurt to remind him where she came from and what her country had been through. Don knew she was half Muslim. He'd said, Don't make a point of it. Her visa application said Christian.

Lula said, "So what's the question you wanted to ask me?" If the question was about sex, let Don ask it now. Saying no would be harder after he'd paid for the meal.

Don shook his head like a swimmer with an earful of water. "Oh, right. About that story you gave Stan . . ."

"What about it?" said Lula.

For a moment, she considered telling Don that someone had sneaked into Mister Stanley's house and finished the story on Zeke's computer. She felt like a child with a secret she wanted a grown-up to know. But she wasn't a child, and if her coauthor was Alvo, Don Settebello's knowing would only make everything more complex. She trusted Don, but only so far. She would wait and see what happened between now and dessert.

"I thought your story was fantastic," Don said.

"Thank you," said Lula. The waiter appeared with a choice of breads. Don waved the waiter away.

"Hey, wait a minute," said Lula. The waiter returned, and

she helped herself to a crusty roll studded with raisins and olives.

"Nicely done," said Don. "I like appetite in a woman."

Lula buttered her roll and took a bite, and with her mouth still full in what she hoped was an unsexy way said, "You were talking about my story."

Don said, "Right. Your story. I took the liberty of showing it to a friend in publishing, and she gave it to an editor friend who, coincidentally, happens to be Bulgarian."

"Bulgarian?" Lula already had a bad feeling about this Bulgarian person.

"Bulgarian," said Don. "Anyway, she read your piece. She liked it very much."

"Thank you," said Lula uneasily.

"Don't thank me," said Don. "But she did suggest that . . . well, that story about the Earthly Beauty and the guy who wins her after going through all that abuse and the part about the grapes is a very popular Balkan folktale. So it seemed . . . strange that it happened to your grandfather's half brother."

Cousin, Lula wanted to say, except that she suddenly couldn't remember what she wrote. Maybe Don was right.

Don said, "She did say that the part about the fifteen kids and the harem was extremely Balkan. And not the traditional ending. I enjoyed that part too."

Lula said, "It's a short story."

Don said, "I thought it was true. Something from your journal."

"I've branched out," Lula said. "I thought you and Mister Stanley knew that. Anyhow, calling a character my grandfather's half brother doesn't mean he was my grandfather's half brother. I could call a character Don, and he won't be you. Have you read Ismail Kadare? The greatest Albanian novelist? He wrote about Egyptian pharaohs and medieval monks to hide the fact that he was writing about our dictator."

Lula shouldn't have mentioned Kadare. It was unlikely that Don would remember her passing off a Kadare plot as a story she was writing, but why take chances? She said, "Bulgaria was Disneyland compared to how we lived. How people *still* live in Tirana. Your Bulgarian friend should visit."

Don turned up his palms, and his fingers curled, groping for . . . what? He didn't care about Bulgaria. He didn't care about Lula's story.

Don said, "Camp Delta was a shock. You think you know, and you think you know . . . but when you see the real thing . . . I'm obsessed. I want to tell anyone who will listen. The loneliness, the pressure . . . Thank God for good friends and good food. I hope my daughter finds that out. Another bottle, please. Pronto!"

"No, thank you," Lula told the bottle pointed at her glass.

"Yes thank you for me," said Don.

Neither spoke for a while. Then something fell on Lula's hand so heavily that dishes clattered. At first she thought that a fat warm brick had landed on her fingers, but it turned out to be Don's hand, pinning Lula's to the table. Lula's instinct was to shake it off, but she waited without moving.

Don said, "You're a beautiful woman." He sounded as if he were shocked to suddenly find that out. He said, "Is it all right if I say that? If I compliment you like that?"

"A compliment is a compliment," Lula said, gracious but not flirtatious. "Always welcome, believe me."

Don looked at her over the top of his wine glass, and there was a moment, a split second, really . . . *lawyer client, lawyer client*, Lula chanted inside her head, telegraphing how much Don was risking merely by touching her hand. And for what? Human contact? Romance? Distracting himself from the pain and injustice of the world with a few hours of sordid, unprofessional, maybe actionable sex?

And then, for no discernible reason, or perhaps for a good reason indiscernible to anyone but Don, something broke the mood. Don removed his hand from Lula's and pushed his spectacles back on his nose. Don the lonely guy vanished, and Don the righteous lawyer replaced him.

Don said, "This morning I woke up and looked in the mirror, and my hair was gray."

Lula tried not to look puzzled. Don's hair, what there was of it, had been gray when she met him.

"I'm quoting Chekhov," said Don.

"I've read him," Lula said. "I don't remember about the gray hair."

"Young people never do," said Don. "Anyhow, by some divine intercession, or more likely thanks to some bureaucratic fuckup, they let me talk to another detainee. This one's a businessman from Mosul with the bad luck to have the same name as some al-Qaeda motherfucker. Of course they don't let me meet the big guns. The guys who actually did something or plotted something and are still entitled to protections, I don't care how Dick Cheney tries to fuck with the Constitution—"

Lula said, "If Hoxha and Milosevic had a baby, and the baby was a boy, it would look like Dick Cheney." She'd been waiting months to say this to someone besides Zeke, but she'd chosen the wrong moment. To Don, it was a nonsensical interruption.

"It's fine if I meet with the innocent guys. Nobody gives a rat's ass what they didn't do. This guy's been in solitary for months. The family found out and got in touch. The wife's going crazy. The three kids are crying for their daddy. The guy just came off his hunger strike. He's down to eighty-five pounds."

Lula said, "What's he accused of?"

Don said, "Nothing yet. The guy ran a charity. Funded religious schools. Helped out widows and orphans."

Lula said, "The KLA bought its whole arsenal that way, going from house to house in Detroit and the Bronx, collecting for widows and orphans."

Don said, "That's the kind of cynical shit everybody says." His scowl made Lula feel terrible for being one of those cynics. She made a mental note to tone down the Eastern Bloc pessimism, or realism, depending.

"I believed this poor bastard. I've been a lawyer for thirty years. I can tell when a client is lying."

Every lie Lula had ever told passed before her eyes, starting with the one Don knew about, her omitting the half Muslim part on her visa application. No one in her family had been religious for generations. That is, if you didn't count the third cousin who got born again and went to Afghanistan to wage jihad. Everyone had a third cousin like that. What if they traced him to her? If just one nosy agent found out, she could be back in Tirana tomorrow.

The restaurant's creamy light made everyone look healthy, rich, and happy to be having lunch with everyone else. How long could her comfortable life here last? She ordered the haddock with grapes and saffron.

Don said, "Thanks. I'm not eating." He gulped his wine like water. Lula wondered if she was going to have to help him into a cab. His office number was on her phone. She could call his secretary.

Don said, "A client of mine got deported."

"The one whose foot got run over?" Lula welcomed the chance to prove she had listened. She hoped it was the same client. The more of Don's clients who got sent home, the less optimistic she felt.

"Good girl," said Don. "But no, another one. Honestly, I start to wonder, Why am I even trying?"

"Don't blame yourself," said Lula. "You helped me get my work visa. You fixed things for Estrelia and—"

"This guy *had* a green card," said Don. "He's a contractor. Bangladeshi. His family's some bizarro evangelical Protestant."

"What did he do?" asked Lula.

"Illegal weapons possession. Unregistered handgun. To be honest, if I lived where this guy lived, on the far edge of Bushwick with two little kids and a wife, I'd find a way to protect myself, permit or no permit."

"Okay, sure, wow," said Lula.

"Is it too warm in here?" asked Don.

How could Don see the droplets beading up on the back of her neck? On TV, the suspects who sweated were either on drugs or guilty or both.

"Allergies," said Lula. She wondered which was more dangerous, ditching Alvo's gun and pissing off the Albanians, or holding on to it and worrying that someone would report her to the INS. The latter seemed less likely.

"It's not allergy season. You should get your eyes checked," said Don. "I was around your age when I started wearing glasses."

What age? she might have asked anyone else. But Don knew her age, to the day. It was on her application. Don already knew so much, she wished she could ask him about the gun. After all, he was her lawyer. But she knew what Don would say: Lose the sketchy Albanian pals, don't answer the door when they knock. She would pretend to take his advice, and she would ignore it.

Lula's haddock arrived. It could almost make you believe in God, or in some higher intelligence that had created this fish that, perfectly poached, flaked apart in buttery layers. She smiled at Don. "Would you like some?" Too much generosity! A remark like that could encourage Don to hold her hand again.

"No thank you," said Don. "I seem to be on an all-liquid diet. Go ahead, finish your lunch. I won't ruin it for you, I promise."

Don was as good as his word. He waited till Lula had cleaned her plate, then said, "It's worse than I imagined."

"Let's have coffee," said Lula. She and the waiter conspired wordlessly to get enough coffee into Don so he could ask Lula to calculate the tip—twenty percent—before he signed the credit card slip.

"Drink up," Lula kept saying, while she plied him with small talk about Zeke and Mister Stanley—the upcoming college trip, Zeke's B+ on a math test. Don drank all his coffee. From boredom, probably, but so what? The aim was caffeination.

Walking Don to his office, Lula glared at the few pedestrians rude enough to stare. It was an honor to hold a hero's arm as he lurched down the sidewalk.

Don could manage the elevator. They shook hands, then made an awkward attempt to hug. Lula took the buses back to Jersey.

She decided not to mention the lunch. But that night Mister Stanley asked, first thing, "So how was lunch with Don?"

"He seems a little . . . sad," Lula said. "He didn't eat much."

"Was he drinking?" Mister Stanley asked.

"Only wine," said Lula.

"I thought so too," said Mister Stanley. "I mean, about him seeming sad. Well, Jesus, Lula, who isn't sad with the state our country is in? This evening, driving home, I heard on NPR that forty thousand people are living in homeless shelters. And that's just in New York City! I worry about Ginger. I don't want her to suffer. Fortunately, she prefers the company of goofballs in Navajo sweat lodges to the company of drunks with the DTs picking bugs from under their skin."

"I'm sure she does," Lula said. "I'm sure she's fine." She went to the sink and devoted herself to washing a fork Zeke had left in the drain.

Mister Stanley said, "What did Don want to talk about?"

Lula said, "My story."

"He told me he liked it a lot."

"He did. But next time I think I'll wait before I let anyone read it."

"We didn't mean to rush you," Mister Stanley said. "I hope Don didn't upset you . . . He's been under a lot of stress."

"Don's a hero," Lula said.

"That he is," said Mister Stanley.

Chapter Six

Just when Lula had given up hope of ever seeing the Albanian guys again, Alvo showed up. He had a gauze bandage wrapped around his hand, and he flinched when he shut the front door behind him. There was something sexy about his wince and the whiteness of the bandage. When Lula asked, he told her he'd cut himself when a saw blade snapped. Being in the building trades was an accident waiting to happen. He said, "The workman's compensation board loves it that nobody's legal anymore, so nobody files claims."

"I didn't know they had workman's insurance here," Lula said.

"They used to," Alvo told her.

"Coffee?" asked Lula. It was noon. She had been delaying the moment of making a sandwich from the last of Granny's red pepper jam and realizing that this would be the best part of her day, and that it was already over. She should offer Alvo something to eat. Zeke's leftover pizza? She could make an omelet.

Alvo said, "I was just in the neighborhood. You want to go get lunch?"

"Do I need to change?" Lula hadn't intended to make him look her up and down. Why had she quit dressing nicely and putting on makeup? Because she had no patience.

"Jeans are fine," Alvo said.

She'd expected to find Hoodie and Leather Jacket waiting in the Lexus. But the SUV was empty.

"Are you okay?" Alvo asked.

Why did everyone ask her that? Was every emotion so plain on her face for the whole world to see?

She said, "At university I played poker. Lots of times, I won enough to buy my friends drinks at this club where we hung out in Blloku."

"What club?" asked Alvo.

"The Paradise."

"I used to go there," said Alvo. "How come I never saw you?"

"I was there," Lula said.

Alvo started the SUV and pulled away from the curb.

"I wish I could drive," said Lula.

"I could teach you," Alvo said. "It's easy. Babies drive. Senile grannies drive. It would take one lesson."

"Two lessons," said Lula.

"One lesson," Alvo said.

Leftover drops from a morning shower sparkled on the fallen leaves and the brownish grass. They drove past a golf course on which there was a structure with three roofs, pointed like witch's hats.

"Look!" she said. "It looks just like that snack bar in the park in Tirana."

Alvo nodded. That he knew which snack bar she meant made her senselessly happy.

Eventually, Lula and Alvo slipped into something resembling a companionable silence, the calm married-couple happiness that Lula, despite the odds and the evidence, still hoped someday to experience. With Alvo? She was dreaming.

The silken GPS voice guided Alvo through a series of turns. Then it murmured: "Approaching destination." Alvo parked in front of a restaurant with a black curtain covering the window. Almost Albanian looking, except for the Asian lettering.

"Old Sam?" read Lula.

"Old Siam," said Alvo. "Old Sam. Very funny."

Lula said, "Go ahead, laugh. Nice guy. How do you know I'm not dyslexic?"

"Albanians don't get dyslexia. It's a disease Americans invented so they won't have to admit their kids are retarded."

"Maybe I caught it since I got here," said Lula. From this point it should have been easy to steer the conversation toward spelling. If only she could find out if Alvo could spell *beauty* and *healer*. That would answer a lot of questions. Or anyway, one big question.

Alvo said, "We should get out of the car."

"Sorry," Lula said.

There was a worrisome scarcity of vehicles in Old Siam's parking lot. Two sips of a sweet umbrella drink—next stop, Bangkok whorehouse. No wonder her social life was in ruins! Who would date a girl who couldn't tell being trafficked from a lunch date? As they crossed the asphalt, her fingertips and, weirdly, the surface of her scalp seemed to be responding, independently of her brain, to Alvo's lanky physical *thereness*. It was impressive, how a few nerve endings firing at once could silence Lula's sensible doubts about being alone with a man she'd met when he came to hide a gun in her house.

Alvo said, "This Thai guy from work told me about this

place. I love that about this country. Some people live here a lifetime, they only eat Albanian. But I like restaurants that serve the real deal from countries Albania never heard of."

"Me too," Lula said. She imagined herself and Alvo, brave culinary explorers, eating their way around the world without leaving the tri-state area. He'd said, A guy from work. Maybe he and the guys ran a crew. Maybe they had Thai workers.

"Queens is the best," said Alvo.

"I've never been to Queens," said Lula. "I'd love to go to Queens."

There were no other customers to spoil the pristine perfection of the tables set with yellow cloths and folded napkins. Someone switched on a sound system, and a girl with a baby's voice cooed and hiccupped her way through a song that sounded like a lullaby but was surely about lost love. If Lula ever had a child, she would play it music like that.

The Asian woman who came out from the back of the restaurant was so glad to see them that Lula was frightened to look directly into her joy.

"Water?" The woman smiled, setting menus before them. They nodded. "Beer? Thai beer?" Nod nod. More smiles. Lula watched her walk toward the kitchen door, where another Asian woman and two blond men in white shirts and ties waited tensely as if to debrief her after a top-secret mission.

"Mormons," said Lula.

"That's what I was thinking," said Alvo.

Lula said, "How did they get in? Even under heaviest Communism you saw Mormons in Tirana."

Alvo said, "Someone paid. Someone always pays."

The walls were covered with mirrors in which Lula saw herself and Alvo beside a canal in Bangkok. An optical illusion: A poster behind them pictured a temple with orange dragons coiled beneath its pincerlike spires.

Lula said, "Have you eaten here before?"

"Never. I like to change things up from day to day. Never the same thing twice." Alvo's tone was unsettling. He hadn't sounded like a laid-back, self-employed contractor wanting to maximize his fun, but rather like a gangster or politician describing security tactics designed to foil an assassination. Or was it a philosophical statement? Lula didn't feel she could ask. Maybe it was personal magic, a secret he had with himself, like the female CEOs wearing French underwear to board meetings. Alvo's gun was in Lula's underwear drawer, wrapped in those filmy garments that might not, after all, have been such a waste of money.

He said, "Also in private life. You don't want to be stupid. The place where lovers get blown away? It's always the lover's lane. The bench overlooking the Hudson. What sane person would go there? Some psycho sneaks up behind you. Blam. The perp's halfway to Pennsylvania before the ambulance comes."

He's paranoid, thought Lula. Another thing they had in common. *Paranoia* was English for Balkan common sense. Lula could live without making out on a bench above the Hudson. But what would it be like to have a boyfriend who never did the same thing twice? Sexually, it could be interesting. Where was she getting *boyfriend*? From one Thai meal? If lunch was a relationship, Lula and Don were married.

But wait. Was that a hair on her plate? No, a thread from her glove. Lula picked it off, but not before her lavender soap, inscribed with a copper hair, hovered like a disgusting mirage above the sparkling china. In seconds it vanished, but not before Lula was able to positively match its color with Alvo's.

She said, "Have you ever stalked someone?"

Alvo said, "Strange question, but okay. You want me to stalk you?"

"Look in the mirror," said Lula. "There we are. Eating lunch in Thailand."

Alvo looked. It didn't interest him. After that there was silence.

Finally Alvo said, "I wouldn't go there. I know this Sherpa guy. Buddhist. Hard worker. Never lies. He told me there's this dog at home that brings down yaks by reaching up their asses and pulling out their guts."

"Urban legend," Lula said.

"That's what I thought," said Alvo. "Then I saw it on the Internet."

"If it's not a hoax," said Lula, "why aren't those dogs the hot new pets for rap stars and Asian drug lords and Mexican narcos?"

"Good question," Alvo said.

The waitress brought their beers.

"*G'zoor*," Alvo toasted Lula.

"*G'zoor*," Lula said.

A few swallows infused Lula with a fizzy optimism. Life was not so bad. Back in Tirana no one was taking her out to lunch, and this place would be fancy, and it wouldn't be Thai. At home there was only Albanian. And Chinese, which was the same lamb, only candy-coated and orange. Just before she left Tirana, a Mexican place opened up, Señor Somebody's, where waiters in cowboy hats served melted sheep cheese and corn chips to missionaries from Missouri. Dunia and the Belarusian model had taken Lula to a Thai restaurant on Rivington Street for her twenty-fifth birthday, so she'd eaten Thai food. Once.

"Why the big sigh?" asked Alvo.

Lula said, "I was thinking about a friend."

"Friend as in boyfriend?" said Alvo.

"Friend as in homegirl. Last night, I couldn't sleep, I got up and went downstairs and turned on the TV and flipped through the channels. The best thing about my boss's house is, the walls are so thick no one hears anything."

"Excellent," said Alvo. "Let's say if you have guests."

Was Alvo flirting? It could be embarrassing to mistakenly assume he was.

"I never have guests," Lula said. "So last night on TV this Albanian girl was talking about marrying a rich mafioso and falling in love with his brother, who took her to Italy, where he beat her with a belt and turned her out as a prostitute until her uncle found her and an Albanian lawyer got her back. Two other girls were interviewed, both with similar stories, ghosts with smeary mascara running down their face. The thing was, I'd been lying awake worrying about my friend Dunia. She was here in New York with me, and she went back, but it's like she left the planet. She smart, she's tough. I tell myself she's okay. But maybe I'm just being lazy—"

"I've eaten lots of Thai food," said Alvo. "But I don't recognize hardly anything on this menu."

Lula said, "Pad thai is all I know. Why is this place so empty?"

Alvo said, "Maybe everybody in New Jersey is too retarded to know that Siam means Thai."

He waved the Thai woman back, then looked into her eyes so warmly he could have been her favorite son stopping by for lunch. The woman nodded and waved her arms, sign language for I'll-take-care-of-you, and disappeared into the kitchen.

"Nicely done," Lula said.

"Some people you can trust," Alvo said. "You know right away. Which we learned growing up, am I right? I read this book about bodyguards who work for the mob and the British royal family and Saudi diplomats. The Arab drivers are the brave motherfuckers. The ones who get sent to Guantánamo."

Lula said, "My lawyer has a client in Guantánamo."

"Too bad for him." Alvo crossed himself. "Too bad for his client."

"You're Christian?" Lula asked.

"I'm nothing. I'm Albanian. Like you."

"Like me. I mean, if there is a God, why is he so pissed off at Albanians?"

"Maybe God has a lousy personality," said Alvo.

"Could be." Neither had anything more to add on the subject of God. The conversation faltered until, even though it was a boring first-date question, Lula asked, "When did you come to this country?"

"1990, luckily for me. Or I'd still be there. You must have some hotshot lawyer to get a work visa after you're already here."

"He's famous." Lula tried not to think about Don's hand dropping on hers.

"If he's so good, why's he got a client in Guantánamo? Crazy country."

"It beats home," Lula said.

Alvo said, "The U.S. saved Kosovo from being ethnic-cleansed by the Serbs. No matter what else, we should be grateful. . . . But you know what? Sometimes I think this country's becoming like Albania, and Albania's becoming like this country. Like we're on opposite escalators meeting in the middle."

"In Albania's dreams," said Lula.

"We should be in the EU. Forget the trafficking, the drugs. If we had oil or even natural gas, we'd be in the EU yesterday! Then you get these deluded Albanian brothers sending the wrong message by plotting to blow up some army base in South Jersey. How does *that* make us look?"

"What plot?" said Lula. "What base?" Mister Stanley must have decided not to call her attention to that news item.

"Born-again jihadis," said Alvo. "It's a problem. No one in our family would go to my second cousin's wedding because he wouldn't allow alcohol or music. What kind of religion would even *think* about a dry wedding? Bad way to start off a marriage."

Lula almost mentioned that something similar existed in her family. Not that she knew her own jihadist cousin well enough to be invited to his wedding, or even to know if he got married. But something kept her from volunteering too much personal information. Who was Alvo, anyway? How had he found out her name? Cousin George? His aunt in immigration? Or was he an INS spy?

Lula said, "Would you know how to locate an Albanian girl if she went back home and vanished?"

"Why? You plan on vanishing?"

"My friend," said Lula. "Dunia. The one I'm worried about." Tears popped into her eyes. Alvo looked alarmed. In their brief acquaintance, he'd already seen her start crying and not be able to stop. He probably thought this was something she did all the time.

"Okay, look," said Alvo. "I know people. Here and there. Maybe I can find out something. No promises . . ."

He handed Lula his cell phone. "Write down her name and whatever contact info you have." Then he thought better of it, took back his phone, and swapped it for a ballpoint pen and a paper napkin, on which Lula wrote Dunia's name and Dunia's mom's address. Alvo read it and shook his head.

"Glad I'm not there." He put the napkin in his pocket, and Lula felt as if she were watching Dunia vanish into the linty darkness of Alvo's jacket.

The Thai woman returned and set down a platter of crunchy fried scraps. Lula helped herself to a mouthful of salty, oily, delicious . . . what?

"Parsley," Alvo said. Lula liked it that he knew, and that he not only ate with gusto but made little smacky noises. Of all the lies people told about sex, about the ratio between hand size and penis size, about the pleasure-delivering capabilities of the circumcised versus the uncut, the only one that was true, in Lula's experience, was the correlation between liking food and being good in bed. The subject was pleasant to think about, only mildly spoiled when she remembered Don Settebello saying he liked a woman with an appetite.

The woman brought more food. Duck country-style, very authentic.

"Thank you," chorused Alvo and Lula.

"Every fall my grandfather shot a duck," Alvo said. "One duck per comrade per year."

Lula picked up a chunk of duck and, with her front teeth, pried the moist spicy meat from the bones. She put aside the crispy skin she planned on saving for last. She caught Alvo watching her lick her fingers.

"My father too," she said. "The annual duck. Wasn't there some national holiday when the comrades were all supposed to go out and get trashed on raki and fire away at game birds and shoot each other in the back?'"

"I don't remember," Alvo said. "No one ever took me along. Hunters were always getting shot."

Lula said, "My father taught me to shoot." Bullet-riddled Madonna vogued in front of her eyes.

"I taught myself," said Alvo. "I had to."

Another missed opportunity. She could have sounded girlie, asking why a contractor needed a gun. She was sorry the subject had come up. What if Alvo wanted his gun back? "So what do you guys build?'"

"All commercial. Supermarkets. I thought I told you. We renovate supermarkets."

"Maybe you did," Lula said. She was thinking about the supermarket to which she'd tracked his sales receipt. Someone was doing construction there. Maybe he'd bid on it and lost. Two and two were adding up. Adding up to zero.

"I wish you'd renovate *our* supermarket," said Lula. "It's very organic and expensive, but there's a nasty smell, like a dead rat in the basement."

Alvo said, "What's it called?"

"The Good Earth," Lula said.

"Near you?"

"Five minutes," Lula said.

Perhaps someday she would know him well enough to tell him about finding the sales receipt and going to the store, hoping to meet him. Alvo would be flattered, or pretend. They would agree it was funny and cute, and then they would have sex.

"Where do you live?" asked Lula.

"Astoria," Alvo said.

"With who?"

"Alone."

"I thought you had a girlfriend."

"Did. I don't anymore."

"Sorry to hear that," lied Lula. On a normal date, you could ask why he and his ex broke up and shift the conversation to a more intimate level. When things got really personal, maybe she could ask him about showering in her bathroom. Then perhaps they could talk about his finishing her story on Zeke's computer. She would tell him that his ending, about the fifteen kids and the harem, was the part her boss and her lawyer liked best.

The Thai woman replaced their plates with bowls, chicken curry for Lula, something meaty for Alvo. Not only did she know what they wanted, she knew when they wanted different things. Did the heat in Lula's chest come from the chilis or from Alvo reaching across the table and chopsticking a hunk of chicken from her bowl? She pushed her bowl toward Alvo. Take as much as you want!

She said, "So how did you get to this country?"

"Boring story," Alvo said. "My dad was an engineer."

Lula said, "Everybody from former Communism was an engineer."

"In Detroit he had a barbershop, another family skill. My grandfather cut hair in his village. He cut the mayor of Detroit's hair, the whole family got green cards. So you could say I've moved up from barbershop to construction, or down, from engineer to construction. Depending on how you measure."

Lula said, "We went down. Any way you measure. Right after Communism ended, my father was crossing Skanderbeg Square, and he saw a woman with a huge bird hopping around on the sidewalk. She said it was an eagle, but my dad knew it was a falcon, big as a three-year-old child. Gorgeous. The woman was starting a business, renting out our national symbol for soccer games and races, weddings and private parties. She already had more orders than she could handle. But she had to hire a staff, rent an office, a phone, there were vet bills to pay. In other words, massive overhead. If my father wanted to invest, he'd get fifty percent in six months. Do I have to tell you what happened?"

Alvo said, "To his investment? No. What happened to the bird?"

Lula flapped her hands in the air above her head.

Alvo said, "Too bad your dad couldn't have found an eagle with two heads. That could have been serious money."

"Too bad," Lula said. She had been alone when she saw the woman and bird. Her dad wasn't even there. Why had she lied to Alvo? Because it was a good story.

He said, "You people who stayed longer went through a lot we missed."

Lula found herself staring at Alvo's hands, wishing she could take both his hands in hers and place them over her heart so he could feel their two hearts thumping in the same Balkan rhythm. "What could I do? My father wasn't an engineer. He made shoes." In a manner of speaking. One of his jobs included fencing stolen Chinese slippers.

"Then how did you get here?" Alvo said.

Lula said, "My aunt inherited some money from an uncle in Detroit. She'd kept it in an American bank, and when she died, she left it to me."

"You got here on a tourist visa? How did you manage that?"

Lula smiled and fluttered her eyelashes.

"The old-fashioned way," Alvo said.

"Have you been back?" asked Lula.

"My mother moved back home," said Alvo. "She lives in Tirana now. She and my dad divorced. I guess his being a barber wasn't good for the marriage. I visit every few years to see her and eat her cooking. That's how I know about the Paradise Club. Where I never saw you."

"I was there," said Lula.

"I would have remembered," said Alvo.

The Thai woman brought sweet coffee and a wobbly orange dessert. "On the house," she said. Alvo took a few bites, smiled at the woman, then pushed the pudding toward Lula, who polished off the whole plate. Alvo drained the last drops of beer, and Lula did the same, though it tasted awful on top of the mango pudding. There was nothing left to eat or drink and no reason to stay.

Alvo said, "Will you be around next week?"

Where else would she be? She would try to fit him into her busy schedule of nothing. "Sure. No, wait a minute. Monday, Tuesday, Wednesday, I'm going on a college tour with Zeke and Mister Stanley."

"Like on *The Sopranos*?" said Alvo. "When Tony whacked the snitch?"

"I saw some episodes," said Lula. "But not that one."

"Before your time," said Alvo. "So you and the boss *are* fucking."

"Separate motel rooms." The question had never arisen. But she knew Mister Stanley. He and Zeke would share a room. She would get her own.

"My father wanted me to go to college," said Alvo. "The nearest community college was in ghetto Detroit. Fifteen percent white student body. The odds of not getting my ass kicked would have been better in jail."

Lula decided not to mention her career at the university in Tirana, though in other conversations—with the waitstaff at La Changita, and with Don and Mister Stanley—she'd taken every chance to boast about her education.

Alvo said, "So is that part of your job? Little Miss Make Everything Right. All you Albanian girls are the same. Mother Teresa was just the smartest."

"Mother Teresa?"

"The best at public relations. She worked a genius angle. Everyone in Albania is saving and scheming to move somewhere better than Albania. Which is basically anywhere. Only genius Mother Teresa moves somewhere worse than Albania. That gets you the Nobel Prize!"

"She's the most famous Albanian ever," Lula said.

"There you go," said Alvo. "Her and John Belushi. Everyone knows what famous people are like when the cameras stop rolling."

Lula had always admired Mother Teresa, cradling the dying,

cupping her wizened monkey hand around the last flicker of life. She said, "I can't picture Mother Teresa throwing her cell phone at a photographer."

"Check!" Alvo pulled out his wallet.

What had Lula said? She should have agreed with him about Mother Teresa. It probably wasn't personal. Alvo had somewhere to be.

"Thanks for lunch," said Lula. "What about the week after?"

"The week after what?" said Alvo.

"We could get together the week after I get back."

"I don't know," said Alvo. "Who knows if the world will exist by then."

"It will," said Lula.

"Why are you so sure?" Alvo said.

"Okay, maybe I'm not," Lula said.

They drove back in silence. As Alvo stopped in front of Mister Stanley's, he kissed her twice, switching cheeks. Very proper. Little Sister.

Lula touched his shoulder.

"See you soon," Lula said, at the same moment that Alvo said, "See you later."

THAT AFTERNOON, ZEKE came home with a bright new pimple flourishing on his chin. Lula tried not to notice, then gave in and stared. He was eating a vegetable tonight, no matter how he complained. Lunch with Alvo had left Lula feeling cross and oppressed by the compulsory niceness that had turned out to be such an important part of her job.

She said, "We're having pizza," without offering Zeke the frozen hamburger option. What a disgusting way to live, eating frozen dog food, when twenty minutes away people were feasting on roast duck and fried parsley. "And salad. You're having salad."

"I hate salad," said Zeke.

Lula said, "Let's go to the other market for a change. The faraway one." She could tell that Zeke heard the needling challenge in her suggestion that he venture beyond the borders Mister Stanley had circumscribed. His unteenage willingness to accept his father's limits made Lula suspect that Zeke himself had his own fears and hesitations. His father's rules provided a welcome excuse not to confront them. Though who could blame a kid for being reluctant to drive to the market where his mother sent him and his dad on the night she disappeared?

Zeke's smile looked less like a human expression than like an orangutan trying to make a rival orangutan back down. "I haven't got time. I have to write some crap paper for English."

"About what?" asked Lula.

"About crap," said Zeke.

Zeke drove them to The Good Earth, where delusional Lula imagined she might run into Alvo, there to ask if the owners wanted professional help eliminating the dead rodent smell from their basement. They bought mozzarella, tomato sauce, pizza crust. On the drive back, Lula said, "We should go to the other market sometime." What character flaw compelled her to keep probing this sad boy's sore spot?

"My dad would have a fit," Zeke said. "I think he checks the mileage."

"He can't check it every day," said Lula. Not until they were home and Lula was about to open the cheese did she notice that its package was puffed up and slimed with white.

Zeke said, "That mozzarella smells like when kids used to get sick on the grade-school bus."

Lula said, "I saw on TV how they take moldy hamburger and smush it around so the red meat is on the outside and the green in the middle—"

"You made me watch that story," said Zeke.

Lula dropped the cheese in the garbage, and Zeke followed her outdoors to put the plastic bag in the bin. Neither was wearing a coat, so Lula chattered to distract them from the cold. "Those bitches change the expiration dates, some poor kid eats a burger at the family picnic and winds up on life support so the supermarket can make . . . what? A hundred bucks, ten bucks, who cares how much. Human life is worth nothing to them."

"Corporate capitalism," Zeke said.

"Communism's no better," said Lula.

"Obviously," Zeke said. "Forget the cheese, okay, Lula? You can use tomato." He sounded so tragic that Lula rushed them back into the warmth.

"Mojito?" said Zeke.

"Definitely," said Lula. She made Zeke's light, as usual, but didn't hold back on her own and drank it quickly, then fixed herself another.

She said, "One night at La Changita these customers played musical chairs. They were the last ones in the restaurant, and they'd run up a giant bill and left a humongous tip. So the staff let them screw around before we kicked them out. The leader turned his iPhone up loud, and the customers danced around the chairs, and when the music stopped they scrambled. The homeliest girl was the first one out, and she burst into tears. They don't play that game in Albania. They play other sadistic games, but not that. Not enough chairs to go around was something we knew from life. No one would have understood what was supposed to be fun."

Zeke said, "Can I ask you something?"

"Sure." Lula drained the last of her drink.

"How come you don't have a boyfriend?"

Did Zeke imagine that was what her story meant? She almost said, I do have a boyfriend. "What kind of boyfriend would I meet here? Even the mailman's married. You want to fix me up with someone?"

"My friends are pretty young," said Zeke.

Lula hovered over Zeke as he ate three slices of pizza, then tossed the rest in the garbage because she didn't want Mister Stanley seeing the wretched meal she'd made for his son. After that she went up to her room. Let Mister Stanley drink his scrumptious glass of water solo.

That night, Lula woke from a dream in which Dunia's streaked face emerged from belching clouds of black smoke. How she longed for Dunia's counsel, her bad hair advice, bad fashion advice, bad boyfriend advice, bad immigration advice, bad life advice. Dunia was the only one with whom she could talk about Alvo. She could ask Dunia to read the tea leaves of bad-boy courtship. But how could Lula even think about her own problems when Dunia might be in danger? Probably Dunia was fine. People changed e-mail addresses. They moved back home and forgot you. Or they bounced back your e-mails as punishment for your staying in New York without them.

Or maybe Dunia wasn't okay. Maybe lazy selfish Lula was just telling herself not to worry. In the bar on Second Avenue at the Albanian World Cup game party, she'd met a woman who ran a nonprofit that rehabbed Albanian girls after they'd been trafficked. The woman gave Lula her card, and Lula checked the Web site, on which you could order pillowcases the rescued girls embroidered, which was not an encouraging sign of their reentry into their old existence, or any existence at all. Wasn't it time for Lula to tell Mister Stanley and Don about Dunia? What could they do? Alert Interpol and the CIA because her friend wasn't returning her calls? Don would pay attention only if Dunia was in some secret U.S. prison, which Lula doubted.

How could Lula find her friend, short of going back? A real friend, unlike False Friend Lula, would do anything necessary. She promised herself not to forget how lucky she was, living her comfy new American life in Mister Stanley's comfy house instead of selling her body to some tuna fishermen in Bari or hiking up her skirt on a service road beside a Sicilian *autostrada*.

Chapter Seven

O<small>N THE</small> morning of the college trip, Lula was ready early, dressed in her peacoat and the cheap secretary suit she'd bought for her very first meeting to discuss her case with Don. By the time Mister Stanley came down, Lula had made a thermos of coffee and packed a bag of low-fat cheese sandwiches, cut in half. Mister Stanley tasted a sandwich half.

"Delicious," he said, taking it along when he went upstairs to wake Zeke. Forty minutes passed before Zeke slouched downstairs. His hair was glued in two hornlike tufts, and his black T-shirt and jeans looked slept in.

Zeke threw on his jacket, opened the back door of his father's Acura, and lay down with his face pressed into the crease of the seat.

"You've got to put your belt on," said Mister Stanley. "We'll be on the highway."

"I'll sit up when we're doing forty," said Zeke.

"Crash test dummies implode at thirty," Mister Stanley said. "I've seen their heads fly off."

"Please, Dad," said Zeke. "I'm tired."

Mister Stanley said, "Of all the moments to regress."

"He'll be okay," said Lula.

Turning to watch Mister Stanley's house recede and vanish, Lula felt as if she were leaving a child who might grow so quickly as to become unrecognizable in her absence. How melancholy the house looked as it watched them go. She tried to see it through Ginger's eyes, as a prison she was escaping, a jail guarded by those tyrannical warders, Zeke and Mister Stanley. What if it were Ginger who'd sneaked into the house and bathed in Lula's tub? The hair in her soap was red. Ginger was a redhead, a clean freak, and probably cagey enough to misspell *beauty* and *heal* and to try to think like an Albanian male. But Ginger was in Arizona. It must have been Alvo. A warm rush melted the ice chip that had lodged briefly in Lula's heart.

Mister Stanley had printed out pages from MapQuest, which he handed Lula. "Ginger was the family navigator," he said.

Lula said, "You should get GPS."

"I wouldn't know how to work it." Mister Stanley tried to sound dismissive, as if a GPS system was a frivolous toy and anyone who used one was a frivolous toy person. But he couldn't carry it off. The Wall Street guys who'd eaten at La Changita were all about their gadgets.

"It's not that difficult," Lula said.

"How do you know?" asked Mister Stanley. "Do you ever use that cell phone—"

Lula said, "All the new cars in Albania, GPS comes standard."

"This car sucks," said Zeke. "I wish we could take the Olds."

"The gas would cost more than your first year's tuition," said Mister Stanley.

"Give me the money instead of school. That's what I've been saying!"

"I'm glad you're sitting up," said Mister Stanley. "Now please put on your seat belt."

One of the favorite after-hours conversations at La Changita concerned the spoiled brattiness of American children, a category in which the waitstaff included the customers. Everyone had a friend who worked as a nanny, everyone had watched some mom bribe her little monster into putting on his mittens. Lula didn't volunteer her opinion, which was that no one knew how to raise kids, they just screwed them up differently in different places.

"Turn that down," said Mister Stanley. "We can hear that racket leaking through your earphones."

"Ear*buds*," said Zeke. "Not phones."

The singer was screaming the same two words over and over. Back pray? Black pay? Mister Stanley gritted his teeth. Zeke disappeared into his music, and Lula felt as if she and Mister Stanley were coworkers trapped in an elevator between floors. She leaned her head against the cool window and let her mind drift back to her lunch with Alvo and its unclear conclusion. Kiss kiss. Little Sister.

"Please, Zeke," Mister Stanley pleaded.

Lula had resolved to stop comparing Mister Stanley to Albanian fathers, with their overly manly approach to raising manly Albanian sons. It was darling, the way Americans put so much faith in going to college, the way American parents bought their baby birds a dovecote in which to roost for four years before their maiden flight out into the world. In Tirana, university students were like neighbors in a roach-infested slum, six to a dorm room, all working the same shitty job, smoking pot, drinking cheap raki, waking up in bed with a guy you sort of recognized from English class.

The traffic thinned as they passed oily black trees and swamps choked with russet weeds. How bleak everything was, even the new mansions like hairless patches of mange scratched from the fur of the mountains. The cold window burned Lula's cheek. She shut her eyes and let the tires sing her to sleep.

When she awoke, Mister Stanley was exiting the highway.

"Some navigator," he told Lula. "Good thing I memorized the directions."

"Sorry," said Lula. Zeke's head was tipped back, and his breath whistled in his nose. They drove past some barns and a meadow. Though she'd always hated those shooting trips with her father, now the memory of them filled her with grief. Twice her dad had slapped her for missing the target. No wonder she'd refused his offer to teach her to drive. It would upset him to know she'd never learned. Alvo had said: one lesson.

"Zeke," said Mister Stanley. "Wake up. Do you really want these schools to catch their first sight of you passed out?"

"You see anybody looking?" said Zeke. "Dad, you're getting like Lula."

Lula said, "Meaning what?"

Mister Stanley said, "Here we are. Harmonia College."

"Great. The gay one," said Zeke.

"Mrs. Sullivan suggested that you and Harmonia would be a good fit," said Mister Stanley. "And that with your grades and SAT scores you'd have a decent shot."

"Mrs. Sullivan is gay," said Zeke.

Lula had expected something brick and ivy-covered. A college in a movie. This one looked like Albania. Windowless, half buried in sod like the dictator's bunkers.

Mister Stanley said, "This place had a rough time during the sixties. Prehistory to you guys. But when they rebuilt, they figured they'd skip the breakable glass. In case the students rebelled again."

"Rebelled against what?" said Zeke. "The skyrocketing price of weed and K-Y Jelly?"

Mister Stanley sighed. "Mrs. Sullivan mentioned that it used to have a reputation as a druggy school, but all that's long past."

Zeke said, "Let me get this right. We're begging them to let us blow one hundred and twenty grand so I can smoke grass and have gay sex."

"Look," said Mister Stanley. "There's the admissions office. Visitor parking."

"Should I wait in the car?" asked Lula. Two young women in identical parkas and jeans walked past the windshield, holding hands.

"What did I tell you?" said Zeke.

"You might as well come along, Lula," said Mister Stanley. "I don't think they'd mind if we bring a friend."

A friend? Was that what Lula was? Friend-of-the-family Lula.

Friend was not how the admissions secretary assessed Lula's situation. The girl in harlequin glasses and a pencil skirt gave her a long, icy stare. Was Lula the dad's young Russian mistress, the son's pedophile older girlfriend? Or was Zeke correct about it being a gay school?

"Ezekiel Larch," said Mister Stanley. The secretary asked if they'd taken the tour. Mister Stanley said no, they hadn't.

"They left about five minutes ago. You can probably catch them if you hang a left and head up the path toward the arts building."

"Thank you," said Mister Stanley, grabbing Zeke's elbow and hustling him toward the door, with Lula following close behind.

"Have fun," called the receptionist. "Let us know if Zeke is still planning to stay over."

Stay over? Zeke looked at his father as if he'd just heard he was being put up for adoption.

"Applicants can stay overnight," explained Mister Stanley.

Zeke said, "Thanks but no thanks. We're leaving right after the tour."

It was easy to find the gaggle of parents and teenagers shifting from foot to foot in the cold as they listened to a Viking maiden in a Peruvian poncho. A peaked, striped knitted wool cap with earflaps ended in hairy blue strings that vanished in the tangle of her yellow curls.

"Welcome," she said. "I'm Bethany. I'm a sophomore. Concentrating in theater."

Everyone in the group checked Zeke out, sizing up the competition and concluding that Zeke was unlikely to offer much competition, so they didn't have to bother checking out Mister Stanley or Lula, although some of the dads checked out Lula and then looked guilty in case she was Zeke's older sister.

Bethany said, "And you're—?"

Zeke tried to think of a way not to answer, but at last gave up his name.

"What a beautiful name. Welcome to Harmonia, Zeke. You'll love it."

"This is like science fiction," Zeke whispered to Lula. But within moments he'd surrendered, dazzled by the high beams of Bethany's smile.

Lula and Mister Stanley trailed behind as Zeke followed on Bethany's heels—sandals in this weather!—into the eggy smelling, overheated cafeteria, past the organic salad bar, the troughs of mystery chunks bubbling in thick ochre sauce, the plastic canisters excreting coils of peanut butter. They toured the sunlit art studios where a group of students were spraying newspapers with red paint, then a theater in which another group was painting a backdrop of a red desert crisscrossed with white picket fences, which, Bethany explained, was for a production of *Our Town* set in outer space.

Bethany extolled the range of vegan dietary choices, the enviable art careers of the faculty, the deep spiritual beauty of the ninety-year-old Egyptian poet with an endowed chair who had mostly quit teaching but who lent his super-beautiful spiritual vibe to college events. It seemed to Lula that Bethany was directing much of this at Zeke, interrupting her monologue with questions designed to draw him out.

"What kind of food do you like, Zeke?"

"Pizza." Nervous laughter.

"This one cook, Mario, makes this amazing three-cheese-and-pineapple pizza."

"Awesome," said Zeke.

"Do you paint, Zeke? Have you ever been in a play?"

"No, but I'd like to," Zeke said. The other kids glared at Zeke as if he'd pushed his way to the front of the line and had already been admitted.

After they'd trekked through a suite of rooms, each containing a grand piano, Bethany said, "Everybody at Harmonia is some kind of artist."

"I like music," said Zeke.

"What bands do you listen to?" Bethany asked.

The parents had begun making discontented clucking noises. Perhaps some sort of protest might have erupted, but Bethany or no Bethany, their kids might still want to go here.

"My Chemical Romance?" said Zeke. "Ever heard of them?"

"I totally love them," Bethany said. "There's this great jazz class here called Noise. Last year one kid put his drumsticks through the snare drum, and the teacher, Bob Jeffers, gave the kid an A."

"Bob Jeffers teaches here?" said one of the fathers. "I used to go hear him years ago—"

Bethany ignored him.

"A class called Noise?" said Zeke. "That is superior."

Lula tried not to wonder why Bethany had fixed on Zeke, hardly the most attractive boy among the prospective students. Maybe she saw something in him. His sweetness, his vulnerability. Love was strange, everyone knew.

Sure enough, at the end of the tour, as they stood before the chapel where, Bethany told them, Harmonia graduates were always returning to marry each other, she reminded them about the Day and Night at Harmonia admissions option, which enabled applicants to go through a day of classes and have dinner and stay in a dorm, if they'd reserved in advance.

"Did we reserve?" Zeke asked Mister Stanley.

"Actually, yes," said his father, for which he was rewarded with the first grateful look Lula had ever seen Mister Stanley receive from his son.

Was Mister Stanley really going to hand over his child to this predatory female? He wanted Zeke to go to college. And this might be the only college that wanted him, a fear that Mrs. Sullivan seemed to have planted in Mister Stanley's mind.

Three other kids, two boys and a girl, stepped forward. That they had also made arrangements to stay made Zeke's going with Bethany seem less like a kidnapping than like an admissions option.

"Everybody have cell phones?" asked Bethany.

Everybody did.

"Your kids will call you first thing in the morning. We'll take good care of them. Don't worry." Then she thanked everyone and repeated what an awesome school Harmonia was, and left with her captives in tow.

"Let's go," Mister Stanley told Lula. "Before Zeke changes his mind."

Lula thought, He won't.

MISTER STANLEY MUST have memorized this segment of the directions. Because without much trouble he found the chain motel by the side of the highway where they had reservations.

"Nothing luxurious," he told Lula. "But it's the only game in town."

Glass doors glided open, admitting them to the lobby. A nervous boy, perhaps a Harmonia student, regarded them fearfully from the front desk. Mister Stanley had reserved two rooms, just as Lula expected. The clerk apologized because the rooms were on different floors.

After they got their key cards, Mister Stanley said he needed a nap. Lula was probably tired too. In the elevator he mentioned that, if she wished, they could meet downstairs for dinner at seven. Well, yes, in fact she did wish. She hadn't eaten anything all day except for one low-fat cheese sandwich. Lula continued up to her floor, where her key card didn't work. Red light, red light. *Buzz buzz*. Don't panic, try again. Green arrow, green light. A chimpanzee could do it. Not until she entered her room did she realize it was almost dark outside. The best thing about the shortest days of the year was the promise that the days would get longer. There was nowhere to go but up. The key in a slot made the lights go on. Cheap energy-saving bastards! Be thankful, Lula told herself. They were trying to save the planet.

She flopped down on the spongy bed, grateful to be safe in this simple, more or less clean room among hundreds of simple, more or less clean rooms, a bed, a deadbolt lock, a phone, towels, TV. No flat screen, but big enough. And most important, all hers.

She took off the floral bedspread they couldn't wash between guests and lay down on the sheet that, she hoped, they could. The pillows were comfortable, and the remote was placed precisely where a mind-reader had imagined Lula's hand reaching. Lula clicked through the channels, pausing at a talk show on which today's subject was marriage. The middle-class couples confessed their infidelities and cried, the poor couples refused to confess and then got trapped into telling the truth when their lovers appeared onstage. Then they cried and shouted. Some of the poor women cried, but none of the poor men. None of the middle-class women yelled, but many of them cried. Had Mister Stanley cried over Ginger? One night, on her way upstairs, Lula had heard a sound like someone sobbing from Mister Stanley's room. Just the possibility that it might be Mister Stanley had upset her so badly that she'd convinced herself she must have dreamed it. But now she thought, Who wouldn't cry? No wife, no fun, no girlfriends, a job he hated, a son who seemed to despise him.

Lula must have slept. Stadium lights from the parking lot shone into her window. Trucks whined past on the highway. She switched on the news and watched a congressman apologizing for his adulterous affair, then a group of senators calling for an investigation into charges that U.S. soldiers tortured prisoners in Iraq, then the president telling the press that the United States didn't torture. It was interesting how everyone lied and only the adulterers got caught. She was lucky to be in this warm motel and not in a smoldering ruin in Baghdad. No sooner had she thought this than another story came on, about a family of refugees from Katrina still living, eight to a room, in a motel outside Denver.

In the desk drawer was a flyer from a pizza delivery chain. Lula hoped the restaurant served steak. At two minutes to seven she left her room and found Mister Stanley waiting at one of a few tables in an area lit by the glowing juice and milk machines. Very Eastern European. Mister Stanley raised his glass of something golden in an uncharacteristically effusive greeting.

"Good evening," Lula said.

On the wall a shrimp and a lobster wearing top hats and tuxedos were jitterbugging to the notes of a song whose lyrics were "Surf and Turf Tonite!"

"We're pretty far inland for the surf," Mister Stanley said.

"I was thinking that too," said Lula. But the pride they took in their wise decision to skip the catch of the day evaporated when the bruised-looking Harmonia-student waitress informed them that their only choice was between spaghetti Bolognese and fried shrimp. She thought the kitchen could do a vegetarian Bolognese, but she wasn't sure.

"I'll have the spaghetti," Lula said.

"Make that two," said Mister Stanley. "And bring us your best bottle of red. For once I'm not driving."

"The wine's forty-eight bucks," the waitress said. "For which it will suck, I guarantee."

"Bring it, please," said Mister Stanley.

Lula said, "There were places like this at home. In the mountains. The cook only prepares one thing, but it's always great, and there's usually a goat or even a cow turning on a spit out back—"

Mister Stanley said, "We can assume with some confidence, there is no goat outside."

The waitress brought the wine, already opened. That wouldn't have flown at La Changita. Lula wanted to object on Mister Stanley's behalf. But that would only make the situation more awkward. Mister Stanley poured Lula a glass, then filled his own and said, "No ceremony here." He seemed disappointed by the spaghetti's rapid arrival and gave the waitress a sullen look, which went unnoticed. She plunked down a shaker of grated cheese and stalked back to the kitchen. Mister Stanley let his pasta cool as he drank the wine, and Lula did the same.

"Have you heard from Zeke?"

"Why would I?" said Lula. "He's having fun."

"What did you think of that Bethany?"

"Super friendly," said Lula.

"It's so strange," said Mister Stanley.

"What's so strange, Mister Stanley?"

"Call me Stanley, please. It's strange how alone I feel. And Zeke isn't even gone yet. Maybe if my marriage had lasted, I could be looking forward to a new phase of life. Ginger and I could be traveling. Poor Ginger! I have nightmares about her drowning and not being able to save her. If she'd been happy with us and hadn't . . . fallen ill, I'd have someone to talk to, someone to share the heartbreak of losing the boy—the young man!—who five minutes ago was an infant in our arms. Have you ever had those dreams in which you're trying to walk or drive and everything's dark and you can't see?"

"I don't drive," said Lula, ungenerously. Of course she'd had dreams just like that.

"May you never have that dream, and may you never discover how closely it mimics real life. Groping around in the darkness, taking all the wrong turns. Don tried to warn me before I took this job with the bank. But I thought . . . I don't know what I thought. The money and the power . . . I thought the additional income would be good for Ginger and Zeke, and that I could somehow improve the lives of all those poor folks who needed my help."

This was more emotional intensity than Lula had heard from Mister Stanley in all their previous conversations combined. It could affect their relationship, and not in a positive way. Not knowing more than she needed to was a policy that Lula tried to follow, not only with Mister Stanley, but also with Zeke and Don. It was how you survived under Communism. Who said you had to be intimate with everyone's personal secrets?

He said, "I always imagined that on the day Zeke left for college I would cheer up Ginger with a surprise—two business-class tickets to Venice!"

Lula tried to picture Mister Stanley's head in Ginger's lap while the gondolier serenaded them with swoony Venetian ballads. She said, "It's not like Zeke's moving to another country."

"Losing is losing," said Mister Stanley.

Now was the time for Dunia's half-full-glass pep talk, but no matter how she tried, Lula couldn't see what was left in Mister Stanley's glass. He said, "After they leave the house, it's never the same. It's not supposed to be the same. *Then* you'd have a problem. Those kids who never leave home and turn into . . . I don't know what they turn into."

Lula said, "They turn into cannibals hiding body parts in the freezer." She stopped. Mister Stanley was looking at her strangely. "That happened in Albania. Also here. I saw it on TV."

"TV." Mister Stanley made a face. "The point is, no one prepares you. Empty nest? Just that word—*nest*—is a joke. Empty heart and soul is more like it. That's why it blindsides you. I know you probably think we're not much of a family, Zeke and I—"

"Family is family," Lula said.

"But what I want to tell you, Lula, and what you'll find out when you're a parent, is that every time I see my child, I'm seeing every moment that child has been alive, every stage of his life, the baby, the toddler, the older kid. Besides which I'm seeing my own life—"

Lula wanted to cover her ears. The sorrier she felt for Mister

Stanley, the harder it would be to leave. Lula was alone too, but she still had a chance to find someone with whom to take that gondola ride. How pathetic, to console herself by measuring the potential brightness of her future against the certain gloom of Mister Stanley's.

He said, "This college admissions process thing is an evil plot to make one hate one's last months with one's child. Even if you know it doesn't matter, you still get sucked in."

At least Mister Stanley was saying *one* and *you* again, instead of *I* or *me*. Lula twirled a forkful of crunchy pasta and tasted the afterburn of chemical tomato, harsh but with a comforting similarity to the pizzas she made for Zeke. She hoped Zeke was having fun.

What was that jangly music-box tune? Lula stared at her purse as if a small rodent was banging on a toy piano inside it.

"Answer the phone," said Mister Stanley.

"I can't find it," said Lula.

"Push the goddamn green button!" Mister Stanley said.

Zeke said, "It's me. It's me. It's Zeke. Tell my dad to come get me."

LULA DIDN'T REMEMBER the motel being so far from the college. Perhaps it only seemed distant, every mile lengthened by her lack of confidence in Mister Stanley's driving and by her terror that they would never find the dining hall entrance where Zeke had said to meet him.

"Where the hell is he?" said Mister Stanley.

Zeke emerged from the shadows and jumped into the back seat. "Let's get out of here. Don't even think about asking."

"Have you eaten?" said Mister Stanley.

"Let's go home," said Zeke.

"You need protein," his father said.

Some guardian angel of paternal instinct must have been guiding Mister Stanley, because after fifteen minutes on dark country roads, they pulled into the parking lot of a diner crowned with the feather headdress of a neon Indian chief. Zeke slid into a booth near the window. Mister Stanley sat next to him and Lula across the table.

Lula was glad she hadn't filled up on motel spaghetti. She ordered a tuna melt, a piece of lemon meringue pie, and a large Coke. No, make that coffee.

Mister Stanley ordered the burger deluxe, then changed his mind and asked if they had a plain can of tuna, no mayonnaise, which they did, though it clearly lowered the waitress's opinion of Mister Stanley. He said, "I'll have coffee too. The hard stuff. Caf."

"Coffee," the waitress said. "And you, hon?"

"I'm not hungry," said Zeke.

"You need a minute?" the waitress asked him. "You can tell me when I bring your mom and dad their coffee."

"How could Lula be my mom?" demanded Zeke, after she went away. "She would have had to have me when she was ten years old!"

Mister Stanley said, "Zeke, you can trust us. What happened?"

No one expected Zeke to answer. Lula was startled when he said, "We were each given a big sibling, you know, instead of a big sister or brother, which is so corny and sexist. Bethany was my big sibling."

The waitress brought their coffee. Sipping his, Mister Stanley watched Lula burn her tongue.

"Careful," he warned her, too late.

"We went back to Bethany's room and talked," Zeke said. "Really talked. She told me about her town in New Hampshire, and how she's the first person to go to college in her family, and I told her about us and Mom—"

"What did you tell her about us and Mom?" Mister Stanley asked.

"The truth. Nobody was trying to impress anyone. It was like we'd been friends forever. We went and heard these kids she knew in a band, practicing. We had dinner in the cafeteria. The food sucked, no one could eat it. But lots of kids came and sat with us, so it was fun, and then we went to her room and—"

"You don't have to tell us this part," said Mister Stanley.

"You *do* have to tell us this part," said Lula. How stupid was Mister Stanley if Zeke was willing to talk? Let Mister Stanley look daggers at her. "What happened in Bethany's room?"

"As soon as we got there, Bethany said she was going to the bathroom and she'd be right back, but after a while this other girl came in and asked where Bethany was, and the girl got all stressed and said she thought I knew, everyone knew, you had to watch Bethany constantly because she would try to kill herself the minute she was alone. Sometimes she got better, but she went through bad times. And this was one of them. Her friends had convinced the school to let her stay if they watched her round the clock. She told me they'd try to find her—"

"What kind of school is this?" interrupted Mister Stanley. "To allow such a thing! To permit a mentally ill girl to give tours of the college. And to put you in such a position! What happened to the poor girl?"

"What happened to *me*!" Zeke said. "I sat on the edge of her bed, thinking how lucky she was to have friends who cared about her so much. Also how weird it was, because Bethany seemed so cool and at peace with herself. Her friend told me to wait there, in case Bethany came back. And if she did I should hang on to her and find a way to let someone know. I started to get really nervous, thinking the whole college was probably searching for Bethany. She might be dead, and it would be my fault, even though no one had told me."

"It wouldn't have been your fault," said Mister Stanley. "It would have been the college's fault."

Zeke said, "Finally I went out into the hall, and I ran into this older dude, some kind of hall monitor. He asked me if there was a problem, and I told him everything. Like a scared little bitch. The dude said, 'Fuck me, are those bastard theater kids up to that shit again?' "

"That person was in authority, and he used language like that?"

Zeke ignored his father. "It turned out they'd done it plenty of times. They call it real-life serial theater. Punking, college style. They do it to kids who are applying. Kids they figure won't get in, so they won't have to deal with them later." Zeke's voice had thickened with tears.

Mister Stanley said, "How could a tour guide and her sadist friends presume to know who will be admitted?"

Lula longed to throw her arms around Zeke and hug him to her chest and promise that soon, sooner than he could imagine, all this would seem funny. Though it was equally possible that it never would. Once, some girls in Lula's neighborhood had locked her in a storeroom. It hadn't made her claustrophobic or done any lasting damage, but still sometimes a bathroom lock jammed, and it all came back. She wanted to tell Zeke that he would grow up and be happy and loved. Today, she'd been mistaken for his sister and his mother, and tonight she felt like both, wishing she could protect him from so much she couldn't control. Maybe that was what family meant: wanting, and not being able, to help the people you love. She used to wish she could get her parents a nicer place to live than a room in her aunt's apartment in Tirana. The biggest apartment in the block, practically a villa, was occupied by the family of the prettiest girl in Lula's class, a girl who early in life had pimped herself out to a Party official.

Mister Stanley said, "Someone should be informed. One can't have . . . I'm sure the college . . ."

"I wouldn't go to that school if they paid me. I want to go home. And if you tell anybody about this, I won't apply anywhere. I'll move to the West Coast and work in a photocopy shop. I'll go live with Mom in Arizona."

"Whoa there, big fella," said Mister Stanley.

The waitress reappeared. "Can I get you something, hon?"

"Ant and roach poison," said Zeke.

"Kids," said the waitress, over her shoulder. "God love 'em."

"That was terrible," said Mister Stanley. "What you just said to that waitress. Zeke, my God."

" 'Ant and Roach Poison' is a song," said Zeke. "A Sweat Bees song. Don't you know anything, Dad? Okay. Miss? When you get a chance? I'd like a cheeseburger deluxe and fries and a chocolate milkshake."

"You got it," said the waitress.

Zeke wolfed down his food and ordered another side of fries. Lula and Mister Stanley each drank several cups of coffee. Mister Stanley tried to persuade Zeke to visit the other two colleges, but Zeke said no way, not now.

Mister Stanley said, "Look on the bright side. Everyone's still alive, no one is sick or in danger, and whatever happens at the other two schools has to be an improvement."

After that, he kept quiet.

Zeke ordered a slice of blueberry pie. Slowly, his mood improved. Mister Stanley said, "The motel has movies on demand. You can stay up late and order in any movies you want."

"I hope it's flat screen," Zeke said.

Mister Stanley nodded.

THE NEXT MORNING they met in the motel lobby and drove home in the rain. Mister Stanley refused to start the car until Zeke fastened his seat belt. When they turned onto the highway, Mister Stanley said, "For the record, we never agreed that you could charge an adult movie."

Zeke said, "You were snoring, Dad. The motel said it wouldn't show up on the bill."

"You believed them?" said Lula.

Zeke said, "Dad promised me it was flat screen, and it wasn't. So who's the liar here, really?"

Mister Stanley said, "I'm sorry, Zeke. But this is a moral discussion I don't have the energy for right now."

"Fine," said Zeke. "Me neither."

The minivan's wheels on the wet road seemed to whisper *sad sad sad*. What if Zeke didn't go to college? Could they stay like this forever, aging year after year into a trio of ghosts haunting Mister Stanley's house? Mister Stanley should have thought twice before getting so upset about his son leaving home. Be careful what you wish for. Be careful what you fear.

When they got back, it was late afternoon. Zeke slammed the door to his room. Mister Stanley sat at the dining room table and began opening the mail. Lula asked if he was hungry, and when he said no, she went upstairs.

Her room smelled faintly of cigarettes. On her blanket was a small red cardboard box. "Little Charmy Puppy," it said, in Chinese-style letters. Lula took out the furry Dalmatian dog and flipped the switch on its belly. She set the puppy on the floor. It barked and waggled its rear, then rose up on its stumpy hind legs and yelped so piercingly that Lula clapped her hand over Charmy Puppy's mouth.

What an adorable present! She hoped it wasn't a thank-you gift. Thanks for taking care of the gun. Lula rushed to the bureau. She unwrapped the gun, to make sure. Did Alvo suspect it slept with her underwear? Let him meditate on that. She counted her money. All there. She switched off the puppy, lay down on the bed, and put the toy near her pillow. Watched over by her mechanical pet, Lula fell asleep.

Chapter Eight

———— ∞∞∞ ————

In the days that followed, Lula rehearsed how she would thank Alvo for Little Charmy Puppy. It was nicer than imagining what she would say if Mister Stanley discovered that Albanians were creeping around his house when no one was home. When she noticed that she couldn't look at the mechanical dog without sighing, she shoved it into a drawer, as if it were Charmy Puppy's fault that Lula was attracted to a guy who would rather stalk her than see her. But then she took it out again and made it do its tricks.

Having lived with relatives in a cramped apartment, Lula had long ago learned how to construct an imaginary wall between herself and the pushy cousin brushing her teeth and spitting into the same sink. Brick by invisible brick she constructed such a wall between herself and Zeke, with whom she still grocery-shopped and ate and watched TV, though now it was as if they were living the same lives in separate buildings. Surely Zeke must have felt the chill. For once, Lula didn't care. She would knock down the invisible wall as soon as Alvo showed up. It wasn't Zeke's fault that Alvo hadn't called, but Zeke was the only one here to blame. She avoided Mister Stanley, except for the brief nightly exchange required to reassure him that his son was still alive.

To pass the time, Lula wrote a true story about having a crush on a neighbor kid and slipping notes under his door, but never having the nerve to write anything, so she'd doodle on the paper and hope he knew it was from her. Soon after, his parents moved out of the building, and later she heard they were terrified that the secret police were tormenting them with encrypted messages that said nothing.

One night, Mister Stanley told her that Don Settebello had asked if he could come for Thanksgiving dinner. "Little Abigail is going to be with her mom. I think that's why Don wants to be with us. His second family."

"I'll cook a turkey," Lula said.

"Have you ever cooked a turkey?"

"Many times back in Albania," Lula lied. Her granny's *peshest*, crumbled cornbread soaked with turkey gravy and baked crisp at the edges, was a legend. Anyway, all you had to do was turn on the Food Network, day or night, and learn some famous chef's holiday turkey secrets. Lula kept hearing a funny phrase: *a successful turkey*. How successful could it be, dead and eaten by people?

But either to spare Lula the effort or because they didn't believe she was qualified to produce this national ritual of the grateful Pilgrim stomach, Don and Mister Stanley agreed to split the cost of a caterer who specialized in festive dinners and whom Don heard was fantastic. Lula tried not to feel hurt. It was less trouble for her. Less trouble was very American, she might as well enjoy it.

No one cooked in this country, though they were obsessed with every mouthful and afraid of how it might harm them.

One bond between Lula and Zeke was the pride they felt in the market among the shopping-cart cornucopias of good-for-you citrus and leafy greens, wheeling their own fuck-you cart, empty except for pizza crusts and frozen burgers. Though maybe only she and Zeke imagined that anyone noticed. It occurred to Lula that her willingness to sign on to Zeke's diet might be an unhealthy sign of regression to someone else's childhood. Or worse, a symptom of depression, a disease that didn't exist when she was a child. Under Communism, suicide equaled a failing grade in the dead person's political education.

On the Tuesday before Thanksgiving, Lula worked beside Estrelia, straightening up, futilely trying to make the house welcoming or just presentable. Was Estrelia trying to say that she stuffed her family's turkey with chiles?

"*Pica*," Estrelia said, giggling as she pantomimed steam rising out of her mouth.

That night, Mister Stanley told Lula that Don was bringing someone. A woman. He said, "I couldn't be happier. Don deserves some fun."

"Great! Who is she?" Lula felt as if a fat cold raindrop had slid down the back of her neck. What was her problem? She didn't want Don Settebello. He'd come on to her, more or less, and she'd gracefully rejected him without anything getting messy. Maybe she should have turned her palm up. Played with his fingers, even. What if Don had been her last chance at romance? At home everyone knew some spinster who'd rejected a suitable guy because she thought she could do better, and no one asked after that. Lula thought of the game of musical chairs she'd witnessed at La Changita. She felt like that girl who'd lost the first round. But why would anyone want a hero like Don when she could yearn after a lowlife who stalked her and left her cute Chinatown mementos?

Thanksgiving dinner was at five, and at three a van full of Mexican guys in baseball caps arrived with a foil-wrapped turkey and plastic tubs of mashed potatoes.

"Microwave?" said one of them.

"I can do that," Lula said.

Mister Stanley seemed dismayed. Perhaps Don had led him to expect handsome unemployed actors.

He said, "I'll bet Don helped those guys with immigration."

One of the Mexicans gave Lula a page of printed directions.

"Microwave," he said.

Mister Stanley sighed.

"Don't worry," Lula said. "This will be great."

Unwrapped, the bird looked gelatinous. No way this buzzard could be cooked from within by agitated atoms. Lula put it in the oven, and, just as she'd seen on TV, took it out early so it could drink back its own juices.

Don showed up at five fifteen. The woman with him was very pretty, a few years older than Lula. Don introduced her as Something Something, the sharpest lawyer who'd worked for his firm in years, maybe the sharpest ever.

"Tell me your name again," said Mister Stanley. "I'm getting old and deaf."

"Untrue, Stan." Don glared at him.

"Savitra Dasgupta," the woman said. The ends of her beautifully cut black hair brushed the shoulders of the pleated man's shirt she wore, tucked into pressed jeans. Lula felt sluttish and frumpy, a bread dumpling neatly sliced by the knife-edge of Savitra's pleats. Lula had gravy stains on her skirt, and she hadn't even really cooked.

The guests stalled in the front hall. Mister Stanley was supposed to ask them in, but that must have been Ginger's role. Mister Stanley should have hired someone else, someone unlike Lula, someone with the domestic talent to make him and his son a real home. Lula saw their pretend home through Savitra's eyes, just as she'd seen it through Alvo's. It was amazing how fast you got used to things and stopped seeing them at all. Where was Alvo spending Thanksgiving? Eating turkey and cranberry sauce? More likely, bellied up to a bar in the Bronx with his homies and ESPN and a keg of homemade raki.

Lula studied Savitra, taking lessons in the art of assuming a posture so regal that by the time they drifted toward the living room, where Lula had set out salami and cheese and sliced apples already edged with brown, Lula and Savitra had swapped places, so that Savitra was the hostess, and Lula the anxious guest. Lula hated these girl-on-girl dominance games, especially now when her hands were tied, because she was not about to repay Don for the miracles he'd worked on her behalf by being bitchy to his new girlfriend.

Savitra gazed at the cheese and wilted fruit.

"How autumnal," she said.

Like an expensive brooch pinned to the edge of Ginger's sofa, Savitra sparkled as she told Mister Stanley about her rise to the top of her class at Georgetown and the cases she'd worked on at Don's firm. Savitra subtly conveyed the fact that she had turned down big corporate money to "give back" to the country that had provided her family with a chance for a better life. Don beamed as if Savitra were his own prodigious child. And indeed he treated her like a delicate, moody girl. Like Abigail, in fact. He kept asking, Was she too hot? Too cold? Was everything okay?

Mister Stanley poured the drinks. Wine for Lula and Savitra, cold black coffee for Zeke. Scotch for himself and for Don.

"A light one, please," said Don, whose hasty glance at Lula was the only sign he gave of remembering their lunch.

Mister Stanley asked Savitra where her family came from.

"Great Neck," she said curtly.

Don said, "Savitra's grandfather is from Bangladesh. Her family owned a textile plant."

Savitra said, "My great-grandfather made silk for Christian Dior." It took Lula a few seconds to understand the conspiratorial smirk Savitra flashed in her direction. As a fellow immigrant, Lula was marginally less white than Don and Mister Stanley.

"I like your shirt," Savitra told Zeke. Zeke was charmed, as were the two men. As was everyone but Lula.

"Dog Breath?" Zeke read aloud, looking down as if to see what his shirt said. "Ever heard of them?"

"No," Savitra said. "But I hope you'll play their music for me sometime."

"Any interesting new cases?" Mister Stanley asked Don.

"Why spoil our dinner?" said Don. "Same psychotic freaks in the White House. Same al-Qaeda maniacs. Same innocent civilians trapped in the middle."

"Sorry to hear that," said Mister Stanley.

Don said, "But listen. Our brilliant Savitra may have found a loophole that could crack open one of our Guantánamo cases."

Lula could hardly bear it! Don's girlfriend was not only

pretty and sexy but a legal genius. Couldn't Lula just be happy for Don and Savitra and the Guantánamo detainee?

Savitra said, "Don's the brilliant one."

Don said, "And Savitra obviously has a mind of her own."

Savitra said, "Don's the one who could wind up in Gitmo."

"If I do, Savitra has promised to bring me samosas," Don said.

The two lovebirds nestled on the couch. Zeke walked behind the sofa and mimed gagging so only his father and Lula could see. Lula asked Zeke to come help her in the kitchen.

"Open the oven," she told him.

"Awesome turkey," said Zeke.

"Big strong boy," Lula said. "Bring this to the table. Make everybody sit."

Zeke picked up the platter with a weightlifter's grunt. Lula scurried in and out the dining room with bowls of mashed potatoes and a basket of rolls she'd made from tubes of dough. It had been fun to watch through the oven door as the gummy blobs swelled into perfect crosshatched grenades.

"Can I help?" asked Savitra.

"Sit," said Lula, which no one had done, no matter how many times Zeke told them. Lula had gone to great trouble to create an attractive holiday table. Organic beeswax candles from The Good Earth, Ginger's best china. She'd even ironed a tablecloth.

"Didn't I tell you, Stan?" said Don. "Aren't those caterers terrific?"

Savitra said, "Shouldn't we call Zeke back? He seems to have given up on us and disappeared."

Mister Stanley frowned at Lula. Wasn't Zeke her job?

Zeke made them suffer a long, tense wait before they heard his footsteps.

"Welcome back," Savitra said.

"Everybody begin," said Lula. "Start eating. I forgot to make the gravy. It will take two minutes."

Savitra called after her, "Are you sure I can't help?"

"No," said Lula. "Please." But Savitra, with that mind of her own, followed Lula into the kitchen, where she posed like a temple goddess with one hip thrust out and one elbow against the refrigerator door. Making gravy was tricky enough without Savitra saying, "May I ask you a personal question?"

"Sure." Lula was glad she could focus on whisking flour into the drippings.

Savitra took a sip of wine. "Did you ever fuck Don?"

"Of course not!" Lula said. How pleasant it was to tell the truth, and how false it sounded. "He's my lawyer."

Savitra said, "So Don claimed. I just needed a reality check. We'd been dating for two weeks before he bothered informing me he was married and had a daughter. This guy's a human rights hero, but when it comes to women—"

"He's separated, I think."

"Married, actually. Legally married. I know what legal is."

"Don's a good guy," said Lula.

Savitra said, "I hear you're a writer."

"Look," said Lula. "The gravy's ready."

When Lula and Savitra emerged from the kitchen to find that the others had started eating, they exchanged a surprisingly friendly and rich communication. Both were thinking that an American girl would have been pissed at the rude American men. But Lula and Savitra came from older cultures that assumed men ate first, after having been waited on, like royalty or babies. They knew better than to expect a hollow show of chivalry from the greedy pigs, though the look that passed between them said, We're American now. The greedy pigs should have waited.

Mister Stanley was telling a story about a guy at his job who rode a motorized scooter to work and everyone in the office thought it was really cool, but last week the guy fell off his Segway and broke his collarbone in two places. Zeke and Don hated Mister Stanley's story, each for a different reason. As Lula and Savitra filled their plates, the three men watched.

"Savitra! Is everything all right?" said Don.

"Lovely," Savitra said, gently squeezing Don's arm.

"How's business, Stan?" asked Don. "Who would have thought that my childhood pal would rise to become a Master of the Universe?"

Mister Stanley shrugged. Seeing Savitra touch Don had so deflated his spirits that he seemed to have lost the will to ever speak again.

Finally he said, "Actually, I wouldn't be surprised if the market goes the way of that hotshot's Segway. This housing bubble, the derivatives, the subprime lending . . ." Everyone watched his pale fingers glide along the table like a scooter and plummet off the edge.

"Are you joking?" asked Don.

"I don't have your sense of humor," said Mister Stanley. "I never did."

"Please," said Don. "Don't—"

Mister Stanley said, "Does the word Enron mean anything to anyone here? Are our memories that short? If I were Joe

Average, I'd be cashing in my pension and buying gold and stashing it in the mattress."

Lula looked around to see how the others were reacting. Having had some experience with economic meltdown, Lula wanted to tell them: Don't think it can't happen here. But Don and Savitra were looking at Mister Stanley as blankly as if he'd just suggested that they might be in danger of running out of mashed potatoes. Nor did their expressions change much when Mister Stanley said, "What we saw with Enron was just the tip of the iceberg. Risk management is a fancy term for what the lemmings do when they hold hands and jump off a cliff."

"Lemmings don't hold hands, Dad," said Zeke. "Lemmings don't have hands."

"You sound like Abigail," Don told Zeke, then glanced worriedly at Savitra to see how she'd responded to his mentioning his daughter.

Savitra asked Zeke what his favorite subject was.

"Subject?"

"In school," Savitra said.

"None of them," said Zeke.

Don said, "Did I tell you, Stan, I was back in Guantánamo last week? The UN guys called off their inspection visit because they're not being allowed to talk to the detainees one-on-one. Oh, and the hunger strike's started up again. The strikers are being force-fed with gastric and nasal feeding tubes. They're reusing the same tube for every guy up and down the line, strapping them into these horrible chairs so they can't vomit up their food—"

Savitra said, "My God, Don! Reusable nasal feeding tubes?

We're eating Thanksgiving dinner. You need to give yourself a break—"

"A break," said Don. "Only the prisoners don't get a break. And those poor kids fighting our wars."

Mister Stanley shook his head. "We do have a lot to be thankful for."

"Name one thing," said Zeke.

"That we're not in prison," Mister Stanley said. "That you're not in the army."

"Not yet," said Zeke.

"When we were your age, there was a draft," said Mister Stanley.

"You told me that," singsonged Zeke. "And you burned your draft cards and went out onto the street and stormed the Pentagon and—"

Don said, "All over the country, American families are giving thanks. As we should, for the privilege of living in this country. We should be offering up our prayers of gratitude for our precious freedoms. It's not about the cranberry sauce. Nor is it about what the indigenous people taught us to grow before we slaughtered them all."

"Not in the Northeast, Don," said Mister Stanley. "Not so much slaughter went on here."

"Stupid fucking wrong-way Columbus thought they were Indians," Zeke said. He caught himself, horrified to have said "Indians" in Savitra's presence.

"Marvelous turkey," said Savitra.

"Thank you," said Lula.

Don said, "I really will have to thank the guy who turned me on to those caterers."

Don and Savitra left early.

Afterward, Zeke and Mister Stanley helped Lula clean up. Mister Stanley said, "Poor Don! Betsy was a piece of work, but this one's going to put him through the wringer." Lula made room for Zeke as he cautiously transferred the gravy pan from the stove to the sink.

Zeke said, "Dad, you just wish a girl that hot was putting you through the wringer. What's a wringer, anyway?"

Mister Stanley said, "Can you two finish up without my help?"

"We're good here," Lula said.

Chapter Nine

———— ∞ ————

THE SNOW seemed apocalyptic, not falling so much as hurled. Bulletins came from the silent world: Zeke's school was closed, and so, more unexpectedly, was Mister Stanley's office. New rules, emergency measures, enabled Mister Stanley to turn on the early-morning TV news. Batting at snowflakes, as if in playful combat, a reporter puffed her cheeks and chafed her arms, while, behind her, a rickrack of broken trucks zigzagged across the highway.

"Record breaking," Mister Stanley said several times to make it clear that he was being kept from work by severe climate change and not by unmanly squeamishness about inclement weather. Zeke faked jubilation when in fact Lula suspected he would rather be at school than home with her and his dad.

The endless day stretched before them. How would they get through it? Everything grated on Lula's nerves. The rumble of Zeke's music, Mister Stanley's footsteps. How could anyone live with anyone else, unless you were tied by blood or sex and didn't have any choice? How tiny the large house had become, and how she longed to escape it.

She said, "I'm going back to bed."

"I don't blame you," said Mister Stanley.

Months ago, Lula had found three sleeping pills in Ginger's

medicine cabinet, and though she was wary of any Ginger-associated medication, she'd saved them for an emergency, which the news had assured them this was.

Lula's sleep was racked by nightmares, most of which she forgot, except for one in which she was visited by her dead parents and Granny, and another dream—or was it the same dream?—in which she sat in a stadium and watched truckloads of pastry flour dumped on Dunia. Lula somehow understood that this was a fundamentalist country in which adulterers were executed by being baked into apple pies.

When she awoke, it was still snowing. The sky was battleship gray. An alarming jingle was blaring from Lula's phone.

"Lula?" said a voice. "Did I wake you up? Wake up! It's afternoon."

Lula said in Albanian, "I was just dreaming about you!"

Dunia said in English, "I hope I was having fun."

"Where are you?" Lula said.

Dunia said, "Twenty miles from you. In Maplewood, New Jersey."

"I thought you were in Tirana. You always talked shit about New Jersey."

"I never got there," said Dunia. "I'm here. Like you."

"I didn't hear from you, I didn't hear from you. I started thinking you'd been trafficked."

"Very funny," Dunia said. "Though in a manner of speaking I was. Ha ha. I'm joking. I'm married. I married Steve. A rich American plastic surgeon. Very romantic story."

"Why didn't you answer my e-mails?"

"That's the unromantic part," said Dunia. "I'll tell you when I see you. Want to meet for coffee? Have lunch? Go shopping?"

"Now? Have you looked out the window? I don't have transportation. I'm stuck here."

"I've got a driver," said Dunia. "I'll come to you."

"A driver?" Lula repeated.

"A driver!" Dunia shouted. "What's wrong with this connection?"

Dunia sounded the same and different. Well, Lula had changed too. Even if nothing happens, you get new cells every seven years, so technically the former best friends were now one-seventh strangers.

"I didn't mean today," Dunia said. "I meant a week from today! See you then. Kiss kiss."

Lula walked to the window. Mister Stanley had shoveled the walk without the help he always asked, and never got, from Zeke.

Zeke was playing like a child in the snow, a big child with no one to play with. He'd made a snowman self-portrait, three white snowballs, the middle one in a ripped leather jacket and with something—shoe polish?—trickled down the sides of its lumpy spherical head to give it vampire hair. Its eyes were two silvery CDs that caught the last light of day. The snowman had its back to the street, an unusual choice. It seemed to be looking at the house, and one silver eye winked at Lula.

LULA HAD PICKED up, from Mister Stanley and Zeke, the good habit of not worrying too much about the neighbors, a welcome change from Tirana, where for many reasons, none of them good, the neighbors were the first thing you thought of after food and money and sex, and often before. Inhabited entirely by schoolchildren and their parents, and a few old relics, Mister Stanley's block came to a sleepy sort of life only on summer weekends when someone held a yard sale. Today it was deserted except for cleaning ladies, delivery guys, and an occasional handyman blowing snow from one lawn to another.

No one saw the Range Rover pull up in front of Mister Stanley's house, and though Dunia moved as if on stage, Lula and the driver were the only audience for Dunia's theatrical scowling at each crumb of snow that menaced her beautiful boots. Where had Dunia gotten such shoes, or the stylish black coat, understated and, Lula could tell, terrifyingly expensive? How had Dunia skipped a step from servant maid to queen, from an illegal-alien East Village mojito-joint waitress to a rich New Yorker, or at least New Jerseyite?

Dunia was always a fast learner. It was Dunia who'd taught Lula how to navigate the fitting rooms and cosmetics counters. Lula told herself not to be jealous. Lula probably had many things that Dunia didn't have, though right now she couldn't think of one. Watching her friend's halting progress up Mister Stanley's front walk, Lula felt simultaneously overjoyed to see her and sick with love for Dunia's clothes. Lula's happiness should have been pure. Dunia was healthy and safe.

The two friends hugged in the doorway.

"You smell great," said Lula.

"Specially blended," said Dunia. "From roses that bloom once every twenty years."

"You're kidding," said Lula.

"Half kidding," Dunia said. "Once every decade."

They hugged again, and Lula pressed her face into Dunia's

cashmere shawl. Only when the danger was past did Lula realize how worried she'd been.

Dunia said, "Can we go inside now? I'm freezing my you-know-whats off."

"Sorry," Lula said. "Coffee?"

"American," said Dunia. "If you have it."

"Starbucks," Lula said.

She started off toward the kitchen so she wouldn't have to witness Dunia's response to Ginger decor and by extension Lula's life. Dunia was an emissary from another world, a messenger bearing a mirror. Meanwhile Lula noted with relief that Dunia's roses had already overpowered the musty dead air of houses like this, where everything fun had already happened in the distant past. Why should Lula make excuses for herself? Let Dunia do the talking.

Dunia followed Lula into the kitchen, perched on a stool, and leaned both elbows on the counter. Her pale breasts scalloped the empty space inside the V of her dove-colored sweater.

"Sweet scene," Dunia said. "Homey."

"It's a job," Lula said. Mister Stanley's house was a step up, many steps up, from the skinny Belarusian girl's walk-up. But the purse that Dunia plunked on the counter was many steps up from Mister Stanley's. They were friends, they loved each other. Why should a pocketbook matter?

"Please don't smoke." Lula's upturned palms cradled the fragile ecosystem around her.

Dunia shook her head but put her cigarettes away. "I'm used to it. It's American. I told my husband I quit smoking. Steve used to bring home photos of cancerous black lungs."

"Tell me about Steve," said Lula.

Dunia said, "What's to tell? Steve is nice. Steve is positive. Steve knows what he wants. Steve is rich. Is Steve hot? No, Steve is not hot. If I met him for the first time, I'd think he was gay. That's what I thought when I met him for the first time. Mistake. Steve is not gay. He's American. He wants me to be American. When I talk about my old life, he looks bored, so I quit. At the beginning, he was fascinated by all the Albanian stuff. But now he wants me to be newborn, he wants my life to have started on the day we met. No past, no friends, English only, except—"

Lula said, "Is that why you disappeared?"

"Not exactly," said Dunia. "But sure, maybe yes. I was trying. I thought, I'll give the marriage a shot. Steve is very controlling. He throws tantrums, but they're easy to avoid. Don't leave the alarm system off or the faucet running. Otherwise, no problem. I get to shop till I drop in return for sex that's always short and always the same. Two, maybe three times a week. Of course his family assumed I was a Russian hooker. A million times his mom and sister and aunts interrogated me about how we met. Obviously they were thinking online, or some ad in the phone book. So now I'm like the Earthly Beauty. I make Steve pay every time he sees me naked."

Lula leaned across the counter and kissed her friend on the cheek. It was too complicated to explain that she'd written a story about Earthly Beauty, but it made her happy to even consider explaining and to decide against it.

"What was *that* for?" asked Dunia.

"I'm glad to see you," said Lula. "So how did you meet Steve?"

"At the airport." Dunia reached again for a cigarette, then

remembered. "I was having a problem with my ticket home. I should have known. I bought it from a bucket shop behind a realtor in the Bronx. The guy at the ticket counter hated me on sight. Our discussion got hot. I called him an asshole. Big deal. He was an asshole. Also a baby. Big Baby Asshole Airline Agent called for backup. I thought, Here we go. I'm traveling to Guantánamo on a one-way ticket."

Lula said, "My lawyer has a client in Guantánamo."

"Sad," Dunia said. "Poor him. Steve was in the business-class line. He got out of line and saved me. He had time before his flight. That's the kind of guy Steve is, gets to the airport three hours early. He was going to Nassau for some plastic surgery convention. We sat at one of those little round tables with high stools. God must have commanded me to travel in a short skirt instead of a sweatsuit. After two whiskeys Steve asked me: If he canceled his trip, would I go home with him right then? The next morning he said he'd take care of everything. Everything. And he did."

"That must have been some night," Lula said.

"For Steve it was," said Dunia. "End of story. He knows people. I'll be a citizen soon. Married to an American doctor. It's a dream come true."

"Nice." Lula chafed her palms together, dusting off the obstacles that ordinary people went through to get where Dunia was. She shivered with self-pity. Everyone else had it easy, everybody but her, everyone got the lucky breaks that whisked them along the road down which Lula was trudging, step by difficult step. She told herself, Have patience, or at least some pride. She had a work visa, she'd have a green card, she'd become a citizen maybe, and all on her own, without having to marry some guy she didn't love. On the other hand, everything could still go wrong. She could be deported back to Tirana, and Dunia would be in her fancy house, shopping for fabulous clothes.

"Nothing's easy," said Dunia. "Tonight at dinner he'll tell me about some brilliant rhinoplasty or challenging butt reduction. But if I say anything, anything at all, he picks up a magazine. Any time I want some body part tightened or tweaked, he'll do it for free. His business partner gave his wife a permanent smile and a killer cleavage."

"So why did you call me now?" Lula said.

"I missed you," said Dunia. "I'm bored."

"It can get boring here," Lula said. How good it felt to say so. From time to time, Mister Stanley and Zeke suggested that Lula must be bored, and Lula always protested. No, not at all, she was finding plenty to do. Alvo and his friends had implied that Mister Stanley's house was a tomb. They'd said it smelled like the grave.

"Anywhere can get boring." Dunia frowned at her pearly lip print on Mister Stanley's coffee cup. Licking her fingertip, she dabbed at the stain like a mother wiping another woman's kiss from her child's face. "So many minutes in a day! At some point Steve will ask the driver—in Spanish—what I did today, so it's good my driver can tell Steve about you, and Steve won't get jealous thinking I went to see some boyfriend. It's like living under Communism. Okay, I know it's not like Communism. The shopping is better. The sex is worse."

"A driver!" Lula said.

Dunia smiled lewdly. "Jorge. Dominican. Twenty-two. Drop-dead handsome."

"I can't even drive," said Lula. "Most of the time I'm stuck here. Unless I take the bus."

"I told you," Dunia said. "Ten miles to downtown if you swam."

Lula said, "You still have an accent. How does American Steve like that?"

Dunia made a face. "He likes to talk during sex. *Then* he likes the accent. He even likes me to talk Albanian. He thinks I'm begging, Fuck me up to my eyeballs! When what I'm really saying is, Tomorrow I have to tell Gladys the maid to clean the refrigerator. Out of bed he doesn't like the accent so much. He says the more American I speak, the more Americans I speak *to*, the more American I sound."

Lula said, "It's the opposite here. Everybody wants me to hang on to my roots. They love all the fairy tales and the sayings and folk songs and crap. You know what? I've started writing little stories about home."

"You always were a creative person. What an imagination! I remember you getting drunk one night after our shift at La Changita and making up some crazy shit about your dad teaching you to shoot Madonna in the heart. Whatever happened to Franco the waiter? He wasn't so cute, but still . . ."

"That was true about Madonna," Lula said. "A *picture* of Madonna."

Dunia said, "I missed you. But listen, no shopping today. I don't have the time I thought. The cleaning guy is coming to pick up the living room curtains. Also I have to go home and talk dinner with Gladys." Dunia kissed her fingertips. "Fried chicken. She worked for Steve before I got there."

It was a sign of power, having somewhere you had to be. In

the same article in which the female CEO advised buying fancy underwear, another successful corporate woman said her secret was to always give the impression that she had even less time than she actually had. Lula too had somewhere to be—right here—and someone who needed her: Zeke.

"We have Estrelia," said Lula.

Dunia slipped back into her coat. "Call me. Call me soon. Meantime you can stop worrying that I'm a sex slave in Dubai."

They hugged and kissed, then hugged again. And then Dunia was gone, leaving Lula feeling more hopeful and less alone, but so physically exhausted that she drifted into the living room and sank into the couch, where she remained until the last trace of Dunia's perfume had followed her out of the house.

DUNIA'S SAFETY AND good fortune were a relief, and yet her visit was like a spray of ice water, shocking Lula out of the coma in which she'd been snoozing at Mister Stanley's. Wake up! Girls found rich husbands or married men they loved. They didn't hide out in a Jersey suburb dreaming that Alvo would find some tough-guy-contractor language in which to tell Lula that he thought about her as much as she thought about him.

It was a welcome distraction to sit at Zeke's computer. Would anyone go for a story about a man who tried to build an apartment house that kept collapsing until he dreamed that the solution was to wall his beloved wife into the foundation? The house stayed up, but the foundation was always wet, soaked with the woman's tears. Mister Stanley and Don Settebello obviously believed that the laws of physics no longer applied once you crossed the Albanian border. It was fortunate that she'd mentioned mixing fiction and nonfiction. When she'd written enough for a book, they would sort it all out, but for now her two American guardian angels could think what they wanted about her pretending her stories were true.

Lula was writing the scene in which the builder explains to his wife why his real estate needs demand that she be buried alive, and when she refuses, he shoves her into a crawl space and, sobbing, mixes the cement. Lula was so lost in her story that when the doorbell rang, she heard it as the clang of the husband's shovel, smoothing out concrete. She ran downstairs and opened the door to find Leather Jacket on the front steps.

"Little Sister, why so sad?" Leather Jacket—Genti—kept glancing back over his shoulder. The unforgiving winter light pooled in his pitted cheeks. Lula told him to step inside, where he seemed even more uneasy. Had he come to ask her out behind Alvo's back? Was Alvo passing her along to his friend, a sick male custom she'd heard of but never experienced first-hand? Did they think she was a hunk of roast lamb to be tossed to the next guy down the table? More likely Genti had come for the gun. Let him stand in the hall and mumble.

"What?" said Lula.

Mumble mumble.

"I can't understand you!"

"Mumble mumble Christmas Eve? My boss? . . . not busy Christmas Eve? He wants to know, Do you want to go out?"

Why was everything a question? Genti sounded like a teen-age girl. Gradually she understood. The guy was playing Cupid! It was all Lula could do not to throw her arms around him and squeeze till his jacket crackled. How touching that Alvo hadn't wanted to risk rejection in person. At the same time, how thoughtless and conceited of him to assume she wouldn't have plans. Christmas Eve was only two weeks away, and she had no plans.

What would happen to Leather Jacket if she told him to tell Alvo she was busy? Most likely the messenger wouldn't get killed if the bad news was about dating. As if Alvo cared enough to give his friend a hard time. He would just send one of the G-Men to ask another girl.

Lula said, "Tell him yes, I'd be happy."

"He'll be here at eight? He said dress nice?"

"Dress nice?" said Lula. "I always do. As opposed to what?" Where did Alvo get the nerve? But maybe it wasn't male arrogance. Maybe it was semantics. Maybe *nice* meant *up*, dress *up*, maybe they were sparing Lula the embarrassment of arriving at a formal event in a T-shirt and jeans. Obviously, she would dress up. It was Christmas Eve. But before she could ask for details, Genti shook her hand and left. Mission accomplished, he could go back to being a busy guy with important business elsewhere.

TWO WEEKS UNTIL Christmas. The winter days were too short and bloodless to sustain the weight of thought required to fathom the meaning of "dress nice." Nice by Dunia standards? Or Albanian nice: too shiny, too tight, too synthetic, and above all, too leopard. Nice like the big-haired singers who traveled the Balkan circuit with their big-haired manager husbands? Alvo was way cooler than that. He'd mean what Lula meant by nice.

Lula had patience and goodwill to spare, especially for Zeke.

On their drives to The Good Earth, they mixed high school metaphysical talk about the purpose of life (Lula assured him that life had a purpose) with the usual chitchat about driving and the other drivers, who, according to Zeke, were getting crazier and angrier as the holidays approached.

"What do you want for Christmas?" Lula asked.

"I don't know. Nothing. Wait. There's a DVD, this vintage vampire film called *Nosferatu*."

"Write it down," said Lula, who had no intention of spending money to feed Zeke's vampire obsession. She'd already bought him a leather belt on St. Marks Place, with rows of studs and grommets, and an iPod Nano for Mister Stanley.

Against her better instincts, she'd been letting Zeke drive to the market even when the weather was bad. She didn't tell Mister Stanley when the Olds slid into a snowbank, and Zeke and Lula had to dig it out, ruining Lula's boots. It would be hard enough explaining that she was going out Christmas Eve, abandoning Mister Stanley and Zeke on the anniversary of Ginger's departure.

She waited for a Saturday afternoon. Zeke had gone somewhere with friends. Christmas shopping, he'd said. Lula found Mister Stanley in the living room, reading the weekend sections of the Sunday paper. Tomorrow's news today. He was wearing his chinos, a cardigan, and a knit shirt, in which he managed to look more stiff and uncomfortable than he did in a suit. He looked like Mr. Rogers, the first American Lula ever saw on her granny's contraband TV.

"I need to talk to you," Lula said.

Mister Stanley said, "I have a wild idea. Let's go for a walk."

"Too wild," Lula said. "It's cold out."

"The air does one good," he said. "You'll turn into Dracula, entombed in this dark house."

A funny remark from the father of a vampire son. He was making a Mister Stanley joke. Trying to be helpful.

"Ha ha," Lula said. "Okay, let me get my coat." Outside, she pointed accusingly at the plumes their breath made in the air.

"Just around the block," said Mister Stanley. "No one is going to freeze."

Lula and Mister Stanley had the street to themselves, unless you counted the inflated plastic reindeer and carolers on the neighbors' lawns. Every so often a car passed, but no one slowed to watch the two of them drift from house to house, pausing to gaze at the Christmas displays, each of which, Lula thought sourly, consumed enough electricity to power all of Albania. But surely the lights were low-wattage. Why couldn't she just enjoy this harmless American custom instead of going straight for the dismissive immigrant envy? Because the decorations were intended to make outsiders envy the happiness inside.

No matter how much Lula had learned about American family life, she still longed to have participated in those family trips to the big-box store, the assembling of the decorations, with Dad and Junior following Mom and Sis's cheerful creative suggestions. Under Communism, one of the few foreign texts they'd been allowed to read was a translation of Hans Christian Andersen's "The Little Match Girl," which was taught as an illustration of class brutality in the West. Like everyone, Lula believed it. But in her new American life, she had learned about nuance. Mister Stanley came from the same class as the living rooms into which they were staring. An alternate title for her memoir could be *On the Outside Looking In.*

When Mister Stanley paused before a plastic sleigh the size of a tractor-trailer, Lula said, "I need to tell you something. I won't be spending Christmas Eve with you and Zeke. If that's okay with you."

"Of course it's okay," said Mister Stanley, too quickly. "So. What are you doing instead?"

"Going out," Lula said. "With friends." If Mister Stanley asked which friends, she would say friends from La Changita.

"Well, that's excellent," said Mister Stanley. "We want you to have your own life." He walked ahead to the next lawn, on which there was a crèche with a life-size camel whose plaster had chipped off so that hunks of flesh appeared to have been clawed away in a fight.

"It shouldn't make any difference," he said. "I think Zeke would be just as happy if we did away with the tree and the trimmings and the holiday cheer."

Holiday cheer? Had Mister Stanley forgotten that last year he brought home a dead tree, and they'd spent Christmas at the mall?

"Are you sure?" asked Lula.

"I don't know," said Mister Stanley.

Lula said, "When they outlawed religion under the dictatorship, people still celebrated. They'd pile up pyramids of baklava that looked like Christmas trees." Her granny had made baklava on Christmas. The pyramid part was extra. "The dictator ignored it because he loved pyramids so much he had himself buried in one. Until they dug him up."

"They dug him up?" said Mister Stanley.

Lula nodded. "And reburied him."

"That's awful." Mister Stanley chuckled, then caught himself. "A little-known fact, I guess."

"Every Albanian fact is a little-known fact," Lula said.

Mister Stanley smiled at his cute Albanian pet.

He said, "You're priceless, Lula. Enjoy yourself while you're young. Okay, let's go home now. You were right. It's freezing."

"LULA, *ESTE* JORGE," said Dunia, wrapping one flawlessly manicured hand around the wrist of the driver who had beeped for Lula to come outside and spare Dunia and her boots another damaging encounter with Mister Stanley's snowy walkway. "Jorge, *esta* Lula. *Mi amiga.*"

"*Buenos dias.*" Jorge's smile lit up the rearview mirror.

"*Buenos dias*," said Lula, glumly. Lazy Dunia could have come inside long enough for Lula to give her the history of her relationship, if you could call it that, with Alvo. Describing her fantasy romance was embarrassing enough without having to do it in the presence of New Jersey's most handsome driver. Even so, she was grateful that Dunia had, without hesitation, agreed to take Lula shopping. Despite everything, they had stayed friends, holding hands across the Grand Canyon of money and class that seemed to have opened between them.

"Don't worry about Jorge," Dunia said. "He speaks fifty words of English, all having to do with local highways. I've been teaching him Albanian. Our secret language, right, Jorge?"

"*Si,*" said Jorge. "Yes."

"Come to think of it," Dunia said, "speech is not his language."

"How is Steve with that?" Lula said.

Dunia slashed her forefinger across her neck and laughed. "I'm joking. Steve doesn't want to know what Steve doesn't know. Very incurious person. So what's the desperate situation?"

"I didn't say desperate. I said serious."

"You said desperate," Dunia insisted.

Maybe Lula had said desperate. "Okay, I meant serious. I need something to wear."

Dunia raised one eyebrow. "That's desperate? Baghdad is desperate. Hurricane Katrina was desperate. Ten-year-old Albanian kids working in a factory disassembling old Kalashnikovs is desperate. Did you hear about that?"

"My boss told me," Lula said.

"Nice boss." Dunia looked Lula up and down. She said, "Okay. Desperate."

"Short Hills Mall," she told Jorge. "*Gracias. Por favor.*"

It was easier once they were moving. Less intimate, in a way. Lula tried to talk without thinking, to just let the story of Alvo and his G-Men roll out. Or as much as she knew of the story. When she finished, Dunia was silent for so long that Lula had no choice but to contemplate the ridiculousness of what she'd just said.

"Let me get this straight," said Dunia. "You're spending Christmas Eve with a guy who takes you to some Thai joint and screws with your head and sneaks into your house and takes a shower and writes shit on your computer—"

"On Zeke's computer. Plus he left me a present." Lula

missed Little Charmy Puppy and its unconditional affection.
She'd made it bark so often that it broke and couldn't be fixed.

"What present? You didn't tell me that part."

Lula smiled. Let Dunia imagine.

"Presents mean nothing," said Dunia. "Take it from someone who knows."

After that they rode in silence. Dunia said, "Bravo, Jorge!
We're here. This is the only decent mall, the others are big
wasters of time."

"Wastes of time," said Lula.

Dunia shrugged. "Look where perfect grammar's got you.
So let's be clear about this: You want to make sure Mr. Psycho
knows he can fuck you if he wants to. Take it from me, he wants
to."

"You're one to talk," said Lula. "You've had some pretty
strange boyfriends."

Dunia's pearl-dusted eyelids fluttered. Lula wondered if she
was thinking of the tough little stockbroker who'd refused to
do it in bed and who was always leading Dunia, flushed and
dreamy, back from the men's room and the alleyways near La
Changita.

"Don't change the subject," Dunia said. "Stop here! Forget
the macho parking two steps from the entrance." She flung open
the door and trotted across the lot. Lula rushed to catch up. Was
Dunia running away? Possibly from the idea of Lula's romance
with Alvo. True love and hot sex, even the chance of true love
and hot sex, was the only thing that could compete with the standard of living that came with Dunia's boring marriage to Steve.
Love, or even the hope of love, gave you status, in a way.

But if so, this slight edge was lost on the women who watched

Lula and Dunia from the mirrored fortresses of the cosmetics counters. Under their scrutiny, Lula's coat turned into a jester's rags, in which she skipped after Dunia, distracting her friend from the saleswomen's grown-up claims on her attention. They sized up Lula and looked away, as if from someone disfigured. Then they trained their come-to-me gazes on the one in the ostrich boots.

"I need a new outfit," Lula said. "Something sexy but elegant."

"Perfume," Dunia told her. "Trust me. Forget the outfit, the short skirt, the fishnet stockings, the unbuttoned blouse, the fuck-me shoes. More wastes of time and money. Dab something expensive in a few secret places, and their testosterone pumps. Steve brought me home a study from a medical journal. Certain scents increase guys' blood flow and give them massive hard-ons. Better than Viagra. Call a doctor if your erection lasts longer than four hours. The problem is, a different smell works on each individual guy. So Steve does his own research and comes home with this million-dollar vial of oil, probably illegal, he says it's extracted from poppies that grow in the kitchen gardens of Afghan warlords. God knows where it really comes from. If I put it where he wants me to, it gives me a hideous rash. So now I have to smell like a hooker and pretend to talk dirty in Albanian. How much fun is that?"

Did the women smiling at the two girls from their glittery counters suspect that the rich one was complaining about her sex life?

"Pheromones," said Lula. "Like with the insect family. That funny odor when you crush a beetle. To another beetle it's the irresistible sex smell."

"The death smell," Dunia said. "The day I met Steve in the airport I was wearing a bucket of Chanel No. 5."

Lula said, "How nice for the person sitting next to you on the plane."

"There was no person next to me on the plane," said Dunia. "No plane. I figured I might as well wear it. If I tried to bring it home to Albania, some customs guard at the airport would have stolen it for his girlfriend."

Dunia trawled the counters, eyeing bottles, raising and dashing the hopes of women who had spent the day seducing an empty department-store aisle. Grasping Lula's forearm, Dunia said, "Concentrate. Focus on this guy. Be him. Figure out what he'd like. Let your instincts guide you."

Now all the women were looking at them. How confident it made Dunia and Lula to stand there deep in conversation, suspended in time and space, feeling no compulsion to get on with the business of shopping. Lula couldn't be this brave alone. No one could. How she needed and loved her friend! Dunia flitted from counter to counter, spraying perfumes on tissue squares and writing, with a stubby pencil, the names of scents until she'd narrowed the selection down to three or four squares. In what exclusive rich-girl school had Dunia learned to do this?

"Smell them. But think about the guy."

"They're all starting to smell the same," Lula said.

"My God, you're hopeless." Dunia kissed Lula's cheek. The perfume ladies goggled. Did they think that Lula and Dunia were Russian hookers spending a stolen lesbian afternoon? She could see why Steve's parents worried about Dunia. How wrong they were, how little they knew. But the lie they believed about her friend was another lie come true. Somehow they'd

transformed her into the ambitious Natasha climbing the social ladder on which their son was the bottom rung.

"I think musky," Dunia was saying. "A guy who stashes his gun with you and pretends to be in construction—"

"Pretends? He's in construction."

"Pretends," Dunia said. "Probably the fastest way to his heart is to pick up your skirt and show him. Look, no underwear."

"That's not going to happen," said Lula.

"I understand," said Dunia. "That's why we're doing perfume. Concentrate. Start again."

Lula sprayed and sniffed and tried to think about Alvo. But try as she might, she couldn't conjure up the scenario in which one whiff of something spicy or sweet gave him no choice but to jump her.

"Check out this one." Dunia sprayed a cold mist on Lula's wrist. "Give it a minute. Okay, sniff."

Lula closed her eyes and inhaled.

In the littered courtyard behind her housing block in Tirana had been a glorious flowering tree that thrived on garbage, weeds, cigarette smoke, and the fried food aerosol that fell on it from the windows. Luckily it bloomed around May Day, so the tree was left alone by the neighborhood committee, which usually ruled that anything pretty or pleasing was Western bourgeois mind poison. The May Day tree bloomed for a week, and people would come downstairs in the evenings and gather in groups or stand alone to breathe in the scent of the blossoms. No one stole the branches to have inside their homes. It was the only time when Communism worked like it was supposed to. After the blossoms fell, it was understood that the kids could

stay out late and have battles, flinging the slimy petals and hard stamens at each other. The perfume Dunia had sprayed on her wrist smelled like those warm spring nights.

"This one," Lula said thickly. The bottle—sapphire blue, like the pharmaceutical vials in which Granny used to keep her gardenia water—reminded her of Granny's story about the woman who went around collecting tears and marketing them as a skin care product. Just thinking about that story seemed like asking for bad luck. Lula decided to keep the perfume in the drawer with Alvo's gun. Let her new smell and his pistol spend some time together.

A voice said, "Shall I wrap it up?"

"My treat," Dunia said.

"I can't let you do this," Lula said.

Dunia brandished her credit card. "Steve's treat," she told the woman.

Chapter Ten

———∞∞∞———

MISTER STANLEY took the day before Christmas off and spent the morning rooting through the closets for some important item that turned out to be a package of tinsel that he draped, strand by strand, over the picture frames. When Zeke woke at noon, Mister Stanley, apparently having forgotten his plans to ignore the holiday, asked if Zeke wanted to go help pick out a Christmas tree.

Zeke said, "What kind of sick trees do you think will be left on Christmas Eve?"

Mister Stanley said, "Probably plenty. There will be plenty of choice."

Zeke said, "Then you don't need me."

Mister Stanley said, "What the heck, does one even need a tree?"

Zeke said, "What the heck, does one even need a tree?" and turned on the TV. Was he trying to exhaust the patience of his patient American dad? No, he was trying to remind his guilty American dad that his mother had abandoned them on Christmas Eve.

At six, when Lula decided to start dressing to go out with Alvo, Zeke was lying on the couch watching the Yule log burn on TV, while Mister Stanley sat in a chair, watching his son watching.

"Oh, look, it's just like Communist TV," Lula said in the grating warble she heard in her voice whenever she tried to brighten the dark air between them. "The newscaster would read us statistics of people starving to death in the West, and a clock would tick on the wall."

Mister Stanley said, "Zeke, do you think we could possibly watch something more compelling?"

"No," said Zeke. "I like this. It's totally compelling."

Mister Stanley struggled visibly not to ask, then asked, "Are you high on something, Zeke?"

"On holiday cheer," Zeke said.

Beckoning Lula into the kitchen, Mister Stanley said, "I think he misses his mom."

"I'm sorry," Lula said, meaning sorry sympathetic but sounding like sorry apologetic. In Albanian they were different words, and the difference could mean life or death.

Mister Stanley tented his fingertips like a priest. "Quite honestly, it was a challenge not to notice the symbolism and anger in the timing of my wife's departure. I told you it was Christmas Eve."

"You did," Lula said. What a heartless monster Ginger was. Yet somewhere in Lula's own heart she understood Ginger's panic. She was sure, or almost sure, that the remorse she felt for leaving tonight would vanish the minute she left.

"I'd better get ready," she said.

Even as Lula told herself that her date with Alvo would be nothing special—really, you couldn't say enough for low expectations!—she not only used all her creams and soaps but every one of the free bath-product samples she had hoarded from her first days in New York. There was a reckless glee in opening the tiny vials and anointing herself with substances so potent that the store had bet those precious drops on making her want more.

She walked naked across the bedroom, opened her under-wear drawer, and gently unwrapped Alvo's gun from its cocoon. She held the silk in one hand, the pistol in the other, hesitating as if she were weighing them, deciding. She lay the gun on a hastily gathered nest of polyester and stepped into the silk panties, fastened the bra, and went to the mirror, braced for a vision of decrepitude and horror. But in fact she looked fit. Like a girl! Her ass hadn't sagged all that much, amazing when you considered how much time she'd spent sitting on it at Mister Stanley's. For a moment she drifted out of herself and floated into another perspective, the warmer, more admiring view of someone like . . . someone like Alvo. She imagined, as she hoped he would, slipping off the lace and silk. The physical symptoms of desire were unmistakable, even after a long remission. Like riding a bicycle, Lula thought, not that she'd ever learned to ride a bike.

Lula needed to calm down. It would be unwise to start out on her first real date with Alvo in a state of high arousal.

Given that Dunia had talked her out of spending money on a new outfit, "dress nice" had better mean her black dress and the heels that made her calves look thin but which she could dance in, if she had to. She put on her makeup, American subtle but heavy enough to convince an Albanian guy she'd made an effort. Even after she'd wiped off three different shades of blush and sprayed on the precise dose of perfume that, she'd learned through trial and costly error, communicated erotic interest without being too aggressive, she was ready twenty minutes early.

Which was lucky, because so was Alvo. Her phone chirped, and a text appeared. *Parked outside*. Short, to the point, and now his number was on Lula's contact list.

She had rehearsed her exit, and it went smoothly, as planned. She grabbed her coat and let the door close tenderly on her "Merry Christmas!" This time she added, "See you soon," to reassure them that she wasn't leaving forever. As she walked down the path, her knight in his shining black charger beeped his horn—honk, honk, hello. The guy had a few rough edges. Maybe he was nervous.

Lula slid across the seat and kissed Alvo on the cheek.

"Merry Christmas," he said.

All Dunia's painstaking olfactory research results were instantly corrupted by the unforeseen variable of Alvo's strong cologne. Despite the fortune Dunia had spent, Lula was glad to let the scent of those long-lost summer evenings surrender without a fight to the peacock pheromones of Alvo's preparations for the evening, which happily did not include the tight, shiny synthetics that so many Albanian boys favored. His black shirt set off the red of his hair, and in his black jacket and jeans, he could have passed for one of the guys who'd blown their trust funds on rum drinks at La Changita. Lula hadn't wanted to go out with those guys, so why did she want Alvo to look like one? Because she didn't want to be the bossy know-it-all, tutoring her fresh-off-the-boat boyfriend in the fashions and customs of their adopted country.

They rode in silence, struck dumb by the awareness that they'd altered their smells for each other. That had to signify something, if only the likelihood that Alvo had calculated the probability of his getting laid this evening. Lula's stomach fluttered. Dunia and her bright ideas. How much harder the perfume made it to pretend this was just a platonic friendly night out, Older Brother and Little Sister reeking like a pair of sex fiends.

"Where are we going?" Lula asked.

"The Bronx," said Alvo. "Where else?"

They crossed the George Washington Bridge, its bright loops improbably strung above the silver cord of the river. Down below, glittering hives of mist swirled around the streetlamps on the snowy banks of the Hudson.

Alvo said, "So how are the boss and his kid spending their Merry Christmas?"

"Watching the Yule log on TV," Lula said.

Alvo said, "Bleak. Very bleak."

"Please. I feel guilty enough," said Lula.

Alvo took the exit for the Whitestone Parkway. Then he said, "Are you sure you're not fucking the boss?"

"Jesus Christ!" said Lula. "How many times do I have to—?"

"Sorry," Alvo said.

Lula said, "What's the point of Christmas, anyway? We never had Christmas at home."

"Now we do," said Alvo. "Now it's a big travel season for Albanians. Everyone's got to come here. To do what, I don't know. Go to Radio City. Sit on Santa's lap. Right now I've got three cousins from Vlorë sleeping on my bedroom floor."

So much for the option of ending the evening at Alvo's apartment. But since when had Lula needed to do it in a proper bed? She'd grown so middle-aged and conservative since she and her boyfriends used to sneak out and rip off their clothes and roll around in the dictator's bunkers.

Alvo said, "I wonder if they ever took a survey: How many Albanian guys and girls had their first sex in a bunker?"

Lula said, "Did you just read my mind, or what?"

"Really?" said Alvo. "That's beautiful." Without taking his hands off the wheel, he bumped his elbow against hers. "You know what? One of my cousins brought me this little vial of water from a spring somewhere in Bosnia. Male water, they call it. Supposed to be Balkan Viagra."

"Do you need it?" Lula asked.

"Not the last time I checked," Alvo said.

Lula saw searchlights raking the sky above an industrial wasteland, beacons to guide their smooth landing in front of a one-story building on which red and green and silver lights spelled out "Merry Christmas, Happy New Year." Another string of bulbs outlined a double-headed eagle over the door.

"I've heard of this place," said Lula.

"Who hasn't?" Alvo said.

Two guys in bow ties lunged for the doors of the Lexus, but Alvo waved them off until he and Lula got out and he surrendered the keys.

"Valet parking sucks," Alvo said. "Paying some stranger to screw with your seat adjustment and mirrors. But in this neighborhood you need somebody to kneecap the junkie before he smashes your window for the pocket change stuck in the seat."

A squad of gigantic bouncers guarded the entrance, checking IDs and exuding random intimidation. One of them recognized Alvo and cleared a tunnel through which Alvo led Lula, a gauntlet of arm-punches and shoulder thumps that Alvo good-humoredly endured while Lula succumbed to the dizzying high of specialness and privilege. Which other girls had Alvo come here with? It almost spoiled her good mood to think about Alvo's life before her.

Lula saw a security guard holding a girl at arm's length, laughing as her flailing arms and fists bounced off his puffed-out chest.

"Spit on me?" he was saying. "What kind of way is that for a nice Albanian girl to behave?"

The coat check girl looked hard at Lula to see how she'd wound up with Alvo. Lula wanted to tell her: chemistry. For some reason she thought of Savitra asking if she'd had sex with Don Settebello. What did Lula know about Alvo's past? She knew nothing about his present.

A blast of noise blew these reflections straight out of Lula's head. As Alvo guided her into the crowd, Lula remembered why this feeling—too many people, too much sound, not enough oxygen, not enough room, a barrage of intense sensation bombarding your heart and belly—was something you might want. Sparks leaped from body to body, each body in a bubble yet paradoxically hyperaware of every other body nearby. It was a highly diluted but still arousing version of the wordless language two bodies speak when they are about to have sex.

As they moved away from the door, the space was less tightly packed, and indeed the dance floor had the forlorn air of a wedding before the party gets rocking. An invisible DJ shouted, "Let's slow it down!" as if it weren't slow enough already, and a soul singer crooned a ballad. A few couples, newlyweds or newly engaged, danced closely, half entranced and half convincing the world and themselves of their passionate future together.

"Let's get a drink," said Alvo, again reading Lula's mind. He found an empty corner and told Lula to wait. He'd forgotten to ask what she wanted. Or maybe it was a guy thing, profoundly cave man and Bronx. You not only ordered for your date but you told her what she liked.

Alvo vanished into the strobe-swept darkness. What if he never came back? How long did Lula have to wait before she called a taxi? There were plenty of single guys here. She could dance, have fun, maybe even find another guy to take her home. But there was no one she wanted to meet. She wanted to be with Alvo. He wouldn't do that to her on Christmas Eve. No one would stoop that low. No one, that is, but Ginger.

At last she spotted Alvo bobbing toward her with a shot glass in each hand. "Sorry it took me so long. I ran into this crazy dude who wanted to start a big fight. He claims we installed his air conditioner backward, and it blew dirt and soot and garbage all over his little baby. Now he wants us to reinstall it—"

"I thought you did commercial construction," Lula said.

"We do," he said. "Like I told you. The dude's hallucinating. This one's yours. *G'ʒoor.*"

"*G'ʒoor.*" Lula took a sip. Raki, the drink of good-bye and hello, of congratulation and consolation. Lula didn't think of herself as a nationalistic person. Mostly, in her experience, country was like religion, an excuse to hate other people and feel righteous about it. But then there was raki. Raki *was* Albania, it had that special taste. Even Albanians with no sentimental attachment to their home country brightened and got teary-eyed when the talk turned to raki. They got high just hearing the word.

"Mother's milk," said Alvo.

"Delirium in a glass," Lula said.

"Hell, yeah. Whoever said money can't buy happiness never got into the top-of-the-line mulberry raki."

"I like the walnut," Lula said.

"That works too," said Alvo. "Expensive."

Lula was trying to figure out what else to say about raki when a blare of static rattled the loudspeakers, and the music turned Albanian. A man sang about a woman he couldn't forget, while behind him the clarinets tried to cheer him up. The volume climbed, while the sinuous thumping of the electronic drum cast a spell on the crowd and dragged the enchanted ones toward the dance floor.

"Another drink?" Alvo asked.

"I've still got some." But oddly, Lula's glass appeared to have emptied itself. "Sure, why not?" She smiled.

"That's my girl." Alvo plunged off toward the bar against the incoming tide of merrymakers.

His girl? Had Lula heard right? It meant nothing besides approval of the pace at which she was drinking. He could have said, My man. Yet she no longer worried that he wouldn't return. She leaned against a wall that seemed to be keeping time with the drum and watched people approach the dance floor as if it were a pool into which they were either about to dive or venture one big toe.

It had been so long since she'd seen Albanian dancing. She'd forgotten how it made you want to join the line even if you were cool and modern and over Albanian dancing. So much individual soul was poured into the simple steps, men and women, young and old, married, single, fat, thin. No one wore the stiff mask of vacancy or anxiety that Lula had so often seen on the faces of Americans inventing their own dances, trying to seem unself-conscious even as they labored to telegraph a message about confidence, sexuality, and whether they were available or taken. How stressful it was when Americans paired off in Noah's ark couples, performing rhythmic preludes or aftermaths to sex, or danced in groups of girls, never groups of guys, writhing, distanced from the bodies they were showing off. Albanians just grabbed the last hand in line and let the music take charge.

Lula was dancing in place when Alvo returned with more raki. As they toasted each other, Alvo smiled so widely that his gold tooth sparkled at her, only at her. Alvo eased in beside her and bumped ever so slightly to the music. When his hip brushed hers she longed to rub against him like a cat.

Luckily, they had double rakis to finish before they had to decide whether to join the dancing, which, as luck would have it, stopped, giving them more time to figure out what to do next. A set of curtains opened, and a guy in a white suit bounded onto a low stage. His first "Good evening" in English and Albanian elicited manic applause. He slipped between languages, playing to both sides, the older people who clung to their native tongue and the kids who'd never learned it. But everyone understood and loved his patter about old friends and new friends, brothers and sisters, all family here tonight. More applause for the names of the stars who'd be entertaining them this evening, and for each of the beautiful cities in which the talent had performed. The applause built as two men, also in white suits, tried out the keyboards, one of which sounded like a clarinet and the other like a drum. The host whipped the audience into a frenzy of welcome for the singer, who strutted out nonchalantly, as if frantic clapping was the background noise of her everyday existence. Then her bright red mouth exploded in smiles, and she bowed from the waist and blew kisses.

Black as Zeke's, but varnished to a high gloss, the singer's hair framed her face in question marks. Curls spilled over the shoulders of her white dress, which had gauzy sleeves and pearl flowers like a wedding gown, only with a miniskirt stretched tightly across her belly. White boots rose up to meet it, exposing a long expanse of thigh, fit and tan in the dead of winter, though her face and hands were pale.

"Miss Ada Culpi!" yelled the MC, and the singer curled her arms, palms up, asking, asking. She sang to each person in the crowd, begging each kind soul to advise her, to tell her what to do about the man she loved but who didn't love her. No one believed this guy didn't love her, but her voice reminded them of every time they'd felt what she was pretending to feel. Lula had never felt that way. Then she remembered Alvo and thought she might be about to start now. She glanced at Alvo, steeling herself for the sight of entranced, hormonal male rapture. Instead he shook his head and shrugged, eloquently conveying his adorable opinion that Miss Ada Culpi was a little much. His shrug said he preferred more normal, less outrageous women like . . . well, like Lula!

Ada Culpi reached for the audience, grabbing them, pulling them in, signaling that the only way they could soothe her broken heart was by dancing. A few people, then a few more, formed a line, and the line of dancers grew long enough to coil once and then again. By now there were two rows, a men's line and a women's line facing one another.

Lula took Alvo's empty raki glass, set both glasses on a ledge, then led him onto the dance floor. The women's line grabbed Lula just as the men's line, led by a guy twirling a red scarf embroidered with a double-headed eagle, yanked Alvo the opposite way. Lula had drunk precisely enough to feel loose but not too loose as the steps came back to her, as natural as walking but less isolated and boring. Why should this seem so pleasant to a person like herself, a person who hated chorus lines, military parades, anything in lockstep? She liked the music, and she liked knowing what to do with her body in response to the drum beat and the hysterical clarinet.

A girl with purple eyelids held one hand, a middle-aged woman the other. The woman smiled, but not the girl. Lula trusted them both enough to briefly close her eyes. Alvo was out there somewhere. No need to fear he'd left the club or found a prettier girl to dance with. They were all dancing together, Lula and Alvo among them. As the lines spooled and twisted, Lula caught sight of Alvo, taller than most of the men. Alvo could dance, it turned out. Confidently, but not arrogantly, his back straight, his head held high. How handsome he was, and how glad she was to be here with him. Why should she care about a gun, some moody weirdness, a certain lack of clarity about what he did for a living? And okay, some low-level stalking.

Did Alvo see her? She couldn't tell. She watched his line snake closer until he was opposite her. He saw her. They looked at each other. That was that. Nothing needed to be discussed, not even inside her own head. Lula loved how the voice of sex drowned out all the other voices, the naggings of reason and common sense, shyness and hesitation. Desire and inevitability were the only voices left, and their interesting questions were the only questions: How and when? When and where? Would it be easy or awkward?

Alvo and Lula danced past one another and looked back, not caring who was watching. Alvo's line turned a corner, so that his back was to Lula, who peered around the dancers between them. There was nothing to do but keep dancing.

At last the music ended. The singer said, "*Falemenderit.* Thank you thank you thank you," and a storm of blown kisses rained down on the dancers, who regretfully dropped each other's hands so they could applaud.

Alvo found Lula and put his arm around her shoulders and steered her toward the exit. He produced a bill and a claim check and gave them to the coat girl, who sensed that this was not the moment for another competitive whole-body appraisal of Lula. They headed out into the cold night, which warmed up when Alvo grabbed Lula and kissed her right in front of the door. The bouncers whistled and cheered. Alvo handed over the parking ticket, then drew Lula into the shadows and kissed her with such force that it took several horn blasts from the valet to detach them long enough to get into the SUV.

Before leaning over to kiss her again, Alvo considerately pushed the buttons that heated the seats, and the warmth beneath Lula flowed into the warmth inside her. It must have started snowing, because Lula was dimly aware of the sigh of the windshield wipers.

"Merry white Christmas," Alvo said.

"Merry white Christmas to you," said Lula.

Alvo shook himself like a wet dog as he separated from Lula. As he drove, he yanked at his clothing with a shy embarrassed smile at some secret he had with himself, a secret that, Lula concluded happily, must be a massive hard-on. After a few blocks, he pulled over and parked on the formerly scary industrial street that now seemed private and romantic.

They kissed and pressed against each other as closely as the console between them allowed. Pausing for breath, Lula watched, from a momentary remove, passion locked in a heated argument with her sensible reluctance to have sex for the first time with Alvo in a vehicle, even one as roomy as this. It was awkward enough in bed, with every creature comfort helping you over the various hurdles, zippers and bra hooks and first seeing the other person naked.

"Not here," her sweet Lancelot murmured.

"No, not here," agreed Lula.

"My place," Alvo said. Then he slapped himself on the forehead and said, "Look how you've messed with my head. I forgot the Vlorë cousins."

Lula had messed with his head. His desire for her—for her!—had erased three entire cousins. Lula waited for Alvo to suggest a hotel. It couldn't seem like her idea, even if it was. She didn't want to look like a degenerate slut who did this all the time.

Typing into the GPS, Alvo said, "She'll tell us a hotel." Then he said, "Motherfucker. I don't have a credit card. This friend of mine got his wallet boosted at a club. Five round-trip tickets to the DR charged before he called it in. So now I only bring cash and my driver's license. I could pay you back—"

"I don't have a credit card," Lula said. "I don't even have cash."

"Big problem," said Alvo, then kissed her again, as if that

might solve the problem. After a while Lula heard herself say, "We could go to Mister Stanley's."

"And what?" Alvo said. "Introduce myself? Hi, I'm a friend of your nanny's?"

Lula said, "They'll be asleep. But we'll have to be very quiet."

"Silent as death," Alvo said. Lula wondered if it was possible to literally faint from desire. Probably not if you were sitting down. As Alvo started the motor again, Lula rested one hand on his thigh. Brushing against his groin, the backs of her knuckles confirmed her pleasant suspicions. She would have to make sure that Alvo left before Mister Stanley woke up.

Alvo groaned softly. "Wait. Slippery weather. I need to concentrate on the road."

Lula sat back and closed her eyes. That last double shot of raki had affected her more than she'd realized. Probably it would sober her up to focus on the challenge ahead: finding the quietest route to her room and figuring out what she would say if by some chance Mister Stanley or Zeke was still awake, waiting to catch Santa Claus squeezing down the chimney.

Alvo said, "Tonight is why God invented four-wheel drive."

The alcohol almost persuaded Lula that this might be the time to broach the subject of Alvo breaking into Mister Stanley's when she wasn't there. This time we'll sneak in together, she'd say.

Only at the last minute did better judgment prevail. Suppose it hadn't been Alvo? He might change his mind about getting naked and defenseless in a house where stalkers wrote Balkan stories on computers and showered, uninvited. As Alvo sped down the icy highway, Lula reminded herself to observe how he acted at Mister Stanley's, to see if he gave any sign of having been there before and knowing how to get to her room without her having to show him.

ALVO TOOK THE Baywater exit, then parked, and they kissed some more. By the time he started the car again, Lula's hesitations had vanished.

Mister Stanley's windows were dark, except for the outside light he'd left on for Lula. She told Alvo to wait behind the tree and crept around to the window to make sure that no one was sipping delicious cold water at the fridge.

All clear! She gave Alvo the thumbs-up sign, unlocked the door, and pushed him away so he wouldn't be groping her till they were safe in her room. Stealth came easily to Alvo. For such a forceful guy, he could be quiet as a kitten. Lula forgot to watch and see whether he knew the way.

She opened the door to her room. What was that smell? Musty, yeasty, with an edge of organic rot. Mice died in the walls in Tirana. Did that happen in New Jersey? Of course. But why now, why here, why on this night of all nights when she had found a guy she liked and was bringing him home? What would Alvo think of her? Maybe he wouldn't notice. She pulled him inside and shut the door. Light shone in from the street. Lula lowered the shade and switched her night lamp on low. She knew men liked to see. In the dark, the costly underwear would have been for nothing.

"What's that smell?" asked Alvo.

Lula said, "The kid's pet rabbit escaped and had babies inside the wall."

Alvo said, "I always wondered how bunnies have so many babies."

"Let's find out," said Lula.

"Not the baby part," Alvo said warily.

"Of course not," Lula said.

Alvo sat on the edge of the bed, spread his knees, and eased her toward him. The sweetness and the expertise Alvo put into his kisses made Lula feel hopeful about the immediate future. Of course there was fear and nervousness, that was part of the high. The silk panties were a brilliant touch. A nice surprise for Alvo.

By the time Lula surfaced for air, the smell had gotten stronger.

"Hey, where are you?" Alvo said.

"Right here," said Lula, demonstrating how right there she was. She had reentered the state of steamy bliss when Alvo pulled away.

"What the fuck?" he said.

Lula turned. A dripping-wet woman, naked except for a towel wrapped around one hand, stood in the bathroom doorway. Lula turned the lamp on full. The woman was smeared with some brown substance that Lula hoped was mud. She was backlit against the bathroom glare, her shadowed face surrounded by a bright nimbus of reddish gray curls. Then she stepped into the light.

"Ginger," Lula said.

"Who the hell?" Alvo said.

"The mom," Lula said. "The mother and the wife. The wife of Mister Stanley. I know her only from pictures."

"You stay away from my pictures," said Ginger.

"Pleased to meet you, Mrs. Stanley," Alvo said.

"Go back to hell, hog boy," said Ginger.

"Nice," Alvo told Lula, as if it was her fault. "Nice manners your roommate has."

"She's not my roommate," said Lula.

"Your boss," said Alvo. "Your boss's wife."

"I told you, I never saw her before!"

"Then what's she doing in your room?"

Ginger took a step forward. Proximity and lamplight were spectacularly unkind. Lula didn't know where to look first, or where not to look ever. Not at the tires of soft flesh stacked around Ginger's middle, not at the sunken loins and sparse pubic hair, the pouched thighs streaked brown, and certainly not at the grotesque mask of the face in the family snapshots.

"It's chocolate," Ginger said. "I had to cover myself with candy to get rid of the sour vibe you've brought into this house, miss."

What exactly did Ginger mean by "sour vibe"? The psychic residue of Lula helping Ginger's husband and son sweep up the ashes after Ginger had burned down their happy home?

"Chocolate," Lula said. "I hope so."

"Disgusting," said Alvo.

"You shut up, asshole." With a dramatic flourish, Ginger shook the towel from her hand, revealing, underneath, a butcher knife that she brandished, first at Lula, then at Alvo. Lula recognized the knife. The last time she'd tried to cook Zeke broccoli, it had sliced through the stem in one stroke. How had Ginger found it? It was Ginger's knife.

"Put that down, lady, please," said Alvo.

"Please, Mrs. Stanley," said Lula.

"Call me that one more time, and I'll cut your face off. I'll kill you both and let you bleed out on the floor."

"For your husband and son to find?" Lula said.

"Fuck them too," said Ginger. "The kid's a fruitcake like his dad."

Where was the Ginger who had sent her son those cheerful postcards implying that the red rocks and the clean Western air were healing her spirit? Where had Ginger really been during her circular pilgrimage to and from New Jersey? What had she done with the money Mister Stanley sent, and how had she convinced him that she was getting better? Lula should have been watching the knife, but instead her thoughts ranged through space and time, until the fog finally parted, revealing an unobstructed view of the truth that had been there all along.

It had always been Ginger. Ginger had a key. How could Lula not have realized that Ginger was letting herself into the house, showering in her tub, writing on Zeke's computer? The morning of the college trip, it had crossed her mind. But she'd instantly dismissed it. She'd wanted to think it was Alvo. And besides, Ginger was sending postcards from all over the country! Little Charmy Puppy had thrown her even farther off, as Ginger doubtless intended. Why would her employer's wife be leaving her cute wind-up toys? The obvious was now obvious, as it always was, sooner or later.

"The crap you let my child eat," Ginger said. "Frozen hamburgers! Pizza. You think a mother doesn't know? You think I didn't look to see the toxic slime you stashed away in the freezer?"

"We got what Zeke wanted," said Lula. "We bought what he would eat."

"First of all, what gives you the right to even say my child's name. Or to feed him poison."

"He's not a child," said Lula. "And it wasn't poison."

"To the mother he's always a child," Alvo said.

"Shut up, you Balkan boy toy." Ginger waggled the knife at Alvo. Why didn't Alvo grab it? He was as big and male and strong as Ginger was female and weak. Perhaps he doubted, as did Lula, that the substance with which she'd painted herself was chocolate. For now, squeamishness trumped mortal fear.

"What kind of house is this?" demanded Ginger. "I'll tell you. A whorehouse. It's Christmas Eve, and there's not even a Christmas tree downstairs!"

"Please, lady, give me the knife," said Alvo.

"In your fat gut I will," replied Ginger.

"We won't hurt you," Lula said, illogically, considering who had the weapon. But Ginger was so vulnerable, so old and crazy and naked. Ginger came several steps closer, smelling like chocolate, but with an undertone of shit.

"Hurt me? You already have. Sleeping with my husband, turning my child against me, undermining everything I worked for—"

Alvo said, "So you did fuck the boss!"

Lula said, "I told you. I never had sex with Mister Stanley."

"Mister Stanley," said Ginger. "Listen to you. Stanley got himself a real servant maid. A real Transylvanian goat girl."

"I'm not Transylvanian," Lula said.

"She's Albanian," said Alvo. "So am I."

"Bully for you," said Ginger. "I'm from Indiana, but I don't go around reminding people every five minutes."

"Albania isn't Indiana," said Alvo.

"Enough!" said Ginger. "This is making me sick! I'm not discussing politics with some camel jockey."

"Hey!" Alvo shouted. "Take that back!"

"Pipe down," Ginger said. "Wake my son and husband up, and it's your jugular, pal."

Lula pictured Mister Stanley and Zeke slumbering in their beds. Her heart contracted with pity for them. For all of them, Ginger included.

Alvo said, "Give me the knife. Slowly and calmly. Nobody panic."

"Where did you learn English? Watching *Law and Order*?" Ginger stepped closer to Alvo, pointing the blade at his neck.

"Why are you threatening *me*?" he said.

"Because you're the threat," answered Ginger. "What could this bitch do that she hasn't done, except two-time my husband under his own roof? Maybe she's done it already."

"Have you?" Alvo asked Lula.

Really, that was it.

"Button your pants," Lula told Alvo. "If you're going to die, you'll want your fly zipped to give a more dignified impression of your last minutes on earth."

"No one's going to die," Alvo said.

"Everyone's going to die," said Ginger.

"Would you like a robe?" Lula asked Ginger. "You must be freezing cold."

"I wouldn't wear your slut clothes," Ginger said. "I've seen what's in your closet."

For a split second, Lula was outraged. But it was only fair. Lula had held Ginger's dashikis and fat pants against her body.

"It's comfortable. Warm," Lula said. "My granny made it

for me." Anyone would forgive her for lying about her granny. Granny would forgive her. She would want her to save her life. Lula cringed at the thought of shit or even chocolate smeared inside Granny's robe. She needed to keep it firmly in mind that there was no Granny's robe.

There was, however, a gun. That Lula remembered it only now proved she wasn't a violent person. Loaded or unloaded, guns trumped knives. Her papa used to say, You don't ever need to use a gun, you only have to show it. What if Ginger had found it? Ginger hadn't found it. She'd be waving it at Alvo.

Not even Ginger could resist the offer of Granny's warm love against her cold skin.

"Sure," she said. "A robe would be nice."

Lula said, "I'll get it."

Lula looked back over her shoulder at Ginger menacing Alvo. A stifled sob leaped from her throat at the sight of Ginger's droopy behind. Some day Lula's would sag like that. Young people weren't supposed to know this, but Lula always had. Even her ass depended on her staying in this country. If she signed up at a decent gym, her muscle tone would hold up twenty years longer than it would in Tirana.

Alvo shot Lula a meaningful glance. He probably thought her plan was for him to grab the knife as Lula helped Ginger into the robe. Which would have worked, if there was a robe. He knew there was a gun, but not where Lula kept it. Because, unlike Ginger, he'd never been in this room with the time and motive and opportunity to look through Lula's stuff.

Ginger was too busy with Alvo to wonder why Lula would keep Granny's robe in a bureau drawer. With all her snooping around, how could she not have found the gun? Maybe Lula's underwear had created a magic force field. If so, it was worth the money, even if the silk against her breasts and the tops of her thighs was now a shaming reminder of her ruined hopes.

Lula aimed the gun at Ginger.

"Drop the knife," she told her in her most persuasive, and, she hoped, least cops-and-robbers tone.

Ginger tilted her chin at the gun. "Right. I'm dying laughing. Shoot me and explain it to my husband and son, then catch a one-way ride to the deportation center." With a shrug, she turned back and waved the knife at Alvo. "You know what? I'm sick of your face. Your face in its present form."

What was Lula supposed to do now? Nothing was going according to plan. A moment passed, another moment.

Lula squeezed the trigger.

The retort knocked her backward. Her papa would be furious to see her stumble and nearly fall. The room began to glitter, as if the walls were mirrored, the air bright with flakes of mica. The last thing Lula saw before she succumbed to a sudden, overwhelming need for sleep was Madonna smiling while a little girl riddled her with bullets.

OPENING HER EYES, Lula smelled incense. No. Gunpowder. Smoke. Ginger was slumped against the wall, stunned but evidently unharmed. No one had been hurt. The knife lay across the room. A trickle of plaster dust sifted from a charred hole in the wallpaper. Alvo grabbed a blanket and gently covered Ginger.

"What the hell?" said Ginger. "Where's my fucking robe?"

"There is no robe," said Lula.

"Liar," said Ginger. "Lying whore. Murderer. You almost killed me."

The door opened. Mister Stanley saw everything in five seconds.

"Jesus Christ," he said. "Jesus fucking Christ."

"Stanley," said Ginger. "Look at me! Your nympho trollop tried to kill me."

"She had a knife!" protested Lula, childishly.

"Hello, dear," Mister Stanley told Ginger. His bending over to kiss his wife on the top of her head was the saddest thing Lula hoped ever to see. He picked up the knife and took the gun from Lula, going from weapon to weapon liked an exhausted mother gathering toys after a playdate. With the gun in one hand and the knife in the other, he went into the bathroom, where he left the weapons and shut the door behind him. For such a safety-conscious guy, Mister Stanley seemed awfully calm. But why should Lula have been surprised? That was how he was. His composure was admirable, but she could see how it might have been part of what drove Ginger crazy.

"Hello, dear?" The cruel precision of Ginger's mimicry reminded Lula of Zeke. "That's what you say? Hello, dear? Stan, you are so *autistic*!"

"Are you a friend of Lula's?" Mister Stanley asked Alvo.

"My cousin," Lula said. "Mister Stanley, this is my Cousin Alvo."

"Cousin my ass," said Ginger. "She and the so-called cousin were getting ready to fuck."

Alvo rose off the edge of the bed and extended his hand to Mister Stanley. "I'm Lula's Cousin Alvo."

Just at that moment a voice in the hall said, "What's going on?"

"Don't let Zeke in," cried Lula.

"Mom," said Zeke. "What's that stuff on you?"

"Chocolate," Ginger said. "Remember we used to have so much fun baking cookies?"

Zeke wore a black T-shirt and plaid boxers. He screwed his fists into his eye sockets like a sleepy child. Look at him! Lula wanted to cry out. But what exactly did she want Zeke's parents to see?

"It stinks in here," Zeke said.

"You're shivering, Ginger," Mister Stanley said. "Your mom is shivering, Zeke."

"I'm freezing inside," said Ginger.

"This is gross. I'm out of here," Zeke said.

"Somebody stop him," Ginger said.

"Let him go," said Mister Stanley. "He doesn't need to see this. Are you comfortable down there, dear? Wouldn't you like to sit in this nice soft chair?"

She's filthy! Lula almost pointed out. But it was Ginger's chair.

"Nobody come near me," Ginger said. Propped against the wall, she pumped her legs under the blanket, and ten dirty toes wriggled against the satin border.

"I didn't know it was loaded," Lula said.

"I didn't know it was loaded," mocked Ginger.

Alvo looked from one of them to the other in such innocence and wonder, no one would have suspected that it was his gun. His loaded gun. He went into the bathroom and returned with the pistol.

"I'll take care of this," he said.

"Thank you," said Mister Stanley. "How did the gun get in the house in the first place?"

"I think it was your wife's," said Lula.

"Fucking liar!" Ginger yelled.

"And the knife?"

"From the kitchen," Lula said, nodding at Ginger again. The crazy wife had come heavily armed. She wasn't taking chances.

"Lying scumsucker," Ginger said, more resignedly this time.

"Thank God no one got hurt," Mister Stanley said. "My God, what a terrible illness."

"I'll say," Ginger said. "And you know what the fatal part was? Being married to you."

Mister Stanley sighed. Then he went to the phone and dialed without having to look up the number. He said, "Is this the doctor's service? This is Stanley Larch. Ginger Larch's husband. I'm sorry. I know it's Christmas Eve. But could the doctor call us back? My wife has come home unexpectedly, and we're having a bit of a crisis."

"A bit of a crisis?" Ginger said. "What kind of faggot talk is that? And isn't it just like my husband to send for that fetal pig, that Wannabe Sigmund Doctor Fat Fuck Freud who did such a fabulous job of curing me the last time?"

"You need to get dressed," Mister Stanley said.

"If you touch me I'll explode," said Ginger. "If you come near me I'll scream murder and rape and all your zombie neighbors will rise from their graves and come running. Hey, listen. Did you hear that?"

"Hear what?" said Mister Stanley.

"The front door slamming," Ginger said. "Elvis has left the building. By which I mean our son."

"Is that true?" said Mister Stanley. "Did Zeke go out?"

"A mother knows things," said Ginger.

Lula was sent to look for Zeke, and when she'd searched everywhere and couldn't find him, Mister Stanley asked Lula and Alvo if they would mind locating his son, who probably hadn't gone far, and make sure he got back.

"Your coats are on the floor," Ginger pointed out helpfully. "Dropped on your stumblefuck way to bed."

"Ginger and I will be fine," Mister Stanley said. "Just make sure that Zeke's okay."

Alvo hurried out to the car, and Lula tagged after him. The SUV still smelled of Lula's perfume mixed with Alvo's cologne. When Alvo put the gun in the glove compartment, Lula felt a deep sadness, as if she and the gun were breaking up after a long romance. Starting the ignition, Alvo said, "Poor kid. I have a little brother that age. He stayed behind with our aunt in Durrës. Big boy surfer didn't want to leave the beach."

"I'm an only child," Lula said.

"Too bad for you," said Alvo.

"Let's check the bus stop," said Lula.

"The buses don't run at this hour," Alvo said.

"Just check it." Lula told him how to get there, and sure enough, they found Zeke huddled on the bench in the shelter.

"Get in the car," Alvo said. "It's cold."

Zeke obeyed without argument. Lula wanted to tell him that he'd be all right, but Alvo's presence inhibited her, and besides she felt dwarfed by the magnitude of what Zeke must be feeling.

That crazy woman in Lula's room was this poor kid's *mother*. Zeke had rushed out in his T-shirt and shorts. Lula heard his teeth clatter.

"I'm blasting the heat," said Alvo. "You'll be broiling in a minute."

As the temperature rose, the mood inside the SUV grew relaxed and mellow, as if they were old friends or even family. Mama, Papa, Zeke. And though Lula was the one who was close to Zeke, the one paid to watch Zeke, the one who cared about Zeke, Papa was in control. Let Alvo have the power. It was a relief to have someone help her carry the weight. Only now could Lula admit how heavy it had been, only now as she pretended that she and Alvo were sharing the responsibilities of raising a teenage son. Borne along on the current of this convivial warmth came the chilling certainty that she would never see Alvo again.

"Better?" said Alvo.

"Nice ride," Zeke said.

"Thanks," said Alvo. "Lula's Cousin George hooked me up with a guy who got me a break on the vehicle."

"Is that how you guys know each other?" asked Zeke.

"Want to drive?" said Alvo.

"Are you serious?" said Zeke.

Alvo hadn't bothered asking if Zeke had a license, nor did Zeke bother mentioning that he wasn't allowed to drive at night. Mister Stanley would kill them. He would especially kill Lula. But eventually he would forgive her for having found his son.

"Would I ask if I wasn't serious?" Alvo said. "I don't joke about my car."

"Then sure. Definitely," Zeke said. "Awesome."

Alvo motioned for Lula to get in the back. And though it would have been simpler for Lula to sit behind Alvo, she went around to Zeke's side so she was standing there, waiting for him when he got out.

"Be careful," she said. "You know what your father—"

"My *fodder?*" demanded Zeke. "What about my *fodder?*" Was Lula's accent so thick? The first time Lula met Zeke, he'd complimented her English. Since then he'd never once corrected or criticized her. Lula might have asked what she'd done to deserve this if she hadn't just seen his mother naked and raving.

"Have fun," Lula said and kissed Zeke's cold cheek, something she'd never done. He shrank away. By the time Lula had fastened her seat belt, Alvo was asking Zeke if he knew where everything was on the dashboard.

"It's a little new to me," said Zeke. "My ride is a 1970 Olds."

"Sexy beast," said Alvo. "They don't make them like that anymore."

If only Alvo could read Lula's mind now as she beamed him the information that Zeke had never driven at night and was doing so for the first time on an icy Christmas Eve in a sixty-thousand-dollar vehicle with a gun in the glove compartment.

"The brights, the dims," Alvo said.

"Got it," Zeke said. "All systems go."

Zeke drove slowly. The streets were empty. At least it had stopped snowing. Lula began to enjoy it. She was disappointed when they reached Mister Stanley's and glad when Alvo said, "Keep driving."

As they passed, Lula stared into the brightly lit windows. Was Mister Stanley still there? Had he managed to get his wife cleaned up and dressed? Mister Stanley's Acura was in its usual spot, but there were no silhouettes on the shade that Lula had pulled a lifetime ago when she and Alvo sneaked into her bedroom.

Zeke didn't leave the neighborhood. Though he was breaking one big rule, he wasn't ready to break them all, and he stayed within the borders his father had drawn. They made a ten-block circuit and twice passed the house. The third time they saw an ambulance parked outside. Zeke drove a few blocks, rounded the corner, stopped, and switched places with Alvo.

"Nice parking job," Alvo said.

"Let's go home now," said Zeke.

Mister Stanley was starting his car and preparing to follow the ambulance. Its unhurried beacon spun a thread of light that spooled out and snapped back, like the string of a yo-yo.

Lula rolled down her window and asked Mister Stanley if he wanted her to go with him.

He said, "That's very kind of you, Lula. But I think we've got things under control. I'd rather you stayed with Zeke."

Zeke yelled, "Merry Christmas, Dad. How's Mom?"

"Merry Christmas, Zeke," said Mister Stanley. "She'll be fine. Are you sure you guys will be okay?"

"We're sure," said Lula.

"They will," Alvo said. "I'll check everything out before I leave."

"I appreciate that," said Mister Stanley. "I locked the front door."

"I've got my keys," said Lula.

The ambulance flashed its lights, and the two-vehicle cortege began its mournful crawl down the street.

"Good luck, Mister Stanley," called Lula.

"I'll let you guys say good night," said Zeke. Lula and Alvo watched him go into the house.

Alvo said, "The badass runaway rebel took his keys."

"The kid is smart," said Lula.

Alvo said, "The dad's gonna turn him gay if he doesn't give him some slack. Do you and the kid really need me to come inside and check the closets and look under the beds?"

"Of course not," Lula said. If only she and Alvo had done that the first time. The last time.

"It's been quite a night," said Alvo.

"First it was fun," said Lula. "Then it wasn't fun."

"Next time, all fun, I promise," said Alvo. "I'll call you."

But he wouldn't. Lula couldn't have said how she knew. But she knew. There wouldn't be a next time, let alone *all fun*. Alvo had the gun back. He wouldn't call. In the end he had decided: She was bad news and bad luck.

"See you soon," said Lula.

"Happy New Year," said Alvo.

Chapter Eleven

———◦∞∞◦———

LULA AWOKE to a grainy cold light and a sky the white of tombstones. The inside of her skull felt like her childhood jack-in-the-box, a clown that popped from its tin cube, banging its drum in terror. Now the pounding played a demonic duet with the clanging church bells. Happy Birthday, Jesus!

All over America, children were hyperventilating with joy, grabbing their mattresses to keep from racing downstairs and ripping open their presents. Lula knew that this was the made-for-TV version of American life, that half the population was sick and alone or homeless, conscious of the holiday only as something they wanted to end, preferably after free turkey in a steamy, malodorous shelter. But how many households were recovering from a Christmas Eve when Mom showed up naked and smeared with chocolate and shit, a night when the lady of the house held hostage, at knifepoint, the Albanian nanny and her date?

Now Lula remembered why her room was so cold. She'd left a window open in an unsuccessful effort to eliminate the lingering stench of Ginger's madness.

Her fingers still reeked of gunpowder. She remembered her father describing one of their neighbors as the kind of guy who fired off one shot and spent the next three days sniffing smoke on his fingers. That's how her dad got sent away. The smoke-sniffing neighbor had been a police informer. Say something like that, it gets back.

Her papa had gone to jail until he promised one of the prison guards a tribal musket, and they let him go. He'd been away for slightly less than twenty-four hours, but from then on he referred to himself as a former political prisoner. Though Lula had been very young, she remembered that day, counted off in seconds and by the nonstop cups of tea her aunt prepared for her mother, who sat at the kitchen table, veering between extremes of panic and resignation, motionless but for the raising and lowering of the tea cup. The memory of those hours had merged in Lula's mind with the Communist TV news, the maddening tick tock of the clock behind the drone of the stern newsreader. And now the clock had slowed again in Mister Stanley's house, marking off the minutes until a father and son awakened to the reality of last night's visit from Ginger. It could happen anywhere, the nasty twist of fate that turns time into your enemy, implacable, mean, and patient, dragging its feet to torment you.

She was surprised to find the presents she'd bought for Mister Stanley and Zeke, still in their Christmas wrapping at the top of her closet, survivors of Ginger's search-and-destroy. No one would feel like celebrating. But even so it seemed wrong to have spent the money and effort and not try to help Mister Stanley and Zeke enjoy their sorry Christmas. She averted her eyes, as if from a wreck, as she bent to pick up her fancy underwear. She stood too fast, and a slosh of bile slapped the back of her throat.

Lula brought the boxes downstairs and placed them beside the other presents on the kitchen counter: an envelope with

Zeke's name on it, a small package addressed "To Dad from Zeke," and a large box, wrapped in silver paper with a card that said, "For Lula, Merry Christmas from Stanley and Zeke." The presents looked stranded and ashamed to have been left on the counter where everyday objects congregated: the mail, the groceries, the newspaper. Even without the tree, couldn't Mister Stanley have arranged the gifts near the fireplace? Everywhere parents were telling their kids that Santa had read their letters and heard their prayers and rewarded them for being good American children by bringing them the latest Barbie, the must-have video game. Not at Mister Stanley's. Their Christmas Eve visitor could hardly have been less like the jolly grandpa flying in from the Arctic.

How would Lula face Mister Stanley, and how would that conversation begin? Good morning, Merry Christmas, sorry about your wife. Her fear of discomfort, awkwardness, and an incapacitating rush of sympathy for her boss warred against her desire to hear what had happened with Ginger. Curiosity won out, and Lula ran the coffee grinder hard. Soon she heard the murmur and splash of Mister Stanley's shower.

Sunday Casual Mister Stanley walked into the kitchen.

"Smells good," he said. "Merry Christmas, Lula. Are you feeling all right?"

"I don't know," Lula said.

"You look a little pale," he said. So did Mister Stanley.

"It's the light," she said.

He poured himself a cup of coffee and, with his back to her, said, "Sorry about last night."

The sadness was almost too much to bear. The sadness and the pity.

"It's not your fault," Lula said.

"I know. But it must have been upsetting. And naturally one worries that a person might reasonably decide not to continue working in a house where this sort of thing occurs."

Where did Mister Stanley think she would go? And who did he think Lula was? A person who would abandon him and Zeke at a time like this? And why was he apologizing to a girl he'd caught in his house on Christmas Eve with a "cousin" who obviously felt so comfortable around a gun that he'd taken it with him, for which Mister Stanley had thanked him? And what was "this sort of thing"?

"How is your wife?" Lula didn't know what to call her. Not Mrs. Ginger. Not Mrs. Larch.

"We were lucky. Despite what my wife believes, her doctor's a human being. He was able to recommend an excellent facility. We were lucky they had a room."

Lucky. Someone had dressed Ginger. Someone had bathed her, or not. But yes, they were lucky that no one had been shot. Lucky that Zeke hadn't disappeared forever into the night. Lucky that wherever Ginger had gone was a five-star resort compared to the least hellish Balkan asylum.

"Well!" Mister Stanley said. "Between Ginger's care and Zeke's college, we're not going to be retiring any time soon."

We? Lula could hardly breathe until she realized that Mister Stanley meant *I*. She was about to make some chatty remark about how this was like Albania, where doctors treated you differently depending on how much you paid. Or maybe she should mention how, under the dictatorship, mental hospitals often doubled as political prisons. People used to say, You meet the most interesting people in the nuthouse. Or anyway, the purest. Normally Mister Stanley enjoyed comparisons between Albania and here. But maybe not at the moment.

"Thanks for looking after Zeke," he said. "Thanks for finding him. Jesus. I hate to think—"

"He wanted to be found. He was worried about you." It was true, it was easy to say, it made Mister Stanley feel better, and it gave Lula a break in which to recover from the memory of Alvo letting Zeke drive his SUV. Nothing could have been better for Zeke. How much heart Alvo showed! She would never see him again. But the breakage of her romance was a hairline fissure compared to the chasms that must have opened last night for Zeke and Mister Stanley.

Lula turned to hear Zeke say, "Is this Christmas? Is this *it*?"

"Zeke," said Mister Stanley. "What a pleasant surprise. We didn't hear you come downstairs. Good morning. Merry Christmas."

Lula scrutinized Zeke's features but couldn't see much difference between his crumpled frown and the face he showed his father every weekend morning. If you didn't know Zeke, or even if you did, you might not conclude that this was a kid whose mother had just had a breakdown in front of the nanny and a cool Albanian dude who let him drive his Lexus. Maybe it would hit Zeke tomorrow morning, or the next day, or maybe in twenty years. If there was one thing Lula had learned from Balkan history and from American TV, it was how long memories could stay bottled up before the cork exploded. Another cloud on the bright horizon of Zeke's future wife.

Mister Stanley said, "Lula, open your present."

Lula said, "Zeke first. It's Christmas. Zeke's the kid."

"Ladies first," said Zeke.

Having only one gift to unwrap, Lula exaggerated the drama of removing the paper, opening the box, and lifting the laptop from its Styrofoam nest. Chromosomes or maybe hormones worked in tandem so that both Zeke and Mister Stanley turned away at the same moment, with the same gesture, ducking as if from a blow, so as not to see Lula cry. The tears were real, but she faked a sob to prolong her time to float on the swell of pleasure and gratitude for this perfect gift, this generous investment in her future. She would deserve it, she would be worthy. She would work like a dog. She would make up beautiful stories and not pretend they were true. She would devote herself to the journal she'd neglected since she met Alvo. There was no reason not to, now. She had nothing to hide. Her authentic new American life would start fresh from today.

"Thank you," Lula said. "Now you, Zeke."

Zeke opened the envelope from his father. "Thanks. I can always use cash." He unwrapped the belt from Lula and slung it around his waist.

"Awesome studs! Thanks, Lula!" She'd underestimated his skinniness. Even on the last notch, the belt slipped down his hips. She had also underestimated the ferocity of the metal grommets that turned the belt into armor, the perfect fashion accessory for the collapse of civilization.

"It can be fixed," said Mister Stanley. "We can punch another hole—"

"You think everything can be fixed, Dad," said Zeke. "Nothing can be fixed."

"Hmmm . . . " said Mister Stanley. "Let's see what Santa brought *me*." He thanked Lula for the Nano even as the earbuds popped out of his ears. Saying he'd figure it out on his own, he stuffed it back into the box from which it would never emerge again.

"To Dad," read Mister Stanley. Zeke's quiet snort was intended for Lula, but Mister Stanley heard, and an echo seemed to linger until Zeke said, "Hope you like it, Dad."

Mister Stanley unwrapped a book. "*The Diamond Sutra!*"

"Buddhist meditations," said Zeke. "Helpful when you're . . . stressed." The last word created a depression in the air that slowly filled with disturbing images from the previous night.

Mister Stanley paged through the book. "That's very thoughtful of you, Zeke. Very unexpected. I'm touched."

"It wasn't my idea," said Zeke. "Abigail picked it out."

"Abigail? *Don's* Abigail?"

Zeke nodded.

"I didn't know you two were in touch."

"She meditates instead of eating," said Zeke.

"That's not smart," said his father.

"Abigail and Shirley and I—"

"Who's Shirley?"

"Another friend."

"But it's such a geriatric name," said Mister Stanley.

"What does *geriatric* mean?" Zeke asked Lula. Why was he asking her? Last night, switching places outside Alvo's car, he had made fun of her accent.

"Elderly," said Lula.

"Shirley's a kid in my class. I'm tired. I'm going back to sleep. I didn't get a lot of rest last night. Merry Christmas. Thanks." Zeke took the belt but left his dad's check on the counter.

"Do you want to go visit your mother?" his father called after him. "I thought I'd—"

"Next time," Zeke said. "Or maybe the time after that."

"Probably just as well," Mister Stanley told Lula.

"Excuse me too," said Lula. "I'm also really tired."

Mister Stanley said, "Before you go, can I ask you one question, Lula?"

"Anything," Lula whispered. Then louder, "Anything."

"How *did* that gun get in the house?"

"You asked me. I told you. I guess your wife brought it with her. I never saw it before. She must have picked up the knife in the kitchen. For backup." Ginger should have thought twice about what she did to her son. Now among the things she had lost was the right to say what had happened. Who would believe Ginger's story, even if it were true?

Mister Stanley said, "That Buddhist book he got me . . . you don't think it might be a sign of . . . I don't know . . . something he inherited from his mom?"

"Some girls convinced him it was cool. He explained that. Remember?"

"Right. I suppose that is a relief," said Mister Stanley. "Be sure and drink lots of water."

Lula sat at her desk until she heard Mister Stanley leave. She watched him shuffle out to his car and drive off. Then she got her new laptop and carried it up to her room. Moments later Zeke knocked and asked if she wanted help connecting to the Internet. Lula said she needed help powering it on.

It made for a pleasant afternoon, sitting on her bed and letting Zeke play with her new computer. For the rest of Christmas Day, neither said a single word that wasn't about electronics.

. . .

THE NEXT MORNING, Dunia called to ask about Lula's date. Had the perfume worked? Lula said her date was . . . interesting. She would tell Dunia more when she saw her. Dunia asked what Lula was doing New Year's Eve. Lula said she wasn't sure, her guy might be out of town on business.

Dunia said, "He's your guy now? And he's away New Year's? I thought you said he was in construction? What kind of contractor goes away on business on New Year's? Is he cheating on you already?"

"We're still in the getting-to-know-you phase," said Lula. "Everything's very new." Lula tried to freight that *new* with unfolding romance and passion. What a good little actress she'd become since she'd found it so hard to tell the visa officer about returning home to marry her fiancé on Christmas. If the fiancé had existed, yesterday would have been their anniversary.

"I see," said Dunia gloomily. "Steve says he wants a private New Year's Eve, the two of us quietly sharing a bottle of great champagne. Just the idea of it makes me want to kill myself and vomit."

Lula made her promise she wouldn't kill herself. They smooched their phones and hung up, swearing to get together soon. It was nice to have a friend, even one she had to lie to. The next time she saw Dunia, she would tell her the truth about her date with Alvo and about Ginger's visit.

In the days that followed, Lula got to know her new computer. She had plenty of time, the weather was cold, she tried not to leave her room. Zeke and Mister Stanley were still on vacation, though Mister Stanley was gone a lot, visiting his wife. A new side of Mister Stanley emerged: the considerate dutiful husband. Once, Lula heard him ask Zeke if he could think of anything his mother might want. Zeke's silence was like a finger poked into his father's chest. It was sad they couldn't help each other through their family hard time.

Instead, Mister Stanley and Zeke argued about Zeke driving the Olds in bad weather. Mister Stanley said they should order in, The Good Earth would deliver. Zeke let his father win after Mister Stanley described how road salt would eat away at the chassis of a vintage sedan and how he didn't intend to pay for body work. Zeke said he wasn't hungry, anyway, and Mister Stanley said everyone had to eat.

The bitterest fight was about New Year's Eve. Mister Stanley wouldn't let Zeke go to a friend's party with the slightly older boy who would be driving. Mister Stanley said he didn't know the boy, Zeke never brought his friends home. Zeke said that maybe now he *could* bring kids home, now that Mom was safely locked up. Lula heard doors slam and howls of murderous rage, sounds that must have reminded Mister Stanley of the place where he'd left his wife.

New Year's Eve came and went. All three of them went to bed early. Lula wouldn't have known it was New Year's if the newspaper hadn't featured a photo of confetti. Probably it was bad luck not to get drunk or have sex or eat some special food supposed to bring you money or luck in the coming year. Maybe it was too late for that. What worse luck could befall them? Lula knocked on her desk.

Lula was under house arrest, room arrest more like it, and she used the wintry hours to write a story about a farm that lay under a curse. Her granny had said there were places like that, dwellings whose tenants all died suddenly, suspiciously, and young. In Lula's story, a guy appeared in Berat one day, claiming his grandpa had left him the farm. He didn't care about the curse. Against all advice, he moved there with his beautiful wife and their beautiful kids, and they began to grow apples, tomatoes, and lettuce and to raise ducks and lambs. The place was their private paradise on which no one would set foot for fear the curse was contagious, though this didn't stop anyone from buying their produce at the market. Not one bad thing happened. And when a series of animal and vegetable plagues devastated the region, their farm alone was spared because they were quarantined by their neighbors' superstition.

Lula spent days trying to think of how the curse finally got them. But she'd grown to like this plucky family, and her imagination refused to conjure up the disastrous fire or flood or earthquake. Instead they lived to a healthy old age, their beautiful children had more beautiful children, and each year the farm grew more productive, its lambs fatter and more playful, its apples more delicious.

Lula spent more time on this story than on anything she had written, and she hated it the most. Because she didn't believe it. If the farmland was that fertile, the government would have seized it long ago, and the family would still be in court trying to get even one apple tree back. Also she wasn't buying the lesson it seemed to preach: Ignore the crowd and go your own way and life will turn out all right. In her experience, you could follow the rules or refuse to bend and you were still at the mercy of the same wicked cosmic dice-roll.

But regardless of what she thought, Mister Stanley and Don would adore it. Virtue, integrity, courage, hard work rewarded——that was the story they wanted to hear. Lula decided not to show it to them. Their approval would only annoy her. She didn't feel strong enough for their praise. On the other hand, the story might be just what Zeke could use right now. Do the right thing, follow your heart, keep on keeping on, and you get the happy family, the juiciest lamb chops, and the sweetest apples.

She printed out the manuscript and knocked on Zeke's door, then eased it open. Zeke lay on his bed, fully dressed, hooked up to his iPod. Lula had to kick the bed twice before he opened his eyes.

"Fleas Bite Dogs," he said. "I love this song. Want to listen?"

Lula said, "Why are you shouting? You should be listening to Buddhist chants. Helpful for stress."

"That was bullshit," Zeke said. "I knew Dad would fall for it big-time."

"He asked me if your giving him that book meant you were getting like your mother." Lula caught herself, too late. She'd always made a point of not telling father and son what they said about each other. Maybe she'd just wanted an excuse to say *mother*, in case Zeke wanted to talk about his.

"Not a chance," said Zeke.

Lula said, "Want to read something I wrote?"

Zeke took the manuscript. A short time later he came to her room.

"Did this really happen?" he said.

Lula nodded gravely. "In my granny's village."

"That is awesome," Zeke said.

.   .   .

LULA KNEW NOT to take credit, but she couldn't help noting: Just a few days after reading her story, Zeke appeared at Sunday breakfast and announced that he wanted to go to college. He said, "I guess it's the only way I'm ever going to get out of this dump alive."

"Dump" made Mister Stanley flinch, but he rapidly recovered and said that college involved more than escaping the family dump. In any case, he was pleased that Zeke was making the right decision. Then the two of them disappeared into the "library," where they remained until late afternoon.

"Progress," announced Mister Stanley, when at last they reappeared.

Lula's job now included helping Zeke fill out his college applications, a tedious and complex task he performed with such rare perseverance that Lula tried not to feel hurt by how badly he wanted to leave. But it wasn't just that. He wanted to grow up. Everyone did. Or should.

When Zeke asked Lula's advice about the application essays, Lula told him to go on the Internet and read the colleges' home pages and figure out what each one wanted to hear. Then he should write that. She was glad he'd asked her and not his father, who would have given him the wrong advice: write what was in his heart.

Zeke showed Lula a draft that began, "I want the freedom to express my full individuality while at the same time being an integral part of a larger community."

Lula said, "Zeke, put on your thinking cap! What teenager sounds like that? You can't just *copy* what they say. I thought you wanted to get in."

The second draft began, "Everything I've read about your

school makes me think it's a place that would let me be my authentic self and still work hard and learn from my fellow students who are also there to grow and learn."

"You nailed it," Lula said.

Now, when Zeke came home from school, he asked if there was mail, and now when the letters slipped through the slot, Lula searched for the fat envelope stuffed with good news. The college that accepted him would be setting both of them free.

The envelope arrived on a Saturday morning. Zeke ripped it open, skimmed the letter, punched the air, and said, "Okay!" Mister Stanley and Zeke high-fived each other.

"Congratulations," said Lula.

The only good-news letter had come from Alice Ames College, across the Hudson and forty-five minutes north. It sounded like a girls' school, but Mister Stanley said it had been coed for years. It wasn't too close, but close enough for Mister Stanley and Zeke to attend the accepted-students tea.

"Will you come with us? It seems only right after all the help you gave Zeke." Mister Stanley must have thought that attending the tea was some kind of reward. Which it was. Going anywhere was better than going nowhere. He was asking for Lula's company and support and trying to make it seem as if he was doing her a favor.

"I'd love to," Lula said.

Chapter Twelve

◆◆◆

Lᴜʟᴀ ʜᴀᴅ studied the brochure, the photos of attractive students of every body type, gender, and race, pausing for amusing, educational conversations as they strolled through the handsome stone cloisters. The pictures had looked real enough, but still she half expected Alice Ames to be a boarded-up storefront in a mall. She'd seen a TV program about a fake online college that promised to prepare kids for medical school and stole their parents' life savings. It had tickled her to see Americans taken in by the sort of scam people thought happened only in Eastern Europe. If she had a dollar for every La Changita customer who told her about not being allowed to drive his rental car to Prague because it might get stolen, she wouldn't have had to work there. But now that she'd come to care about Zeke and Mister Stanley, she'd lost the ironic remove from which she watched Americans get conned, and she hoped that Alice Ames was not a dirty trick cynically named after some grifter's favorite hooker.

They were halfway to the college on the day of the tea when Mister Stanley slowed down and said, "Wait. I'm remembering something. The college had some problem. A very public problem . . . not so long ago . . ." Lula and Zeke sat very still, neither liking his tone, the same tone in which he had forbidden Zeke to go out with his friends on New Year's Eve. But Mister Stanley couldn't seem to recall what the problem had been, and when they picked up speed again, Lula's sense of well-being returned, intensified by its close brush with disappointment.

A perfect meringue of snow glistened on the rolling lawns and filled the crenellations of the castle turrets. The cold seemed cleaner and sharper than the cold in New Jersey, and it made you want to go inside where it would be warm and smell of wet wool, and where young minds would be humming like air conditioners in summer.

At the edge of a parking lot a sign said, "Welcome Class of 2010." Lula refused to calculate how old she would be then. Zeke nodded at a purple balloon bobbing against the sign.

He said, "I hope this isn't a super-expensive mistake."

"It's a godsend," said Mister Stanley. "It will be worth every penny."

A *lot* of pennies, said the pillared veranda overlooking a meadow, a lot more pennies, said the stained glass windows along the staircase that led to a wood-paneled hall. Two girl students, bouncers in party clothes, sat at a table and power-smiled guests into writing their names on sticky labels. Mister Stanley and Zeke complied, but when Lula said, "I'm just a friend," the girls were so flustered that Lula got away with not having to wear a name tag.

The school should have chosen a more intimate space, where the students, parents, and teachers would have looked less lost as they tried to fill its rejecting vastness. The minority students in the brochure must have decided to skip the party. Two long tables held platters of fruit slices and ziggurats of cheese cubes, already in ruins, plus bottles of water, orange juice, and several industrial-size samovars.

Tea, Lula thought despairingly.

Sipping their tea, the parents assumed the hunched, vigilant postures required to balance a fragile cup of hot liquid while chatting with other nervous strangers. Lula noted how often they checked their watches and how hard they tried to conceal it. A few older students scanned the crowd. Would their glances have looked so predatory if not for Zeke's recent experience with Harmonia Bethany?

"Stay away from those girls," Lula whispered.

"Believe me," Zeke said. "I've learned."

A woman with a shiny domelike forehead charged toward them, her proffered handshake so aggressive that Lula's impulse was to jump out of her way. Unnerved, Lula missed the name of the assistant admissions director, who was thrilled— she checked Zeke's name tag—that Zeke might be coming to Alice Ames.

She said, "You'll probably think I'm prejudiced if I babble on and on about how much I love it here."

Lula took this opportunity to slip away and pour herself a cup of tea and find a corner from which to fake interest in the proceedings. But wait. This could be interesting. A man was walking toward her.

"I'm Carl," he said. "Carl Levin. I teach in the philosophy department."

Even better, a Jewish guy. At home girls said that Jewish guys made outstanding boyfriends. To hell with Alvo and his air-conditioner scam, if that was even what it was. Stay cool,

Lula reminded herself. What was her recent past if not a warning against excessive imagination? Besides, this event was not about Lula and her sordid love life, but about the bridge that Zeke was about to cross from his childhood into the world. And it was part of Lula's job to make sure that bridge was sturdy.

"Are you one of the incoming students?" the professor asked. Did she really look that young, or did he say that to all the second wives here with the college-age offspring of the rich husbands' first marriages?

Lula said, "I already went to university in Albania. My friend . . . I mean, my friend's son is enrolling here in the fall."

"Wait!" he said. "You're the Albanian friend! How many could there be?"

Lula said, "What do you mean?" This was how it happened. They knew who you were. They were waiting for you. You thought it was a college tea, but it was an INS sting, the kind where they promised illegals anything from amnesty to a pair of free tickets to a baseball game. And when you showed up, they nabbed you. But Lula had nothing to worry about. Thanks to Don, she was legal.

The professor's lips were moving.

"Excuse me?" Lula said.

This time he seemed to be saying, "Everyone loved Zeke's essay."

"What essay?"

"The one about the family that inherits the cursed orchard, but they keep their eyes on the prize and nothing unlucky happens and they raise the best lambs and apples. Zeke had a sentence at the end about how he'd heard the story from an

Albanian friend, and how it made him realize how important it was to work hard and keep the faith and do what you think is right, and how glad it made him feel to live in a country where people don't believe in curses. The sentiment was so positive. And it was so well written."

Zeke had copied her story. Sooner rather than later, Lula needed to tell him that plagiarism was wrong.

"To be perfectly honest," said the professor, "Zeke's wasn't the strongest application in the pool. But this isn't the sort of place that bases its decisions solely on grades and test scores. That essay got him in."

Mister Stanley hadn't wasted a cent of the salary he'd paid Lula. And was it really so bad if Lula had given Zeke some basic instruction in the relationship, however regrettable, between deception and survival? Once Zeke got where he wanted to be, he could sort out the moral issues. And how did a little all-in-the-family intellectual-property theft stack up against the fact that Lula's story had gotten Zeke the one thing he seemed to want? By the time Professor Carl finished raving about Zeke's essay, Lula had almost convinced herself that Zeke's submitting her work under his name wasn't plagiarism, but collaboration.

The professor said, "One of my colleagues read it aloud. It got passed around the committee. It was by far the most interesting essay we got. I work part-time in admissions, even though I was hired to teach the second half of the beginning survey course. From Machiavelli to Marx. When you don't have tenure, you agree to whatever they ask."

Lula said, "That's the beginning of philosophy right there."

"And also, as you doubtless know, these are unusual times."

Lula didn't know. His unspoken question (what had Lula heard?) made her recall Mister Stanley's reference to some trouble at the college.

"Unusual how, exactly?"

"Obviously, the shooting."

"What shooting?" Lula said.

"It's always the science students. Even here, where we have no science program to speak of. I never taught the kid, but his advisers said he was wound pretty tight. I know that's what they always say. Obsessed with grades. High-strung. No one knows where he got the rifle. He started blasting away at the gatehouse—"

"When was this?"

"Year before last."

"Was anyone killed?" Lula held her breath.

"No, thank God. The guy couldn't aim. A couple of minor flesh wounds. The security guard wrestled him down. The shooter weighed about ninety pounds. Very bloody and messy. Traumatic. But fortunately, not lethal."

"What happened to the kid?"

"Deported back to Singapore. Meanwhile, the freshman applicant pool dried up completely. Parents get nervous. No one believes that lightning never strikes the same place twice."

Lula made a mental note to tell Mister Stanley the part about lightning in case he remembered what he'd heard about Alice Ames.

The professor said, "One more year like this one, and our jobs are on the line. I think that's one reason Zeke's story was such a hit. It was exactly what everyone needed to hear just around now: If you keep on doing what's right and doing it well, the bad weather clears, and the curse gets lifted."

No wonder this place was so eager for students willing to step over some fading blood stains in return for no one fussing about their test scores. Lula felt vaguely injured on Zeke's behalf. If Zeke was going to steal her work, it should earn him something better than a college that no one else wanted to attend. But hadn't she read her own story? The cursed farm grew the tastiest apples. This college was pretty, the students looked happy, the professor was handsome and nice.

She said, "Why do school shootings happen so often in this country?"

"They happen everywhere," Professor Carl said. "And not as often as you'd think. But the media loves them."

"Going postal. Ha ha . . ."

"Your English is flawless." He smiled. "So what do you do now?"

"Okay. I'm not the Albanian *friend*. I work for the family. I take care of Zeke. Until he leaves for college."

"And then?"

"Good question. Any suggestions, Professor?"

"Please," he said. "Call me Carl." In Lula's experience, only a few steps separated "Call me Carl" from asking for her phone number.

"Any suggestions, Carl?" Lula tried to make "suggestions" sound lewd.

"Actually, my wife runs a terrific program that just started here, funded by the school. It helps women, recent immigrants, underemployed single moms with child-care issues, find their way into the workforce. She's a lawyer, she's amazing, she does this pro bono, part-time—"

Lula was still stuck on those two little words. *My wife.* There were many ways in which men signaled availability, but *my wife* was not among them, at least not in that proud voice of ownership, within the first few minutes.

"Let me go find her," said Carl.

"Nice to meet you." Good-bye forever. Oh, where was Mister Stanley? How soon could they leave this crime scene soaked with student-faculty blood?

Before Lula could find her boss and ask when they could go home, she saw Carl returning with a dark-haired woman who looked familiar. Lula struggled to place her, and at the same time to use every bit of sexless body language to communicate that not for one moment had she dreamed of stealing the familiar-looking woman's husband.

"Savitra!" Lula said.

"You two know each other?" said Carl.

"Small world," said Savitra glumly.

"She works with my lawyer," said Lula. How often did it happen, a coincidence like this, meeting the same person twice under such different circumstances? Probably more frequently than Lula might think. In Tirana there were also coincidences, but they usually involved ties of family and blood. The guy she'd sort of recognized from her English class and slept with one drunken night had turned out to be her uncle's nephew by his second marriage.

"Don Settebello is your lawyer?" Carl said. "No wonder! The guy's a hero."

Savitra said, "I met Carl my first day here at the school. We were married New Year's Day."

"Very sudden," Carl said. "A *coup de* you-know-what."

"His head is still spinning," said Savitra. The sweetness with which she smiled at Carl suggested the existence of a loving soul that had been absent or in hiding when she'd come for Thanksgiving with Don.

"Congratulations," said Lula.

"I loved Zeke's essay," said Savitra. "Carl showed it to me, but I never made the Albanian connection. Not until I saw you just now and put two and two together. How beautiful that Zeke should write down the stories you've told him. And write them so well! You've done so much for that kid. It just proves that education can happen in so many different ways. So outside the box."

Had Savitra read Lula's stories when she gave them to Don Settebello? It was amazing, how many secrets you could share with someone you'd met only once before. She and Savitra could have been best friends with years of sworn confidences between them.

Savitra said, "I don't know how much Carl told you about my work here. We've only just started, but I think we're about to accomplish great things, helping women find their way into the mainstream."

"I could use a job." Lula caught herself. She had a job. What if Savitra told Don, who told Mister Stanley?

"I understand, believe me." Savitra mimed a merry, conspiratorial agreement. Then she wrinkled her forehead, pantomiming concentration. Lula used to laugh when Granny warned her against frowning. Once again, Granny turned out to be right. Savitra had better be careful.

Savitra said, "When I see a woman who comes from a place that . . . well, not everyone comes from, and when that person is fluent in both languages, and when one of them is hardly a language everyone speaks, the first thing I think of is a court interpreter job."

"Brilliant!" Carl gazed worshipfully at his wife.

Lula said, "How much work could there be for an Albanian translator?"

"You'd be surprised," said Savitra.

"My God, yes," said Carl. "The coke trade and the heroin traffic and now, I was just reading, organized burglary rings—" He stopped himself in midsentence. Had he insulted Lula's homeland? "Listen to me. I'm sorry. It's like assuming every Italian has ties to the mob—"

"Not at all," said Lula. "Don't worry. Anyway, if our Albanian crime rate means more work for court interpreters—" She smiled so they knew she was joking and would be charmed by her lack of hypersensitivity about her native land.

Savitra's women's group met in the evenings. When Lula explained about not driving and the late-night buses, she was excused from going. It seemed like bad luck to sit in a room with women whose problems were worse than her own, though she knew that many Americans believed this was how your luck improved.

Savitra said she would e-mail Lula about the court interpreter position. Lula wrote down her e-mail address as if she were a person who was constantly fielding messages about job opportunities.

In the car going home Zeke said, "Considering how many

bands there are, what's the statistical probability of finding kids who listen to the exact same music I do?"

A hundred percent, thought Lula. Hadn't Harmonia Bethany liked, or pretended to like, Zeke's favorite group?

Zeke said, "What kind of coincidence is that?"

Lula said, "Speaking of coincidence . . . Guess who I met? Remember that girl Savitra whom Don brought to Thanksgiving? She married a professor at the school. A philosophy teacher."

"I saw you talking to that young couple," Mister Stanley said. "I thought the woman looked familiar, but . . . married already? Thanksgiving was just six weeks ago. I wonder why Don didn't mention it. Though why should he? He's got more important things on his mind."

Lula thought she detected a faint note of satisfaction, possibly because Mister Stanley's fellow single dad had lost his girlfriend to a more age-appropriate husband.

Mister Stanley said, "I'm very glad you met some nice kids, Zeke. But liking the same bands is no reason to go to a college."

Zeke said, "It is, if it's the only school that accepted me. And when did I say that the kids were nice?"

"You chose the school," said his father. "We chose it together."

"It's fine with me!" yelled Zeke. "I like it! Now please leave me alone!"

"You know," said Mister Stanley, "the funny thing is, architecturally, it looks a little like the place where your mom is staying right now."

"Great," said Zeke. "My college looks like a mental hospital."

"A treatment center," said Mister Stanley. "And I'm talking about the buildings, not what goes on inside."

Lula imagined a student staggering from the recoil of a gun and another holding her forehead as blood poured through her fingers. Lightning doesn't strike twice. Lula had to find another job before she turned into Mister Stanley.

The next morning, when Savitra's e-mail arrived, Lula was astonished. "Hi Lula!" the message began. Savitra sent Lula a link to a site with information about New York and New Jersey court interpreters. It wasn't exactly a real job; you only worked when they called you. It was the first time Lula had come across the phrase *independent contractor*. What an appealing expression, with its dual associations of freedom and construction, though *contractor* made her think of Alvo, which she tried to avoid. All you needed to be approved or semi-approved or conditionally approved was to demonstrate that you were fluent in both languages and could speak and read English, especially the English that Americans used in courts. In New York there was an oral exam. You had to watch a film in which actors played witnesses from your home country, and you had to interpret, showing you knew all the technical terms like *plea bargain* and *bail bond* and *plaintiff*, which Lula had learned from TV crime shows.

She puzzled over the Web site's suggestion that would-be applicants attend trials to familiarize themselves with court procedures. No one in Albania went near a court unless they were in handcuffs or were suing to get back their land. Here, except for family court, trials were open to the public. Lula asked Mister Stanley to tell Don that she was curious about how a democratic legal system functioned, and Mister Stanley reported that

Don was delighted by Lula's interest. In his opinion, the Lower Manhattan courts would offer her more than Newark. Mister Stanley also approved of Lula's project, but he still hoped she could get home in time for Zeke's return from school.

"I promise," Lula said.

Chapter Thirteen

LULA WAITED patiently to send her purse along the conveyor belt and pass through the metal detector. It was relaxing to shuffle forward along with her fellow creatures, even the resentful ones who didn't want to be here. The guards didn't care how inconvenienced the prospective jurors were. They cared if their cell phones took pictures. Lula's phone did not take photos, which she announced—boasted, really—as evidence of her innocent intentions. She imagined that the look that passed between her and the guard was fraught with something more personal than his appraisal of her level of terrorist threat. The molecules in the overheated air seemed to thrum with the excitement of this intriguing alternative to watching the timid winter light do its cameo turn on Mister Stanley's lawn.

She gathered from the elevator conversations that her fellow passengers would be shocked to learn that she was voluntarily doing what they so wished to avoid. When the crowd turned in one direction, she headed the opposite way and found herself in a room not unlike the one in which they'd held Zeke's college tea. There was plenty of space on the benches. No one noticed Lula as she found a seat.

The judge's little gray head looked like a smoky bauble balanced on the edge of her desk as she instructed the jury about the seriousness of their duties and how the job they'd been asked to perform reflected the beauty of democracy and of their judicial system. She told them how grateful their country was for the sacrifices they were making. Lula tried not to be cynical, tried not to think the judge was just trying to make everyone feel better about missing work. When the judge asked the jurors to take care of themselves for the duration of the trial, to be careful crossing the street at lunch—at which they were not allowed to discuss the case—she wasn't threatening them with certain death beneath the wheels of the speeding Mercedes that would run them down if they even thought about voting to convict.

An African guy was being tried for resisting arrest after he was caught selling fake designer purses. Everywhere it was a crime not to do what the police said, just as everywhere cops could throw you in jail if they didn't like your face. But this vendors' license thing—that was really too much! The world's sidewalks were clogged with people selling hot dogs and halal lunches, bananas and bracelets. In Tirana you bought everything on the street, from olive oil to tampons. The moment her friend Dunia had fallen in love with the United States was the moment when she'd bought a knockoff Louis Vuitton satchel from a guy on Third Avenue.

The defense lawyer wore a pinstripe suit and a bouquet of dreadlocks, a fashion choice that suggested a proud idealistic character but an unrealistic nature and perhaps a deficient desire to win. Twice he quoted Descartes, maxims with an unclear relevance to the case. Lula imagined everyone speaking Albanian and tried to decide what she would and wouldn't translate in order to keep the African guy from going to jail for grabbing an armful of imitation Guccis and taking off when the cops demanded to see his vendor ID. But her opinion wasn't the point. She'd read on the Web site that the job was to translate without judgment, editing, or interpretation. It would be soothing to shift from language to language without the constant mental yakkety-yak about what was true or false.

The prosecution's first witness was a cop who appeared to be chewing gum even when he wasn't. He was sorry to have to say that the defendant threw a punch. Mr. Descartes asked how someone could throw a punch while running, and the cop explained, as if to a child, that first the defendant threw a punch and then he ran. The second cop, a skinny Asian kid, corroborated his partner's story, which he would have done if his partner said that pigs flew out of the defendant's ass.

There were no witnesses for the defense. No one who'd seen the incident came forward. The judge said, "Mr. Mamdani, do you wish to testify on your own behalf?"

Mr. Mamdani shook his head no.

The lawyers gave quick summations. No one's heart was in it. After more instructions from the judge, the jury retired for deliberations. Lula wanted to find out how the story ended. A guard came over to her and said, "This might take a while. You can go grab lunch."

Lula said, "I hurt my foot at the gym." No one had sworn *her* to tell the truth.

"You take it easy then, baby," said the guard. Lula closed her eyes and rested until the courtroom filled again and the judge asked the foreman to read the verdict.

"Not guilty," said the foreman, a gangly hipster whose wrists showed beyond the frayed cuffs of his sweater. How had they chosen him as their leader, and more surprisingly still, how had they reached the right verdict?

The lawyer hugged his client, who recoiled from his embrace. Only then did the defendant turn and look back at the court. Lula saw that he was crying. What satisfying drama! Justice served, a life saved, the capricious abuse of authority subverted once again. Was there another case that Lula could watch and be home in time for Zeke?

In the next courtroom, a kid was on trial for selling a joint to an undercover cop. In his opening remarks, the elderly defense lawyer informed the jury that though they might not know it, and though he was legally enjoined from saying so, he thought they should be aware that they might be voting to send his client—this boy—away for life. The judge sighed and told counsel he didn't care how close to retirement age the lawyer was, he had half a mind to cite him and he could go to jail instead of his client, because he had sworn an oath to uphold the legal system, whether he agreed with it or not and regardless of the frustrations that must come with being a public defender nearing retirement. The way the judge made "public defender" sound like a synonym for "loser" made Lula think that the two men had a history that preceded this case. When Lula left, the judge was still berating the lawyer.

On Tuesday, Lula watched a consumer protection group's suit against a Chinese manufacturer of toxic baby bottles. In theory it should have been interesting, the health-conscious ideas of one country versus the cowboy production goals of another. But there didn't seem to be any actual people involved;

none of the lawyers were Chinese, nor was there an actual baby who had been harmed by the bottles. So she found a courtroom in which a doctor was being sued for botching a woman's gastric bypass surgery. Lula was transfixed by the woman's narrative of what food did on its way from her mouth to the bag hidden beneath her parrot-green dress, but it depressed her to wonder what she would do if the plaintiff was Albanian, and she had to find the English terms for all the digestive parts.

The next morning, the ice flowers on her window almost persuaded Lula to stay home. But she put on her warmest clothes and a hair-ruining woolen hat and submitted to the three buses and the biting wind. As she came in from the cold, the courthouse lobby seemed especially steamy and vibrant. The briefcases and purses jittered along the conveyor belts like amusement-park patrons waiting for a ride to start. Even the metal detectors looked as benign as garden trellises, and the guards on duty smiled.

Already Lula felt as if she were going to a job she was good at, and loved. A golden aura surrounded the passengers jammed into the elevator, and in its glow she marveled at each person's particular beauty. What a gorgeous variety these American faces had! This morning, at the very moment when she was debating whether the warmth of her hat (which she pulled off, running her fingers through her flattened hair) was worth the insult to her vanity, these people had been in their homes, perhaps in front of their mirrors, making all the tiny choices and adjustments that would determine the faces they showed the world. How wondrous it all was, how mystifying in its vastness and strangeness! What had caused her to feel this sense of promise and even of joy? Did there have to be a reason? Or could you wake up one day and see the world differently without it signifying a brain tumor or the onset of mental illness?

Lula wandered into a courtroom where a woman was suing the owner of a corner grocery because she'd slipped and hurt her leg on a broken jar of pickles. The woman overdid the limp with an aggressive swagger that made it seem as if she were about to shake her cane at the jury—evidence of bad advice, or no advice, from her lawyer.

Why should Lula stop at translator? She was smart, she'd been a good student, she could be a judge! Don and Mister Stanley would help her, and someday she would repay them, not just financially but in ways they would value more than money.

The store owner's lawyer asked why the plaintiff hadn't produced one medical expert, which seemed like a good question, until the plaintiff's lawyer asked if his colleague was aware that expertise cost money, which his client didn't have. Which also seemed like a good question.

With no idea who was telling the truth, Lula was glad to leave it to the jury, another American grab bag, men and women, old and young, black and brown and white, all listening intently and occasionally asking for things to be repeated. When the trial broke for lunch, Lula felt like celebrating.

Luckily, lunch was the number-one topic in the elevators, and even in this short time she'd overheard several debates about where to find the best Cantonese noodle soup. What better way to honor her affection for this country than in an affordable restaurant surrounded by fellow immigrants from all over the globe, gathered at communal round tables to warm their faces in fragrant saunas of chicken broth?

Lula should have known better than to be seduced by soup. If she'd stayed put, as she had yesterday, she wouldn't have been part of the lunch crowd filing out of the building. She wouldn't have spotted Leather Jacket—Genti—on his way in, stalled in the security line, anxiously monitoring the basket in which his beloved coat was about to roll on without him. Genti didn't see Lula, which gave her a moment to decide whether to ignore him and keep going. The flame died under the noodle soup, the healing broth stopped bubbling.

She had to call Genti three times. Finally he heard her. He almost smiled, then looked worried.

"Little Sister, what brings you to this lowest circle of hell?"

Just being in this American palace of justice made her feel simultaneously emboldened and protected. She grabbed Genti's arm and yanked him toward the door, an awkward ballet made clumsier when Genti stopped to rescue his coat from the conveyor belt and shimmied into its narrow sleeves as they crossed the lobby. Lula tried to telegraph the fact that she and Genti were old friends, meeting by happy accident, instead of Albanian terrorists recognizing each other by some prearranged code signal.

She said, "I'm applying for a job in court. And you? Why are you here?"

Genti raised one eyebrow. "Arkon's in serious trouble. His trial starts today."

"Arkon?"

"I mean Alvo."

Lula hadn't even known her fantasy boyfriend's real name. "What did he do?"

Genti checked to see if anyone was listening. "Nothing. Guilty in the first degree of the crime of being Albanian."

"I get that. But what are the charges?"

"The guy fell on his sword for us. Me and Guri are not even implicated in their made-up lies. Even so, little bitch Guri is shitting his pants. He's hiding out in Allentown, Pennsylvania, pretending his granny's deathly ill. If his granny dies, it will be his fault."

"Made-up *what* lies?" asked Lula. Let it be a civil case. Let the guy whose air conditioner Alvo installed backward be suing.

"I told you. Nothing," said Genti. "Not paying off the right guy. Come listen. Our brother's facing serious jail time."

Serious jail time was not about an air conditioner. "What's he charged with?" Lula asked twice more, the first time almost inaudibly, the second time louder than she intended. Fear flashed across Genti's face. The fear of being embarrassed.

"Breaking and entering. Possible sentence fifteen years or more of—" Genti's fingers puppeted violent anal rape. Now it was Lula's turn to look around, embarrassed.

"A dog got injured in one of the break-ins. One of the break-ins we didn't do. A scratch. The dog probably cut itself shaving. Is that even a crime? But they found a bullet in the wall."

"From the gun?" asked Lula.

"What gun?" asked Genti.

"The one you left with me."

"Who remembers?" said Genti.

"I do," Lula said. "Let's go."

Genti peeled off his jacket again, and together they rejoined the line filing toward the metal detector.

The near-empty courtroom seemed like a hopeful sign. Alvo's case wasn't drawing the yelping packs of reporters.

"Where is he?" Lula whispered.

"There," said Genti.

"Where?"

"Over there, goddammit!" said Genti. A few people turned. Was this how it was going to be for the rest of the day, she and Genti embarrassing each other like an old married couple, squabbling and talking too loud as they watched their Albanian brother get put away for so long that when he got out he would be an old man wanting a twenty-year-old girl or probably, after jail, a twenty-year-old boy? Lula imagined visiting him, their palms pressed against the glass. Someone would have to tell her the right name to give the guards.

Everyone faced forward. None of those heads was Alvo's. Or Arkon's. They were in the wrong courtroom. Genti was a moron.

"I don't see him," she insisted.

"There," said Genti. "Look again. The dude dyed his fucking hair."

That was the missing puzzle piece. Alvo's hair was as black as Zeke's.

"His lawyer told him redheads always lose. Statistics. Hair color is everything. Natural blonds are the winners. After that comes gray."

"Where did he find this lawyer?"

"The Bronx," said Genti. "Where else?"

Alvo's lawyer wore a pale suit with a cripplingly tight skirt. Combed in a flawless upsweep, her silvery curls gleamed softly in the harsh institutional light. She approached the judge's bench and whispered in his ear. The elderly judge leered besottedly at the lady lawyer.

"Defense has informed me that a translator has been found for his client, who is insufficiently comfortable in English."

"My man's a genius," Genti whispered.

"Are you aware of that, Mr. Capone?"

You couldn't make up a district attorney named Mr. Capone! Lula felt another surge of love for her adopted country. Mr. Capone pointed out that when the accused was apprehended, he'd shown an excellent command of English. English curse words in particular. When this got a laugh from some cops up front, Mr. Capone mock-saluted them.

"Assholes!" Genti hissed.

The guard who materialized at the end of Lula and Genti's row informed them: One more outburst, and he'd have to ask them to leave. He himself spoke softly yet managed to create a rumbling in the atmosphere that got the whole courtroom's attention.

Alvo-Arkon turned. He looked haggard, but still handsome, even with the bad dye job. Poor guy! For Lula to assume she'd been rejected was pure self-centered pride. Alvo hadn't been thinking about her. A possible fifteen years in jail trumped a catastrophic first date.

Alvo spotted Genti and raised one shoulder in that corny way that always yanked his friends' leashes. Then Alvo noticed Lula. No surprise. No nothing. You wouldn't buy a fish with those eyes. He didn't know her, he didn't want to know her. Why was she even here?

"Sorry," Genti told the guard. Then he said, "I fucked your fat slut of a sister," pleasantly in Albanian so only Lula could hear.

The translator was a parched, round-shouldered gentleman

in a boldly checked suit. Not much competition there. What red-blooded court clerk would call this sad sack once Lula was an option? However long it took to get the job, she could still wear short skirts. The translator kept raising his forearm as if to ward off the hail of English. "Please, more slowly, slowly," he said.

"Mistrial!" Genti whispered.

The clerk read the charges. Not one burglary, but many. All groceries and supermarkets. A firearm had been involved. Lula put her head in her hands. Alvo was also charged with funneling money to terrorist groups in Kosovo.

"Objection!" yelled Alvo's lawyer.

"Objection sustained," said the judge.

"Now he's screwed," Lula whispered.

"That part is definite crap," said Genti. "That I swear on my daughter's life. In my opinion, Arkon could be a lot *more* patriotic."

"You have a daughter?" Lula said.

"A daughter and a son. The lawyers know it's horseshit too. Why are you closing your eyes?"

To read the print on a sales receipt. Orange juice and cigarettes.

Genti elbowed her. "Pick up your head. Sit straight."

Mr. Capone called Mr. Aziz. Yes, he was the owner of Sunrise Market at 411 Avenue C. Tears trickled down Mr. Aziz's cheeks when he described how his employee had called at dawn to tell him that there had been a break-in. Thank you, Mr. Aziz. Did the defense have any questions? Come on, thought Lula, no one got hurt, it was only money and minor property damage. Most likely the guy was insured. So who got stung? Some rich insurance company? Alvo was the Albanian-American Robin Hood.

Was there a camera? An alarm? A guard? No, sir, there was neither. There was a dog. A dog? Mr. Aziz's German shepherd had bitten the intruder. The dog had been shot. To death? No, sir, Rex survived. Lula recalled the bandage on Alvo's hand when he'd come to take her to lunch. Even then. But of course even then. He'd asked her to hide a gun.

"They got nothing on no one. Purely circumstantial." Genti must have watched the same crime shows as Lula.

Alvo's lawyer suggested that her client had been bitten earlier in the day by the dog, which had viciously attacked him, unprovoked, when he'd walked into Mr. Aziz's store to buy a quart of juice. Out of the goodness of his heart, her client had declined to press charges, and now his forbearance was being repaid by this trumped-up case against him.

"Brilliant," Genti said. "Is that brilliant or not?"

"Not." Lula looked at the jury. Disbelief on every face.

The lawyers approached the judge, and the next part played out in hushed voices. The judge declared a recess. *State of New York v. Jashari* would resume tomorrow at nine.

"Jashari," Lula repeated. This judge didn't warn the jurors to be careful crossing the street.

Lula watched Alvo confer with his lawyer until the guards came to take him away. He turned and looked at Lula. This time Alvo saw her. His jaw went slack with longing, and the look they exchanged was almost as good as the sex they never had. With all his heart, he regretted not having gotten back in touch.

Lula almost cried out his name. Passion rose from the embers of their awkward dating history. Maybe things could still work out. Maybe Alvo would get off on a legal technicality. Having realized that he loved her, he would reform, and they would start over, two strangers whom that trusty matchmaker, grand larceny, had brought together in a courtroom.

RATHER THAN FACE the buses and the cold, Lula accepted Genti's offer of a ride home. But even before she climbed into the SUV that Genti retrieved from the garage, she realized that riding with him would have its own discomforts.

"Why supermarkets?" she asked, as Genti darted in and out of the traffic that grew thicker and meaner as they headed up the West Side.

"How would I know?" said Genti. "We didn't do it."

"But why would anyone?" asked Lula, more diplomatically.

Genti's answer was loud music. Fuck you up, Serb bitches. Every boast and threat and off rhyme intensified Lula's gloom.

Genti took the Lincoln Tunnel. The minute they saw the light of New Jersey, his cell phone barked like Charmy Puppy.

"That cop's looking straight at you," Lula said.

"Let him look straight at my ass," said Genti. "Hey, boss, how's it going?" Genti switched into Albanian, but mostly he made noises, humming and clucking the international language that signified too bad, not good, we have a problem. "Okay, not to worry, boss, everything will be fine."

"Was he calling from jail?" Lula asked. "I thought you only get one call."

"Money works everywhere," Genti said. "But only so far. The boss says things don't look great. New charges, new evidence. They're trying to connect him to every unsolved break-in in

New York and northern Jersey. Little Sister, we need to ask you one last tiny favor. We know you have a good lawyer. The one who got you that work visa overnight."

"Not overnight," said Lula.

"Yes, overnight," insisted Genti. "We remember that first time, your bragging about this legal genius. So now the boss is wondering if you could talk to your boy. Get him to pull a few strings. We would never ask such a thing unless it was life or death."

Lula said, "My guy's in immigration. It's a whole different field."

"Lawyers know lawyers," Genti said. "Just like people know people. Kinship patterns, right?"

"Kinship patterns?"

"I'm taking an introductory anthro course at LaGuardia Community College."

"Improving yourself," said Lula. "Hey, watch it! You cut that guy off!"

"I saw the stupid bastard," said Genti, swerving. "One more thing. The boss said for me to tell you that what happened between you wasn't nothing. That's what he told me to say. Look, I don't know what *did* happen, but the boss said to tell you it—"

"Was not nothing. I heard. I'll do what I can. Are you going to the trial tomorrow?"

"If it's still going on. The whole thing could be over, and not in a good way, by this afternoon. Not to put any pressure on you. But we think your time would be better spent going to see your lawyer."

"I told you. There's nothing I can do," Lula said.

"There's always something," said Genti. "Call him. We'll go back into the city. I'll drive you there. I'll wait and take you home."

Staring out the windshield, Lula recalled the look on Alvo's face as he'd left the courtroom. Had his hungry stare been for her—or her lawyer? "I'll think about it. I'll call my guy. He's out of town a lot. He works in Guantánamo, where people have *real* problems."

"Little Sister, trust me. This is a real problem. Tomorrow's too late. I'll take you to his office."

Lula could have said no. She could have tried to say no. Instead she got her phone and pressed Don Settebello's number. Lula told his secretary she needed to see Don in person. Now. For only ten minutes.

"You're in luck," said the secretary. "He's just back from Cuba. His schedule opens up around two, two fifteen. He can give you five minutes tops. This better be important."

"It's life and death," Lula said.

DON SETTEBELLO LIKED to give the impression of a guy who worked out of a dusty back office, like a detective in an old movie. But Lula had long since discovered, not entirely to her surprise, that Settebello, Reitman and Leiber was a huge intimidating law firm with a huge staff instructed not to intimidate clients. The scrubbed young receptionist picked up the phone, and a scrubbed young man whisked Lula through a labyrinth populated by other scrubbed young people, all working for Don, not one of them looking up long enough to envy or even notice Lula, the family friend who could breeze into Don's inner sanctum. She was no ordinary supplicant, come to beg Don's help. She and Don and their families had spent Thanksgiving together.

Don's kiss on the cheek said, Hi! I have five minutes.

"I was in the neighborhood," Lula said.

"What are you doing, Lula?" said Don.

"I've been going to court, watching trials. I like your legal system. Very fair, very humane. I saw a judge tell the jurors to be careful crossing the street. At home that would mean she was threatening them, but here—"

"We try," said Don. "Some of the time we succeed."

"Some is better than never," said Lula. "I was thinking of becoming a court interpreter."

"Good! I heard you met Savitra. Crazy overachiever, but you have to give her credit. I mean what are you doing *here?*"

"How's Abigail?" asked Lula.

"Fine," said Don Settebello. "I've got her this weekend. So what's so life and death?"

Lula said, "I know there's probably nothing you can do, but I need to ask you a favor. I have this cousin from home, he's being framed for robberies he didn't commit."

Don said, "Is this by any chance the cousin who was in your room the night Ginger showed up?"

Ordinarily, Lula admired how quickly Don's mind worked. But this was a little too quick.

"So what have they got on the innocent cousin?"

Lula said, "Some grocery store dog bit him. There was blood at the crime scene. His blood. A guard dog. Actually, the dog bit him earlier in the day."

It was suicidal to lie to Don. But it was worth a try. She and

Alvo were friends. They'd been through something together. Their lives had been threatened—by Ginger. They came from the same place. Blood loyalty was the upside of the tribal psychosis that made people kill nephews and grandsons for fifteen generations.

Don said, "Please. Don't tell me any more. I don't want to know."

Lula said, "It's political. He's an Albanian patriot." Was that even true? Or was it something the court made up? Genti had said that Alvo—Arkon—wasn't patriotic *enough.* "He's innocent. I swear. I mean, about the break-ins."

Don returned to his desk and motioned for Lula to sit. He shut his eyes and massaged his eyebrows. "You know what the most painful part is, Lula? What hurts is how stupid you must think we are. I'm just curious: Do you think all Americans are that dumb, or only me and Stan? Do you think we didn't know you made up those stories you passed off as family history? So fine, everybody takes liberties. Famous writers, as we all know. But now do you really imagine that Don the Dummy is going to believe that your boyfriend or hookup or one-night stand or green-card husband or whoever the fuck he turns out to be is an innocent Albanian patriot framed on a bogus burglary rap?"

"He isn't my boyfriend." If only she hadn't worn that stupid woolen hat! Maybe if her hair looked better, Don would agree to help her.

Don said, "You know what, Lula? If you'd come into my office and said, Hey, Don, I've been screwing this Albanian dude who's gotten popped for B and E. You know anyone in criminal? Is there something you can do? I still wouldn't have done anything. I mean, I would still be horrified that you would ask me to waste my time fixing—refusing to fix—a case like this when the secret jails and black sites are jammed with water-boarded beat-to-shit miserable motherfuckers, a certain percentage of whom have done nothing wrong except be named Abdullah. But at least if you'd said that, if you'd said that, Lula, I would not have felt, as I do now, personally insulted."

"I didn't mean to insult you," said Lula. No wonder Don was famous. He must be a genius at badgering witnesses into saying what he wanted. Lula tried to imagine Don's wife Betsy, whom she'd never met. Then she thought of Savitra, and of Don's hand thumping heavily down on her hand at lunch. A woman would have to be crazy to marry, or even have sex with, a man who would prosecute every lover's quarrel like a criminal case.

Don said, "I haven't gotten where I am without being able to read a situation, and quite frankly, Lula, my reading of this situation makes me feel . . . I don't know what it makes me feel. Tired. Disappointed. It depresses me, Lula. You know that? As we used to say back in the day, it brings me down. You work in the home of my oldest friend. You're family, in a way. You know what I've chosen to do with my life, the problems I've made for myself, the sacrifices, not that they're sacrifices. Someone has to do it. The daily shoveling shit against the tide of government lying, military lying, pointless social lying. And now you're adding your own pathetic little lie about a guy who shouldn't even have been in your room that night Stan's wife went apeshit."

Why not? Lula wanted to ask. Why shouldn't Alvo have been there? Was jealousy the problem? Was it Alvo's criminal past? Alvo's criminal present? Lula's lying was the problem. Did Lula's minimal alteration of the truth make Don think that she didn't know why he'd chosen a hard life over an easy one, or what was at stake for him and this country? Did Don believe that her efforts to help a guy she had a little crush on was a threat to the Founding Fathers and the American way of life? Don was a hero. Case closed. Lula respected him for being brave and honest and always ready to help the underdog. Would Don refuse to keep working on her green-card case because she told a tiny white lie to save her Albanian brother? Don would go on helping her. Don was in every way—well, in most ways—a saintly human being.

"Look," said Don. "I know. People do crazy things for love. If this is love. Is it love, Lula?"

No! Lula wanted to say. Or was it? She didn't think so. This was hardly the moment to analyze the depth of her feelings for Alvo.

"You know a concept I've been having trouble with lately?" Don said. "No, why should you? Well, the fact is, I've been having trouble with simultaneity."

"Simultaneity?" said Lula.

"Two things happening at once," Don said.

"I know what the word means," said Lula. It was maddening that at this late date Don should question her English. Did he correct Savitra's grammar? Savitra grew up in Great Neck.

"What I mean," said Don, "is that at this very moment, this kid I met down there last week, this boy, this child, younger than Zeke, for fuck's sake, the usual story, they confused him with some jihadist piece of shit, they don't believe he's fourteen, the warrant says he's twenty, he looks older than his age. Now he looks like a little old man. They grab him off a Yemeni street and fly him blindfolded and shackled to Guantánamo, where he's been tortured and starved. He spit bacon back in a guard's face, he started acting up. They gave him electroshock until he seized so badly he's paralyzed down one side of his body. He's a kid. He's alive right now, Lula, and maybe right now he's being punched around after days and nights without sleep, at the exact same moment that you and I are sitting in this comfortable high-rent office and you're bullshitting me to save the ass of some loser whose only saving grace is that he comes from your country and at some point you wanted to fuck him."

"Losers are human beings too," said Lula.

Don said, "He's not your cousin. He's not political. And he did the crimes."

Lula said, "I don't know what he did. What if he stole something? Everybody steals. Compared to the crimes you deal with, what's theft? In grade school we learned that property is theft, and then they stopped teaching that, they said it was too right-wing. By the time I got to university, property was good, the more property the better, preferably real estate. Not having property was theft, or anyway, it gave you a reason to steal. Someone emptied a cash register? Okay. No one got hurt! The dog recovered! Let my cousin pay back what he stole. I'll make sure he does. Why take away fifteen years of his life? His whole life is what it will be. What kind of justice is that? Supermarket-owner justice. Aren't you the one who talks about the big lies and the small ones? You Americans and your freedom to give speeches about the truth. You don't know how free you are. In another country, you could piss me off and I could turn you in, or I could turn you in because I wanted your real estate, and they'd send you away to a labor camp, and that would be that."

Don said, "Are you finished, Lula?"

Lula shrugged.

Don looked at his watch. "I'm sorry about your friend. But I've got enough on my plate. I could do twenty years of non-stop habeas corpus before I got around to a breaking and entering case. Unless it was Watergate, maybe. But look, Lula, I've always liked you. And you've done wonders for Stan's kid. That poor boy was a basket case before you arrived. Or anyhow so Stan says. I don't doubt him. You're talented, smart, you're a scrapper. The country needs people like you. We'll forget this whole incident happened. Everyone makes mistakes. We'll just forget it and never mention it and work on your legal status. Then you can become a court interpreter or a lawyer or whatever, and the next time your boyfriend robs a store, you can defend him yourself."

Lula said, "It's not so easy to forget."

"You're young," said Don. "You'd be amazed at how much you can forget in twenty years. I hate to bring this pleasant chat to an end. But our five minutes are up. I'll call you if I hear anything about your green card. It'll be a while. Be patient. Give my love to Stan and Zeke."

Lula wanted to ask him not to tell Mister Stanley. But she couldn't ask, and besides she knew he would tell Mister Stanley. The whole story would come out. Mister Stanley would be furious, and this part of her life would be over. More proof, as if she needed it, of how your secret hope for a change in your circumstances could turn around and bite you. She shook Don's hand and thanked him, and though she assured him that she could find her way out alone, he remanded her into the custody of the same scrubbed boy.

Only in the elevator did she remember that Genti was waiting. The SUV slithered across the street, and she climbed into the passenger seat.

"What did your boy say?" Genti asked.

"He says he'll do what he can," said Lula.

"Good work! Should I pick you up tomorrow? We can go to court together."

"I have errands to do on the way," Lula lied. "I'll meet you there."

"See you in court, ha ha," Genti said.

"Funny joke," Lula said.

That night, she waited for Mister Stanley to mention the phone call from Don. But the subject never came up. How was Zeke? Had he done his homework? Hadn't Don said that he and Lula could just forget it? Maybe there was still a chance that everything could work out all right.

THE NEXT MORNING, Lula got through the line fairly quickly and hurried to the courtroom, where two elderly Filipino gentlemen were shouting at each other, while the judge shouted at their lawyers to make their clients quit shouting. What had happened to Alvo? Despite what Genti said, Lula never imagined his case would be settled so fast. Why hadn't Lula let Genti drive her into the city?

Lula left the court and rushed down the hall, looking in other courtrooms, searching for someone she could ask about Alvo. A guard sent her to another guard, who sent her to a desk, where a woman sent her to an office, where someone gave her a number to call. Exactly like Albania.

It was possible that she would never know how Alvo's story ended. Possible that, for Lula, the story would end here. When she called Alvo's cell phone, a recording apologized: The number was no longer in service. Lula looked around wildly, further alerting the guards who'd already noted her terroristic dash from courtroom to courtroom.

She left the building and went home. Maybe Genti would stop by and give her an update. By now, they had probably figured out that Don hadn't lifted a finger on Alvo's behalf.

No one stopped by. No one called.

Late in the afternoon, Zeke came home. His posture annoyed her. His fake smile annoyed her. The cigarette ash on his black jeans annoyed her. The way his hair sucked up all the light in the room annoyed her. Poor Zeke. Poor little baby. Ginger was his mother. How Lula's heart must have hardened for her to feel anything but love and kindness and compassion.

She said, "You want some hot chocolate?"

Zeke said, "Did I do something good that I don't know about?" His gratitude was depressing. It was scary how easily he could grow up to be Mister Stanley. Under the black dye and piercings was his father's son. But what was so bad about that? Mister Stanley was a decent, well-intentioned person.

"You didn't do anything especially good," said Lula. "You *are* good."

"My dad pays you to say that," said Zeke.

"This is me talking, not him." A voice inside Lula's head seemed to be giving some sort of speech about how grateful she felt for the time she'd spent with Zeke and for how much he'd helped her adjust to a new country. Why was the voice so solemn? Because she was hearing herself deliver the eulogy for her life with Zeke. Lula went to the window, where, she knew, the desolate sprinkle of snow would make her feel even more unhappy.

She said, "We have extra pizza in the freezer. We don't have to go out."

"Are you all right?" asked Zeke.

"I'm catching a cold," Lula said. "Dr. Lula prescribes hot chocolate."

Lula recalled seeing cocoa mix at the back of the kitchen cabinet. The packaging was designed to look vintage, and by now the contents probably were. But thanks to the scientific miracle of preservatives, the hot chocolate was delicious. Had Ginger made cocoa for Zeke? Zeke was not about to let the memory of his mother ruin his precious hot-chocolate moment with Lula.

A little later, Lula heated a pizza and left it out for Zeke. Mojitos were too much work. She could live without one. She went to her room and lay down. She slept and woke in her clothes. She thought it was nine in the morning. It was nine at night. She couldn't face Mister Stanley. They could skip the nightly check-in. Sooner or later Don would tell Stan about this guy Lula was lying about, and how she'd tried to make Don lie too. Her luck wouldn't last forever. It was already leaching away.

She took the last of Ginger's pills. After a while she checked her watch. Hours had gone by. Had she been lying awake in the dark, or had she fallen asleep? She felt achier but less stupid. Smart enough to register the fact that someone was knocking on her door.

"Lula," yelled Mister Stanley. "Can we talk downstairs?"

. . .

MISTER STANLEY WAS disappointed in her. Mister Stanley had been deceived. Mister Stanley had expected more of her. How could Lula have so betrayed his confidence and trust, consorting with thieves and criminals, endangering the welfare of the innocent boy he'd hired her and paid her generously to protect?

Over and over Mister Stanley said, "You brought a criminal into my home!"

The worst part was that Lula could see it from his point of view. She'd been naive and reckless. She should never have let the three guys into the house. She would have liked to tell Mister Stanley that, but another drawback to habitual lying was that no one believed you when you switched to the truth.

Apparently this was too serious for a kitchen conversation, which revealed a flaw in Mister Stanley's thinking. Nothing was too important for the kitchen. Her granny had died at her stove. But tonight Mister Stanley summoned her into the bookless library, the workless office, the dank ceremonial chamber where she hadn't been since he'd hired her and took her there to tell her the rules. Be home in time for Zeke, no drinking or smoking, no driving farther than The Good Earth, make Zeke eat vegetables, etcetera. Lula had broken every rule except the one against smoking, which Zeke broke himself. And the rule against letting him drive farther than the market, which there was still time to break. Mister Stanley had never thought to make a rule against driving Alvo's Lexus.

The library smelled like old people, like old clothes in old closets. It was the principal's office, where bad children were sent. Americans, with their big houses, their special rooms for special events. If her father wanted to have a talk, which he never did, he'd have taken her out to their favorite garbage-dump shooting range. How she missed her papa! There was no one to defend her against Mister Stanley's charges. So what if they were justified? Lula was only human. Humans made mistakes. She hadn't meant to hurt anyone. She'd just been unable to resist the lure of risky entertainment.

Lula watched Mister Stanley pace the room, ranting. If he would only shut up and listen, so much could be explained. Alvo and his friends had practically home-invaded her, practically held a gun to her head and made her ask Don to help. Alternately, she could confess. The gun was Alvo's. Lula had lied when she'd said it was Ginger's. She'd been afraid the truth might involve police and trouble with immigration. But Alvo wasn't a killer. Zeke was never in danger. Ginger had been the danger, sneaking around the house. And Lula had been so forgiving after Mister Stanley's wife had threatened them with a knife. How could Mister Stanley reduce Lula's loving relationship with Zeke to the cheap materialism of a service he'd paid for? Had he paid her extra for making Zeke hot chocolate? She cared about Zeke, she'd been kind to him. Zeke had been a basket case before Lula arrived.

And while Lula was numbering the wrongs committed against her, how could Don have betrayed her to Mister Stanley? What about attorney-client privilege? Did Don think that Lula never watched TV? Wasn't Lula entitled to this legal or basic human right, if not yet as a citizen then as a human being? There were probably grounds for a lawsuit here, if she'd had a green card and a hefty American trust fund.

Lula would have felt worse about her boss's accusations, but she kept being distracted by the way that anger had created or perhaps just unleashed a whole new Mister Stanley. Purple instead of mushroom white, outraged instead of apologetic, he seemed to have expanded into a physically larger presence. Had he occupied this much space with Ginger? It was shocking how long you could live with someone and know nothing about him. Who would have suspected that Mister Stanley could devolve into a jungle creature driven wild by animal instinct to protect his lair and his young? Not once in his tirade did he say "one" instead of "me," and with every word his voice descended from his sinuses deeper into his chest. The idea of Mister Stanley as an untapped reservoir of unsuspected qualities filled Lula with regret. She wouldn't be here long enough to discover even one more hidden aspect of his character.

But Zeke was the one she would really miss. Maybe she and Zeke could stay friends. She could visit him at college. An abyss opened beneath her, a landslide set off by her inability to picture the place from which she'd leave to go see Zeke.

If the mild Mister Stanley had a problem with eye contact, his spitfire incarnation's gaze was a high beam directed at Lula. But at last Mister Stanley blinked and stopped and waited for her to respond.

Lula put everything she had into the ultimate Mr.-Stanley-pleasing shrug. She tried to infuse her rising shoulders with a thousand years of Balkan history, with the what-else-is-new of invaders, murder, pillage, and exile, the what-can-you do of failed monarchies, empires, promises, and scams, the what-do-you-expect of Communism, of decades when you couldn't know anything, couldn't do anything, couldn't say anything, when all you could do was shrug and teach your children to shrug. She turned up both palms with the you-can't-tell-me-anything-I-don't-already-know world-weariness of a person who'd spent the formative years of her childhood under the paranoid leadership of a psychotic dictator, a person who had seen economic collapse and rioting and chaotic violence and everywhere gangsters in control, in the open and from the shadows.

She said, "Zeke was never in danger. Not from Alvo, anyway."

"How can you be sure?" Mister Stanley wanted her to have been sure.

"I'm sure," said Lula. "Trust me."

"I wish I could," said Mister Stanley.

"Then fire me," Lula said.

"Not so fast," said Mister Stanley. "We've had enough drama in this house. Let's think about alternatives. Take our time. Mull things over."

The way he'd said "mull things over" filled Lula with despair. She said, "I should probably quit."

"What makes you think you can quit?" Mister Stanley said, his voice rising again. "Have you considered your chances of finding another sponsor after you asked my childhood friend to sacrifice his integrity, to risk his career, to help some thug you let into my home while my son and I slept?"

"He's not a thug," Lula said. "Are you saying you won't sponsor me if I don't work here?"

"No," said Mister Stanley. "I'm not saying that at all. Though it might be more tricky. Legally speaking. Let's sleep on it. Let's revisit the subject tomorrow night when I come home. There's nothing like twenty-four hours to clarify one's thinking."

Chapter Fourteen

————— ∞ —————

THE NEXT morning, Lula waited until eleven, an hour by which even the most pampered plastic surgeon's wife was certain to be awake. Still, Dunia sounded groggy when she answered the phone. A more thoughtful best friend might have asked how Lula was.

Dunia said, "Please God, somebody shoot me now. I am so hung over."

"Be careful what you wish for," Lula said.

"Old school," mumbled Dunia. "You sound like my granny."

"You and Doctor Steve been partying?"

"What Doctor Steve?" said Dunia. "Doctor Steve was another lifetime."

"Excuse me?" Lula said.

"The marriage is over. It's going to be annulled. Which makes everybody happy. Steve's family included. Steve's family especially. No ugly divorce courts, no bloodsucking lawyers, no scandal. Just a big cash settlement direct-deposited into my bank account. It turns out that Doctor Steve and the versatile Jorge my driver were having a little extramarital something on the side. I don't even want to think what special perfume Steve brought *him*. How could I not have known? Remember I told you that Steve liked me to talk Albanian during sex? The part I didn't mention was that he made me talk Albanian in a low growly voice. Pervert Steve wanted to imagine he was having sex with an Albanian guy! Speaking of which, whatever happened with that Albanian guy you went out with Christmas Eve?"

"Not much," said Lula.

"It's probably better," said Dunia. "Anyhow, no more Steve. What do they say? If it looks too good to be true, it probably is too good to be true? If it looks like a fish and smells like a fish, it probably is a fish. You know me. I'm an honest person. I'm not the blackmailing type. Steve was thrilled when I agreed not to ask for half of everything he's got. Which I probably could have gotten, if I was scheming or greedy."

"Congratulations," said Lula uncertainly.

"Thanks," said Dunia. "Anyway, I was going to call you. Guess where I am now? Twenty-fourth floor, Trump Towers. Overlooking the Hudson. Like Jesus told Peter from the cross, I can see your house from here. I rented a two-bedroom. I was thinking you could move in. Don't worry about the rent, at least for now. I'm bored. I want someone to hang with. Hey, it's your ticket out of New Jersey. We'll max out Steve's credit cards. Then we'll figure out what next."

"There's a job I want," said Lula. As if she had to convince Dunia, of all people, that she was an upstanding future citizen of the United States. "A court interpreter, to start with . . ."

"Fine! I already said I won't charge you rent. When do you want to come and check the place out?"

"I don't know. When would be good for you?"

"Right now," Dunia said.

.   .   .

BY THE TIME Lula got back that afternoon, she was already seeing Mister Stanley's house with the tender detachment of someone who used to live there. Or from the more objective perspective of someone else who used to live there. She wasn't the same person who, only a few months before, had gazed out her bedroom window and monitored the arrival of an SUV full of trouble.

The last remnants of that foolish girl had been blown away by the winter wind off the Hudson, the ice needles and face slaps of cold she'd fended off on her way from the subway to Dunia's overheated lobby, so like a cross between a Las Vegas casino and a grand hotel in Moscow. The uniformed doorman handed Lula over to another uniformed guard, who showed her to the elevator, where yet another lieutenant in Dunia's private army whisked Lula into the sky.

Dunia was waiting outside her door, perhaps to watch Lula admire the depth to which Dunia's high heels sank into the hall carpet. Welcome to America! Finally! They'd come a long way from Tirana. Dunia planted smoky kisses on Lula's cheek, then showed her into the apartment and stepped back to watch her friend's response to the Hudson River and half of New Jersey flinging itself at their feet.

"This works for me," said Lula.

"Look out the other direction," said Dunia, grabbing Lula's arm as they contemplated the skyscrapers poking their glittering heads through clouds of dusty sunlight.

"It's a sublet," said Dunia. "In six months I will have spent every last penny I got from Steve. But worth it, don't you think?"

"I've got sixteen hundred dollars saved up," Lula said.

"Don't make me laugh," said Dunia.

"I like what you've done with the place," Lula said.

Dunia said, "All the little personal touches ordered and paid for before I left Steve. I was thinking ahead."

"Thank you, Doctor Steve," said Lula.

"I thanked Steve, believe me," Dunia said. "Jorge the driver thanked him, too. I think Steve's living with Jorge now."

"The driver was cute," said Lula.

"The driver *is* cute," said Dunia. "Can you believe I put this place together, all by myself, in two weeks?"

"You should have called me," Lula said.

"I called you now," said Dunia. "We'll have fun. Let's wind the clock back a couple of years."

"We deserve it," said Lula.

"We earned it," Dunia said.

NOW THAT SHE was leaving, Lula welcomed the three bus rides home, which gave her plenty of time to figure out how to word her resignation. She knew it would be more professional to inform her boss before she told his son, but she wanted Zeke to hear the news directly from her.

As always, Lula was home before Zeke arrived, and as always she said, "Let's go get some food," exactly as she had every weekday afternoon for, God help her, more than a year. Their drama would play out less tragically in the car. Zeke would be at the wheel of the vehicle that he loved more than anyone, including Lula. He would not be looking at her, and his mind would be partly on the road. Better to tell him en route to the store than on the way home, because if he was upset, he would have to pull himself together before they went into the market full of strangers for whom he would have to wear the mask of unshakable teenage cool. The Good Earth was only a few minutes away. Lula had no time to spare.

They were barely out of the driveway when Lula said, "We'll always be friends. But there are going to be some changes. I'm going to work as a court interpreter, and I found a place to live, nearer downtown Manhattan."

Zeke said, "That's bullshit about your getting that job. So are you moving in with that guy who was here when . . . You know. The guy you said was your cousin. Like anyone believed *that*. The guy who let me drive his Lexus."

"Not at all!" said Lula. "I think that guy's in jail."

"I liked that guy," said Zeke.

"So did I," said Lula.

"What's he in jail for?"

"For being an asshole."

"I didn't know that was a crime," said Zeke. "Especially in New Jersey."

"It can be," Lula said. "The point is, I'm not moving in with him. I'm living with my friend Dunia. She's got a place in Trump Towers."

"That is awesome," said Zeke. "Can I move in with you too?"

"Maybe someday," Lula said.

"So you're just leaving us? Disappearing just like that?"

"You're going to college," Lula said. "You don't need me. You're practically grown up. You can pour your own cereal into a bowl."

"I don't eat cereal," Zeke said.

"Well, you should," said Lula.

Zeke, who had been slumped behind the wheel, pulled himself up to his full height. He said, "Will I ever see you again?"

"Constantly," said Lula. "You'll get sick of me. I'll visit you at college. I'll be your embarrassing old auntie. You and your friends can stay with me and Dunia when you come into the city." Would Dunia still have her apartment by then? They would worry about that later.

"Here we are," said Zeke. "At the store."

"Park close, it's icy," Lula said.

"I always do," said Zeke. "I'm a guy. Anyhow, the parking lot's empty."

Deserted except for a pickup truck, The Good Earth was closed for repairs. A worker wheeling out a cart of broken drywall told them, "Some dirtbags broke in and stripped the place clean. I don't know how those dumbfucks think they're going to fence a truckload of organic cauliflower."

"Let's get out of here," said Zeke. "Everything here is cheesy."

Lula's head felt swimmy. Another supermarket break-in? Alvo was in jail and couldn't possibly have been the dirtbag behind this one. Which proved he was innocent if, as the DA claimed, the robberies were all committed by the same person. Was there someone Lula should tell? Should she mention this to Don? She'd mentioned enough to Don.

From the edges of her consciousness came a sound like a cat choking on a hair ball. Zeke was crying. Gelid tears slipped down his chalk-white cheeks.

"Everything sucks," he said. "Mom going crazy. Now you're leaving. I think I might be gay."

"You'll be fine," said Lula. "I promise."

"Sometimes I wish I was a vampire," said Zeke.

"Why would you want that?" said Lula.

"Because you don't have to live and you don't have to die. It's easy."

"Not for a vampire," said Lula.

"Probably not," said Zeke.

Lula put her arm around him. A stranger driving past might have mistaken them for teenage sweethearts. Lula tried to beam concentrated rays of friendship and reassurance directly from her brain into his, and from moment to moment she felt a warm rush flowing back in her direction, so that it almost seemed to be working.

She said, "Let's try the Shopwell. I know it's further, but the drive would be fun."

Zeke looked at her. "It's too far."

"Don't worry," she said. "No one's going to tell your dad."

"I know that," said Zeke. He smiled his frozen fake smile, and then, as Lula watched, it slowly, slowly came unstuck and turned into a real one.

Lula put her head on Zeke's shoulder as he pulled out onto the street. And they rode like that, without speaking, all the way to the market and home.

IF THERE WAS one thing Lula should have learned from living at Mister Stanley's, it was the folly of comparing your life with how you imagined someone else's life, based on their real estate. Once, passing a house like Mister Stanley's, she might have envied its inhabitants their American happiness, complete with all the American creature comforts. Now she knew better. But still she found it a challenge of the spirit not to sink into the quicksand of envy that lay in the gap between the suitcases into which she was stuffing her possessions and the apartment full of designer furniture that Dunia had earned by being a sex worker of sorts, if not the sort Lula once feared. Well, at least Lula was mobile. She could move across the river without the twenty-foot van that, she hoped, Dunia could still afford when they got evicted from Trump Towers. Lula was like her ancestors, strapping all their worldly goods onto the backs of donkeys and migrating to higher pastures.

The real trouble with packing was that it left so much of her mind free and undefended against the cringe-inducing memories of last night's conversation with Mister Stanley. Lula flinched when she recalled Mister Stanley suggesting they go into his study. Come into my parlor, said the spider to the fly. And Lula, fearing that she might lose her resolve, announced that she was leaving while they were still in the kitchen. Even now, her face flushed when she remembered how Mister Stanley had struggled to turn his shock and disappointment into the legitimate concern of an upper-middle-class single dad dealing with an all-too-common domestic-help emergency.

"One would think you might at least give notice," Mister Stanley said huffily. "After all this time, two weeks seems the least that—"

"I would stay, if you needed me," Lula said. "If you needed someone to replace me. Mister Stanley, no insult, but Zeke is leaving for college in the fall. There's nothing I actually do. He can go to the market and microwave dinner by himself. I'm sorry, but he's growing up. And I'm not sure that it would be the best thing for Zeke to have me here for two more weeks when he knows I'm leaving."

"The best thing for Zeke" were the magic words guaranteed to vanquish Mister Stanley. He said, "I suppose I should have expected this after our conversation last night."

Lula said, "Zeke's a great kid. A very strong and beautiful person. You've done a terrific job with him in a difficult situation." She believed every word she was saying, and at the same time she was aware of how desperately she needed to keep Mister Stanley on her side. The green card was only part of it. Mister Stanley was her sponsor. Sponsor was only part of it. Mister Stanley was family. Mister Stanley would always be part of her new American life.

Mister Stanley said, "You've done wonders for him. We all have to thank you for that."

"Thank *you*," said Lula, inadequately.

"You're an inspiration, Lula. Not just to Zeke but to us all. Watching how you live, your nerve and determination. The courage to leave one life and start a whole new one, somewhere else . . . It almost makes one think one could—"

"You could!" said Lula. "You could quit your job and go back to teaching, if that's what you want. I'm sure a million colleges would jump at the chance to hire you! You could . . ." They both waited for Lula to imagine another positive life change that Mister Stanley could make. "You could . . ."

"I suppose I could," said Mister Stanley. "And given the likelihood of a financial crisis, or let's say a correction, I probably should." Lula and Mister Stanley stared at each other across the kitchen, a look in which, it seemed to Lula, they exchanged more pure unvarnished truth than in all the time she'd worked here. Mister Stanley wouldn't quit his job. He would stay on until he retired or until the crisis he predicted occurred. Zeke would leave home, and Mister Stanley would live here alone, dutifully visiting Ginger, who would get better or not, relapse or not.

Lula looked away. She felt as if the word *hopeless* was tattooed across Mister Stanley's forehead. In Albanian, *pashprese*. *Pashprese* meant an orphan begging on the streets of Tirana. *Pashprese* meant a family of eight crammed into one room of someone's aunt's apartment out near the Mother Teresa airport. *Pashprese* meant seeing your country run by dictators and gangsters and murderous politicians. *Pashprese* was not the same as *hopeless*. *Hopeless* was American, *hopeless* was Mister Stanley alone in his big comfortable house, working and making money so his wife and son didn't have to live with him.

Lula walked around so that Mister Stanley stood between her and the lamp. She memorized his glowing ears so the image would be available in case she needed it to light her way through some dark corridor in the future.

Lula said, "Mister Stanley, you saved my life."

"Call me Stanley," he said. "Please."

"Thank you, Stanley," Lula said.

"You're welcome," said Mister Stanley.

THE NEXT MORNING, as Lula folded and layered her sweaters in a suitcase, she heard herself make a sound somewhere between a sigh of grief and a grunt of self-loathing. But why should she feel ashamed? She had meant it one hundred percent when she thanked Mister Stanley for saving her life. And now it was time to *have* that life. When a door opened, you had to go through. Was it paranoid or realistic, half empty or half full, to assume that the door, any door, might not open twice?

Lula surveyed her baggage, her new laptop in its case. In fact, she wasn't so mobile. When she moved here, Mister Stanley had driven her from the city with all her things, but it seemed cruel to ask him to transport her stuff to Dunia's. Could she find a taxi to take all this? Or did she need a truck? She would have to ask Dunia. Could someone come today? Or would she have to live like this, rooting around in boxes of clothes, breathing in the gritty sorrow and shame swirling around Zeke and Mister Stanley, abandoned yet again? How long would it take to find someone to get her out of New Jersey?

Tires screeched against the curb. Lula ran to her window and saw two vehicles draw up, an old-model American car painted a shiny eggplant color, driven by Guri, and behind it the black Lexus. The perfect timing of the G-Men appearing at the perfect moment inspired Lula to imagine even more unlikely events. For example, Alvo waiting for her in the back seat of the Lexus.

Okay, that was too much to ask. Lula watched the two men lock their vehicles, Guri with a key, Genti with a stagy flick of the remote.

It might be fatally stupid, her being happy to see them. She'd assumed they were the same guys from before. The friendly burglars whose boss had taken her dancing Christmas Eve. The appreciative ones who thought she could save him from jail. The grateful ones who could help her move to Dunia's. But for all she knew, the two bruisers hustling up the front walk were the thugs they'd always been, the violent sons of bitches come to punish her for letting them down. They were here to blame her for their boss being sent away. How ironic, how like the corny stories she wrote for Don and Mister Stanley: In the end, the two villains reveal their true natures. Just when things are finally starting to go her way, they beat her to a bloody mess no man will ever want again. Once you let the devil in . . . She tried to remember Granny's saying. Once you let the devil in . . . then what?

But neither Guri nor Genti was talented enough to fake the bright amiable faces they showed her when she cracked open the door.

"Little Sister," Guri said. "Great to see you! Open up."

"How was Pennsylvania?" Lula said.

"Connecticut," said Guri. "Business trip to Norwalk. Open the door, please."

"You missed all the action," said Lula.

"Let us in." Genti's shoulders were up to his ears. "Come on. It's chilly."

"Why?" Lula asked. "What do you want?"

"To thank you," said Genti. "I swear on my children's lives."

Lula unfastened the chain. She said, "As a matter of fact, you guys couldn't have come at a better time."

Genti said, "That's what I told this lazy fuck. You can thank me for dragging his sorry ass off the couch."

They waited for Lula to ask them in and offer some refreshment. But it was no longer Lula's house. She was visiting too.

"What happened to Alvo?" she asked. "I mean Arkon."

"Whatever your boy did, it worked," said Genti. "The boss isn't going to jail. He's being deported instead. Too bad for us. But he's fine with it. For him it's a free ticket home, where he'll have his pick of Albanian girls. Plus his mom's a dynamite cook."

"Glad to hear it," said Lula. "I wish I could take credit." Had Don made a call, after all? Lula doubted it. Things had taken their course. Some judge came up with a better alternative to the American taxpayer housing and feeding a big strong Albanian boy for the next fifteen years. For the first time since she'd been in this country, everyone was overjoyed about someone being deported.

"Who can say who did what?" Genti said. "Who wants to know? The outcome is what matters. And we want to thank you. Maybe there is a favor we can do for you in return—"

"There is," said Lula. "You can give me a ride. I'm moving to my friend Dunia's place in the city."

"How much stuff do you have?" said Guri.

"Not much. It could fit in the Lexus, easy."

"It's about time," said Guri. "Don't take it wrong, but we always wondered how long our Little Sister could go on living in this tomb."

"It's not a tomb," said Lula.

"It is," said Guri. "It's the house of the dead."

Genti said, "Shut up, idiot. A ride is the least we can do. I'll take you and your stuff in the SUV. Guri will follow behind."

Lula led the guys up to her room, trying not to think about the night she'd brought Alvo upstairs. He had his pick of Albanian girls. His mom was a dynamite cook. The two men loaded their arms with suitcases and boxes. It would only take one trip. Lula grabbed her new computer. If she forgot something, she could get it. She'd meant what she'd said about staying in touch with Zeke.

With the two guys waiting outside, there was no time to get sentimental. Lula went through the house, checking for . . . what? Always when she'd imagined this scene, she'd planned on reclaiming the pitcher she'd gotten from Granny and given Mister Stanley last Christmas. But she couldn't do it. Not that Mister Stanley would notice. But it would feel wrong.

She was saying good-bye to the pitcher when Granny's spirit called her attention to something she might otherwise have missed, an envelope with her name on it, on the kitchen counter. In the envelope were five one-hundred-dollar bills, and a note from Mister Stanley that said, "Not as much as we might have liked, but with all our best wishes, good luck. Keep in touch. Warmest best wishes, Stan and Zeke."

Dear, dear Mister Stanley. Lula hadn't wronged him, really. She had helped his son. She couldn't stay here forever. She was sorry she had let Genti call Mister Stanley's house a tomb. Even if it was a tomb. Which it wasn't. She wished she'd thought to tell him that living human beings lived here.

Lula climbed into the Lexus.

"Got everything?" asked Genti.

"Everything," Lula said.

He pulled out, and Guri followed in his eggplant-colored sedan.

"We're both going into the city," said Genti. "We'll carry up your things. Then we'll be on our way." Lula pictured Genti and Guri trekking through Dunia's lobby as the doormen watched. She looked in the rearview mirror. Being followed made Lula nervous, even when she knew who was trailing her and why.

A few blocks from Mister Stanley's house Genti said, "Another thing. We remembered you don't know how to drive."

"Alvo was going to teach me," she said.

"That was then," said Genti. "This is later. But I can give you a lesson. You have to drive. You need it to be American. You need it more than you need to know who was the first president and how many stars were on the Pilgrim flag."

"You need it to be a human," said Lula. "What human doesn't drive?" She knew better than to tell him, an Albanian man, any man, that there was no Pilgrim flag.

"You'll learn fast," said Genti.

"When?" Lula said.

"Now," said Genti. They were still on a quiet residential street. He parked in front of a house and reached across and opened Lula's door. He said, "Get out and go around and get in."

"Here?" said Lula.

"Where else?" Guri had parked behind them. Through his windshield he gave Lula a hearty wave—of encouragement, she assumed.

"Don't you need a learner's permit?" Lula knew from Zeke that you did.

"No," said Genti. "Don't worry. It means nothing. In this country, you need a license to take a shit."

Lula got behind the wheel. Genti said, "Press on that pedal. Lightly! Okay, now the key." Her hand shook as she fumbled with the key. Lula screamed when the engine kicked in.

"Lesson one, don't scream," Genti said.

"I won't," promised Lula. "I mean I won't again."

"Turn the wheel, ease away from the curb. Good. Little Sister has talent."

Maybe she did have talent, because it wasn't a problem, going straight and sensing the width of the street. Genti found a parking lot and told her to pull in. Guri followed and waited while Lula started and braked and did figure eights.

"You got the hang of it," said Genti.

"I don't," Lula said.

"You'll get it now," Genti told her. Lula turned onto the street. "Look in your mirror. Our brother is behind us. You can brake if you need to. Our brother has your back."

The road fed into a bigger road, more heavily traveled. Genti said, "Don't worry, I'm here. I'm here."

It was what you'd want God to say if you believed in God. Lula didn't worry; she slipped into the stream of traffic, calm even though the sensible part of her knew she could get arrested, she could kill herself, or worse, she could run down an innocent person. A child. But if nothing too terrible happened . . . she was starting to think she could do this. Genti was watching out for her. He would lean over and grab the wheel if she did something wrong.

"Turn right up there," said Genti.

"Onto the highway? I can't!"

"You have to," Genti said.

And then, amazingly, Lula did. She was driving a vehicle! She was very careful, and the other drivers saw that, and they spoke the silent language, the language she'd learned from Zeke when they'd both thought she wasn't paying attention.

She signaled and glanced and gestured like a person, driving. She found a place between two cars and folded the SUV into traffic.

"The law of the jungle," Genti said. "Little cars move over for bigger ones. Survival of the biggest. It's why you want a big one."

It had begun to feel like one of those dreams in which she was driving a car and didn't know how, only this time she did know how. Like one of those dreams in which the airplane turns out to be a safe winged bus that never leaves the ground.

"Take that exit," said Genti.

"No," said Lula. "Not the bridge."

"Take the bridge," said Genti.

Before her was the George Washington Bridge. How majestic it looked, as solid and grand and permanent as the Great Wall of China!

"I can't," said Lula. "I'm sorry."

"Don't be sorry. You can do it. You can trust me," Genti said. "Just watch out. Take it slow."

The traffic was dense, which was fine with Lula, because she could crawl along and concentrate on keeping the greatest possible distance between herself and the car ahead. Let the other drivers cut in front of her. They had a lifetime of practice. She had enough to do, getting the knack of the play between the brake and the gas.

Genti said, "Take the far lane, the far lane!"

Someone honked, but not loud. Lula drifted from the slow lane into a slower one.

When the traffic came to a complete halt, Genti said,

"Good-bye and good luck. If I were you, I'd find somewhere to leave the car. You don't want anyone asking questions. If you know what I mean."

Lula said, "Is the car stolen?"

"Of course not," Genti said. "I'm insulted you would ask. Fully legal and paid for. The papers are in the glove compartment, signed over to you. Sold to you for a dollar. Have you got a dollar?"

"I think so," Lula said. She had twenty-one hundred dollars, counting Mister Stanley's bonus. It made her feel so hopeful that for a moment she felt a rush of friendliness toward Genti, though the feeling wasn't warm enough to tempt her into disclosing the reason for this upsurge of good will.

"Can I get the dollar from your purse?" Genti said. "Just to make it official."

"No, please!" Lula said. The traffic moved again. A station wagon swerved into her lane, and she hit the brake.

"Nicely played," said Genti. "I was just pushing your buttons. A lady's purse—I would never! Forget the dollar. You'll owe me. Okay, we're stopped again. No one's moving for a while. Gridlock. This is it."

"It?"

"This is where I get off."

"Where are you going?" asked Lula, plaintively. "I thought you were going to help me move my stuff to Dunia's."

"Someone there will help," said Genti. "I'm getting into my associate's car. You're on your own from now on."

"In the middle of the bridge? Someone will see you switch cars. How can that be legal?"

"The traffic's stopped," said Genti. "Our brother is right

MY NEW AMERICAN LIFE

behind us. Everybody's got their own problems. No one will notice me moving from car to car. If anyone asks, the wife and I had a difference of opinion, and I decided to ride with my friend."

Then, before Lula could say anything else, Genti got out of the SUV and slammed the door behind him.

"Wait a minute!" Lula cried, as the traffic picked up. Guri's car, with Genti in the passenger seat, passed her on her left. Both men waved and saluted her. When she looked again, they were gone.

The smartest thing, the most responsible thing, would be to stop and ditch the car. But she didn't want to do that. She could go very slowly (everyone was) and be extremely cautious. She would finish crossing the bridge and drive into Manhattan. That would be enough for one day. Tomorrow she could do more. She would get her green card. A job. She would get a driver's license. But what would she do with this big car when she was living at Dunia's? She didn't need a car. She could sell it and keep the money. The money would help her move on. But first she would ask the doorman to watch her fancy vehicle while the other doormen helped her move into Dunia's apartment. Lula would be arriving in the car of a person who belonged there.

Genti had said that the papers were in the glove compartment. But still it would be complicated, explaining to a dealer how she came to be in possession of a fancy new SUV. She would think of something. She would say, I have this Cousin George, a car dealer in Tirana with connections in the States. She would say "connections" or "relatives," depending on who was listening. She would say, I come from a tribe of people to whom such crazy things happen. If you ask around enough, eventually you find someone who doesn't ask too many questions. Flirtation and charm worked everywhere, second only to money.

Rehearsing exactly what she would say, Lula, who couldn't drive, drove across the George Washington Bridge in the brilliant winter sunshine.

About the author

About the book

Read on

Insights,
Interviews
& More...

Meet Francine Prose

Stephanie Berger

FRANCINE PROSE is the author of sixteen books of fiction. Her novel *A Changed Man* won the Dayton Literary Peace Prize, and *Blue Angel* was a finalist for the National Book Award. Her most recent works of nonfiction include the highly acclaimed *Anne Frank: The Book, The Life, The Afterlife* and the *New York Times* bestseller *Reading Like a Writer*. A former president of PEN American Center, and a member of the American Academy of Arts and Letters and the American Academy of Arts and Sciences, Francine Prose lives in New York City. ∿

The Road to the Tower

By Michael Dirda

This review originally appeared in
The New York Review of Books *on*
September 29, 2011.

WITH THE POSSIBLE EXCEPTION of Joyce
Carol Oates, there is no busier or more
prolific woman of letters in twenty-first-
century America than Francine Prose.
During the past decade or so she's brought
out a study of Anne Frank, a short life
of Caravaggio, a guide to "reading like
a writer," a book about the female
"muses" who inspired various male
artists, a monograph on gluttony, and
novels for both young adults (*Touch*)
and grown-ups. These last include, most
recently, *A Changed Man*, which focuses
on a neo-Nazi skinhead, and *Goldengrove*,
which traces the impact of a drowning
death on the victim's boyfriend and
younger sister. Go back even further
into the Prose bibliography and you'll
find fiction about a voodoo queen in old
New Orleans, a creative writing teacher in
thrall to one of his students, and an Italian
butcher who—by the grace of God—won
his wife in a card game.

That last novel, *Household Saints*, was
made into a movie, but *Blue Angel*—the
one about Professor Ted Swenson and his
obsession with Angela Argo—remains
Prose's best-known work of fiction. Like
her latest, the satirical and unsettling
My New American Life, this "campus"
novel is a troubling comedy, sharply witty
but also surprisingly sympathetic to its
protagonist's all-too-human failings. ▶

In *Blue Angel*, Ted Swenson teaches "Beginning Fiction" at
Euston College in Vermont. The poor guy really does try hard
to find positive things to say about his students' various subliterate
compositions, even preppy Courtney's awful "First Kiss—Inner City
Blues" and Danny's tale of a frustrated teen having his way with a
frozen chicken. After one particularly dismal effort called "Toilet
Bowl," the desperate Swenson actually manages to croak out "Thank
you," followed by "It's a brave story. Really. Let's hear what the rest
of you think. Remember, let's start off with what we like. . . ."

For twenty years Swenson has been faithfully married to Sherrie,
the beautiful school nurse, and they've been happy together.
Nonetheless, just lately the blocked writer—it's been ten years
since his last book, the ominously titled *Phoenix Time*—has
started to feel a little weary of his virtuous ways:

> What really bothers him . . . is that he was too stupid or timid
> or scared to sleep with those students. What exactly was he
> proving? Illustrating some principle, making some moral
> point? The point is: he adores Sherrie, he always has. He would
> never hurt her. And now, as a special reward for having been
> such a good husband, such an all-around good guy, he's got the
> chill satisfaction of having taken his high-minded self-denial
> almost all the way to the grave. Because now it's all over. He's
> too old. He's way beyond all that.

> Wrong. No man is beyond all that. It just takes the right other
woman, though on the surface Angela Argo doesn't seem Swenson's
type at all. A new student, she's "a skinny, pale redhead with neon-
orange and lime-green streaks in her hair and a delicate, sharp-
featured face pierced in a half-dozen places." She wears a black
leather motorcycle jacket and "an arsenal of chains, dog collars,
and bracelets." Yet Angela, alone of all the students Swenson has
ever taught, possesses The Gift. The chapters of the punky goth's
novel—reproduced in the book—are terrific.

To his surprise, Swenson finds himself strangely turned on by the
young woman's command of language, by her syntax and diction,
though it doesn't hurt that her book's sexy plot revolves around the
kinky seduction of a teenaged girl by her teacher. Or is it the other way
around? All that really matters to Swenson is that enigmatic Angela

writes like an angel, albeit a blue angel. Before long, however, the good professor finds himself caught up in a genuine *folie à deux*, while simultaneously clashing more and more with his politically correct colleagues. Toward its end, the novel begins to accelerate and things spiral completely out of poor Swenson's control. As Prose succinctly puts it: "Time passes quickly when you're wrecking your life."

Time also passes quickly for Lula, the young Albanian protagonist of *My New American Life*, who is, however, very much in control of herself and deeply focused on acquiring her green card and enjoying the endless bounty of our generous country. In a loose sense, *My New American Life* is the flip side of *Blue Angel*. Where Swenson merely dreams of a new life, Lula does all she can to realize hers. Readers may feel sorry for the middle-aged professor, but Lula elicits our admiration as a force all her own, a survivor, not a victim. And unlike Angela Argo, Lula is a woman with whom it is quite easy to fall in love.

When the novel opens it is 2005 and Lula has been employed as a nanny by Mister Stanley for nearly a year. Her unhappy benefactor currently works long days on Wall Street, having given up his career as a college professor in the hope of better providing for his wife Ginger and son Zeke. Unfortunately, a couple of Christmas Eves back, Ginger suddenly ran away from home, having decided that she needed to live a more wholesome, organic, and spiritual life. Since then the twenty-six-year-old Lula—who speaks excellent English—has kept Zeke company after school and brought a little warmth to a household in which father and seventeen-year-old son hardly communicate. Though neither acts on the only half-acknowledged feeling, both Mister Stanley and Zeke are clearly smitten with the vibrant Lula.

How could they not be? Lula is irresistible and when the novel opens the reader might guess that we're in for an updated version of Turgenev's *First Love* or Calder Willingham's *Rambling Rose*. No innocent, Lula knows that "flirtation and charm worked everywhere" and were "second only to money" in getting what you want. At one point she even recalls having paid for some of her college courses, back in Tirana, with sexual favors for a professor. But she loves America and wants desperately to stay in this gorgeous and exuberantly vulgar country: ▶

Who would choose Tirana over a city where half-naked fashion models and their stockbroker boyfriends drank mojitos from pitchers decorated with dancing monkeys?

While working at an upscale bar in New York, Lula and her friend Dunia, both technically here as tourists, worry constantly about being sent back to Albania:

She told herself not to worry, the government had plenty of people to deport before they got around to her. Busboys like Eduardo, Arab engineering students, hordes of cabdrivers and cleaners. On the other hand, who would a bored horny INS dude rather have in detention: Eduardo, some Yemeni geezer in a skullcap, or two twenty-six-year-old Albanian girls with shiny hair and good tits?

Then, one day, Dunia disappears—perhaps sent back to Albania, perhaps sold into white slavery. Lula regards this latter option as a distinct possibility. But what can she do?

She promised herself not to forget how lucky she was, living her comfy new American life in Mister Stanley's comfy house instead of selling her body to some tuna fisherman in Bari or hiking up her skirt on a service road beside a Sicilian *autostrada*.

As it turns out, Mister Stanley is not only willing to sponsor Lula's application for citizenship but also just happens to be the boyhood friend of the country's leading immigration lawyer, Don Settebello. Lula's life is starting to look up.

And then the young woman notices the black Lexus SUV that is slowly cruising around Mister Stanley's New Jersey neighborhood. One afternoon the ominous vehicle stops and three guys emerge, knock on the door, and inform Lula that they are friends of her cousin George. All they want from her is a small, quite inconsequential favor. Just hide this gun until they call for it. Partly because she finds Alvo, the leader of the gang, to be kind of cute, Lula impulsively agrees.

• • •

By this point, the reader has begun to feel increasingly ill at ease. Who are these Albanian low-lifes? Why do they want Lula to hide the gun? Is Lula in danger? Prose, author of *Reading Like a Writer*, knows that Chekhov famously remarked that if you produce a pistol at the beginning of a play it must be fired in act three. But who, in this case, will pull the trigger? Will Lula be the victim? Or Mister Stanley or Zeke? Will this bright comedy suddenly turn very, very dark?

Matters grow increasingly unsettling over the following weeks: Lula discovers that someone with red hair has been secretly using her shower and Zeke's laptop. Could it be Alvo? She begins to build sexual fantasies about him. Before long, he starts to reappear on her doorstep when nobody is home, each time asking for just a little more from her. What is going on? Have we slid into the distinctly creepy territory of a Patricia Highsmith thriller?

Meanwhile, Lula's mind constantly veers back and forth from the present to the past, recalling the grotesque deaths of her parents, comparing America with Albania: "The true stories of her childhood were tales of grubby misery without the kick of romance, just suffering and more suffering, betrayal and petty greed." In view of such a soiled life "back home" it's little wonder that "Lula was obsessive about her soap, hand-milled in France by monks consecrated to silent prayer and shampoo."

When Mister Stanley requests details of her earlier life in Albania, Lula quite naturally makes up stories, full of exaggerations and elements of ancient folklore. "It was nicer to mine the mythical past." But that's not the only reason. As she once told Zeke, perplexed by the application essays requested by various colleges: "Figure out what each one wanted to hear. Then . . . write that." Lula adds that Zeke's father "would have given him the wrong advice: write what was in his heart."

Providing her own little public with what it wants to hear, Lula tells Mister Stanley that in Albania "blood feuds still raged for generations. Revenges. Bride kidnappings." Back there "courtship was still the fireman-carry and rape." When her fascinated boss asks her to type up some of her longer stories, she goes all out. "I'm writing a short story now," she confesses to Mister Stanley and her immigration lawyer Don Settebello: ▶

The Road to the Tower *(continued)*

"It's about this government bureau that analyzes people's dreams, and everyone has to report their dreams, and they're on the lookout for any dreams that might indicate that someone is plotting against the state." Lula held her breath. Neither Don nor Mister Stanley showed any sign of recognizing the plot of a novel by Ismail Kadare.

By introducing Don Settebello, *My New American Life* adds a further political twist to the story. Settebello is earnest, hardworking, idealist, and even, it would seem at first, a bit of a fool. But he grows obsessed with the horrors visited by the US interrogators upon the detainees at Guantánamo:

You know what the call torture? Enhanced interrogation techniques. You know what they call a beating? Non-injurious personal contact. A suicide attempt? Manipulative self-injurious behavior.

To which Lula responds with one of her favorite expressions: "These things happen." One can almost see the shrug of a woman inured to horror. Lula's other signature phrase is even more casually dismissive of sentimental daydreams: "That's not going to happen."

Like other Prose novels, *My New American Life* is what one might loosely call a comedy of manners. But under this umbrella Prose begins together cultural satire, mystery, a psychosexual thriller, and political outrage. Moreover, surrounded by unhappy, well-meaning Americans, Lula reminds the reader of one home truth after another. Here is a representative sampling of Lula's observations about her new American life:

On paranoia: "*Paranoia* was English for Balkan common sense."

On the plight of the foreigner in America: "She'd seen the guys on Fox News calling for every immigrant except German supermodels and Japanese baseball players to be deported, no questions asked."

On riding the subway: "A woman whose skin seemed to have been baked from some rich flaky pastry shut her book, sighed theatrically, and slid over to make room for Lula, then sighed again and went back to reading *Daily Affirmations for Women Who Do Too Much*."

On hip-hop: "Regardless of the language, it was always the same guys yelling about how tough they were."

At a courtroom trial: "The defense lawyer wore a pinstripe suit and a bouquet of dreadlocks, a fashion choice that suggested a proud idealistic character but an unrealistic nature and perhaps a deficient desire to win. Twice he quoted Descartes, maxims with an unclear relevance to the case."

On patriotism: "Mostly, in her experience, country was like religion, an excuse to hate other people and feel righteous about it."

While Lula navigates her way among the various men in her life, Prose creates a secondary theme, depicting the strained relationship between Zeke and Mister Stanley:

It was as if there were two Zekes: the agreeable boy he was with Lula, and the furious troll he became around his father. Lula told Zeke he should be nicer to his dad, and Zeke agreed, but he couldn't. It would have meant going against his culture.

One evening the teenaged boy tells Lula about the worst summer of his life:

This was after eighth grade. We took a family cross-country road trip. From New York to Chicago Mom and Dad fought about the air conditioner. Dad said it couldn't be fixed, and Mom said that was Dad in a nutshell: Nothing could be fixed. Dad wouldn't let Mom drive, he did the crawly speed limit. We were in Nebraska for like twenty years. We only stopped to sleep or eat or piss until we got to the West, and then we'd stop at every national park, and I'd get out and kick some pebbles, and my mom would cluck her tongue and say weird spiritual shit about nature, and Dad would give me a lecture ▶

full of fascinating facts he'd learned in college geology, and Mom would look like she wanted to kill him. Then I took pictures of Dad and Mom against the natural wonders, and dad took pictures of Mom and me. Then we'd get back in the car and drive fifteen hours to the next national park.

The American dream.

Meanwhile, Don Settebello is working on making Lula's own American dream a reality, assuring her that all will be well with her application for a green card—unless, of course, she were to do something stupid like harbor fugitives or conceal an illegal handgun. In one of the great comic turns of a novel rich in them, the divorced Settebello invites Lula, Mister Stanley, and Zeke to celebrate Lula's birthday at a restaurant:

> Inside, a group of beauties flitted like moths around the glowing lectern that held the reservation book, a shimmering tableau shattered by the arrival of Mister Stanley's party. One girl split off from the rest to guide them toward Don Settebello, who had risen from a banquette and was waving as if to beloved passengers sailing into port.

The lawyer isn't alone, however. He has brought along his bored and sullen teenaged daughter Abigail. The evening's conversation soon veers wildly from Lula's birthday to such subjects as divorce, health insurance, vegetarianism, and Dick Cheney. Don Settebello flirts mildly with Lula, while Abigail and Zeke provide a sotto voce commentary:

> "We want you here," said Don Settebello. "Fresh young blood. You're what keeps our country young."
> Zeke stage-whispered to Abigail, "Fresh blood? That's so vampiristic."
> Abigail said, "Are you actually listening to Dad?"

Later on, when Settebello has found a new girlfriend, Zeke observes to his jealous father: "Dad, you just wish a girl that hot was putting you through the wringer. What's a wringer anyway?"

• • •

All comedy tends to advance toward a tragic denouement—what has sometimes been called the point of ritual death—and at the last moment swerve away from the expected disaster. The god suddenly descends from the machine. The heroine is recognized as the long-lost daughter. The fatal gunshot misses. In *My New American Life* Francine Prose exuberantly shows us, through Lula's eyes, just what luck it is to be a citizen of this rich and childish country. Near the end, she allows Lula's latent exasperation—and perhaps her own—to emerge in boldface, as Mister Stanley suddenly decides that he is a failure:

> Lula looked away. She felt as if the word *hopeless* was tattooed across Mister Stanley's forehead. In Albanian, *pashprese*. *Pashprese* meant an orphan begging on the streets of Tirana. *Pashprese* meant a family of eight crammed into one room of someone's aunt's apartment out near the Mother Teresa airport. *Pashprese* meant seeing your country run by dictators and gangsters and murderous politicians. *Pashprese* was not the same as *hopeless*. *Hopeless* was American, *hopeless* was Mister Stanley alone in his big comfortable house, working and making money so his wife and son didn't have to live with him.

My New American Life is a fast-moving novel, brilliantly demonstrating Prose's ability to replicate every kind of American (or Albanian) speech and conversation. Overall the book feels just a bit ramshackle, and it may try to do too many things at once. Yet it remains exceptionally entertaining, fun to read in its sentences, incidents, scenes. Moreover, it airily raises serious questions about loyalties, ethnicity, love, politics, and, not least, the ability to drive a car. At its end Lula and Dunia are unexpectedly reunited and about to go reside in luxury in—where else?—a suite at Trump Tower. What new American life could be more successfully American than that? ◡

Behind the Book

ALMOST THIRTY YEARS AGO, a young woman told me how she'd been taught to drive by a bunch of Albanian gangsters. Their somewhat unusual teaching method involved driving her to the middle of the George Washington Bridge and insisting she take the wheel. Her anecdote stuck with me, dormant, until a few years back, when I was asked to contribute a short story to a magazine run by Lexus (the car manufacturer). At first I refused, until I had a sort of vision: a waking dream in which a big black SUV pulled up in front of a suburban house. Eventually I realized that the guys in the SUV were the guys in the young woman's story. As always happens, I was about halfway through a first draft in what would become the novel before I understood what I was actually writing about: immigration, how our country looked to the native-born and to new arrivals in the year 2005. I really began writing when I taught, for a semester, at Baruch College in Manhattan, where my students—mostly first-generation immigrants, many with visa problems, and all of them (it seemed to me) geniuses—were experiencing many of the same longings and problems that I gave to my heroine, Lula, whom I came to love and admire in much the same way I came to love and admire my students. Last spring, I traveled to Albania to do research for the novel—a fascinating trip during which I made good friends who were very helpful in the writing of the book and was also invited (unknowingly) by the U.S. embassy to have dinner with political criminals from the Communist dictatorship, which was also very helpful, though of course in a different way. ∿

Have You Read?
More by Francine Prose

ANNE FRANK: THE BOOK, THE LIFE, THE AFTERLIFE

In June, 1942, Anne Frank received a red-and-white checked diary for her thirteenth birthday, just weeks before she and her family went into hiding from the Nazis in an Amsterdam attic. For two years, with ever-increasing maturity, Anne crafted a memoir that has become one of the most compelling, intimate, and important documents of modern history. She described life in hiding in vivid, unforgettable detail, explored apparently irreconcilable views of human nature—people are good at heart, but capable of unimaginable evil—and grappled with the unfolding events of World War II until the hidden attic was raided in August 1944.

But the diary of Anne Frank, argues Francine Prose, is as much a work of art as a historical record. Through close reading, she marvels at the teenaged Frank's skillfully natural narrative voice, at her finely tuned dialogue and ability to turn living people into characters. And Prose addresses what few of the diary's millions of readers may know: this book is a deliberate work of art. During her last months in hiding, Anne Frank furiously revised and edited her work, crafting a piece of literature that she hoped would be read by the public after the war.

Read it has been. Few books have been as influential for so long, and Prose thoroughly investigates the diary's unique afterlife: the obstacles and criticism ▶

Otto Frank faced in publishing his daughter's words; the controversy surrounding the diary's Broadway and film adaptations, and the 1950s social mores that reduced it to a tale of adolescent angst and love; the claims of conspiracy theorists who have cried fraud, and the scientific analysis that proved them wrong. Finally, having assigned the book to her own students, Prose considers the rewards and challenges of teaching one of the world's most read, and banned, books.

How has the life and death of one girl become emblematic of the lives and deaths of so many, and why do her words continue to inspire? *Anne Frank: The Book, The Life, The Afterlife* tells the extraordinary story of the book that became a force in the world—and it definitively establishes Anne Frank as the writer she always knew she was.

"A definitive, deeply moving inquiry into the life of the young, imperiled artist, and a masterful exegesis of *Diary of a Young Girl*. . . . Extraordinary testimony to the power of literature and compassion."
—Donna Seaman, *Booklist (starred review)*

"A lively and illuminating disquisition. . . . An impressively far-reaching critical work, an elegant study both edifying and entertaining. In a book full of keen observations and fascinating disputes . . . Ms. Prose looks in all directions to find noteworthy material. . . . This is a Grade A example of what a smart, precise, and impassioned teacher can do."
—Janet Maslin, *New York Times*

GOLDENGROVE

Nico and Margaret have grown up with their ex-hippie parents in an isolated New England town on the shores of placid Mirror Lake. Nico, thirteen, is still an adolescent, small and pudgy, trying her best to grow up to be like her sister. Margaret, four years older, is vibrant and beautiful, a blossoming jazz singer with cookie-scented skin—born, as Nico says, in the wrong half of the century. When an unexpected tragedy shatters the peaceful life of this middle class family, Nico finds herself suddenly alone with her grief, and teetering on the brink of adulthood.

The only one who seems to understand how she feels is Margaret's boyfriend, Aaron, a gifted painter obsessed with elusive and mysterious Margaret. Nico and Aaron secretly begin to spend more and more time together. But as their friendship deepens and transforms, their tenuous dance takes on a dangerous cast.

With echoes of *Vertigo* and *Pygmalion*, *Goldengrove* explores the treacherous territory of identity and love—both romantic and familial—during one haunted summer lived on the edge of innocence. Narrated in the unforgettable voice of a young girl, Francine Prose's new novel is a wrenching, heartstring-pulling story about adolescence, family, and first love.

"Prose is most astute with her portrayal of the stormy currents of adolescent grief. . . . It's also charged with an . . . element of eroticism, and here Prose is at her very ▶

best. . . . Nico's voice, with its quirky mix of insight and gullibility, will stick in adults' minds, and many younger readers will recognize that voice as their own."
—*Washington Post Book World*

"Ms. Prose is perceptive. . . . Her modest-sounding book turns out to be beautifully wrought. And it blossoms into a smart, gimlet-eyed account of what thirteen-year-old Nico sees happening around her after the loss of the more alluring, glamorous, and manipulative Margaret . . . and yields an unexpectedly rich, tart, eye-opening sense of Nico's world. *Goldengrove* is one of Ms. Prose's gentler books . . . but it's not a sentimental one. . . . It does this with mostly effortless narrative verve."
—*New York Times*

READING LIKE A WRITER

Long before there were creative writing workshops and degrees, how did aspiring writers learn to write? By reading the work of their predecessors and contemporaries, says Francine Prose.

In *Reading Like a Writer,* Prose invites you to sit by her side and take a guided tour of the tools and the tricks of the masters. She reads the work of the very best writers—Dostoyevsky, Flaubert, Kafka, Austen, Dickens, Woolf, Chekhov—and discovers why these writers endure. She takes pleasure in the long and magnificent sentences of Philip Roth and the breath-taking paragraphs of Isaac Babel; she is deeply moved by the brilliant characterization in George Eliot's *Middlemarch.* She looks to John Le Carré for a lesson in how to advance

plot through dialogue, to Flannery
O'Connor for the cunning use of the telling
detail, and to James Joyce and Katherine
Mansfield, who offer clever examples of
how to employ gesture to create character.
She cautions readers to slow down and pay
attention to words, the raw material out
of which literature is crafted. Written with
passion, humor, and wisdom, *Reading
Like a Writer* will inspire readers to return to
literature with a fresh eye and an eager heart.

"Capacious and encouraging. . . . Prose's
little guide will motivate 'people who love
books' . . . to be sensitive readers of their
own and others' work. . . . Like the great
works of fiction, it's a wise and voluble
companion."

—*New York Times Book Review*

"Witty . . . insightful . . . close reading
leads Prose back to the place where
all desires 'to read like a writer' start:
sputtering fandom."

—*Washington Post Book World*

THE GLORIOUS ONES

The Glorious Ones travel the length and
breadth of seventeenth-century Italy,
playing commedia dell'arte in the streets
and palaces with equal vigor. A small
company of players founded by the
ingenious madman Flamino Scala,
they endure kidnappings and passionate
affairs, cabals, riots, disgrace, all manner of
triumph and hardship. Pantalone the miser,
sunny Armanda the dwarf, gossip-loving
Columbina, and evil-minded Brighella
view their myriad shared adventures ▶

through markedly different eyes. Yet not one of them is prepared for the strange twisting of the road brought about by the mysterious arrival of Isabella Andreini, who has come to direct their wayward troupe.

A CHANGED MAN

On an unseasonably warm spring afternoon, a young neo-Nazi named Vincent Nolan walks into the Manhattan office of World Brotherhood Watch, a human rights foundation headed by a charismatic Holocaust survivor, Meyer Maslow. Vincent announces that he wants to make a radical change in his life. But what is Maslow to make of this rough-looking stranger who claims to have read Maslow's books, who has Waffen-SS tattoos under his shirtsleeves, and who says that his mission is to save guys like him from becoming guys like him?

As he gradually turns into the sort of person who might actually be able to do that, Vincent also transforms those around him: Maslow, who fears that heroism has become a desk job; Bonnie Kalen, the foundation's fund-raiser, a divorced single mother and a devoted believer in Maslow's crusade against intolerance and injustice; and Bonnie's teenage son, Danny, whose take on the world around him is at once openhearted, sharp-eyed, and as fundamentally decent as his mother's.

Masterfully plotted, darkly comic, *A Changed Man* illuminates the everyday transactions in our lives, exposing what remains invisible in plain sight in our drug-addled and media-driven culture. Remarkable for the author's tender

**A CHANGED MAN
CD UNABRIDGED**

Available on CD from HarperAudio, this unabridged audio edition of Francine Prose's novel is performed by Eric Conger.

sympathy for her characters, the novel poses the essential questions: What constitutes a life worth living? Is it possible to change? What does it mean to be a moral human being?

"Powerful, funny, and exquisitely nuanced. . . . This story has a continental sweep."   —*New York Times Book Review*

BLUE ANGEL

It's been years since Swenson, a professor in a New England creative writing program, has published a novel. It's been even longer since any of his students have shown promise. Enter Angela Argo, a pierced, tattooed student with a rare talent for writing. Angela is just the thing Swenson needs. And, better yet, she wants his help. But, as we all know, the road to hell is paved with good intentions.

"*Blue Angel* is a smart-bomb attack on academic hypocrisy and cant, and Francine Prose, an equal-opportunity offender, is as politically incorrect on the subject of sex as Catullus and twice as funny. What a deep relief it is, in these dumbed-down Late Empire days, to read a world class satirist who's also a world class story-teller."   —Russell Banks

"An engaging comedy of manners. . . . Prose once again proves herself one of our great cultural satirists."
     —*Kirkus Reviews* (starred review)

THE LIVES OF THE MUSES: NINE WOMEN AND THE ARTISTS THEY INSPIRED

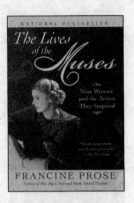

All loved, and were loved by, their artists, and inspired them with an intensity of emotion akin to Eros.

In a brilliant, wry, and provocative book, Francine Prose explores the complex relationship between the artist and his muse. In so doing, she illuminates with great sensitivity and intelligence the elusive emotional wellsprings of the creative process.

"A book of serious ideas that is also addictively juicy." —*Boston Globe*

PRIMITIVE PEOPLE: A NOVEL

What are these barbaric rituals that pass for social and family life? Who are these fearsome creatures who linger in decaying mansions and at glittery malls, trendy weddings and dinner parties? These are the questions that trouble Simone, a beautiful, smart young Haitian woman. She has fled the chaotic violence of Port-au-Prince only to find herself in a world no less brutal or bizarre— a seemingly civilized landscape where dead sheep swing from trees, lightbulbs are ceremonially buried, fur-clad mothers carve terrifying goddesses out of pumice . . . and where learning to lie is the principal rite of passage into adulthood. The primitive people of this darkly satiric novel are not, as one might expect, the backward denizens of some savage isle, but the wealthy inhabitants of the Hudson Valley in upstate New York.

"Francine Prose has a wickedly sharp ear for pretentious American idiom, and no telling detail escapes her observation."
—*New York Times Book Review*

WOMEN AND CHILDREN FIRST: STORIES

These bright and entertaining tales display Prose's special gift for revealing the mysteries and contradictions at the heart of contemporary life; beneath their humorous, acerbic surface, they deal seriously and compassionately with that most modern discovery: nothing is as we've foreseen—not even our own desires.

"Reading *Women and Children First* is like driving down the road with a companion who is so smart and funny and insightful that her conversation transforms the landscape. I loved reading these stories."
—Jane Smiley

HOUSEHOLD SAINTS: A NOVEL

The setting is New York's Little Italy in the 1950s—a community closely knit by gossip and tradition. This is the story of an extraordinary family, the Santangelos. There is Joseph, the butcher, who cheats in his shop and at pinochle, only to find the deck is stacked against him; his mother, Mrs. Santangelo, who sees the evil eye everywhere and who calls on her saints; and Catherine, his wife, whose determination to raise a modern daughter leads her to confront ancient questions. Finally, there is Theresa, Joseph, and Catherine's daughter, whose astonishing discovery of purpose moves ▶

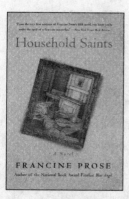

Have You Read? *(continued)*

the book toward its unpredictable conclusion.

"Prose brings off a minor miracle . . . in the rare sympathy and detachment with which she gives life to this poignant story. She writes equally well about sausages and saints, documenting the madness and the grace of God in everyday life." —*Newsweek*

Don't miss the next book by your favorite author. Sign up now for AuthorTracker by visiting www.AuthorTracker.com.